D1390848

You & I, Inc.

The Connection of Sexuality and Spirituality

Waterford City and County
Libraries

AJ Beaber

WATERFORD CITY AND COUNTY WITHDRAWN LIBRARIES

BALBOA
PRESS
A DIVISION OF HAY HOUSE

Copyright © 2015 5683 Legacy Productions, LLC.

All rights reserved. No part of this book may be used or reproduced by any means, graphic, electronic, or mechanical, including photocopying, recording, taping or by any information storage retrieval system without the written permission of the author except in the case of brief quotations embodied in critical articles and reviews.

Balboa Press books may be ordered through booksellers or by contacting:

Balboa Press
A Division of Hay House
1663 Liberty Drive
Bloomington, IN 47403
www.balboapress.com
1 (877) 407-4847

Because of the dynamic nature of the Internet, any web addresses or links contained in this book may have changed since publication and may no longer be valid. The views expressed in this work are solely those of the author and do not necessarily reflect the views of the publisher, and the publisher hereby disclaims any responsibility for them.

The author of this book does not dispense medical advice or prescribe the use of any technique as a form of treatment for physical, emotional, or medical problems without the advice of a physician, either directly or indirectly. The intent of the author is only to offer information of a general nature to help you in your quest for emotional and spiritual well-being. In the event you use any of the information in this book for yourself, which is your constitutional right, the author and the publisher assume no responsibility for your actions.

Any people depicted in stock imagery provided by Thinkstock are models, and such images are being used for illustrative purposes only.
Certain stock imagery © Thinkstock.

Print information available on the last page.

ISBN: 978-1-5043-3216-3 (sc)
ISBN: 978-1-5043-3218-7 (hc)
ISBN: 978-1-5043-3217-0 (e)

Library of Congress Control Number: 2015907117

Balboa Press rev. date: 8/24/2015

In honor of those who have gone before me, thank you
for showing me that fear is meant to be a teacher,
not a guide to lead the way.

Our children, our legacy,
you were the cause and purpose behind every page.
When you see and hear things you don't understand,
may you know it is part of a much bigger plan.

CONTENTS

PROLOGUE

Lessons from a Flower and a Bee

Was it a dream or was it reality? All sense of time and space seemed to disappear as I walked alone in an open field of wildflowers.

It was a beautiful sunny day. The sky was bright blue with hardly a cloud in sight. I hadn't walked more than a few minutes when a bee began buzzing in my ears.

I was not afraid, but at peace, when the bee said, "Listen."

I followed it deeper into the field of flowers, and the bee told me, "These flowers provide for me so that I may provide for you and live. These flowers are supported and nourished by the earth. Without sunlight, the plants would die. Without water and nutrients, they would perish. It is part of the circle of life."

I paused for a moment to consider this.

"You too are supported by me because you were created by me." I realized this was no longer the bee talking, but the wind. As the wind gently blew across my face, I heard it say, "You and I are incorporated, a partnership. Love one another as you love yourself."

I stopped and knelt down in a patch of yellow wildflowers. I touched a single flower with delicacy and tenderness. I asked the flower, "Can a plant feel my appreciation, my love?"

A voice responded, "Yes because you are appreciating that which is from our Protector and our Creator, and we share that appreciation. Yes because when you appreciate us, you appreciate yourself and your Creator; our Creator. We are one."

I then asked, "How are we one?"

The voice responded, "Because you and I were created for a purpose."

I asked, "What is your purpose?"

The voice responded, "To grow free."

I looked at the vast fields of wildflowers in front of me. "You are all living your purpose. How do I do the same?"

The voice said, "You trust your Creator."

"You make it look so easy," I said.

"It's okay for it not to be hard. It's okay to make things look easy," the voice responded.

"Don't you have fear?" I asked.

"No, for I am *free*. When you are *free,* there is no fear. I am *free* because I was created this way; and so are you."

"Aren't you afraid of death?" I asked.

"No, for I will die, and my seed will spread and grow a new plant and I will live again through them. For now my purpose is to be free and wild, to allow my Creator to nourish and provide for me."

A gust of wind blew hard on the flowers, and I thought about the snow that would cover them in the winter and the harsh conditions they must face. As if the flower were reading my mind, it said, "The wind blows, but I am deeply planted into the ground. I am solid. Seasons may change me, but my purpose remains … I am a wild flower."

A Chance Meeting of Purpose

Hurry! Hurry! Hurry! my mind yelled to the train that we all needed to take to the terminal. I looked down at my watch. *Damn! They'll close boarding in nine minutes, and the train will take six, which means I get to run two hundred yards in high heels and I still might not make my flight. Fabulous!*

Having passed through security at Central Florida International Airport, it was a short walk to the passenger rail that would shoot us to the departure terminal. The large glass windows opened into the bright, hot Florida sunshine, where I could clearly see if the next train was approaching. I closed my eyes and tried to relax. *I will make it. I will make it.*

"Excuse me, miss." My thoughts were interrupted, and my eyes opened as an elderly woman pushing an elderly man in a wheelchair tried to move past me.

"Oh, I am so sorry," I said, stepping aside to let them pass.

The woman was moving slowly, and she stopped shy of the hazard line painted in bold yellow on the platform inches in front of the sliding glass doors.

Finally! I thought as I saw the next train approaching. The elderly woman reached down to her man, speaking softly into his ear, barely audible. He reached up and patted her on the arm lovingly. *That is so sweet,* I thought. *That! That is true, genuine love. I wonder if Richard and I will be like that in forty or fifty years.*

The train came to a stop in front of us. The doors on the opposite side opened, allowing returning passengers to exit; then ours opened. The woman pushed the wheelchair onto the train while the crowd behind them waited patiently before cramming in like sardines.

"How long have you been married?" I asked the elderly couple. The woman locked the wheelchair in place and sat down on the bench in the rear of the car.

"We're not married!" the man replied gruffly. "We're living in sin!" His calm demeanor transformed into a sly grin on his wrinkled face.

"Oh, Harold," the woman interrupted, smacking him lightly on the arm. "Don't pay any attention to him, dear." She looked up, bright, cherry-red lipstick outlining her mouth. "We've been married fifty-two years and counting, my dear; fifty-two wonderful, glorious, amazing years." She patted Harold on his shoulder. He returned with his hand on top of hers. She looked down at my left hand, then up again. "How about you, my dear?"

"Almost seven." I stopped, wishing I could mirror her comments of "wonderful, glorious, and amazing," but I knew better. The couple exuded great energy, a sense about them that they played off each other so well.

"Can you tell me the secret to the happiness in your marriage?" I inquired. I so desperately wanted to know why Richard, who never touched me in public, didn't share the same feelings about me this gentleman clearly had toward his doting wife.

"Living in sin!" Harold yelled out again, his eyes smiling along with his mouth this time.

"Pay no attention, dear," she said, shaking her head a little.

She paused for a moment, her eyes slightly closing as if looking deep into the cavernous mass of memories the two must have accrued. Her eyes opened again, looking straight at me. "We run our marriage with plans and goals for our life, like a business. We have financial goals, personal goals, professional goals, and relationship goals."

Harold nodded in agreement.

She continued. "It's worked very well for us, and nearly every couple we know who are as happy do the same. But you want to know the most important secret?" she asked while leaning forward and looking side to side to make sure no one else was listening.

Leaning in closer, matching her moves, I nodded my head in anticipation.

She spoke in a low, soft voice. "We live each day like we are living in sin." Then she winked.

Taken aback and stifling a giggle, I looked over at Harold, who was obviously amused by his wife's comment. He too winked before allowing his Cheshire cat grin to expand from ear to ear. I nodded again, knowingly.

The train was coming to our stop, and I so badly wanted our conversation to continue, but I knew my time was short.

"Thank you so much," I said, looking back at what I hoped my future would look like.

I glanced down at my watch; less than two minutes before they closed boarding. *Crap!*

The doors opened, and I hustled out of the train and down the platform as quickly as possible. My fast walk turned into a skipping jog, the best I could do in heels, until I finally reached my gate.

"You barely made it!" the attendant said, taking my ticket and scanning it.

Can a Man Really Ever Be Trusted?

D ays spent in airports are part of the job. As a clinical research coordinator for a large company, travel is a sacrifice I am willing to make—for the right amount of money. The exchange of long hours spent collecting and reviewing information for study start-ups and scientific trials, then traveling for site visits to ensure the study meets company protocol and federal requirements, is purely to attain a salary to cover my wants in life as well as my needs.

Some days, I wonder if the lifestyle I have professionally is worth the sacrifice to my marriage and my personal life. Richard doesn't seem to mind me being gone so often though. Still, being a married twenty-seven-year-old female, I often feel as if I should be starting a family soon instead of focusing on a career.

Yet there I was walking down my eleventh Jetway in the last three weeks to a plane sitting on an otherwise obscure concourse. My plan was simple: document the day's work and summarize it for management so they could have it by morning, then get some sleep. One might say I'm a glorified babysitter getting paid to keep the kids in line and on schedule while the parents—the ones who keep me employed—take care of the important business, like making sure profits are up and investors are happy; a symbiotic relationship indeed.

Entering the plane, breathless from the run, I was greeted with a friendly welcome from the flight attendant. I managed a halfhearted smile in return, nodding in acknowledgment, while beads of sweat rolled down the sides of my face.

Find your seat, get the report done, then catch up on some much-needed sleep, I repeated in my mind. Rest was a necessity on this flight, since Richard had a company dinner party we had to rush to upon my arrival. This also meant a late night out on top of what had already been a very long day. *Ugh!*

Ticket and bags in hand, I shuffled through the narrow walkway of the plane. Thankfully, my assigned number was an aisle seat located in the front of the aircraft. After placing my small suitcase in the overhead above me, the last vacant spot, I took my seat and noticed the empty chair next to mine. *Hallelujah!* I thought, hoping the vacant space would provide a buffer between the passenger sitting in the window seat and me. My plan was to eliminate the small talk that so often ensues on long flights, and to make sure of it, I immediately pulled out my notebook and began writing furiously in the hope to send a message.

"Are you traveling for work or pleasure?" The woman next to me asked, fishing for a conversation. Her voice was nasally, with a slight southern accent.

Pretending I didn't hear her, I wrote even more furiously in the notebook, furrowing my eyebrows to nonverbally display to her my focused intent on the pages in front of me. However, I knew that if I didn't respond, that would be equally rude, and her curiosity might mean hours of further interruptions.

"I'm on my way home from a business trip. You?" I said, bluffing interest, my eyes still focused on my notebook. I wanted so desperately to stop this dialogue before it started.

"I'm headed to the Rocky Mountains to see my sister," she replied. "I'm so excited to see her. It's been years since we've seen each other. Plus it's my first time away from my husband and children in quite a while." Her conversation was casual, as if she had known me for years. "I'm so excited to relax and take a vacation for myself. Do you live there?"

Nodding but not responding, not making eye contact, I hoped she would get the point. She was relentless, though, and fished some more. "What do you recommend for the best places to visit?"

She waited for a response, recognizing I had not looked up at her. She reached her hand out in my direction, which I couldn't help but see out of my peripheral vision. "I'm Jennifer, by the way."

Oh no, I thought. *This is the obvious difference between traveling for work and traveling for pleasure. Little Miss Sunshine sitting next to me is excited and overjoyed to be on vacation and wants me to share in it. I, on the other hand, have expense reports to fill out. I'm exhausted and simply want to sleep.*

Stopping my writing, I looked up at the woman and the arm that was extended. She was indeed cheerful, with bright eyes and a smile that radiated warmth; she was quite attractive. By her appearance, I would guess her to be in her early thirties. She was obviously genuine in her desire to communicate with me, so I feigned enthusiasm as best I could. Setting my pen down, I returned the handshake. "Hi. I'm Lenea."

"I believe that's my seat," a deep baritone voice interrupted.

Surprised by the voice, I looked up and saw a strikingly handsome man in full pilot uniform. My attention had been so focused on my papers and avoiding the conversation that I hadn't noticed him make his way down the aisle. He smiled and pointed to the space between us. The muscles in his tan arms were outlined by the short sleeves of his pressed white shirt, which was tucked in nicely across his tight abdomen. Suddenly a surge of adrenaline rushed through my body.

"Oh, here," I said, stepping into the aisle, "let me move so you can get in."

"Thanks," he said before sliding between Jennifer and me.

"Sorry, I held things up, ladies," he added. Even his voice was gorgeous. "Just flew a wide-body in and I'm trying to catch a last-minute hop home. Lucky for me they had room." He spoke as if we were in the airline business and knew the lingo.

How lucky am I? I thought, my mood now shifting. There is nothing like physical attraction to spur a sudden increase in blood circulation. I leaned over slightly as he passed. *Oh my God! He even smells gorgeous.*

Even though I had been married almost seven years, and faithfully so, seeing a great-looking man still caused my heart to beat faster and the fantasies to start to roll.

"Are you ready for a great flight?" He put his hand on my knee in a 'friendly' way, obviously flirting and waiting to see my reaction.

My hand moved to deflect his advancement until our eyes met. I stopped. He had bright, playful blue eyes. His look sent a vibration through my body. Quickly I looked down, embarrassed to be caught ogling this incredible specimen of a man. Wanting to giggle like a schoolgirl and flirt

7

back, a quick glance down at his left ring finger stopped the response. A gold band was prominently displayed.

Darn it, I thought, *fantasy over.* With all the extra blood flow, my brain couldn't quite think of anything intelligent to say. I nodded without uttering a word.

"Is Colorado home for you two ladies?" His voice was so low and clear he could have anchored the evening news.

Before I could answer, Jennifer jumped in to recite her story with as much excitement and enthusiasm as she had moments before, this time to a more willing audience. Her body language told me she was also enjoying the new guest, albeit a little more aggressively; she had turned her body toward him and touched his arm for emphasis while responding.

Shaking my head to clear the somewhat jealous thoughts, I returned my focus to the notebook in front of me.

Soon the flight attendants began their announcements while we taxied down the runway. In moments, we made a slight turn before the acceleration of throttling engines pushed me back into the seat. The sound grew loud enough to drown out most of the conversation going on next to me, for which I was thankful.

As soon as the wheels lifted off the ground and the familiar dip that signaled we were airborne occurred, I pushed the button on the armrest and leaned my seat back. My eyes closed without effort.

A burst of laughter from Jennifer and the pilot's own guffaw woke me from a deep slumber. The two of them were chuckling and gasping for air as the pilot continued what must have been a hilarious story. From my half-awake eyes I could see the empty wine glasses on the tray tables in front of them. Looking down at my watch, I confirmed what my internal clock told me. I had slept for nearly the entire flight; we had about twenty minutes left until our expected arrival.

A few minutes later, a flight attendant's voice came over the loudspeaker, directing us to prepare for landing. I rubbed my eyes, yawned to pop my ears, and slowly started to reenter the real world. I sat up and reached for my notebook on the floor in front of me. It was embarrassing that I dropped it in the first place, but then I wondered if I had been snoring as well. *Did anyone see and make fun of me?*

Listening to the snippets of conversation from the two next to me, it was apparent they were in their own world.

"I would love to fly you to Tahiti," the pilot offered to Jennifer in his best bedroom voice.

"Oh that would be wonderful," she responded enthusiastically. "My husband and I love to travel! What's Tahiti like? I've never been there." I was astonished by the pilot's forwardness, given his marital status, and equally surprised by Jennifer, who seemed oblivious to the come on. The pilot was obviously interested in her, not Tahiti, and definitely not her husband.

"No, I would like to take *you* to Tahiti," he growled into her ear loud enough for me to hear, but probably thinking no one else could.

Looking over slightly, I caught Jennifer's response out of the corner of my eye: she was smiling and nodding as the pilot had leaned in closer to her ear, murmuring words only she could hear.

Turning back to my papers, a feeling of disgust reverberated through my entire body. Here was a married man blatantly hitting on a married woman with no shame. And she was playing right along with it.

Her body language demonstrated she was more than interested; she purred words back into his ear and had moved her hand onto his arm. The two continued their conversation more privately as we began the final descent and I tried to concentrate on the final pages of paperwork.

Still, I couldn't help but wonder what the pilot's wife was like. Maybe she was okay with him straying from the marriage. Maybe she had a boyfriend of her own. I would never know the story, but somehow the thought of something like this occurring between me and my husband made my stomach turn.

We touched down shortly thereafter and stopped at the gate. I stood up immediately to grab my bag and get away from the scene. Standing there, waiting for the door to open and the dozen or so passengers in front of me to exit, I heard him ask where she was staying and tell her he lived nearby. He pulled a card from his pocket, handed it to her, and told her she could drop by anytime. She thanked him. Fortunately the door opened and I found myself shuffling off the plane as quickly as possible.

The first breath I took, upon hitting the Jetway, was of the brisk Rocky Mountain air in early March. I was thankful to have space to move my body. Walking through the airport, I couldn't help but reflect upon the romantic interlude I had witnessed. Did this guy think because of his good looks and his uniform he could simply coax any woman he wanted into an affair? What a pig! The more I thought about it, the more

I steamed inside. Then I wondered whether this was an isolated case or whether it was indicative of what happens when married men travel alone. And if the latter, can a man really ever be trusted?

After stopping to go to the restroom, I made my way to the train that would take us to the baggage claim. I entered and moved to the rear of the car; Jennifer and the pilot jumped onboard at the last second before the doors closed. They both stood there and kept whispering into each other's ears. Inside I was disgusted all over again by the scene. *Seriously, can these people just get a room?* I thought.

Moments later the train jolted to a full stop. We all rode the escalator to the arrival area, and I soon found myself witnessing the reunion of the pilot with his wife as well as that of Jennifer and a young woman who must have been her sister.

The pilot's wife could have been a model. He lifted her up to embrace her and gave her a huge kiss. As I walked by, I could hear him tell her how much he had missed her.

Really? I thought to myself. *Oh honey, if you only knew how much your husband missed you! So much so that he asked another woman to join him in Tahiti.* Poor girl, if only she knew the truth. Or maybe she did and didn't care. Maybe, in her world, there was no question of his possible infidelity; it was simply her husband returning home, happy to see her. I could be the one to tell her, "Your husband is a pig!" Then again, so could Jennifer. But neither of us acted on the instinct. We all merely continued separately to our own little worlds. *Besides,* I thought, *no one wants to be the bearer of bad news, especially regarding a cheating spouse.*

Standing at the baggage carousel, I became more and more irritated with the actions of men in general. Moments later, I saw the pilot and his wife walk off together hand in hand, passing right by Jennifer and her sister. There was no sign of recognition between the two. No one would have ever suspected the pilot and Jennifer even knew one another, let alone that they had been engaged in an intimate conversation about an adulterous liaison to Tahiti only minutes earlier.

What is reality? I pondered. Obviously it is whatever we perceive it to be because if questioned, my reality and an outsider's reality of the same situation may be completely different. My thoughts turned to those of my own marriage. *I wonder if Richard was like this pilot since I was gone so often.* I reached into my purse for my cell phone and called him.

3

A Past Has Influence, Not Direction

"What?" Richard answered the phone obviously annoyed.

"Hey, babe, I'm at the baggage claim. Are you here yet?" I looked around the area, hoping to see him.

"Seriously! What do you expect from me, Lenea?" he snarled into the phone. "I'm getting there as fast as I can! It's … traffic. It really sucks. I'll get there when I get there, but probably ten more minutes." The phone went silent.

Great, I thought, *a night on the town with a pissed off husband. Super.*

Normally Richard wouldn't pick me up from the airport. Typically he would be off mountain biking or playing a round of golf. He definitely had never met me upon arrival, lifted me up in the air and told me how much he missed me. No, in Richard's world it was understood that transportation costs are a covered business expense. Thus, he felt it made better "financial sense" for me to find my own ride home, and it was "more convenient" to have my own car or take a taxi rather than to rely on him to drop me off or pick me up.

Today was different. Richard had a special dinner party with his company he couldn't miss. The big event was the fiftieth anniversary celebration of Kiriban Industries, and while he had only worked there four months, he felt the opportunity could propel him to the next level. It was a chance for him to rub elbows with his bosses and socialize with coworkers. The date had been on our calendar since the day he started the job.

I couldn't forget the heated discussion we had had about him going to the celebration without me. I told him that was not going to happen. I wanted us to go together. I suggested he could come get me from the airport on the way to the party. The argument ended with him giving in to my request, albeit reluctantly.

I could tell from his voice he was irritated about picking me up because it was causing him to be delayed. His tardiness was totally expected. I gave up a long time ago being annoyed at Richard's lack of ability to show up on time for anything. It sent me through the roof when we were newly married, but today I've accepted it as part of who he is. Plus, I now had an extra twenty minutes to pull myself together for the evening's event. I knew ten minutes meant more like twenty five in Richard's world.

Luckily I had thought this through and packed for the event in advance. The invitation stated "business cocktail attire." What the heck does that mean anyway? I took a guess before heading out of town and packed the ubiquitous little black dress. Still, I assumed "business cocktail" meant less cleavage and fewer sequins. Picking up my suitcase, I headed to the ladies' room to change.

My knee-length black sheath was perfect for the occasion. The dress was slightly fitted so it showed my curves, but conservative enough not to draw too much attention. I put on pearl earrings and a matching necklace and touched up my makeup. After slipping on some killer high heels, I was ready to go.

I looked at myself in the mirror; my youthful spirit was still with me. *Twenty-seven isn't that old*, I pondered, thinking I looked pretty good for my age. My shoulder-length auburn hair was styled in a trendy bob. My big, hazel eyes were probably my favorite feature. The reflection revealed a few wrinkles by the sides of my eyes—the first signs of aging. But all in all, I was pleased with my appearance.

My body was a different story. After turning twenty-five, I discovered working out wasn't the quick fix it once was, but rather a habit I maintained to keep up my physique. Giving up on the eighteen-year-old body I'd had years ago, I wondered how a woman could have stretch marks and cellulite without ever having a baby. My phone rang; it was Richard.

"Are you here?" I asked.

"Yes, I'm outside at passenger pick up, getting ready to pull forward. Where are you again?" He sounded even more irritated than before.

"I'm at door four twelve," I said, trying to sound happy and change the tone of the conversation.

Taking the escalator down to the fourth level, I turned to my left and walked toward the doors numbered four twelve. They slid open, and I stepped out to the curb as his black 4Runner pulled up.

I envisioned him jumping out of the car, grabbing my luggage, and saying how great I looked and how much he missed me. Instead I was met with "Hurry up!" He yelled through the open passenger side window, "The tailgate's unlocked. Throw your stuff in and let's go. We're late!"

Wow, nice to see you too, I thought. Lifting the rear door, I threw my luggage in, as he suggested, and tugged hard on the strap to shut the hatch. I walked around the car and climbed into the passenger seat, still hoping to get some sort of a reaction. Richard's face held a cold stare. He turned to check his side mirror for traffic.

"We are ridiculously late, Lenea. The traffic out there is horrible," he roared, looking over his left shoulder before accelerating away.

"Okay," I said, anger now welling up inside. "No 'Hi, how are you? How was your flight? How was work?' Instead, you are pissed." There was no response.

Clutching the steering wheel, Richard seemed to be in his own world; he was constantly in his own world. However, it hadn't always been like that. I remember the months of dating when he would open the door, buy me flowers, and leave love notes on my car windshield.

I missed those days. Ever since our honeymoon, it felt as if the game of winning my affection was won and over. Obviously, romance was no longer necessary in his world, but a part of me was slowly dying without it in mine.

As I watched Richard's angry face shift between side mirror and rearview mirror, I couldn't help but wonder how my life had evolved into this. There I sat, with a man who, unless he was being watched, was going to do things his own way and say "screw you" to any authority or rules. Looking back, I see that's what drew me to him in the first place.

Richard had an incredible sense of adventure and independence, always living for the moment. But after a while, that got old for me. I wanted a partner to build a solid future with. Almost seven years after the honeymoon, here we were fighting the same battles: Richard wanting to escape authority and maintain his independence, and me wanting to settle down and establish a lifelong partnership. Never in a million years did I believe "first comes love, then comes marriage," and then comes the day where husband and wife despise each other and stay together for the sake of the marriage contract.

No, I had lived long enough to realize the wedded world is not the Garden of Eden. Many marriages had crumbled around me as a result of various factors, the most common being the crimson mark of adultery by both men and women.

My own parents had divorced for this reason, and I understood deeply the destruction such actions can cause; families are ripped apart simply because a man and woman are still in the process of getting to know themselves and their own wants and needs, let alone one another's.

It wasn't fair. Some kids grew up in traditional families with two parents, a faithful dog, or perhaps a bowl of goldfish in the den. In my world, my sister and I were shuttled from one house to another like cargo in an inconvenient trade.

As a five-year-old, this kind of arrangement was unsettling, to say the least. I remember with fondness the conversations I had with my invisible friend Patty during those times. Neither my mom nor my dad believed in her. Neither accepted the possibility I had a friend to share all my thoughts with, someone who could help me sort out my feelings and deal with tough situations I could barely understand.

Simply because they couldn't see her didn't mean she wasn't real. In my mind, Patty was real and our friendship was too, like that of the blended family I watched on *The Brady Bunch*.

At a young age, I swore to myself that when I grew up and found my Prince Charming, our marriage would be different. I wouldn't experience the kind of hatred that destroyed lives and left children unsure of whether they were coming or going.

Yet here I was in my own marriage, facing what appeared to be a familiar pattern: the same challenges, the same dissatisfaction, and the same unhappiness. At least there were no children to bruise mentally or to treat as pawns in the game of marital chess.

Thanks to many conversations with Patty and years of thought,

I eventually developed my own beliefs as to why my mom and dad divorced. And I was determined that no matter what hell I went through, whatever pain and trouble, whatever discomfort it took, I would damn well make my marriage to Richard successful.

Our marriage really wasn't that different from others, I imagine; I was certain most couples faced similar struggles. Aren't we always in the process of getting to know ourselves and one another? Isn't that what I'm doing right now?

We passed building after building as I contemplated my life in silence. Richard wasn't a bad guy. He had a zest for life. Responsibility wasn't his gig, but that's what I was for. I was responsible enough for three people.

Maybe this is why he felt safe to jump from job to job. Not that it was always his choice; being fired doesn't really count as choosing a different career. Yet this was how Richard viewed things.

There was always some sort of blame or excuse: someone didn't like him, he didn't fit in, he was smarter than his boss, he hated the work, or it simply wasn't what he wanted to do. He felt justified to continually leave and find something better suited for him. His parents would excuse the behavior, saying he hadn't found his "true calling." No kidding. I wondered if there would ever be a "perfect place" for him.

His lack of ambition drove me crazy. Many times I took on extra work or side jobs to stay on top of our bills; I abhorred being in debt. Richard, on the other hand, had no problem with it. He saw credit as a necessary means to an end. Every time we put something on a credit card—this included trips to the grocery store—I cringed. I worried and agonized and lost sleep. He had no discipline when it came to money. Come to think of it, he had no discipline at all!

Sitting in the car staring at his contorted face wrought with frustration, I realized he didn't seem to think twice about the silence between us. Forty-five minutes had passed, and we were only now entering downtown, where the party was. The traffic was horrible. But that was typical during rush hour on a Friday night in a big city. Why someone would plan a major company event at 6:00 p.m. on a Friday is beyond me.

A company party wasn't much of an adventure, but it sure felt good having a night out together, even though the evening started off fraught with tension.

I couldn't remember the last time Richard had taken me on a date.

Seriously, I now understand the people who say they never want to get married, primarily because they don't want to lose the fun, excitement, and romance of dating. I don't blame them.

It's quite pathetic, really, that Richard and I basically live individual lives, bumping into one another because we have a contract called marriage. Marriage. For what? Love? Sex? Procreation? It was comical to think the reason we were married was to have sex. It had been almost seven years, but the sex was almost nonexistent.

It had been very different when we were dating; I remember like it was yesterday. We laughed and played and enjoyed each other's bodies very much. When he wanted sex early in the relationship, I gave him the ultimatum: You don't buy the cow, you don't get the milk. How romantic. Boy, I was young and naive!

I told him I couldn't continue sleeping with a man and giving the best parts of me without a major commitment. Thinking I was being a strong woman by standing up for the virginity I so graciously gave him, I wanted to know his body was for me alone and mine for him. Marriage, I thought, was the key to making this happen. In reality, I loved having sex with him. It felt so right and natural, and I didn't want to stop.

So Richard, only a year older than me, agreed marriage was the next step. I signed the contract of commitment and thought all my fears and insecurities would disappear the moment the ring was on my finger.

If only I could go back and talk to that girl now, I would yell *"Stop! Don't do it! Don't get married just to have sex without guilt!"* But as they say, hindsight is always twenty-twenty.

Six years have passed since the pact was sealed, and I'm still trying to figure out what sex and marriage are all about. Six years with no children was not the typical marriage, at least not for the married friends we had. Maybe that's why I hadn't found fulfillment. It's in children! But something told me deep inside that fulfillment with children was as much of a lie as fulfillment attained via sex and marriage.

Richard's voice broke the silence. "What do you think of my tie?" he asked.

"I think it looks great," I answered nonchalantly, somewhat dazed and confused by his sudden desire to talk.

"Lenea, where's your mind? You seem so distant." At least he feigned concern well.

"Long trip. I'm tired," I responded with an easy out.

"Yeah, me too," he said. "I'm not really looking forward to turning on the charm this evening. Not even sure I have the energy."

"You'll do great," I said, trying to encourage him, but it came out halfheartedly. "Somehow you'll pull it off. You always do."

It's true Richard knew how to light up a room with his charm and charisma. He was a good-looking guy and people were genuinely attracted to him. Plus he was a great conversationalist. He seemed to know something about everything and was able to connect easily with others.

As for myself, I despised small talk. However, I was indeed grateful for his ability to hold conversations and at times even jealous that it came so easily for him.

We turned a corner and slowed in front of our destination. Richard told me the party was on the top floor. I had never been inside the old building and was anxious to get a peek.

As the valet opened my door, I could feel the crisp spring air hit my bare legs, and suddenly my weariness evaporated; my spirit revived. I was ready for a change of atmosphere and excited for an evening of good food, flowing drinks, and lively entertainment.

4

A Party I'll Never Forget

ichard handed the valet his keys, and we were escorted under the covered entrance into the historic building. The big wooden double doors opened, revealing a small waiting area where other party attendees were gathered. It was a private foyer and way too small to accommodate a large crowd.

A long line of people formed in front of a small check-in desk to the left. We took our place in line and stood there moving at a snail's pace. "You look nice," I said to Richard, offering him another opportunity to notice my appearance as well.

"Thanks," he said casually while looking around at others, but never once at me. "You have no idea how excited these people are about this party tonight. They've been going on and on about this event for months." His tone was quiet and reserved. "I did some research on this building. It's actually an exclusive landmark, and the cost to rent this place for the night is insane. You'll see."

Finally, he seemed to show some enthusiasm, and I was happy to see him excited. Still, I was hurt that he once again neglected the opportunity to give me a compliment. Didn't he notice the extra effort? Did he even care? I tried to shake off the feeling my husband didn't seem attracted to me anymore by focusing my attention on the people around me.

Business cocktail attire obviously meant different things to different folks. While some women take any opportunity to show off their furs and diamonds, others showed up looking as if they were headed to Sunday school. Based on my observations, I felt secure in the way I was dressed and proud to be the young, sexy woman by Richard's side.

From the outside, others probably viewed Richard and me as the perfect couple. The funny thing is, no one really knows the truth of a marriage—perhaps not even the couple involved.

As we approached the woman behind the desk, she smiled cheerfully, took our names, and handed us drink tickets for the evening. She directed us toward a small elevator at the opposite corner of the room, where an attendant, dressed in a dark gray suit and jacket with gold piping and big brass buttons, was standing. When we approached, he informed us the wait would be only a minute or two.

Shortly thereafter, the line had grown so long behind us, the attendants told others to stay outside until enough people had entered the elevator.

Standing there, I looked around. The entrance reminded me of a period speakeasy. I read that when going to a speakeasy, patrons would walk through a small, sometimes hidden, door, and the only way out was either back where you came from or through a secret passageway where you needed permission to leave.

"Ladies and gentlemen, if you would please make way for our guests by moving to your right, it would be greatly appreciated. Thank you," the attendant said while pointing in the direction he desired our group to move.

Another group of people waiting for the elevator had formed to the side of us. The sound of a door chime shifted my attention. The attendant's smile gleamed like the buttons on his jacket as he announced the arrival of the elevator.

Finally! I thought.

We all filed slowly into the small elevator, filling every inch of space. Another attendant, similarly dressed, operated the buttons. Standing there in our large group, I felt the floor shift beneath me as we made our ascent to the loft. It was a privilege to be in the building and a part of such a special occasion.

The elevator stopped with a thud, and the attendant announced our arrival. Wishing us a good evening, he held the doors open for our departure.

My heart was racing like a little girl's at Christmas. I was so excited to see what this "exclusive landmark" was all about.

We exited the elevator into a hallway with a large picture window to our left overlooking the city. It was breathtaking; a glittering vision in the night, twinkling from end to end. *This is upscale living*, I thought, gazing out over the buildings below.

We walked down the hall, my heels clicking on the golden maple floor beneath me. The rich color of the walkway perfectly complemented the exposed grayish-brown stone walls of the building's interior. The towering ceilings were spectacular, and my first impression was enough to take my breath away. We were welcomed by an older woman in a turquoise dress who directed us to the bar, encouraging us to drink responsibly.

The bar had an eclectic modern flair, reminiscent of the penthouse suites I had seen in couture magazines. It featured granite countertops and ornate wood accents and was equipped with backlit glass highlighting the top shelf of alcohol. In the space between the glass shelves were three big-screen televisions that displayed rolling photos of the company's employees through the years. It was a nice touch to signify the purpose of the celebration.

Five bartenders were moving gracefully around one another to fill orders. In between their dances, they were chatting with guests and creating colorful concoctions in a blur of motion.

This company obviously enjoyed celebrating with alcohol, for they had spared no expense in making sure their guests were taken care of. We received our drinks and headed to an open cocktail table.

As I took in the surroundings, Richard told me about the history of the building.

"It was renovated during the late 1990s for parties and large gatherings," he said. "But prior to its renovation, it had been used as a dance studio where many of the performers would practice their routines in preparation for productions in the surrounding theaters."

Looking around the room, I focused on the architecture and decor. The stone-covered walls continued past the bar and surrounded a gigantic open area filled with a sea of round tables under rows of enormous and exquisite chandeliers. It was the perfect lighting.

The tables were covered with black tablecloths and accented with gold touches. Sheer golden fabric adorned the room and festooned the open ceiling above. The centerpieces were tall glass cylinders filled with delicate cascades of violets. The hint of purple blossoms against the gold-and-black backdrop provided a sophisticated and elegant environment.

Whoever was in charge of decoration had spared no expense. I wondered why the dress code was business cocktail rather than black tie. I was certain that at any moment I would see celebrities being escorted around the room.

Suddenly my black sheath dress and pearls didn't feel up to par compared to the glamorous setting and the enchanting atmosphere.

"Are you ready to watch the show?" Richard asked, pointing to a stage I had failed to notice.

"Sure, what show are you talking about?" I responded, unaware of the evening's schedule.

"Dan, the CEO, hired a group of dancers to perform for us tonight. He said he chose dancers to keep with the original intent of the building." He stopped to take a sip of his cocktail, each drink fueling his fire. "You'll meet him—Dan. He's the master of ceremonies tonight. He's a good guy."

Richard was right about the venue. It did look like a space where a large performance could take place. It would be the perfect location for a large wedding reception—for the ridiculously wealthy, that is.

"Where will they dance?" I asked, continuing to stoke his enthusiasm.

"Right over there. Come on, I'll show you." He grabbed my hand, and we started walking. We strolled casually through the bar area, which was filled with cocktail tables and crowds of people. Then Richard pointed off to the right, where the open area extended even farther back.

It was a large alcove area. Centered along the back wall was a perfectly symmetrical built-in stage with a huge white screen stretching the entire length from floor to ceiling—similar to what one would find in a movie theater.

With so little of the actual stage showing, I was curious how the dancers could perform. Studio lights hung from the ceiling. Off to the sides were several large speakers. It appeared the stage was part of the building and had probably been used for concerts, small plays, or other live performances.

Looking around for a clock to see what time it was, since he never wore a watch, Richard indicated the show was about to begin and we should find a table close by to have a good view.

Two unoccupied seats were available in the front right corner and we grabbed them immediately. The room was starting to fill up quite nicely.

"You stay here, and I'll go get us another drink," Richard said as I sat down.

The people around me seemed so lively, talking and laughing. It was an enjoyable scene. There was a distinct sense of familiarity between the couples.

Richard returned with our drinks, handing me a glass of white wine while taking his seat. "I don't recognize any of these people," he said in a hushed voice.

"Well, you've only worked here for four months. Give it some time," I responded reassuringly. Secretly, I hoped that this company would be the right fit; that he wouldn't piss anyone off and could make his employment last longer than his typical three- to six-month stint.

The lights dimmed, and a hush fell over the crowd. The air was heavy with anticipation.

A distinguished brown-haired man sporting a goatee approached the stage. A spotlight shined on him as the audience clapped and hollered. He waved casually, stopping in the center. The massive white screen behind seemed to dwarf him.

"That's our CEO, Dan Johnson," Richard said a little too loudly in my ear.

Dan's speech began with enthusiasm and passion. "We are here this evening to celebrate a milestone for Kiriban Industries. Tonight, we celebrate together fifty golden years of prominent business leadership." The crowd clapped and whistled their approval. "We have an incredible lineup of entertainment planned throughout the evening. But first I would like to thank all of the people who made this event possible."

Names were called, and as the contributors stood, we clapped politely in recognition.

Soon I found myself daydreaming, wondering what it would be like to be married to a man like Dan. He was so passionate and enthusiastic. I bet he noticed a woman's appearance. I bet he was great in bed. The fantasies were quite pleasant given the moment.

Mr. Johnson gave a brief history about the building and a synopsis of the evening's events. A theatrical performance would be followed by a buffet dinner, company awards, and accolades. The finale would be live music and dancing. "Oh, and don't forget to stop by the dessert station in the far back corner to my left," he said, a sly grin on his face as he pointed to the table in the back. "You won't want to miss the custom S'mores bar. I had to try it out for you guys. Take one for the team. Toasted marshmallow with cherries and dark Swiss chocolate is my favorite!"

The audience moaned in delight and several people laughed. The thought did make me hungry. I smiled at Richard; he knew S'mores were one of my favorite desserts.

"Without further ado, ladies and gentleman, please put your hands together and welcome our very special guests for the evening, Elemental Charity!" With that, Dan exited the stage.

The spotlight dimmed and the whole room went black.

The sound of a slow, rhythmic drum permeated the space. I could feel the vibration in my chest. My curiosity was heightened as I watched the studio lights transform the white screen into a deep red. The stage and the screen were now both lit with a mysterious ruby glow.

Slowly, three equally spaced, perfectly proportioned women's bodies appeared as illuminated from behind the reddish screen. It was like nothing I had ever seen before. The silhouettes became more distinct anatomically as they stepped closer.

They stopped walking to the beat of the drum and stood motionless for a moment. There was silence.

Suddenly the drumbeat resumed, stronger, and the women stomped their left legs in unison to the beat, pounding their fists toward the ground at the same time. One could surmise that behind the screen they were naked, or at least in form-fitting body suits.

There was something very erotic about watching these women and their movements; I could feel their primal tension and passion energize the room.

The drums stopped, and the music transitioned to a slow, rhythmical number with an ebb and flow like the ocean tide. The women danced about, moving smoothly to the melodic sounds. I was mesmerized by the music and enchanted by the fluidity of the graceful silhouettes. Each woman danced in her own space and in her own way, as if no one was watching.

One song's rhythm led in to the next, each a mere ten or twenty seconds, while the women moved closer to one another.

Eventually they began reaching out, touching and exploring each other's bodies as if they were meeting for the first time, the red light illuminating every curve of their shadowed female forms. Their movements told a story without any words.

When the series of songs ended, the silhouettes grew smaller as the dancers walked backward, away from the screen, and disappeared together in perfect unison.

The stage dimmed to blackness. Before anyone could think, let alone applaud, the stage lights came on, this time covering the stage in a bright emerald green.

Six silhouettes reappeared this time; the same three women were now joined by three male figures. The men looked very muscular. The masculine presence brought a whole new feeling of intrigue.

Looking over at Richard, I could see his eyes were glued to the stage. Turning my gaze to the audience in the green-lit room, it seemed as if the crowd had fallen into a trance. The mass sat motionless, silently gazing upon the beautiful bodies illuminated and moving behind the screen.

This music had a much lighter and happier sound. The fluttering sound of flutes created a whimsical mood as each of the men took turns dancing with the women. The male and female silhouettes appeared blissful in their movements.

Soon the men were lifting the women into the air and twirling them around. I smiled as I watched their love for one another come alive—no sound, only body language. The joy they were portraying on stage was mirrored in my heart. I could actually feel the emotion as I watched what seemed to be young lovers gliding in unison with light feet and not a care in the world.

Even though I couldn't see their facial expressions, I could sense them joyously smiling with adoration for one another behind the screen.

Again the lights went down to blackness.

This time the crowd applauded enthusiastically. I was so elated by this artistic expression of love and bliss that I found myself clapping a little louder than normal.

The sound of the applause faded and the stage was illuminated once again, in an ethereal indigo blue. This color seemed more intense and penetrating than the other two. The music began, and it didn't sound like music at all. Instead it was a loud swishing noise, as if we were being transported somewhere through the cosmos.

Intertwined in the traveling sounds were small, high-pitched chimes, like a bell tinkling through the air. Each time a chime would ring, one silhouette would be vividly illuminated. There was no sense of order to their appearance. An eerie feeling pervaded the space as the dancers repeatedly popped up in chaotic fashion across the stage. There were obviously more bodies than in the first or second act; their sporadic, lighted presence filled the entire length of the stage.

It felt as if we, the audience, were flying and catching visions of bodies flashing in front of us.

The swooshing sounds stopped, and the screen stood bathed in the magical deep bluish light. It was a well-timed dramatic pause.

Suddenly the drum started pounding, and once again, I could feel the vibration in my chest. Then a backlight turned on, outlining twelve silhouettes walking in a perfect chorus line toward the audience. As the bodies came closer to the screen, it became apparent there were both men and women.

When they arrived in their positions, they separated into couples— six distinct pairs of male and female. Each couple reached out to another, hands and arms moving randomly without any sense of choreography.

Then, in unison, the men placed themselves behind their female partners, and simulated tearing off the women's clothes, as though peeling the layers off an onion. The primal sounds of the beating drum grew stronger and stronger as more and more layers were removed until, suddenly, the women's black bodily silhouettes disappeared and became glowing orbs of light.

The music shifted to an intense concerto, swelling as if the symphony were playing its final number. All of the instruments joined in the fanfare.

Meanwhile, the men ran around the stage in confusion while the spheres of light flashed across the screen, rhythmically moving in a sporadic pattern.

It was evident that the male dancers were mesmerized and shocked; they ducked and weaved between the balls of light around them.

The tempo of the music slowed, and following the musical cue, the men lessened their movements. They positioned themselves in a perfect line, all standing completely still as each of the six balls of light came to rest on top of their heads.

The music once again shifted and grew in volume and intensity. The six spheres of light began to consume their male partners, like a forest fire engulfing a tree, until their masculine figures disappeared completely and six distinct, much larger and brighter balls of light remained.

The indigo stage lights were still noticeable. But the six bright white globes, or what looked now like spotlights, were the center of attention.

They began flashing. The strobe effect created a visual signal like six flashlights being turned on and off in mesmerizing sequence. The beat of the music was strong, and soon the high-pitched sound of a trumpet echoed throughout the room.

A sense of climax filled the air as the six orbs converged into one large, glowing sphere of pure white light. The grand finale permeated the room in celebration.

My skin was warm, and my limbs tingled. I felt as if I were in the presence of God.

The warmth was quickly replaced by chills running throughout my entire body. Soon the music and all of the lights went out; there was a brief moment of silence in the still black space.

One by one, a slow clapping began and grew louder as each person realized the enormity and virtuosity of what they had witnessed. Richard and I rose to our feet as the crowd began to whistle, shout, and cheer, demanding more until every member of the audience was standing and applauding.

The house lights slowly rose. I felt a return to reality when the ovation faded away and people turned to one another to discuss their excitement.

Dan, the master of ceremonies walked back onto the stage. With a look of incredulousness on his face, he lifted the microphone to his lips. "Wow, ladies and gentlemen, what a treat! Thank you, Elemental Charity!"

Dan's voice trailed off as I replayed the last scene over and over again in my head, astounded by what I had observed. My body was on fire.

5

An Introduction, a Lesson and a Business Card

The evening continued, following the schedule precisely. A buffet dinner was served while flirty cocktail music played in the background. Small talk surrounded the tables, and it looked as though everyone was enjoying the celebration.

Richard left to retrieve dessert for both of us. I sat at our table and sipped on a decaf coffee while watching the band set up their instruments on stage. Behind them, another set of crew members were removing the final pieces of the white screen.

Several minutes passed, and still no Richard. I looked around the room, spotting him standing over a chair at a table next to the dessert bar. He was talking with a group of three women seated there. *He must have been interrupted on his way,* I thought. They appeared to be having fun and joking with one another—totally normal behavior for Richard. Over the years, he rarely had male friends wherever he worked. He once told me that men in general didn't like him because he presented a threat to them. It seemed like a cocky thing to say at the time, but I figured it must be a "man thing."

When I caught Richard's eye, he made no motion for me to join him and also made no attempt to leave the table of women. It was as if I didn't exist. After waiting almost twenty minutes, he still hadn't come back with our dessert. By this time, I was feeling a little uneasy. Here I was in this sea of people, not knowing a single one, and my husband was chatting up other women and pretending he didn't know me. I decided it would be best if I joined them. Hesitantly, I stood up and pushed my chair under the table.

It crossed my mind for a moment that maybe this was the reason Richard had wanted to come alone to the party. *Does he have ulterior motives with these women?* I shook the thought away and walked toward the dessert bar, stopping at Richard's table, patiently waiting for an opportunity to ask if he would like anything.

I felt awkward standing there by his side, attempting to enter the conversation. The table he was entertaining had now grown into a virtual harem of women. Nevertheless, I merged in, laughing at his stories while he commanded the stage. At a break in the conversation, I politely excused myself to grab dessert. Richard was in his own world of self-importance and never acknowledged my presence or impending absence. The least he could have done was make an introduction.

As I walked to the rear of the line, waiting my turn for a S'more, I noticed a commotion behind the stage. Two tall blonde women in dance attire were walking around visibly upset. I left the line and began walking toward them. Instinctively I knew these women were the performers from the show, and something was drawing me to them like a moth to a flame.

With only a few steps left until I arrived at center stage, I was stopped by a woman's voice. "May I help you?"

Turning around, I saw that a petite woman with long, dark, wavy hair had circled in front of me, as if to block my way to the stage. Her features were very striking—a strong jaw and full pursed lips. She stood uncomfortably close.

"Oh, I'm sorry," I said, trying to back away. The irritation on her face was obvious. I felt like a kid caught with her hand in the candy jar, needing to explain my motives. "I was hoping to talk with the performers and tell them what a wonderful job they did tonight."

The stone look on her face did not change. Her eyes were a deep, dark brown; I couldn't tell where the pupil ended and the iris began. They were piercing right to my core.

"The girls are not available to talk," she said with a hint of a French accent. She had a gypsy-like presence about her, with a long black skirt and matching transparent blouse that revealed her corset undergarment.

Her arms were covered in beads and crystal jewelry, and I got the impression she must be the manager of the dance troupe or somehow connected to them.

"Oh, that's too bad. Are you their manager?" I asked the question, but I wished I had used a better word for "manager."

The look on her face was very mysterious. "You may call me Madame," she responded. This time the French accent was very distinct.

"It's nice to meet you. I'm Lenea." I stuck my hand out, trying to break the ice. There was an awkward pause as her motionless gaze never left my face. Her hands remained still. I returned my hand to my side, searching for better words. "That was one of the best performances I've ever seen," I said awkwardly. "You did a great job with the choreography. It … I mean … I felt as if I traveled to another world."

The corners of her thick lips turned upward producing a slight smile. Then she turned around to face the stage and seemed to purposely ignore my comment. Once again an uncomfortable silence ensued until she quickly spun around, this time a curious look on her face. "And where is this other world?"

Her words took me by surprise. "I'm not sure," I answered. "But wherever it is, it is truly a magical place." The disgruntled look on her face said it all; it appeared she was thinking this wasn't a conversation she cared for. She turned around, again ignoring my comment.

It wasn't my nature to be rude to someone, let alone have someone be rude to me. For whatever reason, I felt a need to make amends to this strange woman, hoping my words would appease her. "It was a very sensual world, filled with love and romance." I looked down for a moment, trying to find words that might get her attention while I spoke to the back of her head. "The scenes did something to my body, transporting me to a place of absolute bliss. I … I really enjoyed it. I felt … happy."

She cast a furtive glance back at me, over her shoulder, then completed her turn before stepping into my personal space to face me once more with those penetrating eyes. "It is sad for a woman to not know the world she desires." She stopped, stepped back to move a plant used as a prop on the stage, and then walked away. She hesitated momentarily and returned to me, this time stopping uncomfortably close to my body, almost nose to nose. Her voice became stern and pointed. "Let me know when you figure out what it is *you* desire."

She reached up, kissed me high on my cheekbones on both sides of my face, handed me her business card, and walked away.

Standing there dumbfounded over our interaction, I was taken aback by her forwardness and realized I had never been treated so rudely by a complete stranger. Yet something inside of me was haunted by her words and that kiss. I had seen French people kiss like that on television, but never had someone, let alone a complete stranger, done that to me. And what did she mean by "the world she desires?"

I couldn't shake the thought of not being able to put this into words, vowing to myself that if I were ever to compliment someone again, I would make sure I knew what I was complimenting them on before I spoke. Otherwise, I would keep my mouth shut. I looked down at the card in my hand. It was black, like her attire. On one side was displayed a silver logo for the dance group, Elemental Charity, and the other contained address information and the following quote:

As your desire is, so is your will.
As your will is, so is your deed.
As your deed is, so is your destiny.
—The Upanishads

Chills resonated throughout my body. I wanted to keep this card in a safe place.

I could see from a distance that Richard had finally returned to our table with dessert. The band was warming up, and the noise of them starting their set made me jump. My mind wandering, I had forgotten all about the reality of where I was and what was going on around me. I walked up to Richard and sat down, the live jazz now energizing the room.

"Hi, Stranger!" I said, feigning interest in him while placing more excitement in the delicacy placed before me.

"I got your favorite," he said, equally disinterested in our interaction.

I wanted to say "it took you long enough!" but I was feeling more confused than ever by the events of the evening, let alone the man seated next to me. "Thanks, babe, you're the best!" I retorted, annoyed and sarcastic.

"Look," he said under his breath sternly while grabbing my hand, "if you are trying to ruin this evening for me, you'd better stop. You're tired, and you've been acting like a spoiled princess since I picked you up. Now knock it off! Maybe you should take the car home. I can catch a cab if you want."

I stared at him, perplexed and hurt. His words cut like a knife. I didn't feel tired at all. In fact, I was ready to dance and party all night long. But there was something about his comment that felt more like a directive than a thoughtful gesture. "Is that what *you* want me to do?" I asked taking a bite of the S'more, though the dessert had now lost its appeal.

"No, but I know you've had a long day, and you don't seem to be having any fun," he answered. "I wanna stay out late tonight, blow off some steam. I don't want you to feel like you have to stay out late with me. That's all."

I sat there and stewed, not wanting to look at him. Perhaps he thought it was a kind gesture; but I knew better. Still, I tried to control my reaction, realizing his words were somewhat true. It had been a long day, and its events had taken a toll on my emotions. Maybe it would be better if I went home and got some rest.

We finished our dessert. By this time, the dance floor was full of people—couples gazing with delight into each other's eyes as they moved with youthful exuberance across the floor. I wondered if Richard and I would ever be like those couples. They seemed so happy and in love, instantly reminding me of the couple I met on the airport train in Florida. I smiled with the memory.

Glancing over at him, trying to diffuse the tension of the moment, I offered, "Do you want to dance?"

He looked back at me, seemingly puzzled by the question. "You know I don't dance," he retorted irritably, remaining seated. He continued to stare at the partygoers in front of him, completely disinterested in me or my words.

I couldn't help but flash back to our dating days, when we would hit dance clubs into all hours of the night. He never said he didn't want to dance then. *What changed?* As we sat there listening to the music, I found myself transitioning from slightly physically tired to completely mentally exhausted. Another song passed without interaction from Richard. I looked down at my watch. *Two more hours of this? No way!*

"Okay, well I'm tired and I think I'll head home now. Do you have the valet ticket?" I asked heatedly.

He stood up, barely acknowledging my words. "I'll walk you to the door."

After gathering my things, we began walking to the elevator. Once we were there, he stopped and handed me the ticket.

"Drive safe. I'll text you when I leave, but don't wait up. Get some sleep, okay," he said, giving me a heartfelt kiss on the cheek. For the first time all evening I felt as though I had my husband back, with his concern for my well-being.

Entering the elevator, trying to make sense of the evening's events, I felt maybe I had overreacted. His affectionate demonstration confirmed that he loved me. *Right now, he is simply a little self-absorbed. He has always been self-absorbed. So why would I spend so much time questioning our relationship? Does it really matter that we don't have a fairy-tale marriage? Who does? What is a fairy-tale marriage anyway? They're obviously fairy tales because they don't happen in reality. I should be happy I have a husband who is honest with me and tells me his plans.*

My mind spun as I thought of my friends who had gotten divorces, usually because their husbands were living double lives. That wasn't Richard. He may have his faults, but at least I knew he would tell me the truth, even if I didn't always agree or like what he had to say.

The elevator bumped to a halt, and the doors opened. I exited into the lobby, which didn't seem as small as it had when we arrived. There were only a handful of people waiting inside for the valet to retrieve their cars. Still, it took a fairly long time. It appeared only one young man was making the run for vehicles. After about twenty minutes, I got irritated from the wait, as did those standing around me.

"Did they park our cars in Kansas?" I asked in a lighthearted manner to a couple standing next to me. The woman smiled politely. The man, on the other hand, simply shook his head while looking down at his watch for the umpteenth time.

I took out my cell phone to pass the time, checking the social status of the world. *What did people do in the days before the cell phone?* I wondered. Finally, the valet came in, his voice exasperated. "Sorry, folks, I had a tow truck blocking my exit. Who's next?"

I almost forgot what I was doing, entranced with a post. "Oh. That's me!" The words took a moment to sink in.

He took my ticket, looked at the number, and looked back up at me. "I'm so sorry for the wait, ma'am. I'll be right back."

YOU & I, INC.

I cringed at the word "ma'am." *Was I really that old?*

I smiled at him graciously. "No worries. I'm not in any hurry." I could feel his frenetic energy, as he obviously knew he was far behind in appeasing his growing line of customers. I tried to balance his angst with a more casual approach and turned my attention to the phone. I was happy to be next in line.

A few minutes later, the valet pulled up with the car and opened the door. I reached into my purse to hand him money and, in a flash, realized I had left Madame's business card on the table.

"Oh no!" I exclaimed in a panicked voice. "I left something inside. I'll be back in five minutes. I promise." My heart raced. I turned to dash for the entrance, not waiting for an answer from the valet.

Anxiety resonated throughout my body at the thought of the cleaning crew clearing the table and throwing away the card. I wasn't sure why, but it seemed like that card was desperately important.

When I exited the elevator into the loft, it was apparent the party had reached a high. People spilled over from the dance floor in between tables, and informal conga lines were now circling the party. Pushing my way through the crowds, I made it to the table and breathed a sigh of relief. There was the black card, set neatly against the centerpiece vase. I picked it up and tucked it safely away inside my purse, silently giving thanks to God. Circling back toward the elevator, I stopped for a moment to look for Richard. When I saw him, my eyes grew wide and my mouth dropped open.

There he was, on the dance floor with a group of young women and two other guys about his age. My whole world started spinning at that moment. I couldn't believe he was out there when less than an hour before he told me that he didn't like or want to dance. My chest began to pound.

One woman had her hands around his neck, moving and gyrating suggestively close to his body. I watched her as she seductively leaned into him and kissed him. He didn't seem to mind. I waited for him to push her away. Instead, he held her closer and returned her kiss with equal passion.

I felt sick to my stomach. I wanted to walk on the dance floor and scream at her to get her hands off my husband, but instead I stood there motionless, dizzy. Tears welled in my eyes. I looked away and started running toward the elevator, lowering my head, hoping not to gain any attention. I stood waiting for the elevator, dumbfounded.

I was able to hold myself together. That is, until I was alone in the car driving home. Then I began to cry hysterically. "You fucking asshole!" I screamed out loud, as if he were in the car with me. "How could you do this? Give up everything we have and have worked for? Just to be with some bimbo? I've done everything to make sure you, *you*, could do what you wanted!" I kept my tirade going until my voice left me. Blinded by tears, I finally made it home.

I turned the ignition off and banged my hands on the steering wheel before opening the car door and slamming it shut as hard as I could. Then I stumbled inside and collapsed onto the couch. There I grabbed a pillow and started pounding it, pretending it was him, before clutching it, a sobbing mess. As I lay there, tears flowing, I thought about what were now obvious signs of trouble: he had received texts from other women, claiming they were work related, as well as business calls he had to take privately during the evening.

Maybe I was blind and didn't want to believe Richard's behavior could be real. I wondered how I had convinced myself that my husband wasn't living a double life. That he was faithful. That he was a good man. Maybe he had a lover on the side. Or, worse, maybe he had asked this other woman to go to Tahiti with him. *Yeah, a trip courtesy of my hard-earned money!* I steamed inside while the sickening visions of him cheating on me played over and over in my mind like sordid tales from a soap opera.

The negative fantasies were spinning out of control. Finally I had enough and sat up. I shook my head, and my thoughts began to change.

Don't be ridiculous, Lenea. This is pointless, imagining all sorts of things when there is no proof! Richard didn't do anything. She kissed him first. They were only dancing.

The excuses kept coming as I justified his behavior. He told me he needed to blow off steam. I knew he wanted to be successful in this new company. He was probably trying to impress his boss.

Even with this change of thoughts, I couldn't shake the jealousy I had of the other woman he held in his arms, and the insecurity of not feeling confident enough to go out on the dance floor and tell her, "Fuck off! Get your hands off of my husband!" Perhaps, if I had more confidence,

I should have just gone out there and joined them in a sordid threesome while blowing off a little steam. God, why didn't I do that?

Continuing to beat myself up for failing to stop this nonsense before it had even started, I tried to deduce why everything had gone wrong. *All I had to do was ask him questions: "Who is the girl, and why are you kissing?" Instead, I'm at home pissed off and he's still having a good time.* I sat on the couch enraged as the battle escalated in my mind.

Eventually I reached what felt like a conclusion. I wasn't going to bed tonight until I had answers. No matter how late he got home, I would wait up for him, strategically planning every move as if it were an all-out enemy attack. I was locked and loaded and ready to lay into him the moment he walked through the door.

Suddenly the words from the quote on the back of Madame's card entered my mind: "As your deed is, so is your destiny." *Is this my destiny? To live with a man who leads a double life? And what the hell did I do to deserve this?* He obviously enjoyed dancing and kissing other women, but not me, his wife. *Had I done something to make him lose interest in me? What was wrong with me? What was wrong with him?* I cried some more and then, for no good reason, pulled the business card out of my purse.

Reading it, front and back, I felt compelled to contact this woman again. I set a reminder on my phone to call her the next day. This was definitely not the world I desired. Maybe there was something she knew that I didn't.

Lying back down on the couch, exhausted from the roller coaster of emotions, I closed my swollen eyes and drifted off into restless slumber.

6

When the Undesired Becomes an Illusion

The moment struck me as completely ironic. Three years later, there I was, a divorced, single woman sitting alone on a loveseat. Shaking my head, I laughed to myself, the cup of coffee in my hands too hot to drink. So much had changed over the last three years.

I was now living in a one-bedroom loft in the city. The wounds of the divorce were still fresh enough to cause daily pain, yet far enough removed to provide hope for my future. Still, anger and bitterness frequently filled my thoughts while I pressed forward with the daily grind of life.

Taking a sip of my hazelnut-flavored bliss, cool enough now to taste, I gazed out at the skyline towering outside my apartment window. A bird flitted by. I began to reminisce on how far I had come in the healing process.

I could only handle so many years of Richard's lies, manipulations, infidelities, and multitudes of broken promises. The hopes and dreams I had of "happily ever after" were crushed each time I believed he would change and return to the man I fell in love with. There came a breaking point in our relationship when I had to ask myself, "Am I better off with him or without him?"

After the separation, we attempted counseling to try to work out our differences. But then I discovered the massive debts he had rung up and never disclosed. I was on the hook for nearly twenty thousand dollars with only two options: declare bankruptcy or work my ass off to eliminate the debt. That was the last straw, helping me realize the answer to my own question: I was better off without the drama, the constant promises of change, and, in the end, without him.

We divorced quietly, without lawyers, each signing the papers one year ago to the day.

My thoughts shifted back to the night of the company party and how I caught him in a series of lies when he failed to come home. I remembered his text: "Got drunk. Sleeping over at a buddy's pad. Home in the a.m."

It was certainly a weird night, except for the dance troupe, Erotic Infusion, or whatever their name was. I remembered how I went to check on the dancers only to be stopped by that woman. What was her name … Madame! That's what she called herself! And her weird, sullen face and voice … with that stupid French accent. "What world is it you desire?" I said out loud, mockingly.

Her words had haunted me for three years. Thinking back to Madame's question, I still had no idea what my desired world was. I thought what I wanted was the same as what I desired and had attained in nearly seven years of marriage to Richard. So how could I ever really know what I want? And what was the point anyway? All it did was make me miserable thinking of wanting something I didn't know how to get.

It is hard not to hold on to anger or look at things in a punitive manner. At times, I find myself watching happy couples around me and secretly wishing that another woman would come into their lives, seduce the husband, and destroy the marriage so she too could feel my pain.

That fantasy ends almost as soon as it begins as I ponder the reality of the downward spiral negativity can take a person on. Maybe this justified my own actions: to feel less pain by knowing other women had gone through or were going through the same situation. *This is sad, really sad*, I thought.

During all of this stress and upheaval, I couldn't help but wonder where my childhood friend Patty was. Several times over the last three years, I would call out to her, hoping she would appear. Occasionally I would talk to her as if she were sitting next to me, again hoping it would prompt her arrival. But she never came. I felt very lonely and isolated with the knowledge that, as an adult with marital troubles of my own, my connection to her was lost.

Something definitely needed to change. And if my best childhood friend wasn't going to show herself and help me, then damn it, it was time to take action on my own and get out of this funk. I was tired of the pain, the misery, and the blame. It was time to get over the emotion and look at things more logically. My emotions were obviously not to be trusted, as I found myself spending days vacillating between crying fits over what could have been to screaming at males as a species for all being pig-headed jerks.

So much of my time had been spent beating myself up over my uncontrolled emotions that I found myself seeking a physician to prescribe antidepressants, hoping they would help create a bridge to future happiness. I remember friends telling me that a divorce was tantamount to the death of a parent or sibling. This justified the use of drugs, in my mind.

Secretly, I spent night after night wishing Richard would die, keeping me from having to go through a divorce. I knew this was a horrific thought. But the pain and suffering he had caused ... it can do strange things to one's mind.

I had become one with Richard the moment he first penetrated me. Since that experience, we were so connected I couldn't remember how free my soul was before we met. I truly understood the analogy of two becoming one in a marriage, not only from the magnetic energy the physical act lovemaking creates, but also from how our hearts, our souls, our hopes and our dreams, had formed solidarity, a union.

Trying to detach myself from years of being as one was like hell on Earth; one of the most painful experiences I had ever encountered. After a year of divorce recovery classes, counseling, and a slew of "I hate men" sessions over wine and cheese with girlfriends, I came to the realization that I could not trust a man to care for my heart, my soul, and, especially, my body.

I had to learn to love myself before I could love again. Certainly, I knew that. But trust? Never again would a man get that.

The saying goes, "If at first you don't succeed, try, try again." *No way! Not if it results in this type of pain!* I doubted I would ever trust another man, form a relationship, and, God forbid, remarry. The more stories I heard of unfaithful men around me, the more I burned with anger and made it my resolute mission to make sure these men paid for the hurt they caused women.

Why do men do this? I constantly pondered. *Why do they feel it necessary to take a lover?* Was it just for sex? Sex—those three simple letters that seemingly consume the minds of all conscious human beings. I began to resent the thought of sex. Not that the act was bad, but it had been used as a weapon of mass destruction in relationships all around me.

I imagined what it would be like to live in a world where sex isn't a part of the equation. Somehow, in that world, life is conceived in test tubes and no one ever knows what the act of sex is or misses it because it has never been part of the game. What would relationships be like without it? Was it all some big cosmic game where God sits above saying, "Okay, let's see who survives this battle today," as He laughs hysterically at His creations? The thought made me cringe.

Personally, it is easier not to play the game. I do not need sex to survive. Social Internet dating became my pastime. There I could privately get to know someone online before deciding to meet him and bare my heart and soul.

When a man and I shared common interests, I would then agree to meet him for a live date. Once I felt that warming sensation of attraction between us, I would stop the relationship from going any further than a good-night kiss. I'd be a liar if I said I didn't enjoy the attention from those men. It was the chase to the bedroom that sickened me—watching the man willingly spend his hard-earned money and time, hoping to receive some kind of sexual favor.

No. I could not be bought for any price.

I would enjoy watching the men leave, obviously frustrated and defeated, when I didn't eagerly provide them with what they were looking for. Several were even brave enough to call back for a second or third date, thinking they could change my mind. It felt as if I were their sport and my body were their prize. I would laugh, thinking that I had won the battle once again. Yes, my body was the prize, and it was for me alone to enjoy! I was not in the sharing mood.

I was determined that for every battle I lost in my marriage with Richard, I would create a win to help balance the score. The problem is, they say it takes ten positive events to cancel out every single negative event in life. That meant a lot of dating in my future. That meant a lot of dinners, a lot of flowers, and no sex.

I wasn't dating to find love. I was dating for validation. And as a woman, for every date I agreed to, I put a mark in the win column, knowing the right amount of attention to give a man to persuade him to buy me dinner. As a reward, for every dinner they paid for, I stashed away an equal amount of money. I called it my rainy day fund. It was the best savings plan I ever had.

Loneliness was only temporary, as I met many wonderful people—but also a few assholes—all looking for some sort of human connection. In the end, isn't that what we all are looking for in a relationship—the physical presence of another to help us listen, share, and learn together?

My girlfriends told me I was crazy to date like this. I told them that by taking sex out of the equation, things get really simple between a man and a woman. Men pay for strippers they can't touch or have sex with. Now they are paying for dinner and a movie for someone they can't touch or have sex with. What's the difference? This way I'm having fun and eating out frequently while also building my savings. It also gave me the time to figure out what a loving relationship is really all about.

Over time, I had stashed away enough prize money to buy things that made me happy. After making the purchase, I would say out loud, "Aw, thank you, Richard, for this beautiful gift. Oh, you bought me a spa package too? You're the best!" It was a quirky way of forgiving myself for the years he took from me. Unfortunately, lost time can never be purchased; not for any price.

The tactic worked for a while. That is, until the longing for a partner and children crept in. I read as many self-help books as possible to reaffirm that it was okay to be a single woman and to know that I had the ability to be as happy without a partner as I was with one. In fact, I could even have a child on my own—no relationship necessary. While the material may have helped to improve my mind and my attitude, the results were always fleeting. My biological clock was ticking.

Feeling conflicted between what I realized I really wanted—a life partner and a family—and the expectation that I could never again trust another man, I was in misery. All of a sudden, something clicked inside. *That's it!* I thought. *I have been in complete opposition to myself all along! I read books on how to feel good as a single woman, but that's not what I really want. No! What I want is a partner; a family. No wonder all this newfound knowledge didn't have any lasting effect! It isn't what I really desire. What I really desire in this world is a lifelong relationship. I want a man I can trust and build a life partnership with.*

A thought occurred to me, and I nearly jumped out of my skin as I flew off the couch and ran to my bedroom. Suddenly I remembered Madame's business card and her words about the world I desired! Memories of the dance performance came flooding back to me; each dancer's moves, each shift in song and each story played out in my head. I got it! It had taken me three years to figure it out, but I knew it was the answer. I rushed to my closet and flung open the doors in search of my small memory box, stored on the top shelf.

Knowing the business card was inside made my heart race. I reached for the small, purple-flowered shoebox, barely visible under a pile of sweatshirts, and gently opened the lid.

How could I have forgotten about this personal little treasure chest? It was where I stored my diaries and pictures from my years in high school and college.

When I opened it, the memories flashed through my mind; it was like seeing a long-lost friend through newly opened eyes. I pulled out the photos and the diaries and began to cry while sorting through them. This was me before I married Richard. This is still the woman I am today. And the only person who kept me from seeing this was me!

I pulled out ticket stubs from old concerts, cards from friends and old boyfriends, and I laid each one down on the bed with a special reverence. Then I spotted it: the black business card with the silver logo! Suddenly time stopped and reverted back to my introduction to Madame. Flipping the card over, I read the quote once more.

> As your desire is, so is your will.
> As your will is, so is your deed.
> As your deed is, so is your destiny.
> —The Upanishads

Instinctively I knew it was time to make the call to Madame. I knew what I desired: to trust a man, be in a committed relationship, and start a family. And if this quote was true, then maybe this woman could help me make my desire a reality.

It was exciting and stressful at the same time. I picked up the phone and dialed the number, completely forgetting it was a Sunday morning. I was too committed to the plan to turn back now.

As the phone rang, I could hardly breathe.

"Bonjour." Her voice still held the French accent I remembered so well.

Closing my eyes, I took a deep breath and spoke. "Hello, my name is Lenea. I have a business card for Madame. Is she still at this number?"

"This is Madame," she answered rather abruptly.

Crap! Now what do I say? I was reminded once again how intimidating this woman was. "Oh, hello Madame ..." The title felt weird rolling off my tongue. "You probably don't remember me. We met three years ago at a performance your dancers gave for a business party downtown."

I paused, waiting to see if she remembered me. There was nothing but silence on the other end of the line, so I continued. "I have held on to your business card because of a question you asked me that night. I realize this may sound ridiculous ... but the impact you made with that one question turned my world upside down." I hesitated, wondering if she was still on the phone. "It's crazy how one question can drive a woman to madness ..." I waited for a response. There was nothing but silence on the other end.

Shaking my head, I looked down at the floor and began to pace. I realized I had so much to say, all to a perfect stranger. But something told me to bare my soul, to reveal what haunted me, to talk it all out in hope of finding the answer. "The question you asked me was, 'What is the world that you desire?' At the time, I couldn't answer you. You told me to call you when I had an answer and handed me your business card." I stopped to catch my breath and then stumbled on. "Well, I have given this question a lot of thought, and I'm now ready to give you my answer."

Though I expected a voice, a sound, or anything that would indicate she was still listening, again only silence. "Madame? Are you still there?"

"Continue," she said, irritation noticeably audible, with the French accent punctuating the displeasure.

"I figured it out! I desire a world where women trust men and men trust women. Where marriages have happy endings and children are raised to believe in love." I said it with so much enthusiasm; it was as if I realized the importance of what I was saying for the first time.

Again there was silence. This time I remained still and pondered my words and where they came from. Then she spoke, her irritation still discernible. "I can help you because I feel your tone, your passion." The sound of her voice penetrated to the core of my being. "Your words are of no importance. If you would like my help, you must come to my studio tomorrow at twelve noon. At twelve oh one, the door will be locked. The address is on the business card. Au revoir." She hung up.

It was like being back in the loft three years ago, only this time instead of her walking away, it was her offering a brusque "Au revoir," followed by a click. That felt awkward. And what was with the "I feel your tone, your passion?" And "your words are of no importance to me?" Could I have told her that I wanted a world made out of chocolate with as much tone and passion and she would have said the same thing?

She was so odd and rude. Maybe it was a French thing. Yet I was definitely intrigued. Suddenly I found myself in the position of the men I had dated. I understood the power of seduction, for I was now under her spell.

7

Things Aren't Always What They Appear to Be

It was a crisp and sunny Monday morning, normal for the middle of May. One of the great benefits of working from home was sitting on my patio, laptop at my fingertips, enjoying the beautiful Colorado weather.

I love my tiny seven-hundred-square-foot apartment. It has the ideal proximity to downtown nightlife yet is isolated enough on the eighth floor to escape from the hustle and bustle of the street below. I chose the location based on views of the mountains to the west and a balcony that overlooks the busy streets. Watching the consistency of the city's patterns fills me with a sense of security; every day is the same routine.

Sitting in my patio chair, watching the flow of well-dressed pedestrians below, I sipped my coffee and finished checking my e-mail. My business attire consisted of my favorite pair of jeans and a light cotton T-shirt—the only way to work from home.

Today was different, though, as I was to meet Madame. Looking my best was top priority. Standing up, I stretched my arms, finished my coffee, and walked inside to prepare for the day.

Setting aside extra time to put on makeup—a rarity unless I was going out in public—I began sorting through my closet. I picked an outfit that spoke to me: a light blue chambray shirt dress with a shirttail hem that hit just above the knee. It had three-quarter length sleeves and was accented by a wide tan canvas belt. The dress resembled a man's shirt, but with a belt that showed off my waist, and a hemline short enough to accentuate my long tan legs. I really wanted to make a great first impression; my attire said class with a bit of flair.

Slipping on red suede heels and matching colored jewelry, I felt confident and ready to meet Madame. The clock said 10:00 a.m. Our appointment was not until noon.

I tried to work, picking up one file in a stack of dozens, but couldn't stay focused. After punching in the address on my cell phone, the GPS indicated the studio's location to be down the street from my apartment. *How convenient,* I thought. I knew the area well. One of my favorite Indian food restaurants was located nearby. Given Madame's warning not to show up a minute past noon, I thought it best to take a stroll and scout out the exact location of the studio to ensure an early arrival.

Walking through the apartment lobby, I said hello to those who passed by. It was exciting to have something to look forward to.

Smiling broadly, I exited the large glass doors and took in a breath of fresh air; it was indeed a beautiful day. Late spring in Colorado is irresistible. The weather is perfect, with glorious sunshine and an iridescent blue sky unlike anywhere I have ever seen in the world. The outdoor beauty and a rush of excitement propelled me with a skip in my step toward my destination. When I arrived at the Indian restaurant, I looked around for the address of the studio but couldn't find the number.

The intersection consisted of two buildings, according to the GPS: a shoe repair store located under a large dilapidated parking garage, and the commercial business building, where the restaurant was located. But where was the studio? I circled the block a few times thinking maybe I was on the wrong side of the street.

Finally I walked into the cobbler's store to ask for directions. The man behind the counter was older, balding, and very pleasant. "May I help you?" he asked in a grandfatherly way.

"I think I am lost," I began, holding up my phone. "I am looking for the studio."

He looked at me suspiciously from behind his horn-rimmed glasses. "Not too many people know about that part of the building. I'm not surprised you couldn't find it." He placed a pair of shoes he held in his hands on the counter. "I can show you the way." He escorted me out the door, turning to lock it behind him, and walked with me across the busy entrance to the parking structure. At the far edge he stopped and turned left. In front of us was an unmarked black door, a door I had walked past numerous times and never even noticed.

"I had no idea this was a business," I said, confusion in my voice. "It looks like the back door to the Indian restaurant."

"I'm not sure I would use the word 'business,' at least not one I know of," he said in a degrading tone. "But it is definitely the address you are looking for." He turned to leave.

"Thanks for your help," I said gratefully. He gave a cursory wave and walked back toward his store.

The way he emphasized "business" in such a negative manner struck me as odd. Indeed, there was nothing indicating an address or business— no doorbell, sign, or even a mail slot. It was simply a large, solid black door situated in a small brick alcove with only a light above. To the right was the back door of the commercial building.

After all the time I had spent walking up and down this street, to suddenly notice and become aware of this door made me feel a bit strange. *Do I knock on it?* I looked down at my watch; it was almost 11:00 a.m. Feeling slightly hungry, I decided to visit the Indian restaurant to grab a bite to eat and hang out there until it was time for my appointment.

After entering the restaurant, I was escorted to a booth with a pleasant view of the street. Noon approached, and a group of women dressed in dance attire walked by. I wondered if they were from the studio.

I paid my bill and stood up to leave, then curiosity got the best of me, and I asked the waitress, "Do you know anything about the studio next door?"

The young girl glanced out the window. "I've been there once," she began, her voice and face showing disgust. "I wondered what it was used for, you know, with all the people that would come and go. I mean, like, really beautiful people, you know—the kind that don't really seem to fit in with the normal crowd." I was slightly taken aback by the comment, but she didn't seem to notice and continued. "When I opened the door to see what was inside, I didn't make it more than three steps before I was told to leave immediately."

She set the dishes down, looked around the restaurant to make sure no one was listening, and leaned forward. In a hushed voice, sounding a bit peeved, she said, "I was told I couldn't enter without a specific invitation, which is fine with me; the place is really creepy and very secretive." She stood back upright, loading her arms with dishes. "Yup, something weird is definitely going on in there. You know, it's like"—she looked around again—"well ... can you keep a secret?"

"Sure." I leaned in closer, acting like a best friend eager for juicy gossip.

"My boss thinks it's a den of prostitution," she said in almost a whisper. She leaned in closer, arms still filled with dishes, her eyes once more scanning the room to make sure no one could hear. "One night, after closing, my boss received a call from the police due to a fire alarm going off in the restaurant. He only lives a block away, so he came down to check it out, you know, and he figured it was, like, a moth or something that had set off motion detectors. But on his way out, he noticed the door to the studio had been left open and a strange red light was shining from inside. Mind you, this happened after two o'clock in the morning."

I nodded, eager to hear more.

"So he went inside, you know, to see if maybe their alarm was going off too," she said, her voice lowering until it was barely above a whisper. "When he walked in, he said he could see a room lit up in a red glow, where naked women were dancing. He left quickly, as it seemed to him some kind of sex orgy was going on. Supposedly, the next day he confronted the woman who owned the place and told her he didn't want her or her clients to eat in his restaurant ever again." The waitress stood proud, content with her boss's response.

"Wow!" I responded, perplexed by the scene that had been painted for me. "That's quite an interesting story; sounds pretty weird to me too." I felt myself blush as I looked down and signed the receipt for lunch.

I wasn't going to tell her about my appointment with Madame at the studio—not after that story! Thanking her for the great food, I exited the restaurant.

Now what do I do? I thought. I crossed the street to make sure the waitress didn't notice me hanging outside the dastardly door of the studio. *Do I go in now? Is it even safe? If the waitress sees me, will I ever be able to eat at my favorite restaurant again?* I walked slowly on the sidewalk, pacing back and forth, occasionally glancing over in the direction of the studio.

Several minutes passed, and I knew the noon hour was fast

approaching. A decision had to be made. I looked down at my watch; 11:55. I stopped, looking up at the black door before making a decision. "Screw it!" I said out loud, and I walked briskly across the street.

Moments later, I found myself standing in front of the big, ominous door. My knees were shaking a little. *What am I getting myself into?* I thought. Taking a deep breath, I reached out to turn the doorknob. Relief swept over me when I discovered it was unlocked. I started to pull, when the door burst open, and I jumped back in surprise.

"Excuse me," a man on the other side said. "I didn't see you there. Come on in."

He held the door open with his left arm. I was slightly shocked to see a male presence at the studio. Then my mind drifted back to the performance from nearly three years ago, and I remembered there had been both female and male dancers.

"Thank you," I said sheepishly, feeling my face turn bright red. The man holding the door was the epitome of tall, dark, and incredibly handsome. He had chestnut-brown hair, an athletic build, and a smile that caused me to melt as I looked into his clear hazel eyes. *The waitress wasn't kidding*, I thought. *This really is the home of the beautiful people.*

"You're welcome," he replied sincerely. My body began to tremble as blood rushed to my extremities. Ah yes, the familiar feeling of attraction. It had been too long.

He gave me the once over, eyeing me up and down as if he knew I must be a new girl. "Well, I've never seen you before. That must mean ..." he hesitated, watching my reaction, which was a combination of surprise and awe. "It must mean ... you're going to have a lot of fun. Relax," he said, smiling before he turned and walked out the door.

I stood inside the doorway, befuddled and speechless.

"That's Mark." A woman's gravelly voice broke me out of my trance.

My eyes hadn't quite adjusted from daylight to darkness; the studio was dimly lit. I looked in the general direction of the voice, wondering if she could see how flushed my face was. "My name's Lenea," I asked, more than told, the voice. "Madame asked me to come by today at noon."

"Come on in," the voice said again. I took a few steps forward toward the outline of what appeared to be a small reception desk. "And don't worry about Mark. He's our resident artist. He doesn't bite ... hard." I saw a figure stand up behind the counter. Suddenly I realized I had no idea what I was doing there.

"I'm sorry, what?" I asked, confused.

The woman answered, "Mark. The guy who opened the door? The guy you were ogling." She walked around the desk to greet me. "He's our resident artist. He paints the women and men of the studio and lives above here in a loft. Don't worry; while he may be beautiful, he's harmless."

I didn't know what to say. I was embarrassed to have been caught staring at this man, and I wasn't quite sure what she meant by "harmless." My mind was in a whirl; it was difficult to think.

"I'm Shannon," she said, sticking her hand out to shake mine. "Are you here for the class?" Shannon was a tall brunette, easily five nine or five ten, with long, straight hair and chiseled facial features. She reminded me of a younger, taller version of Madame, except her demeanor was markedly more friendly; definitely more American.

Not wanting to look like a fool by asking "what class?" I responded abruptly, "I'm here to see Madame," shaking her hand to be polite.

"Oh yes," she responded casually, "Lenea. She told me you would be here. Have a seat, and she'll be with you soon." Shannon turned and walked behind the front counter, sat down, and began sorting through some papers.

By now my eyes were beginning to adjust to the dimly lit space while taking in the surroundings. It was a very old building, judging by the musty smell and the dark, worn wood floors. The foyer I stood in was fairly small, with two women seated in suede chairs on either side of an end table. They each were reading a magazine under the table lamp and did not look up.

The ceilings were extremely low and covered in large planks of wood held up by crossbeams with wide metal connectors. A large bench upholstered in blood-red leather and adorned with tufted velvet of the same color stretched along the front wall.

I took a seat on the bench; the coolness of the leather was a welcome relief. On the other side of the long bench was a striking blonde woman dressed in business attire. It was very similar to what I would wear when visiting a client. She seemed preoccupied with her nails and did not acknowledge my presence.

Directly across from me were other accoutrements. Most noticeable was a large velvet curtain, the same deep red color as the bench, which hung in a manner clearly indicating an entrance of some sort. Additionally, there was an old Tiffany-style light in the center of the ceiling. It cast an eerie glow about the windowless room.

The sound of a sitar played from a speaker hidden in the ceiling, and the air was infused with a combination of musty wood, scented oils, and candles. On the walls were framed paintings of women and men in various stages of nakedness. I felt slightly uncomfortable, wondering if these were the paintings by the "resident artist" Shannon had mentioned.

Another young woman walked in looking as lost as I felt. "Is this where Madame works?" she asked, taking her sunglasses off, clearly out of breath.

"You're in the right place!" Shannon said cheerfully. "Take a seat, and Madame will be right with you." The woman let out a sigh of exhaustion as she walked over to me, sitting down in the middle of the bench.

"Whew!" she said in relief, "I didn't think I was going to make it on time." She turned and looked right at me. "Wow! You're pretty!" she exclaimed unabashedly.

"Hi, I'm Lenea," I said while reaching out my hand to shake hers, slightly embarrassed by her forwardness.

She held her sweaty hand in mine, barely grasping it. "I'm Chrissy. It's nice to meet you." She took another deep breath, followed by another sigh, as she gathered herself and her gym bag.

Chrissy was dressed more casually than I was, wearing jean shorts, a green T-shirt, and flip-flops. Her light sandy-brown hair was tied up in a ponytail, and her demeanor was more laid back than that of the rest of us.

Even though we just met, I could tell she had a comfortable presence about her and, given the right opportunity, we could become friends.

The red velvet curtains began to part, slowly, revealing Madame behind them. She stepped forward in dramatic fashion. She didn't look anything like I remembered, except for that face—the cold, glaring, square-cut statue of a stoic face. Her long dark hair fell in soft ringlets around her exposed shoulders.

She wore a shiny black leather bustier under a long-sleeved transparent black crop top, coupled with matching leather French-cut underwear that exposed her bare dancer legs and her sculptured midriff.

Knee-high black leather lace-up boots completed the ensemble. She looked like a combination of a French dominatrix and a dance instructor. Her face suggested she was in her mid-forties, but her body was that of a twenty-year-old.

I sat rigidly in my seat, nervous and quite uncomfortable, with no clue what I was getting myself into. I wasn't a dancer. *Oh God, please help me!* I thought. My hands began fidgeting with my dress, which now seemed humdrum in comparison to Madame.

"Bonjour, ladies," Madame said in her soft French accent. "Welcome to the studio. Are you ready to change your lives?" she asked, lifting up a black leather crop and pounding it into her hand. Silence filled the room before she continued. "Follow me, and I will show you to our room."

All of us women stood in unison as Madame turned and walked back through the dark crimson curtains. We followed her, silent, like sheep being lead to slaughter.

8

How Can Dance Help Me Obtain My Desire?

We stepped through the plush velvet curtains, and the musty smell became more pronounced in the long, tight corridor than it was in the waiting area. The floor creaked eerily under my heels. In the distance, a large open room awaited at the end of the hallway. *This must be where we are going*, I thought.

Suddenly the story I had been told by the young lady at the Indian restaurant echoed in my mind. My body shuddered. Off to the left and right of the hallway were rows of doors that opened into small private rooms. It reminded me of a massage parlor; I couldn't help but wonder if this was where Madame's clients hung out. I glanced into one of the rooms. It was filled with pillows of all sizes and illuminated by candlelight. *Perhaps the studio was a brothel.* The thought made me cringe.

There were a few crystal fixtures hanging from the low ceilings, which helped throw some light, but it still seemed rather dark for such a tight corridor. The entire building had a mysterious air about it and was definitely a place I wouldn't want to be alone in at any time of day.

We passed by a double staircase on the left. One side of the staircase went down half a dozen steps and ended on a small platform. The opposite side had an equal number of steps leading up to another platform. At the top of the stairway was a painting of a young woman lying naked on a bed with her legs splayed wide open, covered only by a satiny sheet.

Breathing a collective sigh of relief, we came to the end of the hallway and entered an expansive studio. Inside, a parquet dance floor stretched from wall to wall. Full-length mirrors covered three of the walls, and a ballet barre was attached to the fourth. Off to one side of the room were several vertical dancing poles. All sizes of ornately decorated velvet pillows littered the floor.

"Please form a circle in the center of the room and have a seat," Madame directed in her French tone. Quietly and quickly, we followed orders, having an internal awareness of the respect her presence commanded.

Madame turned down the lights and walked to the center wall, stopping in front of a goddess-like bronze statue. She produced a box of matches, pulled one out and lit it, then used it to light a small candle sitting in front of the art piece. Madame bowed her head, whispered a few words, picked the candle up, and began to walk in ceremonial procession to the opposite corner of the room. She stopped at another candle in the corner and bowed her head, whispering a few words before lighting it. She repeated the process until all four corners were lit.

Finally, she returned to the original deity, again whispered a few words, and placed the lit candle into its original holder. She turned on some soft instrumental music, then walked toward our circle.

"You must expand the circle and allow enough space for each of you to move freely," she commanded, directing the group to move outward by gesturing her hands. We all scooted back until she seemed satisfied.

A golden glow shone from the candles, casting shadows that seemed to come to life on the mirrored walls, while the shiny wood floor created one more source of reflection. I adjusted my legs beneath me. Sitting on the hard floor in a dress wasn't necessarily comfortable.

Madame brought out an easel with a large blank white canvas and a set of paints. She then placed it in front of the mirrored wall facing our circle before joining us on the floor. "You've each made a choice to be here today," she began as she looked around at our small group of women. "You have come here because you are searching to fulfill a desire." She looked at each of us, I knew it was the "collective you" she was talking about.

"Your individual desire led you here." She paused. "Now close your eyes for a moment and get in touch with the desire within you." She closed her eyes and folded her hands, as if to set the example.

Get in touch with my desire? What in the world did that mean? I looked around the circle and saw that many girls had their legs crossed and eyes closed in what resembled a yoga position. I imitated the pose as I closed my eyes and listened; the instrumental music reverberated softly.

Questions filled my mind: *How do I get out of here in case of a fire? Why are these other women here? What is it I desire the most? What is this all about? Does desiring chocolate count?*

Madame interrupted my thoughts. She took a deep breath and stood abruptly. "You may enter now," she said motioning to the doorway. A surge of adrenaline pumped through my body as my heart rate doubled; it was the man I ran into while walking through the entrance to the studio. *Oh my God! He is gorgeous!*

"Ladies, this is Mark. He is our resident artist and a critical component of all we do in the studio. Mark captures profound moments of life that occur here and transfers them to canvas." My mind immediately went to the painting of the woman lying naked on the bed I had seen in the hall.

Madame walked around the room, looking at each student from top to bottom, before continuing in a brusque voice, "You must learn how an artist uses his brush to convey emotion, for in the same manner we as dancers use our bodies to paint a picture for the audience to see. In dance, the body is a tool for communication. I would like to demonstrate now what it is I am talking about."

Madame walked over to the sound system and turned on a song that was familiar to me. I recognized the lyrics immediately, then the artist. It was the song "Beautiful" by Christina Aguilera. She looked directly at Mark. "Are you ready?" Mark nodded. She then removed her black see-through tunic, fully revealing her sculptured physique.

Holy cow, she's ripped! I thought, looking at her well-defined abs as she took a few steps forward, stopped, closed her eyes, and began moving her hips to the song. Her hands moved up and through her walnut-brown hair before moving down to her breasts and then finishing at her waist. I understood where the group of dancers from the performance three years ago received their training.

Looking over at Mark, I noticed he held a palette of paint in his left hand and a paintbrush in his right. His eyes darted back and forth between the subject and the canvas, and his hands mirrored the same, moving quickly from canvas to palette and back again.

The music was much louder than the soft instrumental background tunes playing earlier. The energy of the room shifted dramatically as Madame continued her seductive movements.

The music continued, and my eyes were transfixed on Madame. She was dancing with herself in the mirror, her hands still moving; first hair, then hips, then breasts, and then hair again. She appeared lost in the moment. Her grace and ease were breathtaking to watch as she combined her erotic movements with ballet and modern dance. The way she stared at herself in the mirror was powerful.

When the song ended, I looked at the painting Mark had finished, astonished at what I saw. There before us was a canvas full of abstract patterns painted in a wide variety of colors, forming the silhouette of a woman. It was so simple a child could have painted it, yet it had an extremely profound impact on me.

Madame, coming out of her trance, opened her eyes and looked around the room. Composing herself, she regained the face of master and teacher. She cleared her throat and turned back toward us. "What you witnessed, ladies, was emotion in movement; art on a dance floor. And this"—she pointed to the canvas, her brown eyes penetrating—"is a visual representation of that moment in art." She stood with her hand on Mark's shoulder. "This piece of art will last as long as the paint remains on the canvas, even though the moment of emotion has passed."

Madame bent down, picked up her blouse, stood, and walked out the door. Mark followed in her footsteps without uttering a word.

None of us quite knew what to do. No one said anything. But the looks on all of our faces told the story: *Now what?*

I decided to stand up and walked over to the tripod holding the canvas. Looking at the painting, I became overwhelmed by this artist's magical ability to bring colors to life; I was even more turned on than when I ran into him at the door. He had remarkable talent and must be a sensitive, thoughtful guy in order to capture emotions like this. I wanted to chase him down, grab his head in my hands, and kiss him passionately. His presence had permeated the room.

The others soon joined me. We stood there, all enthralled with the creation sitting before us. None of us talked. All of us kept our thoughts to ourselves. *Do they feel the same way about Mark as I do?* I wondered.

"Hi ladies!" A tall blonde dancer said in a cheerful voice. Startled by the interruption, I was quickly brought back to the moment. "My name is Sophie, and this is my sister, Monique. We know you are excited to start your dance lessons with Madame!"

Dance lessons? I thought to myself. *I'm not a dancer!* When I called Madame, I simply wanted her to help me obtain my desires. I wasn't quite sure how she would do it, maybe therapy of some sort or looking into a crystal ball, but I didn't know or even suspect it would be through dance lessons!

Sophie headed to the front of the room. She was tall and slender. Her form reminded me of one of the silhouettes from the performance back in the downtown loft.

"I was once in your shoes," she began, "scared, timid. I had no idea what I was getting myself into." Sophie's voice was calming, her smile sincere. "Looking back, I laugh at those times. There were things I desired. Burning questions in my mind that I couldn't find answers to. This is the sacred space where I found answers to those questions," Sophie said, her arms spreading to signify the very room in which we stood.

Her hands went down to her sides as she looked around at the group, checking the reactions on our faces. "I can tell you, from my own personal experience, whatever happened to bring you here today happened for a reason. No one comes here unless they are invited. To be invited is an honor and a divine appointment. I consider you my sisters as we journey forward together. Stay seated, and Monique and I will come around with paperwork to get you started."

Monique was a tall, thin African American woman with flawless skin and big brown eyes. Her arms were lean, yet powerful, and her leg muscles flexed as she walked around, handing each of us a pen and paper.

What in the world have I gotten myself into? I wondered. *Who are these beautiful people? I'm not like them. Not even close.*

When I looked down at the paper, I realized it was a contract. It was filled with all of the regular lawyer mumbo jumbo about liabilities and so forth. It wasn't until I reached the back page that I saw the description and cost of the dance lessons. The information caused my jaw to drop at the prices they were charging.

The least expensive options were group lessons with Madame, but they increased in cost from private time with Madame all the way to the most costly option of private time with Mark. I was astounded. At least the Mark option included a painting. *Hmm. Okay,* I thought, *maybe the last option is worth the expense.* I imagined Mark painting me, the two of us all alone in a room together.

The moment was broken by the girl to my right, Chrissy. "I'm sorry, but I'm a single woman with hardly any cash left over at the end of the month. Are you saying that I can't get what I desire in life unless I pay you for dance lessons?" Thank God this girl had the guts to say what we were all thinking.

Sophie responded, again with her comforting smile, "I completely understand where you are coming from." Her voice was calm, steady, and reassuring. "I was the same way. My first desire was for the money to pay for the classes. I started with group lessons, the best value we offer, and somehow, someway, the money came together. The rest is history. Let me ask you this: is what you're doing now working for you?"

The words were directed at Chrissy. Chrissy shifted her eyes downward and thought about it for a moment before looking up, and in her matter-of-fact, friendly voice she said, "No, not really."

Sophie responded, "May I suggest you begin with the desire to find the money and then work your way up from there." She winked and smiled. "Once you understand how you get what you desire, you will be amazed at how fast things start happening in your life."

Chrissy's eyes swelled with tears as she returned the smile, and in an instant, it seemed as if they had created a special bond with one another. I guess it was the sisterhood thing this woman was talking about.

The herd mentality had kicked in. I tried to determine if I could do this financially. If I bought into a package deal, it would lower my cost significantly. Luckily they offered monthly payment plans as well. And if there was a chance of receiving my desires and seeing Mark once a week, I could skip out on a dinner date or two and put the money I saved to good use. I signed the contract and handed it to Sophie. The other women completed and returned their paperwork as well.

Sophie collected the papers one by one. "Okay, ladies, it looks like you all signed up for the group lessons. Congratulations! And welcome to your new home. Monique will pass out our expectations regarding the house rules. Please read these over and come prepared for class each week. If you do not come prepared, you will be asked to leave and your money will not be refunded. Please know that how you show up in our house will be a reflection of how you show up in your own life. Don't hurt yourself by being unprepared. We will see you all next week at the same time. Au revoir."

As we stood to leave, Sophie and Monique hugged each of us and extended a personal welcome to the studio.

Oh my, I thought. *Dance lessons? What did I get myself into?*

9

A Sisterhood Is Established, Including All but One

The following Monday, I prepared myself mentally and physically before leaving my apartment. Religiously, I reviewed the list of house rules: Wear comfortable clothing. *Check*. Bring a yoga mat. *Check*. Bring high-heeled shoes for dancing. *Check*. Bring a large bottle of purified water. *Check*. With all items packed in my duffel bag, I headed out the door a little ahead of schedule to ensure I would arrive early. Fearful of the repercussions from Madame should I be late for my first lesson, I left my apartment almost thirty minutes early for the seven-minute walk.

Walking into the studio, I saw the same woman at the front desk. Shannon greeted me by name and directed me through the curtains.

The feeling of the studio was different this time around; it was personal, sacred, and warm. No longer was I the scared, timid girl sitting in the unfamiliar waiting area. I had a sense of knowing I belonged there; it felt like home.

Walking down the same creepy hallway, almost with a skip in my step, I noticed how the architectural features of the wood pillars, stone columns, and areas of tiled floor created a mosaic. Gliding into the dance studio, I saw Chrissy was already there; a feeling of joy swept over me. Something about her presence put me even more at ease.

"Hey Lenea! It's so good to see you!" Chrissy said to me jovially.

She was wearing two tank tops; the top one was white and embossed with a picture of two beer bottles, and the one underneath was a light blue. Her navy-blue shorts had white fringe and sported a picture of the same two beers on her right thigh. As she turned to reach down into her gym bag, I read the words "BOTTOMS UP" across her rear in rainbow colors. She stood up, grabbed two handfuls of sandy brown hair, and made pigtails. "Are you ready to dance?" She asked with a huge smile on her face.

"Ready as I'll ever be," I responded, trying to match her mood.

Two other women entered the room, and Chrissy immediately walked over to them and introduced herself. Chrissy began a conversation that must have carried over from their last meeting, as they all leaned their heads back to laugh.

The first girl was clearly bigger than Chrissy, nearly five foot eight, and outweighed her by at least eighty pounds. She wore a black leotard leading to black spandex shorts and black tights, clearly intended to cover the rolls of belly fat protruding from her midsection. The dimples in her cheeks developed quickly with her smile. Her mountain-brown eyes perfectly matched her shoulder-length chestnut hair. They shared another laugh before the woman reached out her hand to Chrissy, introducing herself as Jessica. Chrissy looked down at Jessica's hand before reaching up with both arms to hug her. Jessica was caught off guard but returned the hug gleefully.

The second girl caught my eye. Her disposition was more businesslike and standoffish. I remembered her from the previous week and still felt slightly uncomfortable in her presence. She reminded me of the beautiful dancers who worked at the studio. She was tall and slender with long, straight blond hair and appeared to be my age. She wore a bright pink runner's top that accentuated her shapely shoulders leading down to long, thin, well-defined arms. The black spandex Capris she wore painted a different picture than Jessica, designed to highlight a perfectly shaped rear and chiseled waistline. I couldn't help but think to myself, *If this group were to be quickly scaled down, we would all be voted off the island except for her.* She fit their "home of the beautiful" mold perfectly.

With a flick of her head and a smile that seemed fake, she interrupted their conversation. "And I'm Samantha." But neither Chrissy nor Jessica acknowledged the woman, so deep were they in their conversation.

Samantha rolled her eyes, shook her head, and walked away to stretch out in the corner by herself.

Looking up at the clock in the studio, I saw it was 11:59. Another woman entered the room and set her things down. I stood up and walked over to her, emulating Chrissy's introduction.

"Hi, I'm Lenea," I said, extending my hand. She returned the handshake, stating her name was Julia.

A little younger than me, she had mousy brown hair cut in a short bob and more of a tomboy look compared to the rest of us. Her diminutive frame was covered by a Metro College athletic gray T-shirt, one size too big, that hung nearly down to her knees. Her matching cotton sweatpants were baggy and had been cut right below the knee; a few threads hung down where they had begun to unravel.

Thinking of an icebreaker, I was about to ask her if she was from around here—a rather dumb question—but was saved by the appearance of yet another woman whose presence commanded our attention: Madame.

Madame was attired in a different dance outfit today. She wore a bright orange midriff tank top covering a black sports bra peeking out from the neckline, little black booty shorts, and five-inch stiletto heels. Her hair was pulled up into a bun. The combination of short shorts and towering heels made her legs look long and lean, like powerful pillars of strength and muscle capable of performing graceful, gravity-defying movements. As I stood there in my gray cotton shorts, light purple T-shirt, and matching tennis shoes, I felt slightly out of place. I guess my understanding of comfortable clothes was perhaps a little off.

"Bonjour, ladies, and good afternoon," she began with her compelling French voice. "We have much to accomplish today. Let us begin."

Madame stood by the stereo and touched a button. Loud, upbeat dance music reverberated against the mirrored walls. She then strode to the front of the room, facing the mirrors, and instructed us to stand behind her and follow her lead. We began with a series of body stretches from a standing position before advancing to floor stretches and back to standing again. The stretching was coupled with graceful dance-like movements, with the expectation for us to mirror Madame's finesse and precise execution.

Am I the only one who feels ridiculous following her? I thought. No way were my steps anywhere close to her graceful moves. She moved as if she were in the spotlight on a stage, performing a professional dance number.

I caught a glimpse of myself in the mirror and was dismayed at my clumsiness. *If these are warm-ups, what in the world will the actual lesson be like?* Then I glanced at the others and breathed a huge sigh of relief as I realized they appeared to be as awkward as I was at doing the unfamiliar steps. Everyone, that is, except Samantha. Her movements mirrored Madame's perfectly—sexy, smooth, and sensuous.

Crap! I thought. *Am I going to have to move like her to get what I desire?*

The warm-ups ended as Monique and Sophie, the dancers we had met at the first class, entered the room. "Sophie and Monique are going to help assist me during the rest of class today. Everyone, please go stand next to a pole and we will begin our lesson," instructed Madame.

The pole? Oh great, I could barely handle the dance floor and now you want to put me on a pole? There's no way!

Reluctantly, I made my way to a pole as techno music filled the air; it was energetic, bouncy and fun. Chrissy was smiling and laughing. Samantha grabbed her high heels and looked ready for action.

"Okay, ladies," Sophie began, a flirtatious grin on her face, "you can't dance pole with athletic shoes on. Go strap on your heels, and let's get to work."

I walked over to the wall where my things were, pulled out my three-inch black high heels, and looked at Jessica sitting next to me. "I wasn't expecting pole dancing," I said to her nervously.

"Me either!" Jessica confided, a matching look of dismay squarely on her face. The moment caught us as we giggled simultaneously at the situation, stood up, and then joined the others.

We walked out onto the floor. Madame turned the music down before barking out her instructions. She demonstrated the sequence of moves we were to learn, and I couldn't help but think, *Wow, she looks like a stripper.*

At the same time, her movements were strong, solid, erotic, and much more deliberate than floozy-like. Each of us stood by a pole and watched her with awe. When she completed the series of movements, we clapped. Next it was our turn. Step-by-step, Madame broke down each move, expressing her words in action.

"First, grab the pole and walk around like this." She duplicated her previous move before ordering the next instruction. "Then spin around.

And when you land … stand up slowly while arching your back … sexy it up, ladies!"

We walked around our poles. In high heels, I had a hard time finding my balance let alone finding my sexy. Instead, I felt like a complete idiot. Madame turned the volume up on the music while she and her assistants walked around the room, offering tips and observing us perform the series of movements.

Sophie approached me first. "Would you like any help today?" she asked with a smile.

"Absolutely!" I bellowed unashamed. "I seriously don't feel comfortable walking in these things, let alone spinning on a pole." I lifted my foot to show her my dress shoes; they were the same heels I wore to meetings when I was required to wear a suit. They were nothing like the fashionable stilettos Sophie was wearing.

"Don't worry, sweetie," she said reassuringly, "it takes a lot of practice to get to Carnegie Hall. Let me show you how it's done, and you relax and try to copy me. Remember, your performance is uniquely yours."

She educated me on how to balance my weight equally and walk with my head up and shoulders back. During her demonstration, she pointed out specific areas for me to focus on. Then it was my turn to demonstrate what I had learned while she watched. Occasionally she would stop to give me praise and kudos for my effort before breaking down what I could improve. The individualized attention was definitely a bonus.

By the third time observing her movements, I made a mental note that different clothes and stiletto shoes might make a difference.

Soon, as I practiced with a better attitude, I felt more confident in my movements and was actually enjoying the process. I caught a glimpse of myself in the mirror, and this time I didn't look as awkward; I looked a little sexy. And I actually felt sexy!

I looked around the room. It was apparent we were all in a similar spot; unsure of ourselves, seeking some kind of self-improvement or even self-awareness. It was comforting and exciting at the same time to know I was in a room with like-minded women.

Each of us started to pick up the dance steps, improving each round, getting into the music and the hypnotic rhythm. We were laughing at ourselves and beaming with pride each time we mastered a complicated move. I was filled with an intense energy, ready to take on the world.

The music ended, and we shared more laughter as we exchanged cheerful high fives, slapping hands exuberantly and complimenting each other in a shared moment of camaraderie. That is, except for Samantha, who walked off to grab something from her bag. She was obviously not a rookie at dance like the other four of us.

The stern staccato of Madame's voice broke up the moment. "Ladies, you must get in touch with where your desire is coming from." She walked around us like a warden in a prison yard. "You all have a homework assignment. Before our next session, you must find a piece of music to accompany the emotion of your desire. Bring it with you, along with anything else you feel is relevant to expressing your desire. Au revoir." She walked out of the room without even looking back.

It was exciting to be a part of this group, a true team. That is, except for Samantha, of course, who made it quite clear that being a part of a team was not her thing. Oh well, she didn't seem very friendly anyway. *It's her loss*, I thought.

The four of us walked out of the studio, bags in hand, laughing and joking about our dance moves when I literally ran into Mark who was hustling down the stairs.

"Oh man, I'm so sorry I keep running into you. It must be fate," he said sardonically, turning back to me smiling that insanely gorgeous grin. He continued shuffling down the second set of stairs, heading toward what appeared to be a basement.

For a moment I thought about stopping him and saying, "Yes, it is fate. Now let's get married and have babies together." I knew this was a fantasy, but it was a delightful thought nonetheless. Whenever I was around him, my knees felt weak and I couldn't think of anything intelligent to say.

Of course, Chrissy noticed my starry gaze and commented on his obvious good looks. Apparently I wasn't the only one attracted to that man. Chrissy wondered out loud if he was single, if he would want to hook up or go on a date. We giggled and chatted all the way out, exchanging phone numbers, and promising to see each other the following week at dance class.

As I walked back to my apartment, I felt exhilarated and enthusiastic about life for the first time in a long time. I had a cozy home and new friends, and I felt attractive again. Truly, there is nothing like the attention of a good-looking man to put me in high spirits. Things were definitely looking up. *Maybe these dance lessons weren't such a bad idea after all.* I went home eager to start on my homework for the next session.

I wondered what Madame meant by "find a piece of music to accompany the emotion of your desire." *Do I really desire to be married and trust a man again?* This is what brought me into the studio in the first place, but divorce is way too prevalent these days, and I doubt getting married and trusting a man will ever happen for me again.

I closed my eyes, took a deep breath, and tried to focus on my desire. *What is it I really want?*

My mind returned to the experience of dancing around the pole and how it made me feel. The thought of potentially dancing like Sophie or Madame intrigued me as well; I considered their grace, their fluidity of motion, the ease of their sexuality, and their confidence.

Confidence.

Yes! That's it! My latest desire is to keep this newfound confidence and capitalize on the positive emotion it brought into my life. I could only imagine the ways I would work to change my body and start to look like the girls of the studio. I imagined that someday I might dance like they did, or even perform. The idea seemed surreal, yet at the same time it was very stimulating. *If I can accomplish this, maybe then I can focus on finding a partner. Yes, I must be confident in me first.*

After some research and listening to snippets of music for nearly two hours, I found the perfect song to accompany my newfound desire: confidence. It featured independent women who were strong and free—a mirror of me and what I desired to feel like every day. I didn't need a man to make me happy. Besides, desires are always changing—at least that's what I remembered Sophie saying.

With the studio homework done, I returned to my regular work-from-home schedule and got caught-up on the business to-do list. This time I had a renewed vigor and tingling excitement as thoughts of what this lasting confidence would feel like if I continued. Blissful visions of the coming week circled repeatedly in my mind. I could hardly wait until my next dance class!

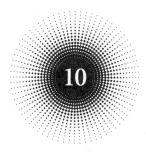

10

A Story; a Connection

The week passed quickly, with clients and coworkers asking about my new outlook on life. Others had apparently noticed the change in me as much as I felt a change within myself.

Soon I was back in the studio, this time with an iPod in hand, wearing black short shorts and a small black spaghetti-strapped tank top covered by a sheer cotton shirt that fell from my left shoulder. Once again, I felt sexy! A new pair of four-inch silver heels completed the ensemble, purchased to reflect my newfound desire of gaining and displaying lasting confidence.

"Wow, Lenea! Don't you look hot!" Chrissy exclaimed, setting her bag down next to mine.

"What? This old thing?" I tugged on my see-through cotton T-shirt and laughed. We gave each other a hug.

"So do you girl! I love your leotard. It's so you," I said, repaying her compliment.

She smiled and laughed in response, then performed a little twirl. "This is a dance class, right?"

Chrissy was dressed in a hot pink leotard with nude tights and leg warmers. She could have been plucked out of any 1980s movie, from her makeup right down to her nude classic character dance shoes. I loved her flair and her ability to wear whatever she wanted without a care in the world for anyone else's opinion. She had that type of personality where she could literally wear anything and get away with it.

Madame walked through the door. "Bonjour, ladies," she began, greeting us in her marked French accent. She stopped before clapping her hands twice. "Please form a circle in the center of the room and bring all necessary materials with you to your space. You will not have a chance to get up once we are all seated. After you are seated, please take a moment to breathe and prepare yourselves to share your desires openly with one another."

What! I have to share in front of everyone? I cringed inside while I reached in my bag for my iPod and realized some people had pages of notes, Jessica in particular. Soon we all gathered and created a circle, Madame put on gentle background music and lit candles in the same ceremonial procession she had performed the first week.

Madame was also attired differently. Today she wore a long, flowing muted green skirt and a matching see-through tunic top over a black corset undershirt; the outfit was very similar to the way she was dressed the night of our first introduction. Her beaded and crystal jewelry once again gave her a gypsy-like presence.

Quietly, we followed her direction and sat in yoga positions, breathing deeply and patiently awaiting further instructions. The room went dark. Madame had turned off all the lights in the studio. Only a faint glow from the burning candles remained. A distinct feeling of reverence permeated the room.

Madame spoke in a soft voice. "Chrissy, I would like you to go first today. Please share with us the deepest desire of your heart."

Chrissy swallowed hard, took a deep breath, and stood up to share. "I desire to find joy in my life. I believe this will happen when I can stop drinking." She paused for a moment, her eyes welling up with tears. "I want to end the alcoholism that runs in my family and not be so damn dependent on something to make me happy," she said irately, the tears now running down her face. Her crying turned into a nervous laugh before she smiled uneasily and took her seat. It appeared her body was shaking.

I was shocked. Here was a girl that, if asked to describe her, I would characterize as joyful. Yet her heartfelt desire in life was to find joy. *Interesting*, I thought.

"Chrissy, you are showing courage, sharing your desire," Madame said. She had been sauntering behind our group, and she stopped only to offer her commendation before continuing her stroll. "Thank you for being so open with us." Madame's eyes followed the direction of our circle, as if to focus the lesson. "And I believe anything is possible. Chrissy, my dear, if you truly desire to break the invisible chains of alcohol addiction that run in your family, I believe you will do it."

That was it? No song? No instructions on how to do it? Simply an "I believe you can" from Madame? I had witnessed others suffer from alcoholism. *Dance classes surely couldn't change things, could they?* I soon discovered who was next.

"Lenea?" Madame nodded in my direction, indicating it was my turn to share.

Rising up, I took a deep cleansing breath, realizing that sharing in front of everyone was a bit frightening. All eyes on me confirmed that what I had chosen as my desire was right—to find lasting confidence. *I definitely could use some right now.* I smiled at the group, and they smiled back, reassuring me it was okay to share.

"I desire to gain a lasting confidence," I said hesitantly. "This past week I have felt sexy and powerful as a woman. I want to harness this feeling and apply it to every area of my life. Many times I feel this, yet it always slips away. I get excited thinking of the things I could do if I could hold on to this feeling." I smiled nervously at Madame and sat back down.

Madame looked deep in my eyes. "I see," she replied in a voice that suggested skepticism. A serious look of contemplation washed over her face while the fingers on her right hand rubbed the end of her well-defined chin. "Did you bring music to accompany this desire?"

Nodding, I reached out to hand her my iPod. She did not reach for it. Rather, she turned away, walking slowly around the circle in contemplative thought, playing with the beaded necklace strung around her neck.

"The music is meant to strengthen the emotion of your desire, if ..." She stopped and turned toward me, her dark eyes and stern face glaring at me, "if ... it is indeed your desire." Her tone was clearly cynical now, and her French accent was discernible as she continued, almost irritated. "We will play your music at the end of class today, and you will have an opportunity to dance the emotion of your desire."

Something about the way she emphasized and then paused on the word "if" really bothered me. Did she not believe me? Was it a bad desire? Why was she judging me? My confidence waned at the sting of her cold response. The thought of having to dance by myself suddenly mortified me.

Julia was next in the circle. She told us the background story of her life. I didn't pay much attention, still focused on why Madame had singled me out and obviously didn't respect me. I tried to clear my negative thoughts, shaking my head and returning to Julia's share. I got the gist of it. She was raised by a well-known family with a hefty fortune, yet with all she had monetarily, her one desire was to be accepted as a lesbian and to get over her hatred toward the people who judged her.

"Beautiful share, Julia," Madame responded, the look on her face much more approving. "A desire that helps you love others is a desire with purpose." Then Madame turned toward me to finish her thought, as if it were not directed to Julia at all. Again her face and glare turned to stone. "A desire with purpose has an end to be obtained, a destiny. You will know when this has happened. And all things are possible to those who believe."

Great! I thought. Now I really felt bad. Here were two women who had shared their desires to better the world, and they made my desire seem selfish and vain. Madame was obviously annoyed with me. Why in the world had I shared that? I should have talked about my original desire to trust a man, which was truly more heartfelt and in keeping what the others had intended. I sighed at the heaviness I felt under the weight of Madame's glare, wishing I could disappear. My mind drifted as Madame began a diatribe, slowly circling the group once more.

Samantha rose without introduction, standing straight, squaring her shoulders, and lifting her perfectly manicured nails on her perfectly shaped hands to run them through her perfectly styled hair. She lifted her perfect chin to the perfect height, cleared her throat, and began. "I desire fame and fortune." Her voice mirrored her body language. It was slow and sultry. She stood alone with unabashed confidence.

"So many people seek recognition and money, but for what?" Madame responded, not recognizing Samantha. Instead, she continued on her diatribe, never breaking her gait. "Our lives are meaningless without contribution to a greater cause." Madame paused and looked down at Julia. "Julia, do you feel your parents are truly happy because of their social status and the money they have?" Madame's question took us all by surprise. I was happy to see someone else on Madame's radar for a change, but I wondered why she returned to Julia rather than Samantha. Yet Samantha stood there, unaffected by the obvious dis.

Julia shook her head, somewhat confused by Madame's question. "No, not really," she responded nonchalantly.

"I want to be an actress and a singer," Samantha interjected, now perky and confident, as if interviewing for a role. "I want to share my talents with the world and inspire others. My gifts and talents are worthy of great sums of money. In sharing my gifts, I contribute to a greater cause." She sat back down in a proud, perched position.

Is this girl for real? I wondered. *What an arrogant statement!* I could only imagine Madame's response to a desire of fame and fortune. And I thought mine was selfish. After hearing Samantha's share, suddenly my desire for lasting confidence didn't seem so vain by comparison.

Madame ignored Samantha completely; her eyes and intent were clearly focused on Julia. The gears in Madame's brain were obviously turning, mulling over Samantha's response before she spoke. "It is within us all to have lofty goals and desires." She turned and continued to circle again, never changing her stride. "And, many times, a desire to benefit others will lead to a benefit to you. In this group, I believe all things are possible. And if you demonstrate and grow your talents here, you will find what it is you desire."

What the hell is this? I asked myself silently. *Samantha talks about fame and fortune and she is rewarded?* I began to hate her even more than I already did. There was something about her that got under my skin. She obviously already had it all. Why was she here? It pissed me off! *Now she wants more?* I could feel my blood boil, looking at her, seething. The thought of her being rich and famous on top of her beauty sent me close to the edge. *Why do I get reprimanded and led to question my desire to feel sexy and powerful? This is ridiculous.* Question after question rolled through my mind in continuous waves. A jealousy and anger at Samantha was building up within.

Madame stopped, gently placing her hand on Jessica's shoulder, indicating it was her turn to share.

Jessica was the all-American girl with round cheekbones and deep-set eyes. She could have been from any Midwestern town, wholesomeness oozing from every pore. She had probably been called a big-boned girl her whole life and was definitely heavier than the other women. Without her speaking a word, I knew her desire would be to lose weight. But to me, her weight didn't take away from the beauty of her face. She could have been a model with her perfectly proportioned facial features.

Jessica picked up a large sheaf of handwritten papers. "I brought these pages from my journal to help explain my desire." Her voice was mousy and definitely didn't match the size of her body. She paused and looked around the circle. "Without knowing my story, you would not understand me. Madame and I have worked together for several years privately. I came to her because of my desire and because of the experience I am about to share with you. When you hear my story, I think you will better understand my desire." Jessica took a deep breath and began to read from the stack of pages in her hand.

"It was raining when I left the restaurant that day. A friend of mine and I had just finished lunch downtown. I was nineteen, full of energy and a zest for life. We had laughed so hard that my stomach ached, and when I got in my car, one glance in my rearview mirror showed a residual smile plastered on my face. In keeping with my energy, I turned up my music extra loud. I didn't even notice the storm clouds building all around me.

"As I entered the freeway to drive home, I lost myself somewhere between the conversations that were repeating in my mind and the beat of the music to one of my favorite songs. It started to rain harder, and cars were slowing down. The visibility was limited. I didn't bother to reduce my speed but continued singing in harmony to the song on the radio.

"Suddenly there was a loud banging sound that brought me back to the reality of the moment. It sounded like a gun went off." Jessica stopped reading, looked up at us and took a deep breath. Then she continued to an audience now caught in her story.

"At first I thought it was lightning. But then my car pulled hard to the left. I was panicked. I realized the front left tire had burst and was now making a terrible flopping sound. I took my foot off the gas pedal and pulled the wheel hard to the right. It felt almost locked. I started begging God to let me live through this. The car fishtailed a couple times before I regained control and slowed to a stop. A few hundred yards ahead, I spotted an overpass I was able to drive to and pulled underneath, using it as shelter from the rain." She turned to the next page, looking to see if everyone was listening. All eyes remained focused on her.

"I pushed the button to turn the hazard lights on, thankful I made it through such a harrowing event, my adrenaline rush subsided. Knowing I needed to call for help, I reached down to pick up my purse and rummaged through it, looking for my cell phone. It wasn't there. It wasn't in my purse or my coat pocket. Trying not to panic, I looked everywhere in the car. Then I remembered I had kept it next to me on the cushion in the restaurant so I could check posts and messages without being too obvious. I must have left it there. I started to cry uncontrollably, banging my hands on the steering wheel and calling myself stupid at least a dozen times for leaving the cell phone at the restaurant."

She paused, took a drink of water from her sports bottle, and continued. "I'm not sure how long I sat in my car shaking, crying, praying for a miracle or some sort of help. Looking up to a noise of squeaking brakes, I noticed a big blue van pull up in front of my vehicle. My first thought was 'Thank you, God. You heard my prayer!' Then I thought, 'Maybe this person saw what happened. Maybe they can help.'

"I saw a man get out of the car. He was Caucasian, clean cut, and of average height. He wore jeans and a dark blue athletic hooded sweatshirt he used to shield himself from the rain. I knew I needed to stay in my car. I cracked my window as the man approached. He introduced himself as Greg. He said he saw my tire was blown out and wanted to know if he could help. I responded by saying thank you, but I didn't have a spare and was really shaken up and trying to figure out what to do.

"Honestly, I kept looking at Greg and thinking this guy was really good looking and he was probably not much older than me. If I had met him on a Saturday night, I would be ecstatic and flirt with him. But sitting in my car with mascara running down my face didn't make me feel very attractive, so I decided to keep the conversation short." She turned the page. Her voice shook as she spoke, and she stopped to take another drink of water.

"Greg looked at me with his piercing blue eyes and asked me if I was okay and if I had anyone coming to help me. I shook my head. He indicated there was a gas station up at the next exit and he would drive me there if I wanted. He told me he understood this was an uncomfortable situation for me to be in and it was uncomfortable for him as well. He smiled, and I felt reassured I could trust him when he said, 'Cause you never know; you gotta be careful with strangers.' We both chuckled a little.

"His humor helped lighten the heaviness of the situation. Somehow I felt safe with Greg, like we had made a human connection. 'That would be great,' I responded. I knew of the gas station, and it wasn't very far. I grabbed my belongings and thanked him profusely for his generosity and time. He responded by saying, 'If you were my sister, I would hate to know you were stuck on the side of the road all by yourself.'

"Immediately I felt a sense of peace and comfort as I got out of my car and followed him to the van in front of us. I was safe and possibly able to make a new friend. Silently I breathed a sigh of relief, for I knew Greg was an angel sent to my rescue. As he opened the passenger door for me, I smiled and thanked him for the polite gesture. If it hadn't been for the reality of the situation, I could have sworn we were on a first date. It would sure make a great story of how we met."

Jessica paused again, her face turning white before she turned to the next page. She reached down for another drink of water, her hands trembling, as she brought the rim of the bottle to her lip, took a long hard swallow with eyes closed, and set the bottle back down. In a short moment, her body language turned rigid and her voice trembled.

"What happened next no one could have prepared me for." Her small voice echoed in the room while pausing to look at all of us, her eyes welling with water as she fought back her own tears. She cleared her throat and continued to read.

"I felt a paper bag slip over my head. Everything went dark, and I could barely breathe. I reached up to grab the bag off my head, when a very strong pair of hands grabbed mine, and pulled them down behind my back. 'Get her in the back of the van!' I heard a different man say.

"The pressure around my neck was intense. I tried to scream for help. But nothing came out and the hands grew tighter. I didn't want to black out, afraid I would die. So I shut up. I knew it was useless. With my arms pinned to the back of the seat, I felt trapped. I jammed my feet into the floorboard in the hope to raise my body and break free. Another pair of hands grabbed my thighs and pushed me back down. I heard their voices yelling at me to 'shut the fuck up! Shut the fuck up or we'll kill you!' At that moment, I felt something hard against the side of my head. It felt like a gun. 'Do you want me to blow your motherfucking head off?' one of the voices said.

"I knew this wasn't a game. I no longer had control. One of the men took my legs and twisted my body into the back of the van. I could feel the blood being cut off at my hands from the pressure around my wrists." Jessica held her left hand up; thick scars were visible a few inches below her wrist.

"I felt a body sit on my chest and pin my hands down, another holding the bag over my head as two sets of hands pulled my pants down, stopping at the ankles, then my underwear. I screamed 'No!' and kicked as hard as I could, but they were too strong. There was no escape.

"I don't remember when the first guy penetrated my body. Thankfully, I can't remember much more… It was as if my spirit detached from my body and was floating above, looking down at the whole scene with pity. There I was, my body lying on the floor, being desecrated by at least four men, each one switching places to have his way with me.

"I came back to my body as I heard Greg say, 'It's my turn, bitch.' He penetrated me hard. It wasn't long before another voice yelled, 'Hurry up, Scott! Let's get out of here!' He stopped. I could feel the tension snap through his crotch as he angrily replied, 'Don't use my real name, you fucking idiot! Now we gotta kill her!' I grew very scared and, for the first time, started to cry and yell 'Stop! Stop!' In a few seconds, which seemed like hours, he let out a big moan as he released. 'Now what?' Another voice said. 'Dump her,' Greg said.

"The van's door was opened, and I felt myself lifted up and thrown out onto the side of the road, where I rolled a few yards down the hill into some gravel. I heard the van door shut, the engine start up, and asphalt shoot from underneath the screeching tires as they drove off. I tried to reach up and pull the bag off my head, but the pain in my body was unbearable. Instead, I curled up into a ball and cried. I was thankful they would no longer hurt me.

"Little did I know, though, that while the pain in my head and body was real, the pain I endured that night would still haunt me to this day."

Jessica set her papers down. The sound of crying echoed throughout the studio. Madame spoke like a parochial mother after hearing a confession. "Jessica, my dear," she paused, searching for the words, "what you have shared today took … a lot … of courage. There is not one woman in this room who will leave here today without being affected by your story. It is powerful. When you are ready, will you please share your heartfelt desire with the rest of the class?"

Jessica took a moment to compose herself. She took a deep breath, sat up proud and tall, and looked around the room at her newfound family members.

She lifted her chin up next, stoically, as she made her announcement to the class. "I desire to find a husband ... and to have children ... and to forgive my assailants. I am tired of being alone and reliving this private hell. I want to find forgiveness and move on with my life."

Immediately, all of us girls left where we were sitting and lunged toward Jessica to hug her. Tears followed, with the passing of a tissue box and a resounding "It's going to be okay" repeated by all of us quite often. The moment continued for several minutes until broken up by Madame clearing her throat. We all went back to our spots on the dance floor, our faces now a mess of mascara. Madame looked at Jessica knowingly and nodded to her. "Your desire has been heard, and you are well on your way to creating your destiny."

Jessica wiped her eyes and smiled; the two embraced. It was the first time I had seen Madame show compassion toward any of the girls. A small part of me felt jealous of their connection. One by one we all stood and circled around the two, tears and laughter flowing like wine at a wedding. Jessica's story had connected us as part of a sisterhood.

Still, as I stood there, I couldn't quite shake the disappointment I felt inside yet again. I knew I had failed to tell the truth about my own heartfelt desire to be married and have children. *How do I go back now?* I thought. *Especially after what Jessica shared? And how could she forgive the men who did that to her? Why would she want to?*

Looking up from the hugging ensemble into the reflection of us in the shadowed mirror, I saw a faintly lighted presence move past the door and into the hallway. It resembled a hologram of a woman. Was I seeing things? I focused harder, and the vision was gone.

I stood there not really knowing what to do. Some of the girls were crying and still hugging Jessica. I was moved by Jessica's story, but at the same time I felt removed and disconnected.

Certainly this was a tender moment for Jessica. But somehow I didn't resonate with all the love being shared. I knew why, though. I had let myself down by not being honest with the group about what it was I really desired; why I was there in the first place. The thought made me feel sick to my stomach.

I glanced up in the mirror and saw the ghostlike figure pass by again. This time a chill went up and down my spine. Goose bumps broke out on my arms. *Did I really see that?*

Greater Awareness

Madame left the group, walked over to the stereo, and turned off the background music. Silence hung in the air. Next she turned on some slow rhythm and blues.

"Please put away your belongings and join me on the dance floor, ladies," she instructed us in her sultry French tone.

A shift of energy permeated the room as we gathered together facing the mirror, lining up like military soldiers ready and awaiting our orders. I focused on the reflections, especially in the direction of the hallway, expecting to see something. Nothing was there.

Madame began swaying her hips from side to side. We followed her lead and copied her fluid movements warming-up our bodies.

"Until you surrender your desires and come to a place where you are secure within yourself, you will continue to think that you will never receive them." Madame paused. "Surrendering control is the first step in the process. It doesn't matter how we get to this point in life. What matters is that we get there. Some people live and die and never get there. Giving up control can be a life-changing experience."

Suddenly she stopped moving and turned around to face us as a group. I could feel her looking straight into my eyes as she asked, "Do you want to receive your desires?"

The response we gave was a combination of nodding heads and a soft "yes" audible only to those within close proximity. We all stopped moving as well.

Then she asked, "Do you feel secure within yourselves?"

Her piercing brown eyes shot right to the truth inside of me. Silence filled the room as no one answered. Until …

"Yes," Samantha said with an air of confidence.

Seriously? I thought. *This girl is unbelievable. No one is perfectly secure within herself, is she?* I waited for Madame's response. There was only silence.

"Are you happy without your desires being met?" Madame asked.

Once again, I felt the honesty within me. A murmur of "no's" and "not really's" echoed in the room; I silently said the same. The murmur was broken by Samantha.

"Yes," she said proudly, this time with a smile on her face.

This girl makes me sick, I thought. Yet a part of me was curious how she could answer the questions so confidently. Mostly, I was envious, wishing I could do the same.

"Regardless of how you answered the questions," Madame continued, "I would like to take you into a place where you can feel secure within yourself." She turned around and started dancing again. We all followed suit.

"Lenea, being a science major, are you familiar with Newton's first law of motion?" she asked continuing our warm-ups.

Her direct question took me by surprise. We had never talked about this. Then I remembered the studio paperwork listing my hobbies and interests. Science was at the top of my list.

"Yes, an object at rest continues to stay at rest and an object in motion continues to stay in motion, until an external force is applied," I answered like a good student.

"That is correct," she said approvingly, pausing for a moment and allowing me to enjoy her praise. "When you move your body, you move your mind. Achieving security within starts with the body–mind connection." She let the words sink in while moving her hips in circles.

I smiled and was relieved to be in her good graces again; a sense of self-worth returning to my own mind.

We finished our warm-ups. I felt loose and comfortable. Madame walked over to the stereo and turned on another song. This one had a strong bass beat and made me feel like dancing. Soon, smiles broke out on the faces throughout the room. It felt good to dance again after such an intense time of sharing.

"Ladies, it is time to move," Madame directed. "Time to get lost in the movement of your body." She waited for our attention before continuing. "I want you to envision your body taking on a life of its own. What would your body do? What would this look like? What would this feel like? There are no right or wrong answers in this exercise. In a moment, I will ask you all to find a place on the dance floor. Make sure you allow yourself enough room to move your body freely. Then I will ask you to close your eyes and surrender to the movement of your body; to the rhythm. Surrender your mind and therefore your desires you have shared symbolically as well."

She stopped to observe us and ensure we had followed her directions. Then she walked around the room. "Please find a space now and prepare yourself within."

Securing my space on the floor, I closed my eyes. My body began dancing, but I felt nervous. "Dance for yourselves ladies, no one else. Dance as if you are all alone and no one is watching." Her words seemed directed at me. Perhaps she felt my apprehension.

I closed my eyes and imagined a completely black room where no one could see me move. I began to loosen up, enjoying the music and the movement. Then curiosity got the best of me as I sneaked a peek at Madame in the mirror. She was moving in the same manner she had in our first class—eyes closed, her hands on her hips and then running up her body.

Suddenly, my eyes were diverted when I saw flailing arms and exaggerated movements belonging to Samantha. She was not moving to the music at all. Her body looked as if she were about to explode. It was weird. I closed my eyes and put the focus back on me. Madame's directive to lose myself echoed in my mind.

Letting go, I relaxed and touched myself, the music guiding my body. Soon, there was no thinking, only a peaceful bliss and singular awareness of the dance. The music stopped mid-chorus.

It was an awkward moment. *Did the sound turn off? Do I open my eyes?* Luckily Chrissy spoke up.

"What happened?" she asked Madame in her casual tone. By now we had all stopped our movements and opened our eyes.

"Why did you all stop dancing?" Madame chided.

"Um, because the music stopped?" Chrissy answered in a matter-of-fact way.

"So you were in motion, and now you're at rest. What external force stopped you?" Madame directed the question to Chrissy. However, I knew it was directed to the "collective you" as well.

"The music?" Chrissy responded, not sure of her answer.

"The music didn't stop you. Physically you all could have continued dancing without the music. Think harder. When the music stopped, what happened in your mind?" Madame scanned our faces for an answer.

"I thought I should stop dancing," Chrissy responded again for the group.

"Yes. And so you did." Madame paused to look around the room. "It is not right or wrong that you danced or didn't dance. I simply wanted you all to understand the power of thoughts as an external force," she said, as if to drive home the point of the exercise. "To finish this lesson, I would like you all to spread out even farther and find a place in the room away from one another. I will pass around pens and paper for our next lesson. Hurry, ladies; time waits for no one."

Quickly we followed her instructions. Madame walked around the studio handing out pens and paper. When she finished, she stopped and returned to the front of the room. Her face remained solemn, but it was obvious she was pleased we moved so fast.

"Thoughts create triggers in the mind," Madame began, hesitating to allow the words to sink in. "One of these triggers can be memories of past experiences. For memories are a part of each one of us." She casually moved about the room handing out supplies as she continued. "Strong emotion is stored in memories, and from these memories we create beliefs; so to protect us in the future. We live our lives based on our beliefs. When we look deeper, we realize these beliefs are based on emotional triggers that we have no control over." She paused again, raising an eyebrow and a pointed finger. "Or do we?"

Waiting to allow us to ponder her words, she gradually moved forward, ultimately stopping in the empty space next to me. Her presence was intimidating. "I want you each to write down five negative memories you would like to get rid of," her voice directed. "Think about this and ask yourself, if you were given the power to erase any traumatic memory … what would it be?"

Fiddling with the pen in my hand, I sat there contemplating what her words meant. A flood of negative memories came to the surface: from my parent's bitter divorce and the fighting between them, to my own divorce and the years and memories with Richard. *Oh God! That night at the downtown loft!* The options kept flowing.

Madame interrupted. "I'll give you a hot tip. The memories you need to focus on have to do with something you are blaming on someone else. Sometimes it is an external experience that you regret."

Her words provided a tipping point, and a deluge of choices came to mind. I wrote furiously, listing my most negative memories. Ten minutes had passed, and with a long list of things written, I went back to reread and see what I was missing. It was only then that I realized everything noted had a common theme: trust. I obviously did not trust men. My thoughts ranged from my father and how he treated me while going through his divorce, to my time with Richard and to each man I ever dated. The bottom line was my belief that men could not be trusted.

Madame could see we were all nearly done and interjected, "Once you identify with a negative belief, I want you to imagine what your life would be like without it."

I sat there conflicted. I doubted if this could ever happen. Still, I took a deep breath, calmed my mind, and tried, if only for a moment, to feel the freedom I would have without this limiting belief.

"Now, in this space, what do you desire most?" Madame's voice was soothing.

Instantly, a thought popped into my head: *I desire a husband and children; to live a life of partnership and love and trust a man.* I wrote down my desire in big bold letters. *That's it! I want to learn how to trust!*

Madame's voice interrupted my thoughts. "Today you have developed a special bond by intimately sharing yourselves and your lives." She walked around the room collecting our papers before returning to center stage. "Thank you for your openness and vulnerability."

Thinking back to the stories we had all shared, I was reminded of the selfishness and regret I had for not sharing my own deepest desire. I felt like a fraud.

Madame set the stack of papers in a basket then asked us all to stand and gather together in the center of the room and form a large circle. We did so quietly. "I want you all to take a moment and look into each other's eyes," Madame instructed.

Doing as she said, I found it uncomfortable to look at the other women directly. At the same time, I felt I had a better understanding of the women who surrounded me—a connection of sorts.

"This bond you all share will help you to create new memories," Madame continued. "These new memories will begin to counteract the old. You are safe to share, and nothing you share will be communicated outside of this circle. Do you understand?" We nodded in response to her question.

"If I find someone has broken this bond by sharing another's story, you will be dismissed from the group, never to return to this studio." Her voice grew stern and pointed. "Do you understand?" A resounding "yes" echoed from the group.

I would hate to see someone on her bad side, I thought.

"Intimacy is developed in a space of safety. The studio is a safe and sacred space." She took a step back, relaxing her face and her body language. "You are welcome in the studio at any time. Please consider this your home. I suggest you all exchange numbers with one another, and any other contact information you feel will strengthen this bond."

She excused the class curtly. Her eyes remained focused on me. "Lenea, unfortunately we have run out of time today for your dance. Would you please bring your music with you next week? Au revoir." She turned to leave, not waiting for my response, and walked out the door and down the hallway.

My eyes followed her as she walked past the same mirror I had seen the apparition in, wondering if it would appear again. *Maybe it was my mind playing tricks on me*, I thought. Nothing was there; only an empty hallway. *Had I imagined things? Where does Madame go anyway? She is never around after class. Everyone seems to just disappear once they walk through that door!*

Curiosity was getting the better of me. I stood to leave, when Chrissy stopped me and asked if she could walk and talk with me. "Certainly," I said. We gathered our bags and headed to the hallway together.

Wanting to be a good friend and listen, I tried to remain attentive, but my mind was clearly preoccupied and my guard was up, hoping to catch a glimpse of the woman I had seen in the mirror. *Was it a spirit? Why did I see it?* I wondered. A childhood memory shot through my mind—a vision of the friend I had when I was five that no one else could see. *Was it Patty?*

We stood outside the studio for what felt like a long time, the intense sunshine beating down on our heads. Finally, Chrissy stopped talking, hugged me, and thanked me for being such a good listener and friend. At the same time, the other girls passed by and waved, saying they would get our information later. They were probably being polite and didn't want to interrupt our conversation. I looked at Chrissy and responded, "You're welcome," but I felt bad. I really hadn't listened to her the way a friend should have. My mind had been elsewhere.

We said our good-byes, then turned and walked in separate directions. In a state of confusion, I stopped for a moment and looked back at the studio. *Wow! What a crazy day!*

There Is Something More to Flashing Lights

The moment I arrived home, the couch called my name. I collapsed on it, duffel bag still in hand, and lay there thinking about the events in the studio. *Why was I questioning my desire to feel strong and sexy? What's wrong with wanting lasting confidence? Why does Samantha want to be rich and famous? I'm sure there was a time when she too wanted to be strong and sexy, because she is. What's wrong with me desiring the same? A woman should feel this way! It's how we are created!*

My thoughts battled against each other before turning to work. Dragging myself off the couch, I set my duffel bag down next to my makeshift desk and picked up a pile of reports. The files seemed blurry with no direction. Five minutes into it, I gave up. *Ugh! There is no way I have the energy to do this today!* I blew off the reports and headed back to the couch, kicking off my shoes and turning on the TV to give myself a well-deserved rest.

Lying there watching the afternoon shows, I tried to zero in on what was really upsetting me. Then, having flipped through several channels, stopping at any show that had romance on, it dawned on me: *Every time I see a happy couple on commercials, or sitcoms, all I want to do is puke. For me, relief and comfort are found in the reality TV shows and soap operas where fighting, cheating, and drama are the norm. Yes! Be mean to each other! Tear each other apart! Cheat on each other! This is reality, right?*

I continued to watch the afternoon dramas, and I felt sad—very sad. *This is not what I want. If I look inside, deep inside, what I yearn for is a relationship with a good man; a partnership. Does a partnership like that really exist? Is it possible in today's throwaway society?*

Turning off the TV, I looked at the clock. Unbelievable—it was already after five. I had spent the last three hours as a couch potato, blowing off an entire afternoon of work, and felt even more drained. Overwhelmed with exhaustion, I lifted myself off the couch to make dinner.

Keeping with the day's theme of sloth, I opened a can of soup, put it in a bowl to heat it in the microwave, and grabbed a box of crackers. I didn't even have enough energy to grab a plate. Instead, I ripped off a piece of paper towel and carried the entire package of crackers and the bowl to the sofa. *No sense in getting off the couch tonight*, I thought. Having already browsed the movies on cable, I was looking forward to crashing for more rest and relaxation, hoping a good movie would revive my spirits.

I set my bowl on the coffee table in front of the couch and glanced into the mirror that hung above the fireplace. It displayed a reflection of the kitchen behind me. A flash of light appeared in the mirror, and I spun around quickly. It felt as if someone, or something, was there. When I looked back, though, the kitchen was empty. Everything was as it should be.

The hair on the back of my neck stood up; my senses were heightened. I took a deep breath to calm my nerves and tried to convince myself the flash was merely the reflection of a passing car. *Relax, it's nothing*, I thought.

I turned on the TV, and the familiar sounds of the movie introduction brought me back to a sense of serenity. I relaxed into the couch, sipping my hot soup and glancing up every now and then into the mirror, expecting to see something.

You're overreacting, I told myself. I snuggled deeper into the soft cushions and finished my meal. Before long, I was laughing uncontrollably, lost in the comical scenes, and forgot all about the flash of light.

After nearly an hour passed, I paused the TV and jumped up to take a quick bathroom break. *It's nice to have a small apartment where everything is so close together.*

The kitchen and living area were combined into one large space with two small hallways: one leading to the entrance door of the apartment, and the other leading to a bathroom opposite my small bedroom.

Walking toward the bathroom, I caught sight of a light passing through my bedroom in my peripheral vision. I stopped dead in my tracks. A million tingles raced throughout my body. Motionless, I stood there staring at my pale face in the reflection of the mirror that hung at the end of the hall. The light flashed again. This time it was familiar to me: it was lightning. My body relaxed. I exhaled.

The curtains on my bedroom window were open, and it was easy to see a storm was brewing. Storms were very common in Colorado this time of year. I laughed as I walked into the room and drew the curtains. Obviously I was too exhausted to even realize what was going on outside the world around me.

Soon I was back on the couch, this time laying my head on the pillow.

I woke up to the sound of the TV blaring and all the lights in the apartment still on. The clock displayed 2:30 a.m. I got up and peeked out the window to see if the storm was still nearby. The starry sky was clear and beautiful. I loved looking out my window at night on a weekday when no one was around. It was so quiet and serene. Streetlights illuminated the asphalt, standing guard as they waited for the hustle and bustle of the morning.

After closing the curtains, I picked up my dishes and placed them in the sink too exhausted to even turn on the water and rinse the bowl. The thought of doing anything made me nauseated. Turning off the TV and the lights, the apartment went dark and silent, leaving only me and my thoughts. *Ugh! How could I have wasted a full day?*

My entire being simply wanted to collapse into bed. Shuffling down the small hallway, I glanced up into the mirror at the end of the hall. An image of light passed behind me. It startled me and shot a jolt of adrenaline through my body. "It's just lightning. It's just lightning," I told myself. The hairs stood up on my body once again, but I was too tired. Ignoring it, I jumped into my bed, pulled the blanket tight over my head, and fell asleep.

••••••●●◉●●••••••

Morning dawned. Opening my swollen eyes, I looked down and realized I was still wearing my shorts and dance shirt from yesterday. "Okay, it is a new day, girl, you can do this," I told myself while leaping out of bed. I showered and changed into my work attire, shorts and a T-shirt, made my coffee and breakfast, and turned on some upbeat tunes. Soon a new day was brightening all around me.

It was time to get to work. I sat down at my desk, the coffee now stimulating my brain. My "desk" was actually an oversized end table placed against the wall in the area intended for a dining room table. It was a little awkward looking but suited my needs perfectly.

If I had friends over, which was rare, I could pull the table away from the wall, remove the computer, and cover it with a tablecloth. You would never know you were eating at a desk. I kept some extra chairs in my bedroom for such an occasion. I hoped to someday bring a date home and cook for him, but that hadn't happened yet.

I sorted through my e-mail, checking headings first, when my attention turned to one from a law firm I didn't recognize. It was marked "URGENT," and as I began to read it, my mouth dropped open; I could not believe what it said: Richard hadn't paid our taxes for the last three years we were married. Furthermore, after being contacted by the IRS, he had "settled the debt" on my behalf, and the notice claimed I owed half of $18,643.67, not including penalties or interest.

"That son of a bitch!" I yelled to no one in particular. Shaking my head in disbelief, the tension in my jaws grew tighter, my facial muscles clenched. I read the e-mail three times, unconvinced each time it could be real.

Without hesitation, I called the number listed at the end of the e-mail, ready to lay into the person on the other line. Anger raged inside me. Now pacing the floor, my heartbeat raced as I tried to determine how I could pay this bill off as fast as possible. *I knew Richard would find another way to screw me.* "Asshole!" Again I spoke out loud to the air around me. "Where the hell am I going to come up with nine thousand dollars?" *Maybe this is all a misunderstanding*, I thought halfheartedly.

Fortunately, the attorney answered. He sounded nice enough and explained how Richard had been audited by the IRS and it was determined both of us had failed to pay federal income tax for three years.

"Wait a minute," I said, anger overwhelming my normally calm voice. "My employer deducted all of my taxes from my paycheck. I claimed zero. How could I owe anything?"

It turned out Richard had claimed a high tax withholding from his paycheck, and even though I recalled signing the tax forms, he failed to file them appropriately for those three years! Furthermore, since we were married, and the divorce decree clearly stipulated that "any additional financial obligations incurred as a result of the marriage that are later revealed will be split in two equal shares," I now owed nine thousand dollars.

Furious, I thought back to our marriage and Richard's lack of responsibility. *How in the world did I trust him with anything?* The one thing I did trust him with was filing our tax returns. *Even a monkey can do that. And now I find out he hadn't paid them?*

Stopping the lawyer in the middle of his sentence, I asked him what this had to do with me. It was an obvious problem for Richard, but I had nothing to do with him not filing tax returns. The government kept my money! I was no longer married to him, so why should I have to pay?

I was met with a long explanation of my part of the responsibility. Since we were married, I was complicit in not filing tax returns. Richard was aware of the audit process and was ready to pay his half of the debt. This was fortunate, since we were married at the time of the infraction. If he decided to skip out and not pay his portion, the IRS could require the spouse to pay the entire amount, even though the marriage ended in divorce and the parties were no longer together. Since it occurred during our marriage, I was liable. The lawyer told me I was lucky Richard was willing to work with me on this. He cited examples of other clients whose ex-spouses had skipped town, not paying their share of the taxes and leaving the entire mess for the former partner to clear up. He told me again that I was lucky Richard had accepted his half of the responsibility.

Great! I am so lucky to be stuck paying over nine thousand dollars because I trusted my husband would pay our taxes. This was yet another confirmation that men could not, under any circumstances, be trusted!

The attorney provided the IRS contact information so I could set up a payment plan if I did not have the full amount currently due. He reminded me the conversation was recorded for the benefit of his client and served as official notice. It was now my responsibility to handle the steps with the IRS and pay my portion of the debt. He sounded sincere when he said, "I'm terribly sorry this has happened to you. Good luck." There was a click as the line went quiet.

Sitting at my computer, staring at the screen that had now gone black, all I could think was, *How did this happen? How am I going to pay this debt?* I had just signed up and prepaid for expensive group sessions at the studio. *Now this?* I considered that maybe I could get my money back and put it toward the taxes.

Tears streamed from my eyes. *How could I have been so stupid to believe that asshole shithead actually paid our taxes? What else could I be responsible for?* I looked up to the ceiling, raising my arms and yelling at God, "Why do I still have to deal with him?"

Reacting with rage, I found myself going back into crisis mode. It felt no different than when I was married, and fortunately, I recognized the pattern immediately. Instead of panicking, I came up with a plan: call the IRS and figure this problem out.

It took the entire morning on the phone, being passed from agent to agent, department to department, before I found what sounded like an elderly gentleman who helped me set up a twenty-four-month payment plan. By early afternoon, my work day was wasted once again.

An idea came to me: Maybe I could walk over to the studio and talk with Shannon or Sophie about the situation. Maybe they would give me my money back so I could pay some of the debt down faster. If there is anything in the world I absolutely hate, it is debt. Plus, if Madame wasn't going to help support me in my desire to feel strong and confident, then it looked like it was time to take matters into my own hands.

I grabbed an oatmeal bar, threw it into my purse, and headed out the door toward the studio. I stopped to look in the mirror and saw a look of desperate determination on my face. "You can do this," I said to my reflection. "They will give you your money back."

13

He Might Change Things

The studio's door was locked. *Great! Why didn't I call before walking all the way down here?*

A light drizzle started to fall from the gray clouds above. *Super; didn't bring an umbrella either.* I could only stand there, hoping someone would eventually come to my rescue. I pulled my cell phone out of my purse and called the studio's number. No answer. I was about to leave, when Shannon came walking up with a bag of what appeared to be takeout from a local restaurant.

"Can I help you?" she asked in a hesitant voice. I looked up; her body language relaxed, and she smiled. "Oh, Lenea. I didn't recognize you. What's going on?"

"I came to talk with you about our classes. Is now a good time?" I asked, despair resonating in my voice. The wet-puppy-dog look only emphasized the moment.

"Sure," she said retrieving her keys and opening the door to let us in. "Let's go inside and get out of this rain."

The warmth of the studio was a welcome relief. The *thump thump thump* of the bass resonated throughout the hallway. I was certain others were there as well. Shannon must have stepped out for a moment to grab a bite to eat because all of the lights were on, and candles flickered in the waiting area. Shannon walked around the counter and set her food on the desk. I stood there and waited for her to get settled before asking my question.

"I'm curious how the pre-purchased sessions work with Madame. Something has happened, and I could really use the money right now more than the classes. Is there any way I can get a refund on the ones I haven't used?" Immediately I realized how sad and pathetic this sounded. "I'm so sorry to sound so desperate. I've really enjoyed the sessions. However, my priorities have shifted. I hope you understand."

Shannon listened and then stood. "Stay here while I grab your contract."

After a few minutes, I took a seat in the chair next to me, picked up a magazine, and began flipping through the pages to pass the time. I became so engrossed in an article that I almost forgot why I was there in the first place. Finally, Shannon returned with my contract in hand and no apology or excuse as to why she had been gone so long.

"Here's your contract," she said, taking a seat next to me. "Let's take a look."

She murmured out loud, her fingers following down the first page before flipping to the second. Again, her fingers moved down the small print before stopping. "Here, read this. I believe this will answer your question."

I looked down and read: "All prepaid purchases are final. No refunds, exchanges, or transfer of sessions are allowed." It also said, "You are fully responsible for attending all classes, and if you are late or miss a class, there are no makeups and no refunds."

Obviously, I wasn't getting out of this commitment. *Why hadn't I read the fine print? Here I go again*, I thought, *trusting people and being disappointed.* It didn't seem right to pay such a large sum of money and not be able to back out because of the drastic change in my life. *What would happen if I were hospitalized? Would I be penalized for that too? This is ridiculous!*

Shannon looked as though she were reading my thoughts. "I know this seems unfair," she began sympathetically, "and you're not the first who has tried to back out of the classes. Madame sets things up this way because she knows that once you make this type of commitment to yourself, resistance hits hard, and struggle is part of the process."

Looking at Shannon, I was puzzled, trying to decide if I should tell her the whole story, hoping it would change her mind, or get angry because no one warned me about the "struggle" part. I was hurt and confused and didn't know what to say.

"Madame said you are moving away from the original desire that brought you here. Is there a reason for this?" she asked, changing the subject.

Oh. Now I knew why she had been gone so long. She must have been talking with Madame about the whole thing. "I don't think so," I said, hoping to get out of the conversation.

"What was your original desire?" She turned to me, attempting to become a trusted friend and confidant.

Pausing for a moment, unsure if I should tell her, I knew deep inside I needed to share it with someone. *Why not a relative stranger?* "I'm divorced, and I don't trust men, but I still desire to find a stable partner." It felt good to reveal the truth. "How crazy is that?" I looked into her face, expecting rejection or some kind of sympathetic gesture. Shannon looked back at me, smiling and grabbing my hand in hers. Tears pooled in my eyes.

"There's nothing crazy about that, sweetie," she said. "Madame said to focus on your original desire and you will create what it is you came for."

She reached out to hug me, and we shared a tender moment. Her support felt genuine. She then stood, went behind the desk, and got back to her work. I took that as my cue to say good-bye and walked out of the studio shaking my head.

Do I really want to trust a man? Do I really want a partner? Why couldn't I simply desire to be sexy and confident? Did I make a huge mistake, once again, in trusting people I don't even know? I turned the corner from the studio, passing the shoe store. It had become the path I now took every time, worried about the embarrassment I would suffer if I were ever caught going into the studio and banned from my favorite Indian food restaurant.

Rounding the corner, I felt as if I hit a brick wall, and I fell backward on the ground. "Are you okay?" I heard a familiar voice ask. The "wall" extended his hand for me to grab. It was Mark. I had literally run straight into him, again!

"Oh my gosh!" he said assisting me to my feet from my fall on the sidewalk. "I'm so sorry." He laughed, nervously.

I wasn't sure what was so funny, and then it dawned on me that this was not our first time bumping into each other. In fact, it was the third. I too started to laugh. "Seriously, dude, if you want to get my attention, there are less painful ways to do it." I was surprised by my own forwardness.

"Me? Trying to get your attention? I thought it was the other way around," he said. "Why is it you're always in the right place at the right time?"

My eyes caught his. He was flirting. My heart leapt in my chest, and my knees felt a bit weak. "I have a habit of doing that—you know, being in the right place at the right time," I said, returning his words with a wink.

He stepped forward, invading my private space, and placed his hand on my shoulder. "Can I take you to dinner to make up for almost running you over?" he asked with a look of playful concern.

Looking up intently into his dreamy hazel eyes, I returned his invitation with a newfound confidence. "Absolutely! It's the least you can do," I said with a smile.

"Great! Meet me at the studio at six tonight, and we'll find someplace close. I promise I won't knock you down again. Deal?" He reached to shake on the agreement.

The moment our hands touched, a noticeable shock and electric tingle raced up my arm. From the expression on his face, I knew he felt it too. There was no doubt of my animal attraction to him. One touch of his hand, and I knew I wanted his hands all over me.

"Sounds perfect," I responded. "I'll have a can of Mace in my purse just in case you decide to get rough."

He raised one eyebrow in curiosity, which made me realize my comment could have been taken as a sexual innuendo. I blushed, knowing this was not the intent of my words. Before I could say anything else, he smiled and interjected, "I'll see you at six." Then he walked around the corner and out of sight.

Not believing what had happened, I wanted to jump up and down and scream from the building tops! In that moment, everything else lost its urgency. No one could steal the excitement that rushed through my veins—not the IRS, Richard, the studio, or anything else.

I practically skipped home like a giddy schoolgirl as I imagined our date. On the way home, I called Chrissy and told her the news. She was equally excited for me and wished me luck. It was great to have a new friend, someone I could share my joy with and multiply it by two. Maybe the studio wasn't such a bad place after all.

Upon walking through the door of my apartment, the neglected pile of paperwork called to me. This time I immersed myself in it, knowing a reward was waiting at the end. I finished the tasks at lightning speed and wrote my reports with ease. I felt happy and energized while watching the clock to ensure an adequate amount of primping time before our date.

At four forty five, I closed the last reports, moved to the bathroom, and pulled out my make-up bag.

Carefully, I coated each eye with mascara, creating a flawless presentation. I chose my outfit with equally careful consideration. *Something sexy*, I decided. *Wait a minute. Not too sexy, not too conservative.* The perfect choice came to mind: a casual, nude-colored dress that belted loosely around my waist and was short enough to show off my well-defined calves. I wore tan flats—a leg-lengthening trick I learned from the fashion magazines. Wearing heels and walking through the city was not an option; no amount of sexy trumped happy feet. My outfit said "vogue meets comfort."

I looked in the mirror, layering my necklaces in precise order, and smiled at my reflection. The look indicated strong and provocative, without being overt. My dark teal purse and sunglasses accessorized the ensemble perfectly. *Maybe confidence is not what I desire. I've already got it. Maybe it is a partner.* The thought of seeing Mark turned my stomach into a chamber of fluttering butterflies.

Gliding out the door, greeting others along the way, I felt a spring in my step, my shoulders back and head held high. Sophie's words from dance class kept repeating in my mind. Giving her words action, I simulated the moves of a runway model.

The extra bounce in my step put me in front of the studio door about ten minutes early. My haste put me in an awkward position. If I waited outside, I ran the possibility of bumping into the waitress from the Indian restaurant, and if I went inside, I might need to explain why I was there. I took my chances and waited outside.

Within a few minutes, Mark walked out the door wearing dark fitted jeans with a tight button-down shirt rolled up at the sleeves. The way he wore his shirt showed off his muscular arms. I could only imagine what his biceps looked like with his shirt off. His Italian black leather shoes showed me he had a keen sense of style. He smiled with that perfect grin of his, then stopped in his tracks when he reached me. "Wow, don't you look nice!" he commented. At the same time, he reached down and grabbed my hand.

"Thanks, you too," I responded, feeling the warmth in my cheeks at the sincerity of the compliment.

"I made reservations not too far from here. Have you ever eaten at Ravens?" His gaze was fixed into my eyes. His hand in mine felt so natural. He held it comfortably, yet with determination; I could feel his strength. I was so caught up by his appearance, the sound of his voice, and the feel of his hand, I almost missed the question.

"Oh, no I don't think so. Where is it?" I asked.

"It's in the L'abeille Palace and Hotel. You're going to love it. I made reservations just in case it was crowded." He matched his step with mine, even though his legs were much longer.

My first thought was, *Wow! I don't think my ex-husband ever made reservations for anything!* But I restrained myself. "Good idea," I replied instead.

The smell of his subtle aftershave wafted in the air. The spicy note of the fragrance lured me closer. We walked, hands melting into one, while he shared stories about the L'abeille Palace and Hotel and the many dignitaries and celebrities who have stayed there.

Hesitating for a moment, now questioning my attire for the environment, I turned to him and asked, "Am I underdressed?"

"No, no, no. You're dressed perfectly!" he replied quickly. "We're having dinner and drinks at Ravens. When I take you to their five-star restaurant, then we can put on the ritz and dress to the nines!"

Again he smiled that boyish grin. My face matched his, and almost embarrassed, I looked down at the ground as we turned in the direction of our destination. I was at a loss for words. Mark had said "when." This obviously meant he must enjoy my company as much as I enjoyed his and that he was looking ahead to more dinners! My hand relaxed into his.

Up ahead was the typical downtown valet scene of one luxury car after another lined up perfectly in front of the hotel. We approached and began to climb the steps. We were greeted by the doorman and valet. The doors were held wide for our entry.

We stepped inside; my breath was taken away at the opulence and elegance of the decor and furnishings. The hotel was built around a large, open lobby. The ceiling stretched several stories high and was topped with an elaborate stained glass window through which the late-day sunlight filtered down in colorful rays. It was magical! The light illuminated the ornate furnishings, marble floors, and rich, dark wood accents. A tuxedoed pianist was seated at a shiny grand piano, playing softly near the base of a regal staircase curving to the floor above. The jazz overture was recognizable, though I could not name it. Music filled the air.

Mark took one look at my face and beamed from ear to ear. He could tell I appreciated what I saw. "Our reservation isn't until seven. I thought you might enjoy a cocktail in the atrium first." He again grabbed my hand, leading the way to the bar. I was too busy appreciating the ambiance to respond.

We walked into the atrium bar and were ushered to a small table. My chair was pulled out for me, and I sat down with a feeling I was living a fairy tale. I looked at Mark wide-eyed and smiled. "Wow! This is definitely elegant. What an enchanting place."

He looked around and chuckled. "I can't believe you've never been here before. How long have you lived in Colorado?"

The waiter walked up, interrupting our conversation. We ordered martinis, the signature drink of the L'abeille Palace before continuing the small talk that so often accompanies first dates. Shortly thereafter, our drinks arrived, and as we sipped, we began sharing our personal histories. I felt so relaxed with him, and I was thankful he thought to bring me here. It was delightful, and I did not want it to end. As Mark regaled me with stories from his youth, his eyes never wandered from mine. It was one of the most intimate, soul-connecting moments I think I had ever experienced with a man.

I also shared one of my stories—an embarrassing moment from childhood my whole family knew. Mark listened with enthusiasm, laughing at all the right points. Again, his eyes did not leave mine. It was as if we had started a dance. Every step we took was matched perfectly by the other.

The cocktail took the edge off, and we were so deep in our conversation we almost forgot about our reservation. Luckily, the waitress remembered and interrupted our waltz ever so politely to show us to our table inside the restaurant.

We were treated like royalty while being escorted to the table. The servers followed behind, carrying our drinks. I sneaked a peak at Mark and saw his confident smile; he looked as if he belonged here. In that moment, being with him and talking to him, I realized how much I desired more. I relaxed and enjoyed the special treatment. This was the first dinner in three years after which I would not put money—money I now did not have—aside for my special fund. Instead, I would simply enjoy the experience.

We were seated at a small, remote table near the window and away from the bar. The atmosphere in the vintage pub was warm, quiet, and intimate. We placed our order for food, and Mark selected wine that would pair well with the dishes we selected. I knew it would be perfect. "I'd like to tell you a story about this room." Mark leaned in. My body angle matched his; our dance had resumed. He began to weave the story. As he talked, I found myself leaning closer and closer and gazing into his eyes, thinking I could look into them for an eternity. I listened intently, prepared to drink in every word.

"This hotel is the second oldest hotel in the city. It was built in 1892. It's rumored that during the Prohibition years in the early 1900s, this room we are sitting in served as the tea room for afternoon parties for the elite." I watched his movements and adored the timbre of his speech.

"What most people don't know is, during the time the hotel was being built, the architects also planned on how to heat the buildings rather discreetly, not wanting the rich and wealthy to be soiled by the loads of coal necessary to feed the furnace for a monstrosity like this." He paused for a moment to sip his martini before continuing. "So they built a bunch of coal tunnels underground that connected a variety of buildings to one another. One tunnel specifically connected The L'abeille Palace to the old brothel at the Mystere building across the street. It is rumored that a different kind of 'tea' was brewed at the Mystere and then carried secretly through the underground tunnels, providing 'tea' for certain L'abeille Palace guests. It is also rumored that the men would use these tunnels late in the evening to access the brothel and return to the hotel undetected."

"Wow!" I said, "That's quite an interesting story."

"What's even more interesting," he continued, "is that I've seen the tunnel. It connects all the way to the basement of the studio. Our building backs up to the Mystere, and I think our studio is somehow connected to this story as well!" He looked at me with passion in his eyes. "Every time I bring this up with Madame, she doesn't want to talk about it. Supposedly only a select group of people have ever seen the basement of the studio. I am fortunate—or unfortunate, depending on how you look at it—to be one of those people." Our dinner was set before us, and Mark tasted the wine to assure his approval with the sommelier.

Without missing a beat, he resumed the conversation. "I stumbled upon the tunnel in the studio's basement by accident. And when I entered, I immediately felt a cold wind push me back, and I know I heard voices shrieking. It scared the shit out of me." He leaned back, comfortable in his manhood; I had to laugh at the thought. He laughed as well, then continued. "I ran out only to find Madame glaring at me. I asked her what was down there, and she made no attempt to explain. I remember her words: 'Your rent does not include access to the basement.'"

His representation of Madame's French accent was spot on. I could actually hear her scolding him. "How or why do you think the stories are related?" I asked. The story had piqued my interest.

"I don't know," he continued, looking around to make sure no one was listening. "But I've done some research. And my belief is that the studio, the Mystere and the L'abeille Palace are definitely connected"—he took a sip of wine—"spiritually."

I was taken slightly aback by his words. My thoughts went to that hologram of the woman in the mirror, wondering if she might have been what Mark was alluding to. Chills went up and down my spine. I recognized I was hearing Mark but not really listening. My mind and focus went back to the conversation.

Mark continued to entertain me with his historical knowledge of Colorado, how he had become a painter, and his childhood fantasy of playing baseball for the major leagues. He asked me about my childhood and was courteous enough to skirt the issue of my marriage and subsequent divorce, focusing more on me and what made me happy in life.

We continued to talk while indulging in a delicious meal and intoxicating wine. Soon dessert was delivered, and I realized we were the only people left in the restaurant.

"What time is it?" I asked Mark.

He glanced down at his watch. "Holy crap! You're never going to guess what time it is."

"Ten thirty?" I guessed.

"Close. Just add an hour to that," he said, surprise still on his face.

"Eleven thirty?" I said it with so much shock it might have come off as rude. I quickly added, "Wow! Time truly does fly when you're having fun."

I reached out to pick up the check that had been sitting in front of us for hours, briefly wondering if he would pull a Richard and conveniently forget his wallet or expect me to pay.

Mark put his hand on mine. "Please, let me get this. It's my treat," he said reassuringly. "Thank you for keeping me company tonight and listening to my stories. I really enjoyed our time together."

Without hesitation, I responded, "Thank you, Mark. Me too."

The server came and closed our tab. Mark and I stood up to walk away from the table, and he reached for my hand once more. We held hands while slowly strolling through the hotel and out the large turnstile doors. The warm summer air brushed against my legs and sent a tingle up my body, leaving me wide awake. I secretly imagined we were guests of the hotel with our own room, where we could retire and make love to each other for the rest of the night. I held and enjoyed the fantasy as we continued to talk and walk back to the studio.

When we arrived in front of the studio, we were confronted with the first awkward silence of the evening. Neither of us wanted the evening to end.

Mark spoke first. "Would you like to come upstairs for some coffee?"

I shook my head smiling, resisting the temptation, knowing what the universal definition of "coffee" was for a man. And while my body was screaming yes, my mind was intent on not sleeping with him until I could trust his motives. "Thank you for the offer," I responded, my body language betraying my voice, "I really don't want to leave, but I need to go. Maybe another time?"

Mark tried to use his charisma and charm to try to change my mind. "Then don't leave. Staying with me is an option ..."

This time I blushed at his forwardness. "Mark, I have to go. But I'm hoping this won't be our last date." I stepped in to give him a hug. His body was warm. I could feel his strong arms as they embraced me and pulled me close. I felt safe; protected. We unlocked our embrace.

He looked into my eyes and said with strong conviction, "All right.

You can leave tonight. But I will get you to stay with me." His face was serious. Then he smiled, opened the door, and made a gesture for me to join him.

I chuckled to myself at his cockiness. Only a man would make a statement like that. I smiled back and waved. We both said good night. He shut the studio door.

Walking home, I recalled our conversations and our stories, practically reliving the entire evening. I wasn't even halfway there when I received a text from Mark: "Had a great night. I really enjoyed your company and conversation. Look forward to getting to know you better. Studio tomorrow night? Same time?"

I thought to myself, *Hmmm*. His excitement and self-confidence were indeed intriguing, yet he seemed a bit arrogant at the same time. I wasn't sure what to make of this type of approach. Interestingly enough I pushed aside those thoughts, knowing I longed to be next to him again. I texted back: "See you then :)"

A Lesson I'll Never Forget

Mark and I went out every night the rest of the week. We couldn't get enough of each other. Each time we were together, it became increasingly difficult for me to leave his side. At the end of the week, I went outside my comfort zone and invited him to Sunday dinner, to which he immediately responded with a yes. *Finally,* I thought, *I get to use my table for its intended purpose!*

We had spent Friday night at a movie, and Saturday night I was reintroduced to miniature golf. When Sunday came, I bounded out of bed early, finished my work in preparation for Monday, and left for the farmer's market to gather ingredients for my grandmother's world-famous marinara sauce.

While shopping for dinner, my mind wandered. I asked myself the questions I believe most women have, even this early in the relationship: *What are we doing? More so, what does Mark think we are doing? Are we in a relationship, and do I even trust him enough to be in one?* My thoughts warred with each other. I knew I would see him at the studio tomorrow. *How was I supposed to act? Were we public? Did he always date the women new to the studio?* The thoughts followed me home. As I prepared the spaghetti sauce, I imagined different situations, trying to determine the best way to approach the conversation.

My questions seemed appropriate to ask. I debated over and over again the best scenario for their introduction. *During dinner? After dinner?* While the sauce simmered on the stove, I lit the candles around the apartment and turned on soft instrumental music. The aroma from the fresh rosemary garlic bread warming in the oven permeated the space. Creating the ambiance for an intimate evening was my first priority.

The doorbell startled me. I looked at the clock. *Wow, he's five minutes early?* I took a cleansing breath, then opened the door.

"Well, hello gorgeous," Mark said in his best bedroom voice as he held out a bouquet of flowers and a bottle of wine.

I couldn't help but hug him even though his hands weren't free to return my embrace. "Thank you," I said. I released him and stepped back, my eyes beaming brightly into his. "Welcome to my pad. Let me give you the big tour." I set the flowers and wine on the kitchen counter, then took him by the hand and led him through my small apartment. As we walked past my bed, a vision of him tearing my clothes off and throwing me on it to make passionate love crossed my mind. I had to shake my head to clear the thought.

We finished the tour in less than five minutes and returned to the kitchen. Mark uncorked the bottle of red wine, sniffed the cork, and poured two glasses. I loved his sense of ease in life. Nothing was forced or difficult with him. If there was an uncomfortable moment, it was because I could feel passionate tension between us. Until now we had struggled to remain social and friendly without taking whatever this relationship was to the next level physically.

However, standing next to him in the kitchen, it was obvious our minds and bodies wanted so much more. We sat down to dinner. It was natural, and I realized in that instant that my small apartment felt perfect; complete. Mark had filled a void I didn't even know existed. I sat across from him at the table, listening to one of his stories from his childhood, glowing radiantly with joy and happiness, and wondering if he could read my thoughts.

"Lenea, I know this may sound premature, but I would love to take you up to the mountains next weekend, if you are available. Maybe for some hiking?" His gaze fixed upon mine, looking for an answer.

"Sure. That would be nice," I said nonchalantly. My mind was elsewhere. I paused and wondered if now was a good time to bring up the status of our relationship. *Better hold off,* I thought, *enjoy the wine and keep the conversation light.*

After dinner we took a second bottle of wine to the couch. We cuddled close together. I was surprised how natural it was for us to get comfortable. In this space, I felt relaxed and more able to turn the topic of conversation to us and the future.

"Mark, I hope this doesn't sound crazy, but I think we should talk about our relationship and the studio." He looked at me inquisitively. "You work for Madame, and I'm her student. I know there are many house rules. Are there any that would prevent us from becoming friends?" It was a start, and the best I could think of at the moment. He looked me in the eyes and put his hand on mine. Instantly I felt a rush of sensations. My heart began to trip. If I were standing, my knees would have buckled. Suddenly, I was aware of stirrings in places I had not felt for quite some time.

"Is that what we are, Lenea? Friends?" He asked in a slow, deep voice. Looking into my eyes, I could feel his desire as he leaned in toward me. I reciprocated his advance, my heart pounding; our mouths united. He kissed me slowly at first, seeking to tenderly touch every part of my lips, then passionately and deeply. Our tongues joined in, tangling together like two vipers fighting before slowly circling and retreating.

Mark soon began exploring more of my body. His one hand delicately traced my collarbone and neck while his other supported the back of my head as he continued to possess my mouth. My insides were flooding with sensations. Everywhere he touched felt as if it were on fire. I was damp and ready for more.

I rested my hands over the top of his shirt, outlining his strong shoulders and arms; I could taste the wine on his tongue and smell the scent of his musky aftershave. Suddenly, it was as if all the reasons I had denied myself of bodily pleasure evaporated, leaving me open and wanting him, free to indulge in this carnal delight.

Mark unbuttoned my blouse with one hand while touching the lace of my bra with his index finger. His touch was gentle as if making a holy introduction to each part of my body. After his reverent exploration, he cupped his hands around my breasts, his fingers circling my nipples. My mouth parted, and I moaned in pure pleasure. His hands were strong, and his grasp felt as if he were pulling me into him. The animal inside me came alive as his lips left mine to trail tiny kisses down my throat, along my neck and across my exposed chest. His mouth claimed first one nipple, tongue circling slowly, then the other. His teeth came together and he began lightly biting. Both nipples hardened in response.

My head rolled back as I held him tightly against my bare breasts. Feeling him touching my skin made me heavy with longing and wet with desire. I reached down to stroke him, unbuttoned his jeans, and felt his heat. Intoxicated, I wanted more; his masculine energy was now my drug. He stopped me. His lips traveled down across my belly to the top of my jeans. Before I knew it, both our pants joined the growing pile of clothes on the floor.

Mark now stood in front of me, his calves wrapped around mine. He was hard, and the sight of his erection took my breath away; clearly he was created to pleasure a woman. I leaned back into the couch and spread my legs, longing to receive him. Evading my invitation, he knelt down before me and began kissing my stomach, inch by inch working his way down my body. Gently his hands slid between my thighs, massaging and caressing me. His touch was warm, hitting all the right places. My clit was swollen and throbbing with anticipation.

I tugged on his shoulders in hopes to raise him on top of me. I wanted him inside of me. He resisted, placing his head between my thighs as he began slowly licking and probing with his wonderful, hot tongue; one hand reached up to knead my breast, causing me to gasp. His other arm wrapped firmly around my waist as he buried his head further between my legs, now sucking wildly. I shuddered and arched my back, rocketing toward a climax.

Mark lifted his head up, gazing at me and loving my body with his eyes. I had lost my sense of time and space. Surrendering all inhibition, I opened my legs even wider, touching myself and granting him private visual access for his enjoyment.

Moments later, something inside of him seemed to unleash as he grabbed my arms forcefully, his biceps flexing, lifting me up and pulling me into a position on top of him. I straddled his lap, and he entered me a little at a time while holding my body up with his strong arms. Bit by bit he settled me on top of him. He was thick; I stretched willingly to accommodate.

The instant he filled me, our energies merged. We moved in unison, meeting each other thrust for thrust; each time harder and more pronounced. Faster and faster, rocking and pounding each other's pubic bones. Our rapid breathing grew in intensity.

I whimpered, not from pain but from pure pleasure, as my muscles contracted around him. Every thrust caused me to clench tighter and tighter. Soon I didn't know where he began and I ended.

The fire ignited.

We disappeared.

I buried my head in the cologne-infused furrows of his neck, letting out a deep, guttural scream as orgasm shot through my entire body, wave after wave.

His shoulders grew tight, his head leaning back, and he began to shudder. The sound of him releasing hung in the air as I leaned forward to capture his lower lip between my teeth. Together we rolled until he was on top of me, his arms stiff as he hovered above me, staring with devotion into my eyes. Lost in our gaze, he settled down upon me, slightly to my side. We held each other tightly, neither of us wanting to let go.

Gradually our breathing returned to normal. Every sense of my being was heightened, from the rhythm of our heartbeats to the inner vibrating calm that filled my body and mind. I felt satiated, my desires fulfilled. It was the greatest, most meaningful sex I ever had. *This is what it should feel like!* I thought.

Mark sat up and rested his head on one elbow, looking deep into my eyes; his other hand running gently through my hair before turning and pressing the back of it lightly against my cheek. He stopped, smiled as if on cue, and stood. His legs were wobbly at first, causing him to reach out to the couch to steady himself. Once settled, he grabbed the wine bottle and poured slightly less than half.

After handing me my glass, he reached for two couch pillows and placed them behind me. He settled down and gathered me in his arms, stopping briefly to pull a lightweight throw over our glistening bodies. My back rested against his chest.

We finished our wine without conversation. None was necessary; the spicy liquid whispered its own story down the back of my throat. Held in his embrace, his muscles flexed, his masculine energy made me feel safe and protected, enhancing the enjoyment of the intoxication.

With the last drops savored, we set our glasses down on the end table. I moved to his side and nuzzled my head into the nape of his neck. His arms held me tight; secure. Wrapped in each other's warm bodies, we fell asleep.

......••●••........

I woke to light streaming in the window and a cup of fresh hot coffee on the table next to me. I stretched and found I was a little sore from the previous night's festivities; the thought put me in a wonderful mood. Mark walked out of the kitchen dressed fresh from the shower. *Boy, did he look good!*

He grinned knowingly, then greeted me. "Good morning, Sunshine." He leaned in and gave me a gentle kiss. His eyes were beautiful, as was the rest of his body. The thought had my blood stirring once again.

"Good morning," I replied, like a schoolgirl caught admitting a crush on her teacher.

"Last night was amazing." His gaze fixed upon me. "You were amazing. We were amazing! I would love to stay longer, but I have to get to the studio early for a sitting. I waited to leave until the last moment so you could sleep." He turned and picked up his T-shirt off the ground. He carefully, and oh so slowly, pulled it on over his head, covering his sculpted abs—one last show before dropping the curtain. "I will see you later today. Have a great day, Beautiful!" He bent over, kissed the top of my head, and, before I could say anything, walked out the door.

I watched the moment unfold, not quite knowing what to say. The door handle gently clicked with his departure. I looked around; the empty space of the apartment grew. His presence had filled and completed my universe, and now it felt vacuous. I shook the cobwebs out of my head and decided it was time to move on, get a shower, get dressed, and ready myself for the day.

I walked into the bathroom and opened the medicine cabinet to pull a single pill from the packet of twenty eight—day seven. I was thankful I had kept up the daily routine. Placing it on my tongue, I turned the cold water on, cupping my hand to take a sip of water before swallowing. Out of the corner of my eye, I noticed the toilet seat had been left up. *Men*, I thought.

Once finished, I turned on the shower and entered. Standing

underneath the flowing water, the entire night replayed like a movie in my head. I closed my eyes and could feel his hands all over me again. My lips were still pulsating from the intensity of his mouth and tongue. I beamed, knowing everything I felt and had desired was equally returned by him. A new door to our relationship had opened, and we had explored the unknown eagerly. In the light of day, what exactly did this mean? Where would it go from here?

I dried off and got ready for the day: hair first, then makeup. I was eager to see him again. I found my mind reliving each moment over and over as I spent the early part of the morning cleaning the apartment, smiling at the mess of pillows and used wine glasses. I finished a report and checked e-mails, eagerly watching the clock, waiting for noon.

At 11:35, I decided to change into something seductive for class that day: a short denim skirt covering booty shorts, and a white tank top with a hot pink sports bra peeking from underneath. The outfit completed by my sexy knee-high black leather boots with five-inch heels. I looked in the mirror and liked the woman I saw staring back at me. *Confident and sexy, that's me!*

At the door, I grabbed my iPod, remembering the need to bring my song with me. Walking to the studio, I rehearsed how I would tell the girls my true desire. I felt that "confident and sexy" was no longer something I had to achieve. It was a part of who I am. And this woman was here to stay. It was time to share with them my true deep-seated desire: to trust a man and have a partner in life. I was ready to test the words on the back of Madame's business card and make this my destiny.

·······●●●●●●······

When I walked into the Studio, Chrissy came running up to me to ask about the date. Like twelve-year-old girls, we giggled and laughed as I told her the story. She was genuinely happy for me. She begged for me to tell all.

When Madame walked in, all the giggling and laughing stopped. There was something about her presence that brought respect, bordering on fear, from those in the room with her. She turned on slow, erotic music, turned the lights down, and lit the candles. The five of us gathered in the center of the dance floor, awaiting her instructions.

Today, looking around the room, I felt more connected to these women. Even Samantha, who normally turned my stomach with her holier-than-thou demeanor, didn't seem to bother me. Instead, I felt her equal, as if she were part of me; we were both sexy and self-assured.

Madame didn't hesitate as she walked to the front of the class and started our series of warm-ups. I enjoyed the process of moving my body with the other women. It was true, they had become my sisters and our feelings of insecurity were like a wall crumbling between us each time we met.

"Okay, ladies, we're done." Madame's words signaled the end of warmups. "Lenea," she looked at me, "today you will be dancing to your desire. Did you bring your music?"

My heart beat wildly at the announcement. I nodded and went immediately to my gym bag, unzipped the top, and reached for my iPod. My hands were trembling. A wave of fear swept over me. But what was I afraid of? A simple dance? After all, I truly desire to get married and have children and a dog; I want it all!

My fingers crossed the metal casing, and I pulled it from the bag. I turned and walked slowly toward Madame, looking down at the screen and searching for my song. I handed it to her and went back to my spot. I was nervous to say the words of my desire out loud and began to fidget with my clothing. What if it didn't happen? I'd look like an idiot. Worse, what if the marriage I so badly desired ended? *Oh, God! I can't go through the pain of another divorce.*

The girls' reassuring smiles helped calm me down some, reminding me of their openness to share their heartfelt desires. I knew this was my chance to tell the truth.

The music stopped, and Madame looked at me, her eyes prodding me onward. I swallowed hard before sharing, "Actually, Madame, I've done some thinking." I stopped and looked around at the women in the room. "I would like to apologize to you, all of you. You each shared your personal experiences, and I did not share mine. I would like to share with you my true desire."

I told my story of my upbringing, my parents' divorce, and my marriage to and subsequent divorce from Richard. As I did so, their looks of comfort and understanding gave me courage.

After a lengthy explanation of why I wanted what I wanted, I finished by saying, "I desire a world where women trust men and men trust women. Where marriages have happy endings and children are raised to believe in love." The words left me with a sigh of relief.

Madame paused, as if to contemplate what I had said. "Lenea, thank you for your honest share. A desire that helps you love others is a desire with purpose. A desire with purpose has an end and can be obtained. You will know when this has happened, and all things are possible to those who believe."

Her words made me feel like I was part of the group again. I remembered her comments from the week before, and I was proud of myself for sharing my real desire. A shot of confidence surged though my body. She turned on some upbeat music. *Confident and sexy, that's me,* I thought.

The music was louder than normal. Madame had to raise her voice to deliver her instructions, "Ladies, let's get to work on those desires. You all remember Mark, don't you?"

Mark walked up to the front of the room. *Oh my gosh!* I thought to myself. *How long has he been in here?* Looking at Mark now was a totally different experience than the first time I saw him in the studio. Something about knowing what his body looked like and felt like under those faded jeans and T-shirt made my knees go weak.

Chrissy looked at me and chuckled. She must have been reading my mind. Madame interrupted my thoughts. "Ladies, Mark will be walking around the room today and watching you all dance. If he feels inspired, he will stop. And with pen and paper in hand, he will sketch what your moves convey to him." She paused for a brief moment. "In life you have to learn to dance as though no one is watching. In pursuing your desires, you have to forget what is going on around you and learn to focus on your goal. Ladies, life doesn't stop for us. It does not wait for us to get our shit together. We have to work with what we have and make what we have work!"

Her words were absorbed around the room. "Now show us what you've got!" She bellowed. The music played even louder. I could feel the beat of the bass thumping in my chest. Not to mention the anxiety I felt dancing for Mark in a room full of other women. *Did Madame know about us?* I couldn't help but wonder.

Mark had his clipboard and pencil in hand. He looked so good. First he approached Jessica, who was in the back of the room. Sensing the nervousness in her movements, I decided to step up my game and see if I could direct his attention away from the others.

An inner part of me was unleashed as I allowed myself to dance more seductively. The music's erotic message and lyrics were a perfect accompaniment to my motive. Looking in the mirror for his reaction, I saw him standing next to Samantha. Mark was sketching frantically. Samantha was moving effortlessly, seductively; even pulling up her tight cotton shirt to show him her well-toned body.

I didn't know what to feel at that moment. She knew she had his full attention, and she was obviously enjoying putting on a show. She pulled off her shirt, leaving her tan body exposed, wearing only booty shorts and a matching sports bra. Her moves were perfect. Her body was perfect. For each move Samantha made, I tried to match and outdo it; focusing as much sexual energy as I could muster to shift Mark's attention to me. All the while I was watching the scene play out through the mirror in front of me.

I felt a cold breeze sweep past me and something caught my eye. There was a figure in the mirror standing in the back of the room; it was a woman shaking her head. It wasn't anyone I recognized. *Where did she come from?*

She had long dark, raven-colored hair. She looked like someone from the early 1900s and was dressed in saloon finery. She appeared to be walking around inspecting the scene from the back of the class. *Was she here to observe us as well?*

My attention kept floating between the raven-haired woman in the mirror, Mark frantically sketching, and keeping my dance moves going. The woman shook her head again and walked out the back door. *How strange*, I thought to myself. *I didn't think anyone could just walk into our class. Who was that woman? Did anyone else see her? Did I just see what I thought I saw?*

My gaze shifted down to my right; Mark was now sketching me. I gave him my best sultry look, bringing my hand up through my hair, and stopping to make sure he had my full attention. In return, his face was stone and resolute. He stopped and smiled slightly before moving his charcoal rapidly across the paper. I could feel his presence as he came closer. My dancing became more exaggerated as I moved to the beat of the music and reliving our night together in my mind. I beamed from ear to ear watching him sketch, my movements much slower and more methodical than Samantha's.

Knowing I had his full attention, I was determined to put on a show. I pictured us together the night before and let my body tell a story of unbridled passion and ecstasy. I truly felt as if no one else was watching; as if it was only the two of us in the room.

Wanting to touch him, I didn't know if that would be appropriate. I fought the urge and restrained myself. Unknowingly, I closed my eyes and echoed a moan from the previous night. Opening them, I saw his face turn slightly red, a bead of sweat upon his brow, his gaze still fixed upon his draft book. He finished the sketch and looked up at me, his stare intense. My heart melted.

My focus shifted back to the mirror, in which I watched Mark stop between Julia and Chrissy. I enjoyed the feeling of success I had gained in capturing his attention. I closed my eyes, lost in the moment, and enjoyed the scene, the music, and the dancing. That is, until I heard moaning out loud to the music.

What the hell is going on? I thought. My eyes popped open. It was Samantha. I looked at her in the mirror and noticed she didn't appear to be in her right mind. She wasn't dancing the same way. It was very different than how she had been with Mark, almost as if she were hypnotized; her eyes were completely black and vacant.

I felt a tremor of fear. Samantha was dancing erratically now, like a puppet controlled by a puppeteer. I had never seen anyone possessed by evil spirits, but I imagined this is what it would look like. All the women stopped and turned to watch. Mark was the last one whose attention was finally diverted as Samantha's moves turned her into a dervish.

Mark walked toward Samantha, just as captivated by her moves as the rest of us were. The moment he got close enough to her, she took the clipboard out of his hands and threw it on the floor. She took his hand and began to dance with him. He followed her lead. She had her hands all over him, grinding her hips into his.

My blood ran cold, and anger raged within. I didn't want to watch the scene, yet there it was, as plain as day. *How could she do that?* I stayed focused on the image in the mirror, hoping this would create an illusion and I wouldn't have to deal with the reality of this bitch dancing so seductively with my man. Lost in a dance or not, it was not okay!

Mark closed his eyes and seemed to be enjoying the moment. By now everyone had stopped what they were doing and were staring at the scene in front of them. Quickly, my eyes were diverted as I looked past Mark and Samantha in the mirror and saw the raven-haired woman appear in the back of the studio again. She was shaking her head.

I looked at Madame to see if she too was shaking her head. Instead, she was sitting in a chair in the back of the room, her chin up and an unusual look of bemusement on her face. She didn't seem to notice the raven-haired woman. In fact, no one seemed to notice her but me.

In the mirror, the raven-haired woman's gaze met mine. My face became sullen and my body went still; I knew she was not from this world. She had a glassy look in her eyes. Chills ran through my body as a different type of fear set in.

Then, as if she understood I knew her secret, she glided out the door. I closed my eyes and shook my head. The music was over, and Madame and the others were clapping wildly. *What the hell just happened? Was that real?*

"Bravo! You are gems!" Madame said. "Today you have all demonstrated how to pursue desires, and some of you even got others involved in the process! Splendid! Ladies, take a good look at yourselves in the mirror and remember this moment."

Following Madame's directions, I opened my eyes to the reflection of the ladies standing to my left and right. I saw Samantha and the expression on her face. She displayed haughtiness and arrogance, overly self-confident. I knew Madame was talking about her.

How could dancing create our desires? I stopped to ponder. *Was there anything I could have done differently to make myself more the center of Mark's focus versus Samantha?* Had any of the other women danced like that, sadly, I think I would have been happy for them. But something about Samantha rubbed me the wrong way. Maybe it was the natural luster in her long blond hair, or her flawless skin. Her perfection made me sick.

Celebration filled the room. All of the women were hugging one another. I joined in reluctantly—a theatrical performance on my part— feigning enthusiasm with an emotionless smile. I continued with disdain. Chrissy stood nervously laughing while tears flowed from her eyes. *Is there something I'm just not getting here?* Then reality hit.

I had seen an apparition in the mirror—a ghost. My focus on the raven-haired woman was a distraction from the dancing. The thought of her made the hairs on the back of my neck stand up. Who was she and why was she there? Why was she looking at me? Or had I imagined her?

Then I remembered the rumors of the haunted studio; they were true. She was a ghost.

15

The Explanation Makes Sense

fter the session, I meandered around the studio, slowly gathering up my things, waiting for the others to leave before I approached Madame. I wasn't sure what to say. She never looked up or acknowledged my presence. I stood there waiting for an opportunity.

"Lenea, what does trust between a man and woman mean to you?" Her question startled me. Without waiting for my answer, she continued. "I would like to invite you to find a song that moves you. And work with me privately to create a dance that represents this desire. You can talk with Shannon about scheduling. Au revoir." She turned away and walked out of the room.

A dance that represents this desire? I didn't have time to think. I could hear heels clicking down the hallway in my direction.

"Hey, Lenea," Shannon said casually, entering the studio with a smile on her face, "I hear you are interested in private lessons with Madame. We're running a special right now. Does morning or evening work best for your schedule?" She looked down at the scheduling pad in her hand, awaiting my response.

"I guess evenings are best, since I work from home during the day." The words slipped out before I even had time to process exactly what I was agreeing to.

"Wonderful. Tuesday at six p.m. or nine p.m.? Or Thursday at six p.m.? Which one works best for you?" Shannon looked up for my reply. I must have seemed like a deer caught in headlights, blindsided by what had happened. *I hadn't asked for these lessons in the first place!*

"Honestly, I have no idea what you're talking about." I could feel the blood rush up to my head, as if caught in a lie. Shannon handed me a copy of the same brochure from the first class. I didn't need to read the cost. I remembered exactly how expensive private lessons were. There was no way I could pay what they were asking for a private dance class. Hell, I didn't even spend that kind of money to get my hair styled regularly.

As if Shannon were reading my mind, she broke the tension. "You know, we do have a special when you commit to multiple classes." She pulled another piece of paper from her pad and handed it to me. "It's a special we have for students already enrolled in classes with Madame."

I read the prices. It was indeed an incredible deal.

"And if you prepay for five classes"—she pulled the brochure from my hand and flipped it over—"you save nearly fifty percent."

My mindset suddenly switched from "I don't have the money" to "how can I get the money?"

"Let's do this," Shannon said, looking down at her scheduling book. "Let's book you for Thursday at six p.m., and you can cancel at no charge with twenty-four hours of notice. Sound good?"

The smug look on her face, like the deal was already done, brought me back to the reality of my finances. Again, I was upset. I decided to be strong and confront her. "Shannon, I was just here talking to you about wanting to cancel my classes. Why in the world would I sign up for private lessons? You know my current financial situation."

"Because you were invited," Shannon replied quickly. "Madame doesn't extend personal invitations to just anyone. It's an honor to be invited. She must see a benefit for you to be here or she wouldn't have asked."

Shannon's words resonated with me, and I calmed down. I remembered my phone call with Madame and how proud I had felt when she personally invited me to the studio. I also realized that had it not been for Madame's invitation, I might never have met Mark. *What if she was meant to bring Mark and me together? What if she had some cosmic knowledge about my future?* The lessons would be totally worth it if I could trust a man again and find a partner in life. *This is an investment in your future, Lenea!* I convinced myself.

Shannon had been very patient with me, watching the drama play out in my mind. I nodded to her as if to say, "Yes! Let's do this!" and handed her my credit card.

When the plastic was taken from my hand, doubts crept back in. *How can five sessions of dance class change my life? Then again, if five sessions can teach me trust for a man, find me a partner for life, and allow me to have children and grow old and happy, it will be a worthwhile investment. Plus extra time in the studio means extra time near Mark.*

Again I focused on all the benefits of making this choice. *Yes! Maybe Mark and I will start going out for coffee afterward. Or maybe even watching a movie in his loft upstairs. Or, better yet, staying over all night! Waking up and having breakfast together! I will be able to watch the morning sunlight glisten off his chest as we lie on his bed!*

And this building! This wonderful, architecturally inspired house of bricks! If only they could speak and tell the stories of everything that has gone on here for a hundred years. I so badly wanted to know more of its history. *Yes! This is a great choice, Lenea! You are doing the right thing!*

We walked down the hallway toward the reception desk to complete the transaction, and I was reminded of the ghost. The hair on the nape of my neck went up and I glanced back into the mirror where I had first seen the raven-haired woman. At first I was afraid to look back. But as I did, it reflected only the studio and me. Still, I couldn't get the picture of Her out my mind. I grabbed Shannon by the arm and she stopped and turned. "Shannon, this is going to sound ridiculous, but … are there ghosts in this building?"

She looked at me, smiled and continued to walk down the dimly lit hallway. The smell of incense filled my nostrils. "I'm sure there are. This is an old building, after all." She stopped, turned, and looked me in the eyes, very serious. "But I've never seen any." She leaned in closer, "However, I have heard Madame say this area of the city is spiritually connected— something called an energy vortex. And"—she leaned further, her voice barely audible—"there are many times I feel a presence." She returned upright. "But it has never felt haunted or threatening. Why do you ask?"

"Curiosity, that's all. Old buildings are kind of spooky to me, and you always wonder about ghost stories." There was no way I was ready to share what I had seen with anyone, let alone Shannon.

Now my mind wondered if it had played tricks on itself. Certainly, though, there was no benefit to mentioning the raven-haired woman to Shannon. Maybe Mark.

We passed into the waiting area. I looked to my right and saw Mark sitting on the red velvet bench across from the main desk. *Had he been waiting for me?*

"There you are!" he said happily, rising from his seat to give me a hug. Stepping back, he held my hands in his. "Do you have time to grab lunch?"

"I believe I do!" My excited smile matched his, albeit with some reluctance. My mind replayed the scene in the mirror of him and Samantha dancing together only moments before. His actions had me baffled; confused.

I stopped a moment, looking into his eyes. I could tell he was happy to be with me. Maybe his dance with Samantha hadn't affected him. Maybe it was common for women to flaunt their sexuality at him. If that was the case, Samantha's dance wouldn't really faze him. I hoped.

I decided it would be best not to mention it and possibly look like the crazy, jealous girlfriend. No way! Instead, I would certainly keep a watchful eye on Samantha and her motives.

Mark opened the door for us to leave. "Have fun!" Shannon said as we walked outside. The street was filled with glorious sunshine and clear blue skies.

⋯⋯•••●●●••⋯⋯

Hand in hand, we walked amongst the hustle and bustle of the city. My body tingled as it surged with energy. Joyful noise filled my head. It was exhilarating to know our one night of passion was, maybe, something more. It was a welcome relief to find a man who wanted more than just sex. No worries if he would call or even if he felt the same way. His actions spoke louder than any words. I knew I was one of the luckiest girls in the world to have the attention of this beautiful man—my own Prince Charming!

YOU & I, INC.

We arrived at a delicatessen and he opened the door for me, "After you, m'lady." He lifted his hand in a wave and bowed ever so slightly.

"Thank you, m'lord." I half-curtsied graciously.

Entering the eatery, the smell of fresh baked bread made me hungry. We each ordered a sandwich, and without hesitation, Mark pulled out his wallet. "I've got this. I invited you to lunch," he said, handing the clerk his credit card. He must have been able to sense my anxiety with letting him pay. His eyes told the story; he enjoyed being with me and wanted to treat me to lunch simply because he wanted to be with me.

I understood his intentions, yet it still didn't feel right. Something about this didn't feel right. The use of men for meals as a savings plan seemed far behind me. I wanted to reciprocate somehow; to be an equal in the equation. When I looked into his eyes, my thoughts evaporated. He signed the receipt and moved to the pickup side of the counter. "You find us a seat. And please"—he leaned into me—"find the most romantic one here." He kissed me on the cheek.

Moments later, I had found a booth as far removed from the crowd as possible. Shortly thereafter, he strolled up with the tray of food and sat down. We ate and chatted about the class. Then he brought up the dancing from earlier. My body stiffened in response, and my breathing grew shallow. I took a sip of water, focused on calming myself down, and started to breathe again.

Enjoy the moment, Lenea. You are out, appreciating life with this wonderful man.

Boom! The vision of the raven-haired woman was like a blown-up photograph in my mind's eye. I wanted to tell Mark what I had seen. I wanted to tell anyone, really. Still, it didn't feel like it was the right time.

He continued to talk about how much passion he felt while walking around the studio, sketching each of the women. "Today's class reminded me how intense this can be for you women. The class Madame led two months ago was very similar to the session today. I felt the need to draw one of the women in that class over and over again. She had the most amazing body!" His remark repulsed me, and suddenly I found myself disconnecting from him. "She was so passionate in how she conveyed her desires through movement. You should have seen her."

His comment reminded me of Samantha's actions today. *Didn't he know it was clearly her intent to seduce him with her fucking incredible body?* The excited look on Mark's face and how smitten he was with women with amazing bodies confirmed my fears.

My mind began screaming, *Hello! I danced too! What made her so much better than me? Asshole!*

Then I heard a voice in my left ear; it was subtle, elderly, and firm. "He's playing you. Don't trust him." I felt a cold breath on the back of my neck; the words made me shudder. I looked to my left, but no one was there. My eyes drifted vacantly ahead.

"Hello? Earth to Lenea. Wouldn't you agree?" Mark waved his hands in front of my face.

I hadn't been paying attention. "What?" I said quizzically. "I'm sorry." My thoughts turned to anger. *You think I want to have a conversation with a man about how incredible another woman's body is?* my mind was screaming to tell him, but I held my tongue.

Again I felt the cold breath on my neck. "Men like him cannot be trusted." This time the voice spoke into my right ear. Goose pimples rose on my arms. I could feel a cold sweat on my forehead. I looked to my right, then all around me. No one was there.

"Lenea, are you okay?" Mark asked, concerned. "You look pale, like you've seen a ghost."

"I'm … I'm … sorry," I said, a tremble in my voice. "I'm not sure why I'm so upset at this, but …" I searched for the words. The voice had truly clouded my mind, and I wasn't quite sure how to react. I had lost track of Mark's conversation, although it certainly seemed to be fixed on Samantha.

Knowing that a voice from a spirit had communicated with me, right in front of Mark, was too much. I looked at Mark; his face was confused and concerned. I stumbled, trying to get the words out. "I … I … I think I need to go to the bathroom. My head's very dizzy, and I feel a little sick. Can you excuse me?" I stood, grabbed my purse, and hurried to the ladies' room.

I checked both stalls to ensure no one was there and locked the door. I turned the cold water on, soaking a paper towel before laying it across my forehead. It felt good to gain clarity as the cool liquid cleared the sweat formed only moments earlier. I looked in the mirror. The whites of my eyes were redder than normal. My pupils were certainly dilated. My skin tone was whiter than usual, with a very slight green hue.

YOU & I, INC.

I pressed the water button again, getting it as cold as possible. My eyes closed. Suddenly the hairs on my arms and the back of my neck stood on end. "Don't trust him," the voice whispered in my right ear, only inches away.

Immediately I opened my eyes, straightening upright to look around. No one was there. Nothing. "Hello?" I said to the vacant emptiness of the cubed room. My voice reverberated in the tight space. I opened each stall, ensuring again I was alone. "Is anyone here?" A slight echo came back in the hollowness.

I realized the droplets of water were now dripping from my face. I shook my head to clear it, walked over to the paper towel dispenser, and reached for a dry section. A movement caught my peripheral vision in the mirror. I turned around sharply. Again, nothing. Empty.

I tore the paper towel and covered my face to dry it. "Do *not* trust him," the voice said louder now, and behind me. I opened my eyes. In the periphery of my right eye, I could see the raven-haired woman in the mirror. Something inside told me not to look at her directly and not to fear her.

"How do you know?" I said to the apparition, not moving my head, ensuring I did not have direct vision of her.

"No man can be trusted," the voice responded. "He will use you for his folly, then discard you like the paper you hold in your hand."

"But I want to trust him. I … I … I think I love him," I continued, keeping her sight fixed in the corner of my eye.

"Then you are a fool!" the voice yelled, angry and irritated; it then vanished.

Turning to look into the mirror, I saw only my own reflection this time. My heart had been beating fast; it was slowing now, albeit louder and stronger. Gazing at my reflection, I could see color return to my cheeks; the whites of my eyes also began to clear. I took a deep breath through my nose and exhaled slowly and steadily through my mouth. One more breath, this time focused on my diaphragm; again I exhaled.

When I returned, Mark had turned the napkin into his canvas and was busily sketching with a pencil. His tongue was slightly sticking out of the right side of his mouth, his focus intent. It was a drawing of a couple walking on a beach; the woman was holding the hand of a toddler at her side. The scenery was vivid, and he was not aware of me standing over him, watching his story being revealed.

127

I interrupted the moment. "That's a very beautiful drawing."

"Oh," he said, folding the napkin and pushing it to the side. "I didn't see you there." His face turned red; embarrassment was something I had not expected from him.

"What were you drawing?" I asked coyly, taking my seat and leaning forward. A Cheshire cat grin spread on my face as he looked around like a little boy caught with his hand in the cookie jar.

"Nothing … I mean … Well … not nothing." His face turned serious, and his eyes became focused and intent. "Have you ever dreamed of having a family? Finding your true love? And living the storybook dream?" His energy penetrated deep into me as he revealed his soul. "Is it old fashioned to think marriage can be forever? That a mom and a dad can raise children together? Take walks on a beach and swing their child, knowing that tomorrow will be like today, only one day older? With happiness, joy, and fulfillment? Can it happen, Lenea?"

I realized at that moment my face had turned to shock and dismay. I wasn't expecting to hear this from Mark. I looked into his face, focusing on his eyes, manner, and timbre. A flood of emotions came rushing through me as I recalled asking myself those same questions days before I got married, and then again as I read through the divorce papers. I felt like crying! I felt like screaming! I felt like laughing and jumping up and down, saying, *"Yes! Yes! It can happen! But you have to choose me! Choose me!"*

"Well?" he said, interrupting my thoughts, "Do you think it's possible?" He waited for an answer—an answer I didn't have. I reached down to grab the napkin he had pushed away, unfolding it and pressing it flat to make it visible and clear. I turned it toward me. His detail was immaculate. His artwork, even this simple sketch, was that of a brilliant mind able to capture a story with ink on this humble medium.

It was beautiful: a couple walking on the beach, swinging a child between them. A small house in the distance. A boat tied to a buoy. Waves breaking nearby. A pair of seagulls in flight. Even the sand had character and shape. I looked up into this man-child's eyes. They had shifted from hazel to a brighter blue, and desperation now controlled his presence as he awaited my response.

"Mark," I said slowly, clearing my throat for clarity and to search for the words. "I think … I believe …" I didn't know what to say. I didn't yet trust him enough to open my heart. Not yet. "I think we should go."

We stood, taking the trash from our table, not saying a word to one another before placing it in the receptacle by the door.

Mark gently grabbed my shoulder, turning me toward him. "May I come over and bring you dinner tomorrow night?"

I felt the cold breath in my left ear and heard the voice again: "Say no." I turned to locate the voice; there was nothing.

Mark noticed my reaction. "Are you okay, Lenea?" he asked, his concern obvious.

"No. I mean yes," I responded confusedly, my face betraying my words. "It's just … look … I like you, Mark; I really do. I'm simply a bit distracted right now. I'm sorry." I clambered around for the words. "You see, I have a lot on my plate with work. And I recently began private lessons with Madame on Thursday nights. I have so much to do." I looked for an escape hatch—anything to get me out of the moment. "Could we make it dinner on Thursday? After class?"

The words came out so fast I didn't realize I was saying no to his request. With the sudden uncertainty of Mark's motives and his irritating passion for Samantha, I really wasn't in the mood. "Thursday …" Mark contemplated. "Yeah. Yeah, I can do that. It's just … I don't want to go a day without seeing you; without hearing your voice." He leaned in, cupped my head in his hands, and kissed me softly on the lips. The smell of his aftershave wafted ever so slightly; my senses were heightened by my closed eyes. A pressure valve had finally released and my body relaxed.

Mark opened the door, and I stopped for a moment to cast a furtive glance back at the entirety of the scene: the table we sat at, the mirror on the wall, and the entrance to the ladies' room. The moment hung like the mid-August air as I captured each detail. I turned to Mark, smiled, and stepped onto a sidewalk busy with pedestrian traffic. The afternoon air was refreshingly brisk.

·······•●●●●•·······

Something about him saying he didn't want to go a day without hearing my voice was weird. Guys don't talk like that. The walk back home took about fifteen minutes. Not a word had been spoken between us as we parted; there had been merely a single wave good-bye as we went in opposite directions.

The time simply allowed my thoughts to spin. *Was the raven-haired woman sent here to help me? To guide me? Or is she the devil's advocate? Why is she talking to me? Why is she stalking me?*

I neared my building, and suddenly the thought of going home to an empty apartment didn't feel comfortable. I did not know when or where the raven-haired woman would appear again, and the thought of her showing up terrified me. Who could I call? Who would believe me? Chrissy came to mind, and I dialed her immediately.

"Hi, this is Chrissy."

Thank God she answered the phone. "Hey, Chrissy, it's me, Lenea." I was unsure of how to begin. "Chrissy, I need help from a friend. Something happened to me today …"

"Oh my God, Lenea," she interrupted, "did someone hurt you? Are you okay?" She must have heard the fear in my voice. Still, I continued. My words tripped over each other as the story poured out. No detail was too minute; everything was put on the table.

"Look, Lenea," she responded in a calm voice, "I have had similar experiences. This is a process many divorced women go through. It's part of what is called transference, where we actually transfer the feelings and emotions we had from our previous relationship onto a new one." Her voice sounded empathetic. "It is very common when beginning a new relationship, especially like the one you've started with Mark. We create imaginary friends to help us cope with the situation. That way we don't have to take responsibility for our own thoughts."

Moments as a five-year-old raced through my brain, as if explaining Patty's existence for the first time. "Oh my God, Chrissy, you're right! That's what I'm doing! How did you know about this?" I asked excitedly.

"Part of being a recovering alcoholic means you spend a lot of time in therapy. And if you pay attention, you learn a lot about yourself and others. These are things my therapist told me. It's definitely not weird or uncommon."

"Thank you, Chrissy. Thank you so much." I felt our connection, even miles apart. "Can you tell me something? Is counseling helping you?"

I could hear her trying to cover up the phone as she broke down. I waited. Finally I spoke, "Chrissy? I'm so sorry to ask. I … I didn't mean to make you upset."

"It's okay, Lenea. It's not you." Her voice sounded thin and fragile. "But you want to hear something amazing?"

"Yes, tell me."

"Since I started focusing on my desire to find money for the lessons, money has come from out of nowhere. It's incredible. If I get to keep going to these classes, I really think I can stop this horrible addiction."

Tears of joy streamed down my face and we both laughed nervously. "Lenea, we are sisters on a journey, all of us. But one word of advice, sister: go with your heart and do *not* listen to those voices. Thank you for calling me."

As we both hung up, I realized how much Chrissy's words made perfect sense to me. I felt normal again, as if someone had lit a candle in the darkness and my fears had been banished. After entering my apartment, I set my purse down, turned on my music, and immersed myself in my work.

•••••••••

The bright white of the afternoon had slipped into the dimming orange of evening by the time I could see the end of my pile in sight. "Two more pages of reports," I said out loud. I was interrupted by the ring of my cell phone. I looked down; it was Mark. My hands tingled with excitement while grabbing the phone. "Well, hello," I said with my best bedroom voice. Chrissy's cautionary directions resonated in my head: *Listen to your heart. Listen to your heart.*

"Is this the sexiest woman alive?" he replied deeply, almost growling.

I could feel a surge of adrenaline rush through me; my face turned warm and red. "Mmm," I groaned into the phone, "of course it is. Who is this?"

"This is your massage therapist. And I am calling to schedule you for a personal appointment, say, Thursday night? After dance? My place?" I imagined his strong hands rubbing up and down my naked back, moving down my legs.

"Mmm," I groaned again, arching my back, wishing he could visualize my body language through the phone. "You know where my favorite place to be massaged is, don't you?" I waited a few seconds; I

131

could hear his smile on the other end of the line. I played along, enjoying the energy. "I'll give you a hint: after dance, it's very … very … tight."

"Oh yes," he responded, "gotta be the deltoids." He waited a second for my answer, "The trapezius?" His voice turned more jocular.

"Uh-uh. A little lower," I purred.

"Gotta be the scapula," he cajoled. He changed his tone. "Lenea, I wanted to tell you how much I enjoyed seeing you today. And I can't wait for Thursday night. But I only had a quick moment between sessions and wanted to wish you … good night."

I sat up, confused, thinking we would continue our banter. "Okay, my prince, good night." The line went dead. He could have just sat there breathing in my ear without saying a word, and it would have been enough for me. Even though we were not physically with one another, the visualization of us together created enough energy to make me feel his presence. *Time for bed.* Dreaming of our next encounter all night long was imminent.

16

Experience Is More Than a Word

Thursday arrived, and the day passed quickly. I had clarity in my mind as I breezed through the necessary office reports. My conference calls went more smoothly than normal, and I was able to catch up on all the work I put off earlier in the week. Strong and confident was how I felt. And that was how my week was going. The anticipation of seeing Mark was the invisible energy pill; the sound of his voice lingered in my conscience.

I ate a small dinner and carefully planned and packed an overnight bag, assuming the massage invitation was also an overture to spend the night. The vivid details of the imagined scene had danced in my head ever since our phone call Monday night.

I allowed myself enough time to sift through my lingerie drawer, giving careful consideration to my undergarments. Luckily, a recent purchase included a deliciously playful bra and panty set—hot pink animal print with black lace, never worn. I giggled while removing the tags, recalling my desire at the time for a man to see this on me. My dream was coming true. *Maybe Madame is right. Maybe desires can become destiny.*

I cleaned up the apartment and, before leaving, glanced at myself in the mirror. I looked deep into my own eyes. "You've got this!" I declared to my reflection. It made me feel so good to leave with all work complete, the house in order, and a bag packed with new lingerie. I closed the door, locked it, and made my way to the studio knowing Madame and Mark were my reward for the hard work.

When I arrived five minutes early, the door was locked. I knocked twice before Madame quietly opened the door.

"Ah, Lenea, bonsoir. You passed your first test," Madame said, as if providing an answer.

I walked in the door and thought to myself, *First test? What in the world is she talking about?*

She closed the door, turned to me, and asked the question, "When something you desire is waiting for you, do you wait until someone opens the door for you, or do you knock, expecting an answer?"

I knew it was a rhetorical question and did not respond.

The studio looked exactly the same at night as it did during the day. With the absence of windows, the lighting never changed. Madame was dressed in a short black wrap skirt, similar to what I've seen ballerinas wear, paired with an unusual black leotard. From a distance it would seem her appearance was that of a professional dancer. However, there was a slight deviation at the neckline of her leotard. It was made of fishnet, exposing the curvy flesh of her breasts underneath.

The netting was woven into asymmetrical shapes that, upon closer examination, appeared to be hieroglyphics. The top, coupled with her five-inch black heels, gave her an exotic appearance, to say the least. Once again, I felt terribly underdressed by comparison.

I wore a pair of tight black spandex shorts and a muted rock concert tank top revealing my black sports bra underneath. *How does she always look so coordinated and sexually intriguing at the same time?* I wondered. I hoped to figure it out one day in order to achieve the same type of look.

We traveled the dimly lit hallway into the studio. It was dark, and I could barely make out a large white cover over the mirrored wall in the front of the room. Madame lit candles around the space, and soon the room was filled with a soft orange glow. As I suspected, there was indeed a large white canvas that stretched from one side to the other. I wondered what it was for. Visions of the white screen from the downtown loft entered my mind.

Our session began similarly to the group sessions. She turned on Indian Bollywood music and lit some incense. I felt a sense of reverence and wasn't quite sure what to do next. Madame instructed me to grab a pillow and sit down in the middle of the studio facing the covered mirror, leaving enough space for the dancers. Confused, I followed as directed.

While sitting and adjusting my legs, two dancers, one male and one female, walked in the back door. I didn't recognize their faces. But as they walked, their bodies reminded me of the silhouette dancers the night I first met Madame so long ago. Madame stepped to the back of the room, whispered into the ear of each dancer, and then returned and stood in front of me. "Now," she said sternly, "tonight you will sit and watch a performance. You will need these." She handed me a purple pen and a journal covered in purple leather. "You must use these to record what you feel. Write down your deepest innermost feelings from this performance. When you fill five pages, you may stop."

The sweet fragrance of incense filled the room. I opened the journal to the first page and tested my pen. Madame had stepped to the side, and as she walked back toward me, she carried a beautiful ornate dish exquisitely decorated with chocolate truffles. My eyes lit up at the sight; I love chocolate.

"Help yourself, my dear," Madame encouraged.

She held the dish in front of me, while I selected a delicate chocolate. She stood there holding the plate, smiling slyly. I popped the small truffle in my mouth, swallowed, and hesitantly reached for another.

She pulled the plate away quickly. "Uh, uh, uh. You had the opportunity to help yourself, as I told you. Yet you chose only one truffle. Hmm." With that, she emptied the others into the trash. *What a waste*, I thought.

I settled into my pillow, embarrassed that I had failed her test but now significantly more alert, wondering what events were next. The Indian music stopped, and a song came on that I recognized. Madame turned up the volume while I tried to place the artist and the song's name. The male and female dancers walked to the front of the room with an armload of paintbrushes, each carrying two buckets of paint. They stood at separate sides of the blank canvas; both were barefoot, wearing only white pants and tight white T-shirts. If it weren't for their heads and bare feet, they would have blended right into the background. When the first chorus of the song began, I finally recognized it: Air Supply's "Making Love Out of Nothing At All."

The artists dipped their paintbrushes into the buckets of paint, dancing erotically against the canvased wall. Every motion of their hands produced a brush stroke of color against the white background. Each dancer held two paintbrushes, one in each hand; they were extensions of their arms, like hands and fingertips. The dance was modern, and though it looked choreographed, I could tell the dancers were simultaneously losing themselves in their movements. As instructed, I wrote these thoughts in the journal sitting in my lap.

The man had two different colors. In one hand he held a paintbrush covered in red, and in the other hand, blue. Both of the paintbrushes held by the woman were covered in yellow paint. Together they represented the three primary colors.

As the dance progressed, the couple not only painted the canvas, but also began to touch each other with their paintbrushes, marking their clothing as well. Each time their colors started to diminish, they would dip the paintbrushes in cans and create more vibrant strokes, all part of the dance.

At the music's crescendo, the dancers looked at each other longingly, walking toward one another like star-crossed lovers, dragging their paintbrushes along the wall beside them.

They circled one another, staring deep into each other's eyes. The music intensified. Their movements grew more pronounced and bold, as if the combining of their energy had sparked a fire. Their colors combined and moved across the canvas like the dance. Their bodies intertwined momentarily, blending the color even more. The canvas was so covered in paint that it was difficult to see where one color began and the other ended.

The flickering of the flames from the candles exaggerated the intimacy of the moment. I was a voyeur, and these two dancers were making love to one another, their body movements erotic and sensual.

Many new colors were created on the canvas, especially in the areas where their bodies had rolled up against it. Now vividly before me stood a beautiful painting where, as the song lyrics indicated, there was once nothing at all. It was so inspiring and artistically creative, yet animalistic and ritual. As the music started to fade, the couple held each other in the center of the painted canvas, finishing the performance in a dramatic embrace. The music stopped, and there was silence except for the sound of their heavy breathing. I had tears in my eyes and no idea why.

Madame interrupted the moment. "Thank you, Elemental Charity."

The two dancers picked up their brushes and buckets and walked out the back of the studio hand in hand. I sat there in awe of the experience.

"Did you write down any feelings, Lenea?" Madame's words echoed like thunder.

I snapped out of the trance, looking down at the pen and paper in my hand. I responded, "Yes. But not as much as you asked me to."

"And?" she asked. "How did this performance make you feel?"

"It was … incredible. So … beautiful." I replayed the fluid motion and harmony in my mind, astounded I was able to take my eyes away, even for a moment, to write down my feelings; any feelings.

"How did it make you feel?" she asked again, this time more demanding.

"Oh, well"—I took a deep breath—"I guess it made me feel … inspired."

"Okay. Inspired." She mimicked slowly, slightly irritated. "Then tell me, Lenea, what does 'inspired' feel like?" Madame's interrogation continued.

I wasn't quite sure how to reply. I searched deep in my mind, trying to find the words that would describe what I felt. "Well," I started, "it felt … good."

Madame shook her head. "No, no, no. Look into your heart, dear," she tapped her pointed finger above her left breast. "Go deeper."

Go deeper? What the hell is she getting at? Deeper? I wasn't quite sure where this was heading, but I tried to keep my composure. "I felt happy, like … I saw something new," I tried to answer, more positive and upbeat, "and it made me feel good. Really good."

Madame was obviously looking for a different answer. "What was the first thing I instructed you to do when you walked in?"

I stopped for a moment to think. I sank in my pillow, recalling the chocolate lesson, "You asked me to help myself to chocolate," I responded with hesitancy.

"No, no. Before that! What is the first instruction you received when you came inside the studio, before the chocolate?" she asked.

I took a moment and thought back to the series of events. "Sit on the pillow in the middle of the room?" I answered. She grabbed a pillow and sat across from me. She crossed her legs, sat upright, closed her eyes, and took a deep breath. I relaxed a little, knowing we were at an equal level. I could look into her eyes.

"Yes, and how does the pillow feel?" she asked in a smooth tone.

"It feels soft and … comfortable?" Again I answered with a question, not sure how I was supposed to respond.

"That's a start," she said. "Write that down in your journal. What part of your body was touching the pillow?"

I opened my journal and started writing. "My legs," I said as I scribbled quickly.

"Okay, now. What did I give you to eat?" She paused for effect. "How did that make you feel?"

"You gave me a chocolate truffle." I wanted to say, *"It made me sad because you obviously were teasing me and testing me,"* but instead I answered with, "It made me feel happy because I love chocolate." I spoke the words out loud while scribbling them as fast as I could, hoping she didn't sense the truth behind my lie.

"Better! But use your words! Use your vocabulary!" she urged. "You saw how they painted! They started with primary colors, then got more and more creative to paint a masterpiece. Fill in the words, Lenea, and paint the picture of what you felt." The timbre of her voice rose higher. "Now, describe the taste of the chocolate!" She almost sang the instruction with the tonality of her voice.

"It was creamy and sweet and melted in my mouth, exploding into a very pleasurable sensation on my palate," I answered quickly, searching through every word in my vocabulary bank while trying to emulate her excitement. At the same time, in my mind, I had no idea where this conversation was going. *How did any of this have to do with trusting men?*

"Good, write it down!" I could feel her intensity "Was there a scent in the air? What did it smell like? Write that down," she said.

I closed my eyes and took a whiff of the burning incense. "It smells sweet, like freshly picked citrus, with a tinge of cinnamon or currant." I turned to the journal and wrote again.

"What music was playing during the performance? How did it make you feel? What did it sound like?"

"The music was 'Making Love Out of Nothing at All,' by Air Supply,"
I answered knowingly. "The lyrics tell the story of a couple making love.
It sounded very intimate and very passionate." This time I answered out
loud, but I felt uncomfortable sharing my experience nonetheless.

Madame continued, "What did you see during the performance?
How did it make you feel?"

I wanted to say, "voyeuristic," but I knew that was inappropriate. So
I wrote, "A couple making love in a ritualistic dance that was magnificent
and beautiful. It made me feel happy." When I finished, I reread what I
had written for Madame.

Then she spoke as a teacher to a student. "I see. So you have written
down what you experienced with your five senses—touch, taste, smell,
hearing, sight—and how each sense made you feel. What would happen if
I were to take one of those senses away? Let's say … hearing. How would
that affect your experience?"

I thought about it for a moment and answered, "I don't think I would
have understood the meaning of the dance without the lyrics of the song."

"Would you say the experience could have been perceived differently?"
she asked.

"Yes," I answered, "I think so." I paused and took in the idea of not
being able to hear. Things really would be much different.

"What if I were to tell you there is a missing sense. Missing from how
you perceive the world every day. Some call it our sixth sense," she said,
attempting to pique my interest.

Instead my mind went to the movie *The Sixth Sense* and the paranormal
scenes of dead people. *Oh my God! Does she know about the raven-haired woman?
Maybe she can explain what is going on around here.* I hung on every word she
said, hoping I wasn't seeing dead people.

"The sixth sense is based on what some people call a hunch or
intuition," she began.

I sighed deeply as the words left her mouth. Inside I thanked God
we weren't talking about ghosts. I was glad to have that part figured out.

"During our private classes together I am going to teach you more
about your intuition, the sixth sense. Right now you don't have to worry
about it. But you must know that it is part of your perception of your
experiences." She picked my hands up and held them in hers. Her eyes
were serious, staring deeply into mine. "Once you learn to use this

sense, your perception will change and broaden your appreciation of life."

I wasn't quite following where she was going. I'm sure she could see the confused and curious look on my face, but still she continued. "Today you had a life experience. When you leave here, you will have many more. Life is a series of experiences, Lenea." Her voice had turned very serious, her gaze never wavering from mine. "And every experience is perceived through your senses. All experiences create sensations and emotion within your body. When you write about an experience and what you are feeling, you are able to get in touch with your senses and therefore your perception or mindfulness about the experience."

She set my hands down, leaning back on her pillow, again closing her eyes to take a deep breath. "I realize that's a lot to take in for one day." She opened her eyes and exhaled. "Let me leave you with some homework, and we will continue this discussion next time. Agreed?"

"Agreed," I responded. She stood first, and I followed.

"The journal is yours to keep," she said, her right hand indicating the purple pages I held in my hand. "Over this next week, I want you to write about different life experiences that stand out. Write about your emotions, sensations in your body, and your perception of the experience. I also want you to find a song that represents your desire to trust. Bring both your journal and the song to our class next Thursday. Until then, au revoir."

She leaned forward, kissed me on both cheeks, and walked off to the back of the room. I reached down and picked up my pillow, confused by her words, before setting it down in the corner with the pile of others. As I walked out of the studio, I murmured a thank you, to which she responded with a cursory wave.

I walked down the dimly lit hallway, trying to figure out what happened tonight. I didn't quite understand my assignment, flustered even more by all the new lessons. Still, I looked forward to journaling my experiences.

As I exited the hallway into the reception area, I felt a hand softly touch my arm. "Going somewhere without me?" Mark's voice bellowed. I unknowingly passed him sitting on the red velvet bench in the hallway. He had been waiting for me and our date. My heartbeat quickened at his sight, and my mood changed just as fast.

"No way!" I said, trying to recover. "But I have something important to tell you."

"What's that?" he asked.

"You're gonna remember tonight," I purred.

17

A Book Reveals a Clue

Part of me needed to get out of the studio; too much thinking and feeling. I was relieved to find Mark waiting for me. He was devilishly handsome in his faded jeans and kelly green T-shirt, which seemed to be his preferred outfit. With his physique, it was my favorite as well.

"Before we go, I need to change. Can you wait here?" I asked.

"As long as you promise not to walk by me again," he retorted, returning to his bench. I walked down the hall to a small door I had barely even noticed before. It led into an intimate powder room. The room was painted a rich maroon color, so dark it made the room appear smaller than it actually was. The toilet and sink were old, and there was an ornate gold Victorian-style mirror illuminated by a small crystal pendant light hanging above the sink. It was the only light in the room.

After opening my bag, I dug through to find my favorite Capri-style jeans. Baggy and faded, they had a worn look that matched well with a solid gray V-neck T-shirt. I paired it with a couple sterling silver necklaces, earrings, and a bracelet before wrapping a dark gray scarf around my neck. The ensemble was complete as I slipped into tan Roman sandals. I looked in the mirror; my outfit conveyed cute and comfy.

I carefully folded my dance gear, putting it neatly into my duffel on top of my new lingerie. I couldn't help but smile as I zipped the bag and turned around. A plaque on the side of the wall caught my attention. It was a framed saying. I could barely see the writing, but it appeared to be a quoted passage of some sort. I leaned in closer, and saw the text and the strange drawings around the long passage and read to myself aloud:

> It was said of old: The self, which is free from impurities, from old age and death, from grief, from hunger and thirst, which desires nothing but what it ought to desire, and resolves nothing but what it ought to resolve, is to be sought after, is to be inquired about, is to be realized. He who learns about the self and realizes it obtains all the worlds and all desires.

> As your desire is, so is your will.
> As your will is, so is your deed.
> As your deed is, so is your destiny.
> —The Upanishads

Recognizing part of the saying immediately from the back of Madame's business card, I pondered the words. *What in the world is "the self?"* I made a mental note to look it up later, for now I had a hot date. I opened the door and welcomed the space. Walking down the hall, I could see Mark talking with Madame from a distance. *Well, I guess it's not going to be a secret any longer,* I thought to myself. I took a deep breath and walked into the middle of their conversation.

"Are you ready?" Mark asked as I entered the room.

"I am!" I said with a resounding joyousness in my voice.

"Well, we are out of here. See you later!" He waved to Madame, opened the door, and escorted me out. I looked back as she smiled a curious smile.

"Enjoy your evening," she said coyly.

The door closed behind us, I felt the chill of the Rocky Mountain evening air. It was after eight. I assumed we wouldn't be going out for dinner but was still curious where we were headed. I loved the fact Mark was always ready to go. He was a man with a plan and led with confidence.

"I was thinking we would head over to the L'abeille Palace again for dessert and coffee. Does that sound good to you?" he asked.

This time I grabbed his hand. "Sounds fantastic," I responded. It felt so good to be outdoors; to be walking next to my stunningly handsome date.

Arriving at the hotel, the doormen greeted us and led us through the large gold turnstile doors. It was busier than the last time. Mark and I entered the crowded lobby and checked in with the hostess. I assumed this was the five-star restaurant he had spoken about. He asked the waitress about dessert and was assured it was the best around. He smiled and thanked her. I loved the way he dealt with people, so relaxed and in a down-to-earth manner. The woman ushered us into the lounge directly across from the restaurant. She sat us at a cozy table for two with drink and dessert menus, mentioning a server would be with us soon.

"What are you in the mood for?" Mark asked, playfully looking at me from across the table.

"Everything sounds good," I said, smiling at his innuendo and pretending to read the menu.

"Ah, the power of decision," he said, sounding eerily like Madame.

The waiter approached and offered to take our order. He was an older gentleman, balding on top, with gray sideburns and slight in build. I quickly stated my choice: "I would like an Irish coffee and a plate of the various cookies."

"Wow! That was fast," Mark said. "That sounds good. I think I'll have the same." He looked up at the waiter and handed him the menu.

The lounge was a warm, intimate area much like the restaurant, but smaller. It was filled with men smoking cigars and drinking scotch. Only one other woman was there, seated at a table of four next to us. Several TVs were tuned to various games, making the room more of an upscale sports bar with its dark wood, elegant furnishings and art.

As we sipped our Irish coffees and ate our cookies, we talked about the day, about work, and about anything random that came to mind. The more time we spent together, the more comfortable it felt. He was becoming a best friend. We laughed at each other's stories and talked about the future as if the two of us were a part of it. He always used the words "we" and "our" in his conversation, which made me feel instantly connected to his life. It was endearing.

Upon finishing our dessert, once again Mark accepted the check.

We got up from our table and walked into the lobby where we spotted a small glass curio cabinet holding objects exemplifying the history of the hotel. Candles, beeswax, honey, tea, and several books graced the shelves. I was curious about all of the bee paraphernalia and walked closer. Mark excused himself to use the restroom.

As I stood there reading the information and looking through the books on display, my eyes rested on a small red book in a white box. The book's cover was decorated with a red illustration of a woman lying on a bed, wearing saloon clothing hiked up to reveal a corset, with her legs splayed wide open. Chills ran through my body. The woman had raven-colored hair and looked exactly like the woman I had seen in the mirrors of the studio and the sandwich shop. *Oh my gosh! The painting at the top of the stairs! That woman is painted in the same pose!*

The hair on the back of my neck stood up. I leaned in closer to examine the picture's details, and goose bumps covered my arms. *It is her! It is definitely her!* I thought to myself. *Oh my God, am I seeing things? No, surely this can't be!* My face must have registered the shock I felt as Mark, now back from the restroom and seeing my expression, put his arm around my shoulders and asked, "Are you all right?"

"No!" I responded quickly. I then changed the subject, not knowing if I should tell him what I really saw and why I was reacting the way I was. "I mean, yes. It's just … I'm curious about these books. I wonder if they are for sale."

"Probably not these," he responded, "but there is a coffee shop in the front of the hotel that sells books. I bought a fascinating one there about the history of the hotel. Shall we go check out what they have?" He motioned to the doors.

"Sure," I said, rubbing the goose bumps that covered my arms, "let's do that."

We walked toward the coffee shop, and I was thankful for the loud piano playing in the background, as it made conversation difficult. My mind was going a million miles a minute as I tried to connect what I had just seen with the two instances in which I had seen the raven-haired woman.

When we got to the coffee shop, I went straight to the book section and spotted the one I was looking for right away. I stood in line to make my purchase. Mark grabbed the book and jokingly asked if I was planning a life of prostitution.

YOU & I, INC.

I gave him a strange look before noticing the title of the book: *Prostitution in the Wild, Wild West.* I didn't care about prostitution. What I cared about was finding the answers to why this woman, the one in the illustration, kept showing up in my life. What I wanted now was a quiet spot to devour the information in this book. I made my purchase and turned around to Mark, who was waiting for me.

"I'm sorry," he said. "I was kidding with you. You know the history about the old Mystere building across the street, right?" He gestured toward the back wall window.

"Not really, only what you've shared with me," I said as he opened the door for me.

We walked outside and down the steps toward the building across the street. We gazed at the picturesque facade, and Mark divulged the story. "The building was built in 1880. It originally opened as a private all-girls school. Around 1889, the school was purchased by two gambling men, and they turned it into a 'hotel' they called the Bourgeoisie." The passion in his voice resonated; his arms and gestures were like paintbrushes on an invisible canvas. "The building was used as a gambling hall. The story goes that during one particularly bad night of gaming, the building was offered as collateral for a wager. The owners lost, and the deed was transferred to the two men who had won the bet.

"The new owners were jokesters who had a very specific plan for the use of the building. They were wealthy Frenchmen and lovers of wine, women, and song. The Mystere became a 'private club' for wealthy men"—he put his hand to his mouth, looking left and right to make sure he wasn't offending anyone with the volume of his voice—"and this city, with its newfound wealth, had a *lot* of rich single men." He stood upright again. "They also included an upscale restaurant—another great way to make money.

"Now, this is where the rumors about underground coal tunnels come in." He smiled warmly. Still, his excitement grew. "Supposedly, an adjacent tunnel was suggested by the owners of the Mystere and built in a way that would facilitate other forms of, you know, 'human energy' to be transported without being seen by guests in the lobby. You get my drift?" I nodded silently, in awe of his knowledge and hoping something in this conversation would point to the raven-haired woman.

"Of course, it wouldn't look right for prominent men to be seen going into the Mystere to solicit prostitutes, right? So an arrangement was made that was mutually beneficial to both owners of the buildings. The average Joe on the street assumed the tunnels were built for the transport of coal. Instead, women and liquor could also be transported back and forth without anyone's reputation being damaged. It was a huge win-win for all involved. And, most important, it was a nice cover story."

"Wow! How did you learn all of that?" I asked, overwhelmed by it all.

"Oh, I read too!" He smiled. "And I pay attention to local info. What else do you want to know?"

What I wanted to ask was why some dark-haired woman spirit or ghost was following me and haunting me. However, for some reason, I didn't feel this was the time or place to share that experience with him. Instead, I decided to ask more questions and keep him talking, hoping he would provide an answer.

"Okay, so let me get this straight. A wealthy married couple would check into the L'abeille Palace. Would they stay in the same room?" I queried.

"Oh no." He shook his head. "Typically they would have two different rooms, sometimes on different floors."

"Okay, so what did the wives do? Weren't they upset?" I could tell Mark was going to enjoy answering the question.

"Well, that's a good question that leads to a good story. You see, back then it was considered political suicide if you didn't publicly oppose prostitution. Men and women both took a strong stance against it. Getting caught soliciting a prostitute was even worse. But wealthy men knew what they wanted, and they knew how to get it and still maintain their reputation." His voice grew to a fevered pitch. "Yet privately the whole business was alive and well due to funding through these same people. The 'restaurants'—back then they were known as saloons—created a boom in the economy through taxes, fines, and even bribes. Many times these funds supported the city's infrastructure itself. So rather than condemn it, they kept it all hidden and quietly condoned it. The money being filtered through these establishments and back into a town or city resulted in growth and wealth. Everybody wins!" He was growing more and more animated as the story continued.

"So I bet you are wondering why it stopped?" He paused for effect. I nodded, curious. "A group of British women had traveled to the

Wild West and learned what was going on. Back home, they feared for their daughters' morality and created a reform movement against such establishments as the Mystere. They called it something like the Moral Purity Movement, and it worked its way over to the US, spreading all the way to California.

"You see, it was a movement of refined women who believed it was important to repress sexuality on all levels. Refinement equaled repression. The movement spread like wildfire across the nation, and activists everywhere demanded repression of every form of sexuality. Additionally, they demanded equal voting rights, abolishment of slavery, and ultimately prohibition of liquor." He grabbed my hand and we started walking down the street.

"So as this movement grew, it made its way to the socialites in the city who really embraced it. In fact, did you know that Colorado was one of the first states in the Union to give women the right to vote through popular election?"

"Oh my gosh! How in the world do you know all of this history? Is it from the book you bought from the coffee shop?" I asked.

"I like to study history, especially local history because I believe it helps me understand my own experiences in life," he answered.

There is that word again—"experiences." I thought to myself as he continued talking.

"As an artist, I capture moments in time. Before there was still photography, there were painters and artists. It was the only way to capture life in a still frame and contemplate its deeper meanings." He stopped and turned us toward one another, looking deep into my eyes. "There are memories of the heart and mind ... and there is art. Both create emotion."

This was my moment. I finally asked, "Did you paint the photo of the dark-haired woman? The one with her legs splayed wide open that hangs in the staircase leading to your apartment above the studio?"

He stopped for a moment, perplexed. The question must have caught him off guard, as he answered, "You know, I don't know where the painting came from. I've always been curious about it myself. It looks pretty old. I could find out the artist if you like? Why do you ask?"

I decided to show him the cover of the book. I pulled it slowly out of the plastic bag from the coffee shop. "Look," I said, pointing to the cover. "Don't you think this is odd? I think this is the same woman in the painting hanging in the studio. Except in the painting she is naked."

He took the book from my hands, carefully inspecting it. "I think you're right. Let's go back and check it out! Now you've got me intrigued." He grabbed my hand, and we turned back toward the studio.

Mark continued to talk about his excitement to help me find answers to this odd coincidence. He also spoke about the passion a painter experiences from creating artwork. I couldn't help but fall in love. He was so intelligent, so intriguing. I drifted off into a daydream of how wonderful our life would be if we spent it together always; how moments like this could be captured in paintings. *Yes! This is a man I could spend my life with; I want to spend my life with.* The thought didn't even scare me. My perspective had changed. Maybe the spirit was still a transference issue and my subconscious had picked up on this image of the dark-haired woman the first time I saw the painting in the studio. *That has to be it!* Nonetheless, it felt good that I wasn't alone anymore trying to figure out this mystery. It was fun to have a common interest to explore together. I felt like Nancy Drew and her partner, Ned, solving the crime. It was fantastic!

18

Sexual Energy; Spiritual Energy

We turned and walked back to the studio hand in hand. The more he talked, the more my love for him intensified. Without prompting, he opened the door to the studio and we both walked in. I followed him into the hallway and knew we were also on our way upstairs to his place. My heart was beating wildly. We heard what sounded like a group of voices and footsteps, but where were they coming from?

Several couples came walking up from the staircase that led into the basement. The couples were some of the most beautiful people I had ever seen; their appearances were akin to those of models on the covers of magazines. They held each other lovingly and gazed into each other's eyes as they passed us in the hallway.

The last couple to come up the stairs was followed by Madame. She didn't say a word to us, but stopped and glared. Mark broke the silence.

"Are those new dancers, Madame?" he asked. We all turned our heads watching them saunter down the hall.

"Actually, they are your new project," she said in a business-like manner. He had a puzzled look on his face. She continued, "You have two groups to paint now."

"Two groups—what do you mean?" Mark asked. I was happy I wasn't the only one out of the loop.

Madame turned her focus to Mark. "They are my new group, the second one I have put together. The twelve single dancers of Elemental Charity and now the four couples in an ensemble I call Supernal Sacrament." Her eyes squinted, and her face remained solemn. "Mark, I would like you join us next Thursday for an introduction ... if you are available." Her eye shifted to me with the last words.

"Yes, I'm available. I look forward to it. May I bring Lenea with me?" He paused, looking over at me. "That is, if you want to join me." My face blushed, and I looked down, bashful.

Madame answered. "Of course, I would have asked you privately if I didn't already see that coming." She looked at me and smiled. There was a sparkle in her eye. "Elemental Charity is also here tonight, practicing a new routine. Would you two like to join us?" I looked at Mark for confirmation.

He looked at me. "It's your call."

It seemed like such an honor for Madame to ask us to watch the rehearsal. I quickly responded, "Yes! I would love to."

"Then follow me." She motioned with her hand as she turned and walked toward the studio.

We followed, stopping to glance up at the painting. We looked at each other briefly and smiled. "It can wait," I said. Mark nodded in agreement.

I could hear voices coming from the end of the hall, and there was a mysterious red light glowing from within. I swallowed hard, consumed by nervous excitement, my heart beating faster, not yet knowing what exactly we were getting ourselves into.

We entered the studio. Madame motioned to us again. "Please take a seat in the back of the room." We walked to the back, Mark stopping along the way to grab two pillows for us to sit on.

The twelve dancers were in full black body suits made of a very thin nylon material that hugged every curve of their bodies. I assumed this was what they wore behind the white screen during the dance number I saw years ago. It looked more like black body paint, as their perfectly proportioned bodies were visible, yet veiled. The red lights made the whole scene erotically mysterious.

Indian music featuring a sitar was playing in the background. If I closed my eyes, I would have envisioned the scene as a prelude to a belly dance. The intimate proximity to the dancers, the glow of the diffuse red light and the black-suited bodies were collectively intriguing. I was anxious to see what would come next.

Madame spoke, "Ladies and gentlemen. Tonight we have guests here to watch your performance. I would like to see your best efforts demonstrated for these young, impressionable minds." She turned and pointed to a couple. "Steven and Sophie, you can sit this one out tonight. Mark and Lenea will be taking your place." The dancers giggled, murmuring to each other in the background. Their confidence was intimidating.

What does she mean Mark and I will take their place?

Mark held my hand and kissed me on the cheek, his lips stopping next to my ear. He softly whispered, "I think you'll enjoy this." He pulled his pillow closer to mine and rested his hand on my knee.

The music stopped, the lights were turned off, and the room was plunged into darkness. I could hear the sound of people shuffling around, possibly moving into position; perhaps their cue to get ready.

The music blared, startling me. Suddenly, red lights penetrated the darkness once again. It was similar to the music we listened to earlier, but with darker tones and a quicker, deep, resonating drumbeat. With the room illuminated in an eerie ruby glow, the rumors of the restaurant owner from next door flashed through my mind. The dancers were in a crouched position, all lined up against the mirror. A few moments after the music began, one woman stood up from her position, turned around, and seductively walked toward us.

She was a gorgeous blonde dancer, tall and slender with a square jaw and steel-blue eyes. Her sports bra concealed her full bosoms; her abs flat and toned. She came right toward me and took my hand to help me stand up before leading me to a chair in the center of the dance floor. My pulse quickened. I could feel my face flush, uneasy and concerned about what she might do. I sat down in the chair and looked over at Mark; his eyes were glued to mine.

The woman was now dancing around me. It felt very ritualistic, yet also surreal, sitting in a room where this beautiful half-naked woman was treating me as if I were the only person there. Maybe it was the effects of the Irish coffees, or maybe Mark's reassuring looks, that allowed my mind and body to relax into the energy of the moment. Soon my mood shifted, and I actually allowed myself to enjoy the attention, feeling even slightly aroused. Mark must have felt the energy as well. He looked into my eyes from across the room and smiled to reassure me.

The music changed, more to an African tribal number; much slower with deeper, constant beats. Another chair was brought out and placed next to mine. A different female dancer walked toward Mark and grabbed his hand. He stood and followed, being led to the chair beside me. It was clear he was comfortable with the attention. I couldn't help but feel like he and I were students and the dancers were the teachers we were to obey. With Mark sitting so close to me, the energy in the room heightened.

My heart and body synced to the rhythm of the music. I looked over at Mark; he was watching the girl in front of him, drinking in the visual display only inches from his eyes. Both women were moving in tandem. He seemed so relaxed, enjoying himself. My body softened a little, mirroring the same.

My attention shifted fully to the girl who was now in front of me. We made eye contact, and it simply felt … right. She knelt down, putting us eye to eye, and placed her hands on top of my knees. I shuddered with the excitement of her touch. The room was now pulsating.

Her white-gloved hands felt strong. She laid her head in my lap; her long hair brushed across my thighs. Then she stood up fast, her hair flipping across my lap, simulating a whip. The growing wetness between my thighs confirmed it: I was definitely turned on by her overt sexuality. My cheeks grew flush.

I watched her walk away; the sway of her hips was hypnotic, the curves of her body exciting. *A woman's body really is a beautiful piece of art*, I thought. Suddenly I had clarity: *She is a piece of art. She was created for me to enjoy.* I couldn't help but nod to myself as it dawned on me: I too was created in the same image.

The music roared to crescendo. Both dancers took a deep breath. The blonde turned toward me and stared into my eyes once again. Instantly she transformed into a zealous hunter, and I her targeted prey. Her intense focus was exhilarating. Our eyes locked, but only for a moment.

I found myself distracted as she pantomimed ripping off her clothes in a seductive striptease; the thought piqued my interest. I closed my eyes, lips slightly apart, and exhaled; a slight moan resonated from my throat at the thought of her naked body. I could feel her sexual energy in front of me; no sight was necessary, thus heightening the sensation.

YOU & I, INC.

She sat down on top of my lap and circled her hips over my thighs. I smiled, my eyes open wide behind my closed eyelids. Then her soft face pressed against mine and she whispered in my ear, "Relax; free your mind." Feeling her breath caused me to gasp. Without eye contact, I knew she was still in charge, guiding me into the unknown; the line between fantasy and reality had blurred.

She pressed her breasts against mine while she continued to circle her hips closer and closer to my stomach. I could feel the throbbing of my own body as it swelled with intense pleasure. The moment was overwhelming. My skin tingled as the blood rushed further down my legs, causing titillating sensations.

I found myself spreading my knees apart, opening to receive the warmth between her legs and mine. Letting go, I slipped into the world of ecstasy. The dancer must have felt the shift in my body language and began to then grind her hips into mine. Immediately my head fell back. I inhaled deeply. My breasts were heaving, my heartbeat racing; I was longing to be penetrated by the energy around me—her energy.

Drawing in the awareness of her heat against mine, I sighed heavily. I had never felt so in tune with my body; energy flowed in waves of perpetual pleasure. Then she slowly rose from my lap and positioned herself behind my chair, caressing my arms and neck oh so softly. It was as if she wanted to protect this moment and allow me a safe and sacred space to savor the experience. Her light touch tickled my shoulders, stroking me to the beat of the music.

I opened my eyes.

The dancer walked around in front of me and blew me a kiss.

I sat there in stunned disbelief that I could be so sexually aroused by a woman, and confused by the fact that I had never wanted to be a man so much in my life! My body shook. I smiled back at her knowingly.

It felt as though we had shared an out-of-body experience. Our energies had connected, melding with one another, creating a feeling of being more alive with another than alone. I was dizzy. Somehow I knew her erotic demonstration was like a permission slip given to unleash my own wild side. "Now it's your turn." I heard in the silence. My breathing deepened. I looked around, regaining a sense of reality, and realized we were not the only two people in the room. Mark's eyes hungrily met mine. His look sent powerful vibrations up my spine.

155

A new song began, still tribal, but with much deeper bass. All of the dancers stood and circled around us while at the same time entwining with one another, each of them touching us as they walked by. The men suddenly turned our chairs, placing Mark and me knee to knee, facing one other. The instant my legs touched his, I felt electricity shooting through my body. One look into his eyes and I knew he felt it too.

The dancers then grabbed our hands and began to move them for us; treating us like puppets. It felt completely surreal not to be in control, attempting to relax my arms while complete strangers used my own hands to touch my partner; we were soon pawing each other wildly.

The song intensified, and the dancers placed our arms around one another dramatically and artistically. Mark and I locked eyes and started to kiss while shifting to the edges of our seats to get closer to one another. Soon I couldn't help myself and straddled Mark's lap. I could feel him hard beneath me; all I wanted was to feel him inside of me. The music reached its resounding finale, and the puppet masters danced wildly in unison around us. I forcefully pushed my hips into Mark's lap, grinding him as if we were unclothed. I couldn't stop myself; faster and faster, harder and harder.

Our actions seemed to ignite the dancers' passion as well. Their erratic energy was like a lightbulb being turned on, surrounding and infusing our experience to the height of human awareness.

Suddenly, without warning, I arched my back, moaning loudly as I orgasmed throughout my entire being. It felt as if my soul had been penetrated with the acceptance and the open sharing of sexual energy. I came alive, and my whole body buzzed with excitement.

The fire ignited.

All disappeared.

Mark held my waist firmly, not letting me go, allowing me the time to fully enjoy the experience; savor the moment. My heart was pounding in my chest. I leaned forward. My eyes adjusted as I opened them, sitting upright. I was back in the studio. The music had ended and the dancers sauntered back to their original positions, crouching in the same pose they had started in.

Instantly, I was aware of the difference I felt between participating with the dancers openly tonight versus the first time I watched them behind the white screen. The feeling inside me now was an intimate connection; I was one with them, harmonious, rather than simply being turned on from a distance. Yet their rhythmic moves were the same—so erotic and mysterious. I thought how wonderfully different close proximity and the absence of a veil could be.

At the conclusion of the music, Mark and I leapt up from our embrace and clapped our hands in recognition of the performance. Madame turned up the lights, bringing the room and occupants back to reality.

"Thank you, Mark and Lenea, for standing in with us tonight. Wow! Great job! Ladies and gentlemen, please give them a round of applause." She lifted her hand in a single wave, introducing us to the cast of performers.

The dancers applauded loudly, shouting and whistling, giving us a standing ovation. It was an awkward moment, since I didn't feel we had done anything to warrant this type of response. Still, Mark and I smiled at one another, took each other's hands, and dramatically bowed. The applause grew louder, we bowed again, turned, and walked out the door.

We laughed at our dramatic exit while playfully walking down the hallway toward the staircase. Stopping, we turned toward one another. Mark grasped my hand firmly and said, "It's time for me to give you a tour tonight."

19

Does She Have Eyes for Him Too?

With Mark's hand still in mine, we ran up the stairs to his loft in the spirit of little children at play. Stopping on the platform, I glanced at the painting. Mark, in his excitement, pulled me along behind him, indicating he had more important business for us to attend to. We turned quickly and continued up the second set of stairs, giggling all the way. Now I was in new territory—another encounter with the unknown.

The layout in the long hallway was almost the same floor plan as the studio but with fewer doors and, like downstairs, no windows. The exposed brick walls and old wooden floors created an indescribably sexy vibe—or perhaps that was the feelings inside of me projecting outward.

We stood at the door of Mark's apartment. *Hallelujah!* I thought. *Dreams really do come true every day!* I had dreamt of this opportunity from the moment I knew he lived here, and now, standing here, I was prepared to live the dream.

He inserted his key into the handle, stopping momentarily to look back. "Wait here one second. I want this to be special." He didn't give me a chance to respond as he slipped behind the door. Several moments later, he returned. "Are you ready?" He asked with a big grin on his face.

"In every way possible," I replied in my sexiest voice. We crossed the threshold hand in hand, and it felt as if I were being ushered into a religious space. There were lit candles in every part of the loft, flickering and casting eerie shadows on the open ceilings. The walls contained black-and-white framed art, which I found surprising, as I had expected to see his colorful paintings of women. In fact, none of the walls held even one of his paintings. A standing easel and half-painted canvas in what appeared to be his art room off the living area was the only giveaway of his profession.

His furniture was colorful: the fabrics in the pillows, chairs, and accessories. The brick walls provided an impeccable backdrop to the black-and-white prints, but it was the combination of the old textures with the shiny stainless steel appliances and granite countertops that made my heart swoon. I loved the feeling of sophistication and comfort he had created.

Mark dropped his keys and set his phone in the charger on the kitchen counter and took me in his arms to welcome me. He kissed me, slowly at first, and then released me and looked longingly into my eyes before turning and walking into the kitchen.

"Did you refurbish this yourself?" I asked as he opened a bottle of wine.

"No, I was lucky. The previous tenant fixed everything up as it is. You like it?" He subtly looked up from his task and grinned. He brought the glasses of wine to the coffee table and made a motion with his shoulder for me to join him on his black leather couch.

"It is absolutely fabulous!" I gushed. "Seriously, Mark, this place is incredible."

He went back to the kitchen to grab the bottle. On his way back, he stopped at his stereo system. I saw the blue light of the on button illuminate while he searched through his collection of music. He turned the overhead lights down and lit a few more candles. Moments later we were relaxing next to each other on the couch, enjoying our wine.

"I'm amazed Madame invited us to join the dancers tonight, and even more amazed she asked us to meet her group next week." There was that word again: "us." I loved hearing it. "She led a couples group a few years ago, and I was dating someone else at the time. I asked Madame then if I could paint the couples, and she said 'no, it isn't time yet.' So"— he shook his head in disbelief—"this is a pretty big deal."

"Why is that?" I asked.

"She may not have thought I was ready. I've always wanted a partner, someone to live my life with, to get married and have kids with. I don't want to die an old man with nothing but paintings around me." His eyes moved around the room. "I want to share my passion."

I was blown away to hear this eligible bachelor talk the way he did, incredulous at the words he had spoken. "That surprises me," I said. "So let me get this straight—a hot single artist like you is really looking for happily ever after ... love? I thought it was all about the sex."

"Don't get me wrong; the sex is great too." He laughed. "But I'm ready for more. How about you, Lenea? What do you see in your future?"

I looked down, searching for words. I wasn't sure if I should fully divulge my heart's desire this soon in the relationship. But he seemed so genuine. "I have been hurt before," I started, "and I'm not sure I'm ready for another marriage just yet." I could see his mood shift downward a little. "But I am definitely open to explore more in the area of relationships." I moved my hand to his knee to reassure him of my growing affection.

Propping my elbow up on the couch, I kicked off my shoes, tucked my legs underneath, and settled in comfortably. He moved forward, lifting my hand and putting it in his. "I think I might be able to change your mind," he said. The words out of his mouth were exactly what I wanted to hear. I was so delighted with his pronouncement that I shivered.

"Oh, really? Why is that?" I asked demurely, smiling into his eyes.

He removed the wine glass from my hand and set it on the table. He stood, scooped me up, gently placed me on a plush rug in front of the fireplace, and handed me several satin-covered pillows for my head. The loft was cool enough for him to turn on the fireplace, and the gas flames emitted a rosy glow in the candlelit room.

He settled next to me, staring into my eyes. "Because one of the marks of a great partnership is great sex," he cooed softly while stroking my arm, his touch tender and soft. "I feel like we experienced this in a very unique way tonight. It isn't often two people can be united so thoroughly through a kiss."

My eyes looked up to meet his. "Mmm," I purred. "During the dance tonight, all of my senses were on fire. From the moment our eyes met and knees touched, I felt our passion and our magnetism in a way that is ... well ... the experience was ... spiritual."

Our heads moved in unison toward one another as our mouths parted slightly. We kissed deeply, wrapping each other in our arms. My body tingled with excitement; the energy of his touch surged from head to toe.

His hands moved up my shirt and under my bra, touching my breast, kneading gently as his tongue explored the depths of my mouth. Carefully, and with great dexterity, he began unfastening my bra. I lifted my shoulders as he pulled it away, our tongues still entwined. His hand was immediately behind my back. With a quick jerk, he expertly removed my shirt and tossed it somewhere. In my mind I was back in the studio, now privately open to explore, in the flesh, with this man.

I could feel the hardness through his jeans as he thrust his hips into the side of my leg. Our lips separated. He tucked his face into the side of my neck, nibbling, kissing, and giving a playful bite. I tilted my head back, exposing the nape further, desiring more of his rough play.

"That feels good," I told him. His teeth pressed down hard against my jugular. I liked it. He didn't hesitate to give me what I wanted. I could feel his desire unleash; then nothing.

My eyes opened. He was unbuttoning his shirt quickly while staring me down with hungry eyes. I knew it was my turn to reciprocate. Wildly I grabbed his shoulders and pushed him onto his back. I kissed him long and hard before heading for his neck. I kissed lightly first before playfully biting. The deep resonance of his "mmm" felt like a tiger's purr as the flicker of the fire painted brilliant orange and browns across his face.

I ripped off his shirt, exposing his sinewy muscles and heaving chest. I moved down slowly. Each kiss had purpose; I moved from his neck, to his collarbone, to his muscular pecs before settling into his little button of a nipple. It grew from a pea size into a hardened knob, my tongue circling and nibbling ever so gently. I took my nails and dragged them down the side of his rib cage.

My body settled down further as my kisses traced his sternum, down toward his stomach, stopping momentarily to play with the circle of his belly. His heat and strength felt wonderful settling between my naked breasts as I moved a little lower.

The top button of his jeans opened with ease and I looked upward, smiling a sly grin. His gaze cast downward. He nodded slightly, leaning back as I carefully pulled the zipper down …

Hours later I was awakened from a deep slumber by a cool breeze passing over me. *The fireplace must have shut off,* I thought. I turned on my side, snuggling close to Mark, and closed my eyes.

Again I felt the cool breeze, this time brushing past my face. My eyes popped open; the hair on my arms and neck stood on end. I knew this sensation. *It couldn't be Her, could it?* I forced my eyes closed, hoping the feeling would pass. I shivered. Seconds felt like hours. *Please go away; please go away,* I thought over and over.

Then I felt Her cool breath in my ear.

In and out.

In and out.

My eyes were closed tighter now. The breathing continued.

In and out.

In and out.

My body was paralyzed with fear. I opened my mouth, eyes still closed. Somehow the words spilled out, in a whisper; "What do you want from me?"

The breath grew colder; heavier.

In and out.

In and out.

"Check his phone," she whispered, barely audible. "Check his phone." My eyes popped open. I pulled away from Mark, grabbing his T-shirt to cover my naked body. He didn't move. The coolness of Her presence disappeared. *Was it a dream?*

I looked around the room. Many of the candles had gone out; a few lingered, dancing, casting odd shadows. No one was there.

Suddenly I felt Her presence over my left shoulder. "Get up and check his phone!" Her voice demanded in a stern whisper. I looked over at Mark. He was fast asleep. The candlelight flickered, painting light yellowish orange hues across the sharp angles of his jaw.

I recalled Mark setting his phone on the kitchen counter. I looked over again, making sure he didn't wake as I carefully stood, my gaze fixed, watching him for signs of awakening. I moved a few steps back. My heart was beating hard and loud; my palms were sweaty. I turned, tiptoeing across the hardwood floors. Every step that created a slight creak caused my body to tense in response.

A faint blue light emanated from the counter; a beacon guiding me.

It was Mark's cellphone. I stood in front of the phone, looking down at it, before shifting my gaze upward to ensure Mark had not moved. *What if he wakes up and asks me what I am doing?* I thought. *Getting a glass of water? Maybe a snack? God! What am I doing?*

I reached for his phone, glancing up twice, swearing I could hear him stir. I swallowed hard, picked it up, and wondered if it was locked with a password. To my surprise, it opened right away. The glow from the phone shone like the spotlight of a police car honed in on a criminal. Shocked by the brightness, I hid it under his T-shirt. My muscles tightened. I looked around, listening for the slightest sound, waiting for the raven-haired woman's voice; nothing, no one.

I tiptoed back into the living room simply to make sure he was still asleep. Satisfied he was, I carried the phone into the bathroom. I wasn't quite sure why, but somehow it felt more secure there.

I read text message after text message with no cause for concern. I moved on to the call log. What I saw made my heart leap into my throat; the third name down was "Samantha." I couldn't breathe. *Could it be Samantha from the studio? She called him? Did he give her his number?* My blood began to boil as I recalled the two of them dancing. I could picture the whole thing over again looking up into the mirror. The raven-haired woman was there, clearly, shaking her head in a disapproving manner.

At that moment, dots began to connect in my mind. *Maybe the raven-haired woman knows something about Samantha that I don't. Maybe She's come here to warn me about her? And she wanted me to see this because she must know what is going on with Samantha and Mark? Oh my gosh! Yes, that's why she was in complete disapproval the whole time!* The lightbulb went on as I realized the truth—that the raven-haired woman must be a spirit. The thought sent chills down my spine. *But she's not here to haunt me; she's obviously here to help in some way.* Another realization swept over me. *Could it be I still have access to my imaginary friends and their advice?* I smiled at the idea then laughed. And here I've been scared this entire time. The thought of rekindling my relationship with my imaginary five-year-old friend eased a part of my mind. Yet, at the same time, I could feel an anger rising up within me. The reality of Samantha seducing Mark crept back in.

Who the hell does Samantha thinks she is to call him? I shook my head to clear the thoughts. *Maybe it's not the same Samantha.* That thought didn't last long. My mind painted very vivid pictures of Samantha and Mark secretly meeting together. Suddenly, I remembered the raven-haired woman's words: "Don't trust him."

Images of the two of them walking down the street together, arm in arm, with her leaning her head back, laughing at his jokes, kept playing in my head. I wondered if he had picked her up in his arms like he did with me tonight. *Did he kiss her the same way, so softly? Or was it more passionate and deeper. Ugh! The thought! And all while he was sleeping with me?* My stomach roiled at the possibility of being played again. I couldn't get the image of the two of them out of my mind.

As I stood to leave the bathroom, I flushed the toilet, in case Mark was awake, and opened the door quietly. The apartment looked the same, but I felt different. I felt like an investigator with a handful of clues, not sure what to do next. *I've been here before. Why would I do this to myself again? Is this all some plot of Madame and Mark to get more money? I knew he was too good to be true. He must be some male prostitute hired by Madame to make women think their desires have been met, only to leave us when we stop paying to be her student.*

I burned with anger at the thought. Between the feelings of shame from sneaking around, the rage at the idea of Samantha and Mark together, and the regret in not listening to the spirit's voice, I reeled with disappointment. Walking back into the kitchen, now unconcerned about the noise I was making, I returned his cell phone to the charger and moved back across the creaking floor.

Mark was still breathing deeply, sound asleep. *How would I ever bring this up to him?* The last thing I would do is tell him I went through his phone. And I was definitely not about to reveal to him the raven-haired woman and her words. My stomach churned inside.

How could I be so stupid to have sex with this man? He must be a great actor, I thought. Yet somehow it seemed we both felt the sexual experiences we had were intense and meaningful. *How many women has he slept with? Is this what he does? Is he simply a player? Have I been played again?* I felt disgusted with myself as the litany of questions filled my mind.

There was no way I was lying back down next to this man. I needed to take a shower and get him off me.

Showering quickly, I vigorously cleansed and rinsed my body and any reminder of our night together down the drain. I dressed and left my hair wet before going back into the living room to gather my things. The sight of his phone plugged into the charger suddenly nauseated me. Mark began to stir.

"Are you leaving?" he mumbled.

"I'm having a hard time falling asleep," I said, barely looking at him, "I have a big project due in the morning and … I think I'll sleep better at my place."

Mark stood up, naked and unashamed, stepping into his jeans, as if to walk me to the door. "Wait. You seem upset. Did I do something wrong? Are we moving too fast?" He began buttoning up his jeans. It was obvious he could sense my discomfort.

"No, Mark, it's not you." I hesitated and looked around. "I've simply been hurt in the past, and I'm not sure I want to go there again." I said it! Wearing a stone-cold face, with courage and calmness, I said it.

Mark walked over to me, shirtless, his tan body outlined by the moonlight from the kitchen window. He took my hand. "Can you sit down for a moment? I really want to talk with you." He directed me to the couch, and I sat down reluctantly, not wanting to be touched by him or hear his words. He sat down next to me, his body weight leaning forward, and turned toward me. His face showed he was obviously hurt. His gaze was very intent as he looked into my eyes, which were now welling with tears.

"Look, I know our relationship is new," he began, "but part of today and tomorrow is remembering and talking through your past … but not reliving it. Does that make sense?" He paused, waiting for a response. "So, now, I know it may be painful, but I really want you to tell me about your past relationship that's caused so much hurt in your life. And I will listen. Please, tell me."

What do I have to lose? I thought to myself. *I've told dozens of my female friends what happened, but never a man. Why not? He's gone tomorrow anyway. At least I will have the opportunity to get a man's perspective.*

The words came slowly as I explained how Richard and I met, how I had felt, the joy of the wedding, and on and on. I had told the story so many times it seemed as though I were speaking the lines of a well-rehearsed play. I told him about my trust issues with men and how my ability to have faith in men was completely destroyed—even the repulsive details of the night I met Madame. I let myself cry at that point. Emotion overwhelmed me. It felt as if a three-day-old scab had been torn off, leaving nerve endings pulsating with pain.

Unbeknownst to Mark, I had used what happened with his cell phone as the impetus for the intensity of my story and emotions. Mark had no idea what I was really crying about. It felt good to let it out.

When the story came to a close, Mark leaned forward, gathered me in his arms, and rested my head on his shoulder. "You don't deserve any of that, Lenea. I want to help take care of you," his voice was strong and steady. "I want to give you everything you desire. You deserve a partner who loves you. I love you." The warmth of his chest was comforting; I could feel his heartbeat.

I looked at him incredulously. His face was serious; his eyes, clear. He had spoken the words without hesitation. They resonated as truth. But my doubts about him still lingered. No man had ever allowed me to cry and share my deep-seated fears and still stay by my side. *Could he really love me?*

The strength of his arms around me felt comforting, but I couldn't completely shake the phone call to Mark from Samantha. I wasn't sure I trusted his intentions, and I so badly wanted to share what I had discovered, to ask him about Samantha. But this was neither the time nor the place. I looked at the clock. It was now 4:01 a.m. I stood to leave.

20

There Is More to a Book Than Its Cover

C losing the door behind me, I left Mark's loft, my head still in a fog, and headed downstairs. It felt awkward to go from loft to studio so quickly. I had replayed the scene of Mark and I making love in his room over and over again in my mind, then me spending the night and leaving with a smile on my face, like a fairy-tale dream every girl has of meeting her prince and living happily ever after. This night, however, had ended with a very different scenario. Now I wasn't quite sure what was next for us.

I crept down the narrow staircase, hoping not to run into anyone. I paused to stare at the painting of the raven-haired woman with her legs splayed wide open on the bed. It was a very erotic painting. Suddenly I remembered the book I had purchased at the L'abeille Palace. I pulled it out of my duffel bag. The woman on the cover of the book was the same woman, in the same position as that of the painting! The only difference was in how she was dressed.

In the painting she was naked, covered only by a satin sheet. On the cover of the book she was dressed in saloon attire. It was her all right, the raven-haired woman. A chill moved up my spine. *Maybe it will contain answers or clues about the raven-haired woman and why I keep hearing her voice!* I was eager to get home and start reading. There had to be a reason for this strange coincidence.

When I got to the bottom of the stairs, I looked to the right; the studio was only a few steps away and was lit up in mysterious red lights. Exotic dance music in a language I didn't know, almost gypsy like, filled the room. The smell of incense permeated my nostrils. Movement caught my eyes. Taking a couple steps toward the studio, I could see Madame and Samantha dancing in the mirrored reflection.

What are they doing here? The sun isn't even up yet. The thought occurred to me to run back upstairs to Mark, knowing I would be caught. I tiptoed one step backward, and when I turned to leave, the floorboard creaked. I froze.

"Bonjour, Lenea," Madame's voice bellowed.

Damn it! I thought. *How did she know?* I stopped and turned around to face her, seeing only her reflection. She was standing, breathing heavily, her hands on her hips. I was nervous about what would come next.

"Good morning," I said, as cheerfully as I could, hoping Madame wouldn't mention anything about last night's dance, especially in front of Samantha.

Samantha was to her right and stood slightly behind. She didn't seem to notice or care about my presence, other than to slowly shake her head from side to side in a disapproving manner.

I was definitely aware of Samantha, though. Her long blond hair was slightly curled on the ends, and along with her flawlessly made-up face, she looked as if she were ready to audition for a Broadway musical. *Ugh!* Standing there in her high heels and expensive dance attire, she had that smug look on her face like, "I know where you were last night."

A wave of shame swept over me from the previous night's events. Madame spoke once more. "Lenea, there is something I want to tell you." Her face was emotionless as she spoke at me through the crimson mirror. "When you choose a song to represent your desire, don't think about it ... feel it."

Her words had me completely perplexed. Then Samantha chimed in, "Yes, feel ... sexy. Men like sexual women. They'll do anything for sex." Samantha's voice was smooth and sultry. She smiled with a look of worldliness in her eyes.

Madame's gaze shifted back upon herself as she closed her eyes and wrapped her arms around her body as if to demonstrate to me what she meant. I could see Samantha reflexively do the same.

Why did Samantha say that? My curiosity grew, pondering the possibility that she and perhaps Madame were part of this as well.

Their movements were almost synchronous, as if they had done this dance before. I began to get irritated. "Okay, I will," I said, merely to placate, before turning to walk down the hallway and out the door.

The morning air hit like a slap in the face. I took a few steps and stopped. Standing in the middle of the pavement, away from it all, my tears flowed like water from faucets. *This is ridiculous*, I told myself. *Stop this crying.*

The walk home was terrible as the world around me turned gray. I couldn't help but wonder if this was some kind of sick game that Mark and Madame were a part of. Was it a scheme to make more money? The thoughts made me ill.

My phone buzzed with a text from Mark: "Thank you for a wonderful night. Have a nice day. I will call you later."

I was so confused, having received so many mixed messages. Obviously if Mark didn't want others like Samantha to know about our relationship, it seemed he would try to hide me from Madame and anyone else at the studio. But he didn't. Each horrible thought began with an exaggerated question, and I searched for answers. By the time I got home, I still hadn't solved the dilemma and still did not feel any better.

Being in my own place was a welcome relief. I threw my bag on the bed and headed straight for the shower; I needed another one. After I turned on the hot water, the steam released and filled the bathroom. I drew the curtain and stepped inside. The water was the right hot. Meanwhile, my mind kept questioning the connection to the times I had seen the raven-haired woman. There must be a connection. Scene after scene ran through my mind as I tried to remember what had been going on each time she appeared: the moments in the studio, the sandwich shop, the L'abeille Palace, and now Mark's apartment. Standing there under the steaming water, it hit me again: *I have to read that book!*

Rinsing my hair quickly, I rushed out of the shower, dried myself off, and swiftly dressed. *Screw work! You're on top of it, and today you need answers!* I told myself sternly. I pulled the book out of my bag and sat on the end of the bed.

When I saw the photo on the front cover, vibrations filled my body. *Who is this woman? Why is she posing on the cover of a book and a painting in the*

171

studio? I took the book with me into the kitchen and grabbed a glass of water before moving to the couch to read.

The words were eloquently written and filled with flowery prose—surprising, considering they were stories about prostitution in the Wild West. I learned about the sex trade—the "flesh business" as many would call it. Mark's stories about the Mystere building were spot on. He was right about the saloon girls and the years of prohibition; the documentary was truly fascinating. I read stories of the hurdy gurdy girls, otherwise known as dance hall girls or saloon girls. They were simply young women trying to make money in a booming economy the only way they knew how.

The flesh business exploited these girls, certainly, as so often occurs when rapid wealth is acquired. However, it turned out not all of the women were prostitutes. In the 1900s, men outnumbered females almost two to one, and they were desperate for companionship. Some of the women learned how to parlay that into a financial advantage.

I read a story of a very smart couple, a man and woman who were business partners. They created an establishment where the men could purchase a dance card, and for a dime a dance, they enjoyed nonsexual female companionship. Hence, the "dancehall girls" concept was established. As long as there was no illegal activity occurring on the main floor of the establishment, no inappropriate touching or kissing, the police would look past any activities that occurred on the floors above.

Upstairs was an entirely different story. "Ladies of the night," "soiled doves," and "women of ill repute" were some of the names given to the girls who lived and worked there. The establishments of the rugged West were known far and wide for their wild activities.

It was intriguing to read the stories of these women's lives, especially given the advantage of modern insight. The dance hall girls, as an example, displayed acute business acumen, quickly determining it was better to exploit others than to be exploited by them. Showing off a little leg was a great way to make big money and didn't necessarily mean you had to go further and corrupt morals. The money generated would cover shelter, clothing, and food, as well as provide security so desperately needed in the harsh new wilderness. It was not a hard job for the desired benefits.

The prostitutes, on the other hand, were more like slaves. Their lives were controlled by a madam, who would act as an intermediary, negotiating fees and hourly rates with the customer based on the age-old axiom of supply and demand.

Each time I read the word "madam" throughout the book, I thought of the studio.

The following chapters were devoted to the "occupational hazards" of physical abuse, pregnancy, addictions, and venereal disease prostitutes faced. Reading tragic story after tragic story, I couldn't help but feel sorry for the women who had to endure such hardships.

The book received my complete attention, and I devoured page after page. It was so interesting that I forgot the real reason I was reading it. I turned the page at the height of a compelling story, and there she was: the raven-haired woman. Goose bumps raised up all over my body; a breeze of cool air brushed past my left cheek. The world went on pause, and I refused to look up, intent on finishing the story that began on the next page with the title "Lady M: The Queen of the Red Light District."

Lady M, otherwise known as Margaret, or Mattie for short, was a madam. And not simply any madam, but the best of the best at what she did. At the age of nineteen, she opened her first brothel in Kansas. She was an excellent businesswoman and figured out what men would pay to satisfy their needs. During the moral purity movement of the 1800s, she was driven out of town. She subsequently joined a wagon train heading west telling others she was a young widow. The story was certainly plausible and kept her from being cast in a negative light.

Traveling to seek a new home, entrepreneurial spirit coursing through her veins, she seized a profitable opportunity in traveling as a "wagon madam." Basically, she provided women for the miners living outside the cities by delivering the merchandise to the men in the field. Her business plan was simple: if the men couldn't get to the whores, she would take the whores to them.

She made a lot of money yet grew tired of the lifestyle. Financially secure at the age of twenty-eight, she looked for a place to settle down. She had passed through Colorado a handful of times on the way to the miners. It met all her needs: plenty of clients, plenty of money, and plenty of opportunity.

A year later, having studied the demographics as well as having established numerous potential business connections, the opportunity to purchase a brothel from the heir of an owner who had recently succumbed to tuberculosis availed itself. It was a fire sale, as the building owner didn't want to lose the lucrative lease that had been signed as well as the perks that accompanied the transaction. It was unheard of in those days for a woman, let alone a madam, to own an establishment. Females had always been relegated to the role of business associate to the male owner.

Mattie was intellectually astute and financially savvy. She also understood that the best way to keep the politicians and police out of her business was to befriend them. She became intimately involved in the politics. Some would say it was because of her ability to win over an audience. Others were more convinced it was the perks she provided to the legislators. Regardless, she was known to have connections in high places.

Her establishments were reputed to have "the prettiest girls, the most upscale service, excellent food, and the best whiskey." As her reputation grew, so did her business and she opened several "parlor houses" along the red light district. They came to be known as the "finest establishments a rich, lonely miner could partake west of the Mississippi." Her story didn't end there.

Mattie was young and beautiful and fell in love with a handsome foot runner named Cort Thompson. He was a man who made his money running foot races, the predecessor to modern-day track and field. Their relationship was fast and furious, and after only a few weeks of seeing one another, he asked her to marry him. She was love-struck and said yes. They set a wedding date for a month later.

The following week, Mattie interviewed a potential employee who was known to have recently worked for Mattie's competition, Kate Fulton. During their meeting Cort came bounding in the door with exciting news. Mattie apologized for the interruption and introduced Cort to the girl as her fiancé.

The young prostitute recognized him and was aghast. Everyone in the other brothel knew Cort as the longtime boyfriend of Kate Fulton, and she could not believe Mattie didn't know. She decided to hold her tongue until Cort left the room. Wanting revenge on her previous boss, but also thinking she might get hired by gaining Mattie's trust, she revealed Cort and Kate's relationship.

Lady M became furious. She dismissed the girl, saddled up, and immediately rode to the other madam, confronting her and challenging her to a duel. But not simply any duel. Mattie always had a flair for the dramatic and was constantly looking for a way to capitalize on the moment to advertise herself and her business. She suggested they fire at twenty-five paces, topless. Kate Fulton agreed.

The next day, hundreds gathered to watch the event as the two met in a "bare breasted shootout." When their bullets missed each other, they decided to call a truce. Instead, they agreed to settle their dilemma with the flip of a coin. The winner got Cort. The loser had to leave town.

Lady M won and ended up marrying the man shortly thereafter. The other madam was driven out of Colorado.

The publicity of the topless shootout was excellent for Lady M's business. Unfortunately for Mattie, though, the man she loved turned out to be nothing more than a gold digger. Still, she was smitten and overlooked his indiscretions as well as his mounting gambling debts. Her desire and love for him outshone the money losses, and she ignored his many failings.

They ran with the movers and shakers of the political machine. Lady M continued to earn her reputation as not only the most successful madam in the American West, but as a very astute business owner and capitalist. Her investments grew considerably and made her one of the richest women in America.

Unfortunately, time tested their relationship. She could overlook the financial miscues but couldn't ignore the sexual indiscretions, having caught her husband spending too much time with one of the girls. Ironically, she filed for a divorce claiming "moral impropriety." The year was 1891.

He, of course, wanted all of her wealth and money, but he ended up walking away with nothing. She had the wisdom and foresight to invest in her name only before and during the marriage, and the divorce left him with little recourse but to accept the pittance she had offered him, knowing full well he would squander it.

She looked into his eyes and realized he had suffered enough; she still loved him terribly, and she forgave him. She survived well into the twentieth century, although he passed away shortly after their reconciliation.

By 1910, the Wild West was starting to close its saloon doors. But Lady M refused to believe that the Old West would bow before the march of civilization. In 1911, she purchased the famous House of Mirrors from the estate of another madam who had once usurped her title as queen of the red light district. To declare her victory, she had her name, M. Silks, inlaid in the tile on the doorstep, thereby demonstrating once again that Lady M reigned supreme.

The closing epitaph was succinct: Lady M would be known as "A woman of sound judgment—except when it came to the men in her life. It's obvious she was an intelligent, sharp businesswoman. She made it in a man's world. However, we don't know what she thought, what she felt, or what motivated her. It's a tragedy that she left no diary or letters."

Closing the book, my arms covered with more goose bumps, it suddenly dawned on me: Lady M sounded like me. I wasn't simply transferring my own relationship issues from Richard onto Mark. Instead, I was being visited by the spirit of this woman for a reason! Maybe she chose me because I would understand her story.

Putting the pieces together in my mind was the challenge, wondering how The Mystere, the L'abeille Palace, and the studio were all related. Even though there was no recorded history of the madams of the Mystere, the missing pieces clearly were connected. Who else would run the most expensive bordello? A great weight was lifted off my shoulders. Everything was beginning to make sense. Now the goal was to confirm why she chose me.

Reflecting upon my own personal situation, including memories of my life from growing up to now, it was clear to me I was being visited by a spirit from the past. Until recently, I had no idea what a spirit was. *Was She like my imaginary friend when I was five?*

Taking a seat in front of my computer, I searched the Internet for the information using certain keywords: "ghost," "spirit," "past lives," and more. Each topic led to other links and other words to search. Before long, early afternoon had arrived. My work was going to have to wait until tomorrow.

After making a grilled cheese sandwich for dinner, I sat back down at the computer to continue my search. Devouring my meal, I learned all about spirit manifestation. Surprisingly, there was a lot of speculation and conjecture, but very little hard evidence, when it came to the paranormal—in this case, ghosts. And, in order to understand how ghosts manifest themselves in the physical world, it was necessary to learn about the two main types of haunting: residual and intelligent.

If the ghost or apparition is appearing in the same place and performing the same task every time, chances are that it is a residual haunting. The theory behind this type of haunting is that certain minerals, usually limestone or quartz, can act as a type of recording mechanism that takes an imprint of highly emotionally charged events and can play them back if the atmospheric conditions are right. In many ways, it is like having a direct window into the past, in that you are witnessing an actual event, repeated before your eyes, even though it actually occurred several years ago.

With these types of manifestations, the apparitions interact with the environment as if it were in their time, not necessarily current time. For example, if a person lived in an old place that had been renovated over the years, you might see a ghost walk up an invisible set of stairs or pass through a solid wall. According to residual haunting theory, this could be because there might have been stairs or might not have been a wall present when the spirit was living. You are merely a spectator, and the entity doesn't even know you are there.

Intelligent hauntings, on the other hand, happen when the entity a person encounters interacts with the person or otherwise seems aware of his or her presence. These ghosts manifest by pulling energy out of the environment and using it to manifest their image to the living. Thus, the location where an apparition or entity has been spotted will usually be ten to twenty degrees colder than the surrounding environment. Apparently this is because the entity pulls the heat and energy out of the atmosphere to facilitate manifestation, creating a so-called cold spot.

My eyes widened, completely fascinated, as I continued my search. Reading about energy and how it can neither be created nor destroyed according to the first law of thermodynamics, something called entropy, was interesting. I read of an attempt to explain why batteries and other electronic equipment sometimes go dead when a ghost manifests. It was also suggested that paranormal entities have the ability to pull electric energy from the environment, which might explain why energy-supplying equipment stops working in the presence of ghosts.

This also seemed to be the case with electromagnetic fields. Our brains, and by proxy our whole bodies, are run with electromagnetism. It is believed, due in part to the fact that Earth itself is covered by an electromagnetic field, that paranormal manifestations are accompanied by a flux or abnormal change in that field.

The information kept flowing. I enjoyed the process of discovery, allowing the scientist in me to come out. I love science. Proven facts have so much more truth than emotions.

Next up was an article about paranormal investigators and how they use the electromagnetic field detector as part of their toolbox, taking base readings in an environment so that any spikes in the field can be noted. It was recently hypothesized and subsequently discovered that wherever there are high levels of electromagnetism and a human crosses the threshold, it induces feelings of paranoia, sickness, or even hallucinations in that person.

Suddenly I began to recall my own personal experiences of what I felt at the deli, the studio, and Mark's loft after having been visited by the raven-haired woman. I remembered how it had started with coldness in the air, followed by nausea, and finally it felt as if I had been hallucinating.

Everything I read matched up perfectly. But I still had no answer as to why a ghost would choose to manifest before me. *Why would she choose me?* I shifted on the couch, placing a pillow behind my neck for support.

I read several stories of others who experienced this type of activity. It helped to know I was not alone. The interesting correlation I made between the stories was that none of the ghosts were there to do physical or mental harm. Rather, they were probably trying to figure out a personal problem from their physical existence on Earth and were being delayed in this realm until the answer was revealed and they could move on into the light.

Then a link took me to story after story of spirits attaching themselves to humans, trying to live vicariously through them to find answers they didn't receive in their own lifetimes. I felt an inner vibration, a knowing; this seemed to be my situation. The raven-haired woman, in spiritual form, was Lady M. In her life, she had issues trusting men. *Yup, it sounded just like me.* I looked up to the ceiling, talking out loud as if she could hear me: "I will find an answer, Lady M." I waited a moment for a response, a validation that my thoughts were real; nothing.

Still, I was so excited about my findings! I took great solace in the possibility that I wasn't going crazy and this was definitely not a new situation. The thought crossed my mind that, with a little help from a local medium, I could more than likely find answers.

I typed "spiritual medium" into the search engine and spotted an ad that didn't look too threatening. I picked up the phone and called the number. Chills filled my body once again, knowing this was indeed the connection to it all.

A woman answered the phone in a pleasant tone, a faint Southern accent noticeable. "Thank you for calling Spirit and Source. How may I help you?"

"I am curious about the sessions you offer for understanding spiritual connections," I began, not really knowing what I was talking about, but using the language from the ad as my guide. "Is this something you can help me with?"

"Oh yes. Lillie is the name of our medium connecting us to the spiritual realm," she responded matter-of-factly, as if I knew how the whole medium thing worked. "The initial visit is seventy-five dollars, and we can work out plans for anything scheduled into the future." Happy with a reasonable fee and knowing additional sessions were optional, I booked my appointment for the following Tuesday morning.

The moment I hung up, my phone buzzed. It was a text from Mark: "Still working. Be done around 5. Dinner?"

My fingers quickly replied to the text: "Yes!"

He must have felt my energy through the phone, and responded with a smiley face emoticon.

Looking at the clock and seeing there was still plenty of time before dinner, I opened the refrigerator and saw the fresh cooked chicken and raw vegetables I had picked up for the weekend. "Oops," I said aloud, "I totally forgot about you."

I picked up my phone and texted back: "My place. 6 p.m. Chicken and veggies. You bring the wine. :)"

His text came back: "Looking forward to it! To you. ;)"

Rapture coursed through my veins as I turned on my favorite music and turned my attention to cleaning the apartment. The energy was flowing.

Mark and I spent Friday night together, then Saturday and Sunday. We laughed, shared stories, watched movies, and acted as if no one else in the world existed except the two of us. We left the bedroom only to grab food and drink. It was truly wonderful to live off each other's energy, making love both physically and emotionally. Monday morning came too fast.

21

How Do We Work with This?

Monday morning began as a repeat of the previous week. Mark went back to the studio early in the morning, and I worked until it was time for class. When Mark left this time, there was an undeniable love for one another between us; this was something much more than a one-night stand or a fly-by-night relationship. This seemed more like the beginning of a partnership with a man I could spend the rest of my life with. He was someone I definitely envisioned myself having babies with.

The morning tasks were completed in record time. After closing my computer, I grabbed my gym bag and headed out to the studio. I entered the street level, the air was crisp and clear. I was giddy thinking of the week ahead, knowing all Mark and I had planned together. Seeing the girls again too was joyous. Even the thought of Samantha didn't bother me now. I realized the disgust with her might be more related to Lady M than me.

Entering the studio, I felt empowered, strong, and sexy. I was excited to see what Madame had in store for our session. I looked up and saw Chrissy and couldn't wait to share with her about Mark. Today was going to be a spectacular session.

Madame paced around our group sitting on the floor, gently swatting a riding crop in her hand in concert with her steps; her eyes glared down, focusing on each of us from across the circle. "We have a celebration today, ladies," she began in her stern French voice. "One of our own has had a very enlightening experience she would like to share."

For a moment I thought she was talking about me, but Julia stood instead. I was relieved and excited to hear what she had to say. We didn't really know each other that well, since she was much more reserved than the rest of the group, but I had respect and honor for her as part of the "sisterhood," as Madame called it.

"I finally figured out what has made me so angry about the people who don't support me," she began, her voice wavering. "I never realized that my anger with them was simply a reflection of anger within myself." She paused for a moment, looked around at the intent faces with their eyes fixated upon her, and continued her soliloquy. "Once I figured out the source of the anger, thanks to Madame and our private lessons, I was able to release the anger, forgive those who hurt me, and make peace within and, therefore, peace with all." She sat back down.

We all clapped and congratulated Julia for her courage to talk and share her experience.

Julia definitely appeared younger and more vibrant than I had ever seen her before. Something had truly changed in her. I'm not sure I really understood or connected to what she was saying about a "reflection within herself," but nonetheless I was happy for her.

Madame began to pace around our circle of five again. We all sat motionless, wondering if we would be called upon. She continued with the riding crop, again pounding in cadence with each step of her slow march. Her eyes and face were stone as she stopped and looked across the group. "I believe Jessica also has something to share."

Jessica sat next to me on my left and stood up quickly, her body language very different from Julia's. Yet she also looked happier and healthier. It seemed she looked lighter too, like she had lost weight, compared to the last time I had seen her.

She cleared her throat, looked around at everyone, and her eyes began to well up with tears before she spoke. "I have been working with

YOU & I, INC.

Madame privately over the last three years. Since then, I have started to lose weight and gain confidence in myself. My fear of men and the fear they would harm me sexually has been replaced with love." Tears of joy were now running down her face; she wiped them away. "During this time, a loving man has entered my life. Madame helped me deal with my emotions surrounding this relationship. And now"—she hesitated, taking a deep breath—"we're engaged to be married in the Spring! I have no idea how all of these dreams have come true"—she stopped and gestured at the standing figure across from her—"but I have Madame to thank for everything." She began to cry freely, and Madame walked over to hug her. They rocked back and forth several times; Jessica's crying grew more intense.

Madame reached up and whispered something into her ear. Jessica turned to the circle, pumping her fist into the air and screamed, "I'm free!"

The primordial nature of the sound took us all by surprise, but I could tell it was from her heart. "And I deserve this!" Again she yelled in a loud voice as she held her left hand up, pointing at the diamond ring that twinkled brightly on her ring finger. We all stood up and took turns hugging her before returning to our seated positions.

Madame paced around the circle once more. This time she stopped across from Chrissy. "Chrissy?" She pointed with her whip.

Chrissy was beaming from ear to ear. "I also have an announcement to make too," she said as she rose up to her feet. Taking a deep breath, she closed her eyes; she then opened them to look at all of us. "I have been sober for two weeks now since working with Madame, and I've felt more joy in my life than ever. I love all of you, and I'm so thankful for your friendship."

Again we all clapped and she returned to her seated position. Julia reached over to hug her. I was truly happy for Chrissy; for everyone who had shared today. While I didn't fully understand how they had accomplished these things, the gratitude they showed Madame as their guide was genuine. It gave me hope I could accomplish my goals as well. I looked over at Samantha, who looked at me. We both knew we were the only ones who had not yet made our desires a reality. I glared at her as she glared back in competition. Now I was definitely determined to make this happen.

Madame began her march around the circle again, this time more relaxed. Maybe she was humbled by the praise she had received. Maybe she would go easy on us tonight during our workout. "Ladies, thank you for your inspiring stories. For those of you who have not yet fulfilled your desires … keep with it. Every day dreams come true."

She turned and walked over to the stereo to turn it on. The dance music blared, with bass resonating throughout my chest. On cue, we all stood and walked to the middle of the floor to begin our warm-ups.

It felt so good to move my body to the music. Closing my eyes to stretch, I pretended Mark was watching me and I was trying to seduce him. I was inspired by these women and their success, and it seemed as though I was very close to a breakthrough of my own—trusting a man again.

This woman must do some kind of magic, I thought. It didn't matter what it was; for the first time in my life, I was seeing results and wasn't about to quit. Soon it would be my turn in the circle.

The vibe in warm-ups was more intense than in the past sessions; there was more joy, more excitement, and more effort from all. Everyone was enjoying the music and the atmosphere. A new song started to play, and Madame instructed us all to go to our poles. It was thrilling to build on what we had learned and I was anxious for the new moves I hoped Madame would teach us today.

"Now"—Madame paused to ensure she had our attention—"we are going to learn how to climb." Standing before our poles, we were all eager to follow her instructions. "It's not enough to dance the emotion of your desires. In order to make your desires a reality, you must climb the ladder to grasp what you can see, though it appears slightly out of reach." She pointed upward. "I have attached a stuffed animal to the ceiling at the top of your pole. The stuffed animal represents your desire."

Looking up, I could see a small white unicorn attached to the top of my pole. It never dawned on me how high the poles reached—maybe eleven or twelve feet.

"For those of you who have already achieved your original desire," Madame continued, "think of a new desire to accomplish, and place that thought at the top of your pole. Ladies, desires never stop. They are placed in our hearts for a reason. And fulfilling them is our destiny, our purpose." She used the crop for effect, pounding her hand with it, then pointing at us. "We climb by defying gravity and testing our strength."

She set the crop down, then put her words into action as she climbed effortlessly to the top of her pole, unharnessed the small pink stuffed elephant, and slid back down with grace and ease. "Okay, ladies, you saw how it's done. Now it is your turn." She turned up the music in an effort to intensify our determination.

I stepped to my pole and jumped on. *Hand over hand, like Madame, that's how I'm going to do it!* It was much harder than it looked. She definitely made it look easy. Struggling terribly, I tried to pull myself up the pole, but I slid back to the floor. Looking around the room, I saw that everyone seemed to have the same struggle, with the exception of Samantha.

Samantha had waited for someone to watch her, apparently, before beginning her climb on the same pole Madame had used. As I made eye contact with her, she nodded her head with a "watch me" look of confidence, grabbed the pole with both hands and wrapped one leg around the base, then ascended to the top with ease. She touched the ceiling where the stuffed animal had been before sliding back down.

Ugh! Sometimes I so badly want to be like Samantha; she makes everything look so easy! Staring at my pole, I was more determined than ever to make it to the top. *That stuffy is mine!* I thought. Again I made my attempt, only to run out of strength and energy barely short of my goal.

Madame walked around, helping those of us who couldn't quite get it. "You must use your legs to form a base and your arms to climb," she shouted above the din of the pulsating music. "Do not let your mind tell you that you cannot attain your desire. Focus. Focus on your breathing and your body. Your mind will quit long before your body does." She stopped to support Chrissy, saying something barely audible as Chrissy nodded in understanding.

The music shifted to a Samba beat, I looked over and watched Samantha climb the pole. Again, she did it with little effort. She was very fluid and serpentine in her ascent. I decided to try to copy her moves. *You can do this!* I told myself.

It took me three tries, but soon I was perched at the top of the pole. I felt so proud of my achievement and began to unharness my stuffed unicorn. The ribbon was knotted and wouldn't untie. My legs began to shake as I clung tightly, trying to keep my base. Soon I became very frustrated. Looking up and into the mirror, I could see Samantha had climbed her pole again; this time she leaned back to slide down, stopped short of the ground, put both hands out, and cartwheeled off onto the floor into full splits. She did it so gracefully.

"You must focus!" Madame's words brought me back to reality. "If you pay attention to others and not your own desire, you will never attain it. You'll simply waste your energy."

"It's stuck. It's in a knot," I whined, hoping to gain some sympathy. I should have known better.

"Do you want someone else to get your desire for you, Lenea?" She pointed in the direction of Samantha, who was already at the top of the pole again, frozen in a position nearly identical to mine. "Maybe she also thinks he's hot!" Madame yelled, "Maybe she can't believe he's single! Maybe, just maybe, she desires the same thing!" She whipped her hand, this time harder. "Is that what you want?"

Madame shook her head in disgust, frustrated, before turning and walking over to Julia, spotting her in preparation for a backward waterfall.

I was pissed at Madame's words. *No fucking way is anyone taking my desire!* The thought gave me renewed energy. My fingers squeezed on the ribbon, unable to untie the knot. It made me sick, the thought of Samantha dancing for Mark, swaying her hips seductively to entice him as he held his palette in his hand. My legs were shaking badly as I looked at myself in the mirror; my reflection began to blur. A chill passed over me.

The mirror continued to shift and transform until a grayish darkness appeared. I could feel the sweat on my face and forehead as my face felt pale. There, walking through the grayish haze was the translucent hue of several women, each appearing in different sections of the mirrors throughout the room. They were the women I had seen in the photos of the book. I swerved my head left and right. They were everywhere, walking toward me slowly, the raven-haired woman leading the group.

My legs gave way first, my arms flailing for the pole. It was too late. I slipped and fell hard to the ground. Immediately I reached for my right groin as a shooting pang, like that of a stabbing knife inserted in my inner right thigh, caused me to wince. "Ow! Ow! Ow!"

Madame and the rest of the class rushed over.

"Oh my God, Lenea. Are you okay?" Chrissy exclaimed. Madame was right behind her. As long as I had known her, she remained stoic with virtually no emotion. Now she showed genuine concern.

"I'm fine," I said, trying not to grimace. "That's obviously not the way to get down." No one laughed. All the girls were around me now.

"Okay, Ladies," Madame said, taking control of the moment, "this is a great example of how we must always be in our bodies when we are dancing, especially when we are climbing on a pole. I want all of you to climb three more times, and I'll be back." She turned to me, concern again on her face. "Let's get some ice on you." She helped me to stand, and we walked over to the kitchenette area, around the corner.

I sat on a chair while she opened the freezer door, pulled a tray of ice cubes out, and proceeded to empty the tray into a plastic bag she had pulled from a cabinet drawer. She tied off the end, grabbed a kitchen towel, and set the bag in my lap.

She squatted in front of me and put her hands on my knee, looking very seriously into my eyes. "What scared you, Lenea? Did you see something?"

Indeed, I was scared, but I wasn't quite sure what had happened. Also, I was uncertain if I felt comfortable enough to tell her I had seen ghosts coming out of the mirror. She'd probably think I was crazy.

"Nothing," I responded, my face betraying my words. "I didn't see anything. I just ... I just slipped. I'm clumsy."

The look on her face changed as she carefully observed my actions and reactions. She let the words digest for a moment. Then she leaned in toward me, her dark brown eyes very serious. "Look at me, Lenea. I know you can see the spirits." She waited for my reaction, which must have been incredulous.

How did she know? How could she know? She paused for effect to let the words sink in and then continued. "But you must not let them frighten you, for that is not why they are here. They are here to teach you. Do not be afraid of them. Listen to what they are telling you, and you will learn. Do you understand?"

Nodding, still pale from the pain, I wasn't sure how to react to what I had just been told.

"You keep that ice there and rest until the class is finished." She stood and walked over to the girls, barking out instructions for more pull-ups. Madame closed the class by congratulating the group of women on their accomplishment, for they had all finished the task. They were beaming from ear to ear.

As I sat there in utter disbelief, the ice began to soothe the throbbing of my inner thigh. *What did she mean? And how did she know I can see spirits? Can she see the spirits?*

The class ended shortly thereafter. All the girls came to check on me. All except for Samantha, that is and whom I didn't see leave, which was good. I wanted nothing to do with her. They all patted me on the back and gave me hugs, wishing me a speedy recovery. Chrissy promised to call later.

Everyone had left. Madame turned the music off, blew out the candles, and walked over to me. "Let's see if you are able to walk. Stand up." She put her arm under and around my shoulder to provide support. My right leg was throbbing, and it hurt to put my full weight on it. Still, I could walk with a slight hobble. "Okay. You are able to walk. That's good. But if the pain continues, you may need to see a doctor."

"Thank you, Madame," I said, gathering up my things. "I'm sorry I disappointed you."

She stopped, her eyes half squinting introspectively. "You haven't disappointed me. You have many gifts, Lenea. The spirits aren't here to hurt you; they are here to help you find your desires. But the lessons you are to learn are complicated. I hope you feel better. See you on Thursday." She reached up and hugged me. I hugged her back, feeling warmth from her for the first time.

"Madame, why are they here? What lessons are you talking about?" I asked. Now that she had opened the door, I eagerly awaited an answer. Somehow the thought of Madame knowing about the spirits made me feel I wasn't alone anymore and maybe I wasn't going crazy.

"We will talk about this more at your next private lesson. I do not have time to go into detail. For now, know that the fear you are experiencing is meant to be a teacher, not a guide. Therefore, there is nothing to fear. Au revoir." She walked out the door, her heels clicking down the hallway.

I stood there half-shocked. *What do I do now?* Part of me was happy to know the spirits were nothing to fear, but why? Hobbling down the hallway, the questions in my mind kept coming. *How does she know the lessons I need to learn? How does she know there is nothing to fear? Even more, why am I apologizing to this woman? She should be apologizing to me. This is ridiculous!*

I came to the end of the hallway and saw Mark standing in the waiting area. "Hey Len!" he called out in a delighted voice. He reached down and kissed me on the cheek. It was fulfilling to hear his new nickname for me, but I wasn't sure how to explain my injury to him. Fortunately, he didn't seem to notice. "I've got a few sittings this afternoon and evening. I'll call you later, okay? I simply wanted to give you a hug and kiss before you left." He leaned in and did just that. "I've got to run," he said, darting out into the afternoon haze. It was a relief not to talk with him about my injury, but sad not to spend our normal time together.

The pain intensified as I limped home. By the time I got in the door, I could hardly walk. It was excruciating. I made my way to the bathroom to inspect the injury. When I pulled down my panties, I could see a knot about the size of a marble had formed on the right-hand crease of my groin and upper thigh. It was huge, and I could feel it move underneath my skin. It hurt like hell. Feeling very scared, I debated going to the emergency room. Instead I picked up the phone and called my doctor's office. Luckily they had a cancellation and could see me right away. It was a challenge, but I made it to my car and immediately headed there.

As I drove, I couldn't stop thinking about Madame and her knowledge of the spirits and her implication that Samantha had the same desire for Mark that I did. It was Samantha who had made me so pissed off that I lost focus. Maybe she had something to do with the spirits. Maybe she was in cahoots with Madame. Somehow, someway, I saw Lady M and what must have been her "girls" marching toward me. *Were they trying to send me a message? Were they coming to help me? Maybe she was there to warn me about Samantha. But why a group of women? What could they teach me?*

The traffic was light that Monday afternoon, allowing me to drive to the doctor's office in no time. After parking the car, I checked in at the reception desk and looked for a seat in the packed waiting room. *Ugh!* I thought. There's nothing worse than being in a doctor's office with sick people all around you; especially when you're the only one who is physically hurt. I reached for a magazine to pass the time.

I couldn't stop thinking about the session. *Why did it seem that every time I talked about Samantha or even when she became the focus of my attention, Lady M appeared to warn me?*

A nurse opened the door and looked down at the chart in her hand. "Lenea?"

Raising my hand, I set the magazine down and stood to follow her into the exam room.

The doctor's diagnosis was an inguinal hernia. He said it most likely happened because of a weakened area in my abdominal wall, and the injury created a tear that allowed my intestines to poke through; that was the bulge I was feeling. Unfortunately, this hernia was larger than most, and even though it wasn't life-threatening, it would require surgery to have it repaired. In the meantime, I was to limit my activities: no heavy lifting or exercising. Even going to the bathroom could be painful until I had the surgery. Until then, I was told not to engage in strenuous activities.

When I told him about my dance classes, he said moderate movement was okay, but definitely no pole. He also informed me that bending over, lifting heavy objects, coughing, and having sex were discouraged. *Great,* I thought, *there goes my sex life.* He also encouraged me to "see a specialist right away," warning me about further complications that could result if I didn't get it repaired soon. Finally, he gave me a prescription for pain medication.

Carefully sitting in my car, trying not to strain myself, I shut the door, grasped the steering wheel, and looked straight ahead, seething with anger. I screamed in frustration and anguish. All I wanted to do was feel strong and sexy, and now I had a piece of my small intestine protruding, causing burning pain. *Super! No sex, no dancing, and definitely no confidence. What the hell?*

Picturing the conversation I would have with Madame, the questions poured forth: *How are we going to work with this? Now how do my dreams and desires come to fruition with an injury like this?* I raged at her, reminded of how she had us climbing the poles that set me up for this injury. *Why didn't she tell me about the spirits before? And now, another bill! How much is insurance going to pay for this? Will they even cover it?*

Looking in the rearview mirror, I saw a crying mess of a woman. *This is not what I wanted!* I thought. Wiping away my tears, I turned the ignition on and headed to the pharmacy to pick up my prescription.

The only good thing that happened all day was finding a parking spot by the elevator to my apartment. Every other step to the apartment only made my groin hurt worse. I opened the door and walked in, my phone rang. It was Mark. *Ugh! I didn't want to answer it.* On the last ring before voice mail, I hit the green button. "Hey Mark!" I tried to sound upbeat instead of pathetic.

"Hey, Sunshine, how are you? I miss you," he said playfully.

"Not so good," I answered. "I got hurt today in class. I fell off the pole. The doctor said I have a hernia and I'm going to need surgery." I tried to hold the tears back, but it was no use.

His voice turned to concern. "Oh my gosh, Lenea! What can I do for you?"

"Nothing," I replied, half sobbing. "I think I'm going to go to bed early tonight and see how I feel in the morning."

"I'm coming over!" he insisted.

"No, Mark, you don't understand. I ... I ... I need to be left alone for now. Can you respect that?" The pause on the other end lasted for several seconds. "Do you understand?" I asked, wondering if he was still there. It wasn't that I didn't want to see him; I simply wasn't ready to tell him all of the details.

"Okay," he agreed reluctantly, "but if you need anything—*anything*—you call me. See you soon."

It felt good to put my feet up on the coffee table. Shortly thereafter, I took my pain medication and fell asleep, trying to make sense of what had happened that day. *Why me?*

22

A Look Into The Mirror

A loud knock on my door woke me from a deep slumber. Looking at the clock, I realized it was 8 a.m. *How did I sleep so late?* I thought dragging myself out of bed and walking over to the door. I looked through the peephole. It was Mark, with flowers in hand. Hurriedly, I ran my fingers through my hair and pinched my cheeks in the mirror to freshen my appearance before opening the door.

"Hey, Sunshine," he said. He walked in and gave me a warm hug. "These are for you." He handed me the bouquet of colorful wildflowers. "I promised not to come over last night, but you didn't say anything about this morning," he said with a sly grin on his face.

"Thanks," I said, recognizing his literal humor. "I can't believe you're here. Don't you have classes today?"

"I got a pass for the day. What can I do for you?" he asked.

After pausing for a moment, I responded, "Now that I think about it, my bathroom could use a good cleaning. You'll find the toilet brush under the sink," I said, trying to add levity without feeling sorry for myself.

"That sounds like a *crappy* job. What a *waste* of time."

His reply shocked me. It took me a moment, and then I got the humor. Though I wanted to come up with some great comeback, my mind got stuck and I couldn't think of any. I rolled my eyes and shook my head.

"What? Can't keep up with me?" he joshed further. "I see your cheeks are getting *flushed*." The Cheshire cat grin grew more obvious as the twinkle in his eyes grew brighter.

This prompted me to laugh out loud. It was obvious he wasn't about to stop there.

"Look," he said. His face turned more serious, pausing dramatically, lifting his hands as if to stop the conversation, "I can see you're getting *pissed*." He took a deep sigh. "Relax. *Shit* happens!"

Mark had me laughing so hard I had to hold on to my sides. He turned theatrically and acted as if he were going to walk out the door.

"I'm sorry. I can tell this conversation is headed *down the drain*," he continued.

"No, don't go!" I said, seeing he might be serious.

He ran over to the couch like a little boy excited to play his next video game. "You like my humor? That's a good sign. Most people can't keep up. It's my curse—or blessing, depending on how you look at it. Now *wipe* that smile off your face because I am *pooped*."

"Oh my gosh. You are hilarious. Where did you learn how to joke like that?" I asked continuing to laugh.

"It's a family thing. Believe me, when you meet my family, you'll understand." He smiled, closed his eyes and nodded knowingly.

He wants me to meet his family? I thought to myself. *That is usually a good sign; a very good sign.*

His face turned serious. "What happened yesterday, Len?" he asked. His face showed concern; he was intent on listening.

Closing my eyes, I took a deep breath, ready to level with him about everything. *If this is a man I can trust, he needs to be tested.* "Mark, I have something to tell you." He looked at me inquisitively, adjusted himself on the couch to better hear me, and focused his attention on my words.

Not quite sure what to say, I hesitated. "Well …" The phone rang, interrupting the conversation. The cell phone screen displayed the caller ID: the studio. "Excuse me; I'd better get that."

"Lenea? This is Shannon." Her voice sounded hurried. "How are you?"

"I'm fine," I said, not really wanting to get into things over the phone.

"Oh good. Madame told me what happened. She asked me to call and make sure you were okay," she responded. "Also, she wanted to know if you could switch your class on Thursday night to Thursday at noon."

"I don't think I can dance with this hernia." I looked at Mark while saying the words, reminded of the injury.

"No worries. There is no dance necessary," she said trying to reassure me. "Madame can still work with you and your desires. Does noon on Thursday work for you?"

"Yes, yes, I suppose I could do that," I replied, checking my mental calendar.

"Thanks. Great. Well, take care of yourself, and we'll see you then." She hung up.

"It was Shannon from the studio changing my class with Madame to noon on Thursday," I explained to Mark.

"Probably because of the couples class on Thursday night," he explained. "You're still coming with me, I hope?"

"Yes! I can't wait to see what the class is all about. I wonder if it will be anything like our experience the other night." I couldn't hide the delight in my voice.

"Knowing Madame, she most likely has something up her sleeve. I'm not supposed to say anything, but this new group is primarily married couples." Mark looked away. "She's always had a desire to work with couples. For many years her work has focused on single men and women. I'm excited to see what she has planned."

Mark had an unusual look on his face; it was more serious than normal. He appeared to be contemplating something significant. He looked at me for several moments, not saying a word. He looked down before again looking up at me. "Lenea," he began, "do you ever want to get married again?"

The question took me by surprise, numbing my mind. I wasn't quite sure how to respond. "Well," I searched for the words, "the answer is yes, sort of. You see, I'm not sure I could ever trust a man again after what I've been through. I don't think it would be fair to my partner if I doubted him." Recognizing him shifting uncomfortably, I changed my tone. "But I am working on it. Madame is hopefully going to help and work some of her magic. So the answer is yes, I do want to be married again."

"Well, the studio and Madame are the right place for that help. When I met Madame many years ago, I had just gone through a divorce as well. I didn't trust women." He looked up and into the distance. "I've had several relationships in the past few years, and some I thought were headed toward marriage. They all ended because the woman found someone else or couldn't handle who I am." He looked over at me. "Have you ever heard of the peacock theory?"

"No. What is the peacock theory?" I asked, wondering where he was going with this.

"The concept was first introduced by Charles Darwin in his book *On the Origin of Species*. It was part of his theory of natural selection. The concept of sexual selection refers to the process of choice, typically by females over males.

"Bird species are a great example of sexual selection. Due to their lightweight body structures, fights between males are ineffective or impractical. So, instead, male birds use other methods to try and seduce the females. For example: color, song, or movement." Mark was getting worked up telling his story. "In the peacock world, male birds with the most ornate and colorful feathers win. The theory behind the ornamentation of peacock trains is that the more extensive his fan is, and the more he shakes his feathers toward a peahen"—he stuck his hands out and shook them—"the greater the likelihood there is of snagging her. Researchers found that peacocks with drab fans and little to shake got left behind and never, you know, mated. Peacocks aren't monogamous, so the females all want to mate with the male whose feathers are brightest or most attractive."

His extensive knowledge on the most inane subjects never ceased to surprise me. Then again, maybe he had told this story before. It was different, though, to hear him talk from a male perspective. Thinking he may have been launching another round of jokes at first, I waited for the punch line; but he was serious. All I could do was listen, learn, and nod my head in understanding.

"Ever wonder why you never see a peacock in a cage at the zoo?"

I shook my head.

"If you put a peacock in a cage, he loses his colors. The peahen then quickly loses interest in the peacock and will not mate with him at all. The peahen can't be coaxed out of this state in any way. All the peahen cares about is a peacock with bright feathers. You get my point?" He looked at me, waiting for a response, but I was confused and slowly shook my head.

"Lenea, it's an analogy for human marriage. We, as men, do all we can to shake our tail feathers: go to the gym, wear nice clothes, buy a nice car. Then, when we get married, we trade the sports car in for a minivan. Nice clothes become a new pair of sweatpants. Going to the gym is something we do once a year, to renew our annual membership. We get a little belly, start to lose some hair, and next thing you know, another peacock comes around shaking his bright feathers, and *boom!* She's off. The woman craves and desires marriage, but after a few years she starts asking questions like, 'Where's the man I married?' What she is saying is that she really wants to be married to a peacock, not a peahen. Do you get it?"

Listening to his analogy made some sense, but I had never really thought about it this way.

His voice grew to a fevered pitch. "We are then left in the dust as she goes off and has an affair or, for no apparent reason, decides to get a divorce. But if you dig deeper, you find *she only wants to mate with peacocks!*" He smiled and shook his hands over his head for effect.

"Yes, but couldn't that go both ways?" I argued. "I see just as many men leave their wives for better tail feathers, if you catch my drift." The passion in my voice matched his.

He cleared his throat. "You're right; it's sad," he said wistfully, ruminating as he spoke. "People don't get the difference between sex and the power of sexual energy. If only they could get the training we've had." He smiled again as he looked into my eyes.

I wasn't sure what he was smiling about. This didn't seem like a humorous conversation. I cocked my head to the side and asked him, "Do you think people can stay married and faithful to one another? Is it even possible?" I asked, as much to myself as to the man in front of me.

"It's definitely not our nature to stay true to one another," he replied, "and definitely not over the course of forty to fifty years of marriage. You see, I don't think it is divorce that's ruining this country, or even adultery, but the hatred and lack of trust men and women develop for the other partner when they're trapped in the cage of marriage."

Thinking about what he said, I couldn't tell if there was a purpose to this conversation or if he was simply stating facts. "Mark, you've said you want to get married again. You've hinted that you enjoy our partnership. Hypothetically speaking, if we were to get married, would you want me to sleep with another man? Are you saying you would have sex with other women?" I couldn't believe the bluntness of my own question, but I was confused by his talk and wanted to know answers.

197

"No," he said immediately. "Look, in a world of disease, unwanted pregnancies, and exploitive relationships, I wouldn't want to run the risk personally. I've had this happen to me. I know it's not sex people are looking for; it's the feeling of attraction, sexuality. I will always feed off this energy and use it in the benefit of marriage. Unfortunately, many people don't understand this and get caught in the lie of adultery. Marriage wouldn't give me a license to possess you, and you wouldn't possess me. We would be free to live our own lives, make our own rules; it's the same as dating, but with a more exclusive contract. I see marriage like a business, a partnership. Do you get it?" He smiled.

Suddenly my mind flashed back to the couple I met in the Orlando airport. Yet I wasn't sure I totally got what he was saying, "Like a contract or an agreement?" I asked.

"If you really want to get technical," he said, continuing his line of reasoning, "it's like the business of prostitution."

I tensed up at the word. My mind turned to the spirits at the studio. And, for the first time, I wondered if he had ever seen Lady M or her girls.

He continued. "So prostitutes have sex in order to earn money to live a desired lifestyle. How is marriage any different? Two people sign a contract to have sex in exchange for money and security. Why else do people get married?" He shrugged his shoulders as if the thought were completely useless.

"Well," I said, trying to defend the institution, "because they want to have kids together and continue the species." This is where the real test for Mark came in, and I was thankful the subject was brought up. What I really wanted to know was if Mark wanted kids.

"Ah, yes. Children. Procreation. Okay, bear with me." I could tell he had thought this out, and I listened. "Let's say two people meet, traditionally marry, and have children. And because of the additions to their 'assets,' so to speak, they now have even more to be possessive of. The only reason for bringing children into this world is to further life. They are no more possessions than a husband or wife. Yet if people stopped having children, our human world would cease to exist as we know it. Hence our burning desire to procreate."

"Jeez, Mark, when you put it that way, it sounds so romantic." I was being sarcastic, but inside I was truly disappointed. While he did not

YOU & I, INC.

come right out and say he didn't want kids, he certainly indicated that. "What's so wrong with the romance of creating children out of your love for one another and wanting to share that in a new life; to be married faithfully and live the happily ever after?"

"I'm a diehard romantic!" he exclaimed, holding his hands up defensively. "Don't think I'm not. I'm simply telling it like it is. For example, look at a typical divorce situation. Two people get married and have children. Years down the road, they decide the other is not making them happy. Now the assets of the marriage, including the children, are to be split. In marriage and divorce, it's about people and, therefore, emotions. People drift and are no longer happy. This often causes hatred and animosity that grows. And this is what our children see and ultimately model? So much for the next generation doing any better! Do you see the theory of evolution here?" He asked, waiting for an answer.

The turn of the conversation made me feel uneasy. Mark could most likely sense my discomfort. He turned to me, took my hands in his, and looked into my eyes. "I'm not saying it's right; I'm just speaking the truth as I see it."

"That's just sad," I said, shaking my head in disbelief. "Why would you even think about wanting to get married again if what you say is true? If that is how you feel?" I asked.

"I think because I see marriage differently," he said. "I'm not looking for someone to complete me. I'm not looking to cure my loneliness. I'm not looking for a woman to possess. I'm looking for a relationship that is a partnership; where we are on the same team, looking to accomplish the same goals. Not everything is going to be perfect. But if we communicate, we can go further together than we ever could apart. It's a universal truth that two people working together toward a common goal or desire have a better return on their labor than when working alone."

"Yes, but don't you think all people who desire to be married want that? I don't think anyone would get married if they didn't believe that at the start," I said, playing devil's advocate.

Mark smiled. I could tell he was enjoying the conversation, and he continued his thought. "Sure they all want it. Some even fool themselves into thinking that they have found it. Yet they still don't understand the secrets behind that kind of love. It's a paradox, like the limits of religion or society. Religion and society have limits, rules, and boundaries. These limits are meant to provide freedom. We're supposed to love others by first loving ourselves," he said, as if citing doctrine.

It became obvious he could tell I didn't fully understand what he was saying. He leaned in toward me and smiled as if he could help me make sense of it all. "Here's an example: my ex spent all her time and energy trying to please everyone else, loving others, right? She couldn't see that she was performing—performing in order to get love back. It didn't matter the kind of love she was looking for. Love comes in many different forms: applause, affirmation, financial security, gifts, acceptance, self-esteem. She counted on these to make her feel valued and loved. As she learned, if you count on others for love, you are going to be sorely disappointed in life. We can't control anyone else's actions or reactions. If we think we have control, we're disillusioned.

"People change. Circumstances change. There's only one constant in life, and that is you—the universal you. I believe that every relationship here on Earth provides a mirror in order to teach us how to love ourselves. In looking into the mirror and learning to love ourselves, we love others, not the other way around. That's the paradox." He grabbed my hands and looked me directly in the eyes.

His maturity blew me away. It was obvious that he too had been through pain and struggle in a relationship. He felt so human to me as he shared his weaknesses and strengths. I connected to his story, and somehow, this made me feel safe to share with him more of my own.

"Mark, I have something to tell you," I began hesitantly, not sure I was really ready to tell him about my recent visits by spirits. But after Mark's revealing comments about adultery and marriage, I knew it was the right thing to do. "I've had some experiences in the studio and around you that I can't quite shake …" I was keeping my remarks a bit veiled to judge his reaction before I told him about Lady M.

Mark sat quietly, his eyes focused intently on me, and listened. "Remember our dessert night at the L'abeille Palace and the book I wanted so badly?" I began. He nodded. "I've been reading about the past, and I think that some of those women have come to me in the form of spirits, maybe to teach me something. They keep showing up at the studio and …" I hesitated, reluctant to continue. "And sometimes … when I am with you."

Waiting for his response, I expected shock and awe. Instead, his focus remained on me; there was no change in his face. "I know they can't hurt me," I continued. "This all started when I joined the studio. I just feel better telling you the truth about what has been happening. Please know I'm not crazy. I have an appointment with a spiritual medium tomorrow with the hope to get some things figured out." Everything came out in a rush, not knowing what to expect from Mark.

Mark leaned back, put his hands behind his head, while looking off into the distance, and then looked up. "Wow! You have had quite an experience! I'm glad you shared this with me. I think seeing someone who has some experience with that sort of thing is a good idea."

Not being able to tell if he was being supportive or sarcastic, I suddenly felt insecure at the moment and wished I could rewind the scene and take the words back. My gaze shifted downward in an attempt to hide my disappointment.

"Hey, Len." He leaned forward and put his hand on my chin, lifting my head up until my eyes met his. "Don't worry about this. A few spirits don't scare me. If it makes you feel better, you can stay with me. And I'll take care of you. Maybe that's being selfish on my part, but it would sure make me feel better if you were there by my side." His words seemed genuine.

"Thanks. I think I'll wait until tomorrow after I see the medium and let you know. I appreciate the thought." I loved his honesty and his offer to take care of me. Sitting on the couch, I knew the next topic was going to be even more difficult. Swallowing hard, I jumped in.

"Hey, Mark? You talked about loving yourself and that other people are mirrors to reflect your love, right?" I wasn't sure I quite got it, but I kept on. "I'm curious about boundaries we make for ourselves. Is that part of love?"

"Absolutely," he said.

"Well"—I hesitated, taking a breath—"my boundary is that I can't have sex until after this surgery. And given my financial status, I'm not quite sure how long it will be before it gets done." I waited for a response, not quite sure what to expect, but I anticipated the worst.

"Lenea, sex with you is amazing! It really is great! But it's not why I'm with you. Sex can wait." Again, he grabbed my hands, holding them in his. They were warm and strong. "We all have baggage. None of us can escape unharmed. I prefer to look at it, sort through it, and then lock it away somewhere where we don't allow it to affect our future. I love you."

"I love you too." The words came easily to my lips.

We kissed each other slowly, lovingly. It was the first time he had said the words. Hearing them felt so good, so natural, so right. There was no doubt I had found a partner in Mark.

The conversation continued for hours as we shared stories of past hurts and current issues. We watched movies, made popcorn, and held each other in a loving embrace. By the end of the night, we understood what we both wanted: a long-term partnership and to trust the opposite sex. But both of us had been burned badly in the past. We were two wounded individuals wanting to be together, with hopes and dreams of a brighter future.

I was joyous as he held me on the couch, lying in his arms. We talked about what the future would look like. It was wonderful to think about his ideas of marriage and partnership and what this could mean. Maybe we would be like that old couple I met, playing off each other's energy so well. The thought made me smile.

23

A Spirit and its Source

The next morning Mark woke up early, headed to the supermarket, and returned with enough groceries to keep my refrigerator stocked for several days. He checked to make sure I didn't need anything else before he left to go back to the studio.

"Please call me after your appointment today," he said, leaning down to kiss me softly on the cheek. "You're welcome to come and stay with me, really."

"Okay. Thanks. I promise I'll call you," I said reluctantly, shutting the door and locking it behind him.

The beautiful wildflowers sitting on my kitchen counter were a living reminder of his love and how, even without his presence, it still surrounded me. I leaned in to smell them, and smiled, filled with gratitude. *How beautiful. I really do love this man.*

••••••••••

The ad for Spirit and Source listed an address that appeared to be relatively close. When I checked the GPS, I realized it was only a few blocks south of the studio. My inner thigh still felt torn and stretched, and it hurt when I made too much movement. Babying my injury, I opted to drive the short distance rather than walk, arriving quickly at the medium's office.

Expecting some kind of shady building or something like a tattoo parlor with crystal balls and dark rooms, I was surprised to find a typical retail space more like a dentist or physician's office. Upon entering, I saw that the space was bright, clean, and fresh, with candles and figurines of angels decorating the shelves and counters. Only a few steps were necessary to get to the reception desk, where I introduced myself to the stocky woman sitting behind it.

"You must be Lenea," she said courteously. I nodded in response. "I need you to fill out this paperwork on the clipboard and bring it back to me, please. You can have a seat in our waiting room if you'd like." She was pleasant but nonchalant in her manner.

I hadn't expected to fill out paperwork, but I did it, answering questions ranging from a basic health history to my reason for being there. Other questions included boxes for subjects including past spiritual connections, relationships with family, lovers, and my occupation. The questions were extensive, including some that didn't seem pertinent.

Oh well. I shrugged, taking a deep breath turning page after page for several minutes. Answering as honestly as possible, I hoped the medium would be able to help me sort things out and provide some answers. When finished, I handed the clipboard to the receptionist.

A few moments later, a petite plump woman with long brown hair and a homely, round face appeared through the arch leading to the hallway. It wasn't obvious if she was the medium or a client leaving. Then I heard the receptionist say, "Your next appointment is here." The woman glanced briefly at the first two pages on the clipboard and walked over to me. She stopped in front of me, closed her eyes, and put her fingers to her head. "Wait a minute!" she seemed to say to herself. "I'm getting something. Yes. It's coming to me ..." She opened her eyes, sticking her hand out. "You must be Lenea."

Standing to shake her hand, I was confused by her actions at first; then I noticed that familiar gleam in her eye—sarcasm.

"Hello, I'm Lillie. Relax! That was a little medium humor; simply trying to break the tension. That I do feel, by the way." She gave a knowing smile.

My body was indeed very tense; my face must have been too. Her humor did break the ice as I reached out to shake her hand. It was very warm, and immediately I felt a surge of electrical energy course through my body.

"Please, come have a seat in my office and we will begin our session." Her voice had calmness to it; it was reassuring, soft, and quiet.

The small, intimate office contained a few chairs, a window, a desk, and a couple plants. The only wall decoration was a seventies-style landscape. It could have been any business office in the United States, with no discernible characteristics indicating her profession. My expectation was kewpie dolls, tarot cards, or something really far out that would indicate she was working in the spiritual realm. Instead, it was like walking into my boss's office.

"Take a seat." She motioned to a plush couch positioned across from her. She sat in her own chair, put a set of reading glasses on, and reviewed my paperwork. Occasionally, she would stop to mark areas with a red ballpoint pen. "As a medium, I connect with the energy of souls and spirits who have departed the earthly plane," she began, her eyes still focused on my paperwork. She flipped a page, marked three times, then glanced up, her eyes above the horn-rimmed frames. She took a deep breath. "Think of me as a portal of sorts. I use my gifts of clairsentience and clairvoyance to accomplish this." She set the pen down and crossed her hands, both elbows on the desk. "My gifts allow me to feel powerful emotions from the departed spirits and receive visions in my mind's eye. The visions may come as colors, people, symbols, places, or situations. Once I have connected with those who have passed over, I cannot force the spirits to communicate, answer questions, or reveal specific information. I can only request that, through their spiritual energy, they come forward and communicate in whatever fashion they wish." Her glare was intense, and her words seemed well rehearsed. "Many times the communication feels like a vibration. I request connections in a space of love. Love is powerful and is something I feel in every session. Frequently, this love can be felt by the person requesting the connection. It is my reason for doing what I do. This is what I have to offer you today. Do you understand?" Her question seemed rhetorical.

"I think so," I responded in a mousy voice. The moment was a bit overwhelming, and I was a little nervous. "It is what I want. I need answers. I need help. I'm ..." My voice cracked holding back the tears. "I'm desperate."

"As we begin this journey, I will be asking you several questions," she continued without emotion, ignoring my concerns. "I will then quiet my mind and request a connection with the spirit you are seeking answers from. Do you understand?" Again, she wasn't looking for a response.

Still, I nodded solemnly.

"Good. Then we shall begin." Her posture and head position never varied as she asked several personal questions about my past, current issues, and especially my hernia. I had no idea how any of it was connected. Abruptly the questions stopped.

"Shh. She's coming to us," she said, her face sullen. Then she leaned back in her chair, her body upright. Her eyes closed and started fluttering, her arms fell to her sides.

Sitting up on the edge of the couch, my heart racing, I looked from side to side, expecting the raven-haired woman to enter the room. Terribly afraid, yet at the same time exhilarated at the prospect of our meeting, I felt safe knowing I had someone on my side who could communicate with spirits in a space of love. Closing my eyes, I took a deep breath.

"Welcome, Lady M. Thank you for joining us today," Lillie said in a low, sultry voice.

Nervously, I opened my eyes and saw that Lillie's eyes were closed, still fluttering, and now rolling in the back of her head. Looking around the room, I noticed there was no Lady M to be seen. *What?* I thought to myself. *How in the world is she here? Where is she?*

Lillie continued talking out loud, seemingly to no one in particular. "Why is it you have come to Lenea?" Her eyes continued to flutter and roll to the back of her head. It was pretty weird looking, and I wasn't sure if I was more afraid of her or the spirit. Lillie's eyes flew open as she looked at me, her pupils fully dilated. "I have seen Lady M! She has dark black hair, like a raven. She has deep brown eyes … She says she has tried to warn you and help you. Is this the woman you seek?" Lillie had described her in full detail. I was convinced.

"Yes, that's her," I replied softly, barely above a whisper. "I am here to listen to any answers you can give me."

"She is here, and you may begin your questions for her." Lillie sat upright again, resuming her eye fluttering and rolling.

Clearing my throat where a tickle had formed, my mouth dry from nervousness, I asked, "Why did she come to me? Why now?"

Lillie's facial reactions looked as if someone was speaking to her and she was listening intently. "She says it is because you need to heal your past and forgive in order to live in the present."

No kidding, I thought to myself. "What about the stories of the L'abeille Palace and the Mystere? What do they have to do with me? Do I have a connection to the past?"

Her voice changed now, becoming more monotone, guttural, and otherworldly. "Locations contain memories. Heal the memories and live in the now."

Lillie's body jerked forward a little, her eyes popping open. "She has left us now." Her voice returned to normal. She reached down for a glass of water, taking a sip before wiping her brow, now dampened with small beads of sweat. "Do you now understand why she has come to you?"

I nodded my head to appease her but then shook my head, being honest.

"She wants you to love yourself. Do you understand? That is her purpose." Lillie's eyes were returning to normal, and her voice was genuinely concerned.

I felt better after hearing the words come out of Lillie's mouth. *Oh, thank God!* It was indeed a relief she wasn't there to hurt me.

Lillie answered like a knowing mother, "Take it one step at a time child. No one runs before they learn to walk. Once you understand the overall objective, we can focus on the steps to get there."

"How long does that take?" I asked.

"It depends on the client. One gentleman has visited my office for over twelve years, coming to me on a weekly basis to contact the deceased and gain more information and understand the love. Rarely does it happen overnight in one or two sessions."

I got where this was going and grew irritated to find myself involved in yet another financial commitment. Deciding to make this seventy-five-dollar session worth every penny, I asked for clarification. "Well, I have a number of other questions for you. Are all spirits good and of love as you say?"

"Basically," she answered. "Every human soul, every spirit, is full of love at its core. But, I must warn you, and I need to know you understand, that once you have placed a label on a spirit as good or bad, it can attach to you and can even possess and guide you in that manner. Good … or bad."

Now I wished I hadn't asked the question, having heard the response. The pleasant feeling Lillie's words originally gave me started to slip away. "Is Lady M attached to me?"

"Yes, child," Lillie nodded her head, closing her eyes bricfly. "Otherwise, you would not be here today." She leaned back in her chair, pausing, as if to analyze me and my body language. "I want you to understand that she cannot physically harm you; it is only your perception of her that stands to harm you. Once you understand this, then the attachment will dissolve.

"The attachment to this spiritual energy can be strong and can even be passed down through generations. I call it the invisible chains. Breaking the chains is what I help people accomplish; a detachment of the spirits. Let me ask you a question: what happened when you got the hernia?"

Shifting in my chair uncomfortably, I recalled the fateful event. "I saw the spirit, Lady M. She came to me when I was doing pole fitness. I was at the top of the pole, trying to untie a stuffed animal as part of a challenge my teacher set up for us. I looked in the mirror, and it was like it had gone dark and ... there she was." Trying to sound confident rather than scared, I continued. "There also appeared to be a group of women behind her, walking toward me. The vision scared me, and I lost my focus and grip on the pole. That's what caused me to fall and injure myself. Now I have an inguinal hernia."

"So you allowed the spirit to harm you?" she asked.

"Not intentionally," I said growing defensive. "It just happened. It was an accident. I was ... the scene ... the women ... they really scared me."

"Nothing in the world simply happens, my dear. You," she said, her finger pointing at me, "you labeled the spirit as bad; scary. And now it is affecting your life, your body. Your negative perception of the spirit caused you to do something that hurt you physically. I present to you a different question: what if the accident was an answer to your problem?"

She leaned back in her chair for a moment and grabbed a book from the desk behind her and flipped through the pages. "Ah, yes. Right here. Inguinal hernia. It says an inguinal hernia is an indication of repressed sexuality." She took off her glasses, laid them on the desk, and looked up at me. "Are you blocking your sexual energy in some way?"

Not quite sure where she was going with this line of questioning, I could tell our time was about to end. But now I was mad. "You think I caused myself to fall so I could create my own hernia? Excuse me, but why in the hell would I do that to myself?"

"Be careful, my dear"—she looked left and right—"and don't let a stronger attachment form. It is not *your* hernia. Your label—or the attachment, so to speak—feeds a part of you that desires to understand. Sigmund Freud called it the ego. We all have it. Our ego allows us to lie to ourselves. It provides labels and attachments for everything." She touched her hand to my head, then my chest. "Open your mind and heart, and you will discover the truth. I'm sure you know the accuracy of the old saying 'The truth will set you free?' Here is a truth for you to consider: we are much more than our physical bodies. That is why you have come to me. Do you understand?"

Shaking my head, I grew more irritated.

"Baby steps, my dear. I can teach you how to walk. In the meantime, remember that we are human beings in spirit and source, and are deeply loved. Namaste." Hands together, she bowed to me. A timer went off, signaling our session had ended.

Sitting there dumbfounded, not sure what to say next, I wondered if my questions had been answered. *Was this woman trying to scare me? Is this Spirit now attached to me and I can't do anything without Lillie's help?* Now I was terribly confused.

She stood up, and I followed her to the door, thanked her, and walked into the reception area. She had a client waiting for her, and her receptionist was busy on a call. Stopping shy of the desk, I looked at Lillie and politely told her I would call again, but I think we both knew I was never coming back. This woman was obviously very talented, but she was off base. Lillie closed her eyes, nodded, and moved to her next client.

I walked outside. The fresh air felt so good on my face, but my hernia still hurt terribly. Putting my hand over it and gently pushing on the bulge to see if that would relieve some of the discomfort, I thought about Lillie's words. Anger seethed through my body. I wouldn't do this intentionally. I wouldn't hurt myself.

My mind replayed the events of the session as well as Lillie's words, and I couldn't help but wonder why Lady M had not shown herself. *Why didn't she tell me what she wanted?*

Remembering I read that some mediums had been found to be

fraudulent by creating fear in clients, asking questions only they knew the answers to in hopes of creating a perpetual client, her words "It could be years before we accomplish the objective ..." echoed in my head.

After opening the car door, I sat in the driver's seat, slammed the door, and began sobbing, feeling duped by yet another "trusted" professional. "Damn it, Lenea! You got suckered by a fake again!" I yelled to myself as the realization of the afternoon's events and wasted money set in. "You can only trust yourself," I shouted, putting the car into reverse for the short trip home.

When I arrived home, I went straight to my computer, knowing I could do the research myself to find answers. "Spiritual attachments" was my first Internet search, and I was shocked to see how much information was available on the subject. The first article I read stated, "Earthbound spirits that are trapped often feel confused, lost, and afraid. They are looking for help and are sometimes drawn to living people."

If they died in physical or emotional pain, these pains can appear within the person they join and with whom they resonate and feel comfortable with, or within a person they think might be able to help them. They will reside in a person's energy field, in a house or location that they resonate with in some way. They most likely will cause unintentional problems for those they are linked with or attached to. When told they are possibly hurting the person, the response is often distress because they didn't understand they were causing problems. Quite often, they don't actually realize they are dead.

All of a sudden, I realized it could be true. Lillie wasn't off base. These spirits could cause problems even if it was not their desire to do so. My head was spinning and my body was aching. *What if Lady M is truly attached to me and never leaves? What if she stays with me forever? Should I go back and start sessions with Lillie?* Then it hit me: I know the location of Lady M's presence and history.

Lady M was a high-end madam of the Mystere. She was a well-respected, well-connected, intelligent woman who obviously died in physical or emotional pain. She was married to a man who cheated on her, and as a spirit, she was now linking herself to me. Still, I didn't know the reason why she had done so, but I recognized that I too, though not a madam, was a successful businesswoman who was once married to a man who cheated on me. Now I was in pain. *Could this be the link? Could*

my success, coupled with Richard's unfaithfulness and our divorce, be the connection?
How do Samantha, the L'abeille Palace, Mark, the studio, and Madame fit in?

Goose bumps broke out on my arms and legs, and I shivered from the chill of the revelations. There was most definitely a series of connections, but what were they and why? Lillie's words echoed in my head: "Locations hold memories."

This reminded me of the information about residual hauntings, where certain minerals, usually limestone and quartz, can take an imprint of highly emotionally charged events and play them back if the atmospheric conditions are ideal. In many ways, it is a direct window into the past. During a residual haunting a person may witness an event happen right before his or her eyes, even though it actually happened years ago.

The analytical side of my brain kicked in, and I remembered reading that these spirits and their memories were purely energy. I thought back to the past few days of studying Einstein, Galileo and Sir Isaac Newton and how I had researched ideas of connectivity, including the theories of energy, the laws of physics, and the laws of gravity. The more I read on the Internet, the more I felt a connection between the scientific world and the spiritual world.

Einstein, in his theory of special relativity, concluded the laws of physics are the same for all non-accelerating observers. He also hypothesized that the speed of light within a vacuum is the same no matter the speed at which an observer travels. As a result, he suggested that space and time were interwoven into a single continuum known as the space-time continuum. Events that occur at the same time for one observer can occur at different times for another.

Chills filled my body as I realized this was the most logical explanation of the connection. It appeared that I was somehow attached to Lady M's mental energy in a different time. This energy manifested by crossing the space-time continuum. That would explain why the Mystere building, the studio, and Mark's loft, with its limestone walls, were able to hold on to the images created by the energy. This facilitated the connection between the Mystere and the studio, probably through the tunnels and, somehow, Madame.

It must have been her memories or mental energy left behind that mimicked my own and attached to me. *The big questions are, how is the L'abeille Palace connected, and what about Mark? And, especially, why is Lady M invoked every time I am around or mention Samantha and her relationship with Mark?* I contemplated further about the connection of this energy. What are the basics of energy? I turned back to the Internet for answers.

As I read, much of what I learned in college science courses came flooding back.

The material suggested that humans are a mass of organic matter transferring energy. All matter, at its core, is made of energy. Thinking, or thoughts, are also a form of energy. So, since energy cannot be destroyed, it can only be changed or transferred, the big question was, how could I change mental energy from the past or a different time, or turn it into a different form? I laughed to myself as I realized I was using an extraordinary amount of mental energy working through all of this.

Another area to explore was matter. All matter consists of energy. I knew matter can be cancelled out or eliminated by antimatter. Maybe that was the answer! I went back to the computer for a quick refresher in matter and antimatter.

I wondered if human spirit was a form of matter? I continued my research. I typed, "Is the human spirit matter?" and discovered there were conflicting views. Some believed that spirit was a different form of matter: slightly denser, some lighter or more ethereal. It was pretty much unanimous; when it came to understanding the human spirit, there was no physiological explanation. There was also no scientific evidence of a mind–body connection, which left only a spiritual explanation of the thoughts or energy of the human mind, with religious, theological, and philosophical teachings as the main faculties for this kind of spiritual learning.

Being a science geek by nature did not help this situation; I needed hard-core physical proof. My research on spiritual teachings continued.

It was interesting that none of the faculties agreed on the explanation, other than that there is a spiritual nature of man and that this somehow explains mental energy. I had seen what looked like the spirit of Lady M. *If it was only spiritual, could the same concept about the charges that energy carry as particles of matter apply?* I believed it was possible.

Leaning back from the computer, I turned my chair and looked out the window. All the learning and thinking exhausted me. Suddenly, an idea of the connectivity and how to break Lady M's attachment came to me.

If Lady M's memories or mental energy were particles in the form of spirit matter, ectoplasm, then all I had to do was present the anti–spiritual matter, and thus the memories would disappear. Lady M told me that Mark was a player and not to trust him. A lightbulb went off in my head. *That's it! Perhaps the opposite of particles of negative mental energy is positive mental energy? If so, the two opposite particles would annihilate each other and she would disappear. But where can I find anti–spiritual matter? What is anti–spiritual matter?*

Back to the computer I went to find answers on how to annihilate Lady M's negativity. I knew I needed something opposite; something positive. Whatever it was, it would have to be a form of positive mental energy, or memories, and was most likely invisible. I began to research the religious, theological, and philosophical teachings once again and realized there was one universal spiritual truth.

The universal spiritual truth suggests there is an invisible force of positive spiritual energy that all of the faculties agree on: love.

Love. Could love be the answer? It was a shot in the dark, but I felt better for knowing and working on a more fact-based plan.

Standing up, I rolled my neck from side to side, happy and relieved a potential solution was in sight. I was proud of what I had learned and what I was doing. Maybe this was what Lillie had revealed during her various sessions. All those loving angels in her office, and her company name, Spirit and Source—it all made sense now. She had spoken about the one important thing being love.

We create the negative through our negative thinking and negative perceptions. She made it sound so much more complex and could have drawn out the process for a very long time, each visit costing money. *The moment love and the negative spirit come in contact, it will be* boom! *Bye, bye Lady M! To think, I saved myself thousands of dollars and hours of time by relying on myself!* I was elated. This had nothing to do with sexuality. It was about logic. And logically, this made total sense.

Remembering Mark's offer to stay the night at his place, I felt as if I needed to respond and not leave him hanging. I reached for my cell phone and called him. Listening to the ring, I imagined Mark reaching for his phone. A smile of anticipation came over my face as I looked forward to the sound of his voice.

He answered, "Hey Len, I was just thinking about you. How did your session go today? How are you feeling?" He sounded as if he had been awaiting my call.

"Great," I said. "I'm doing a lot better. I think I've found some more connections with the spirits and energy. It's a long story. I've been doing a ton of research this afternoon, and I can't wait to share what I found out!"

"I'm looking forward to hearing all about it!" Mark replied with excitement in his voice. "You sound much better. Are you coming to stay with me tonight? You can tell me the whole story then, perhaps this time in the bedroom?" Mark offered, hoping to entice me.

"Mmm. Sounds like an offer I can't refuse," I said, mustering all the sexiness I could. "But I still have a ton of work to get done tonight. How about tomorrow night? My place?" I asked. I wasn't quite sure why I didn't want to see him tonight. Probably it was because I didn't feel like leaving the house. The hernia didn't help things.

"Darn! I was hoping to give you that massage you missed out on last week. But I understand. Work comes first," he said. He then remained quiet. I wasn't sure if he was being sarcastic or understanding. I still couldn't read his humor.

"Okay. Tomorrow night it is," he answered curtly before I could say anything. "I'll call you in the morning. Okay? I'll let you get back to work. Good night," he said.

"Good night," I responded. The click of the phone on the other end came too soon.

Wow! That was a quick conversation, I thought. I had expected it to last longer. While I truly did miss him and wanted to be with him, in hindsight I thought maybe I should have gone over. *Is he upset with me?* I realized I might be reading too much into the call and decided to get the work done that I had intended to do.

24

What Does She Know That I Don't?

Waking up refreshed Wednesday morning, I lay in bed staring out the window at a brilliant blue sky. I felt at peace. My body reverberated with a special anticipation for the day ahead. I was bound and determined to not let this hernia keep me down.

Sitting at my computer to start the day, my thoughts drifted back to the phone conversation Mark and I had the previous night. I couldn't help but think maybe I had upset him. To ease my mind, I pulled out my cell phone and sent him a text: "Good morning! Thinking of you. Miss you. Hope you are having a great day! Look forward to seeing you tonight :)"

Waiting for a reply, I was soon lost in my work. No response came. The day flew by. My focus was especially keen finishing report after report.

Deciding it was time to take a break, I stood up and leaned back for a big stretch. I looked at my watch and down at my phone and realized it was close to lunchtime. Mark still hadn't texted back. That wasn't like him.

With my work nearly done, I decided to extend the break and call Chrissy to see if she wanted to join me for lunch. Luckily she happened to be available. She suggested we meet at the corner café downstairs from my house so I wouldn't have to drive. She was so sweet and thoughtful. I was eager to have girl time with her alone, outside the studio. Additionally, I was hoping it would give me a diversion from my worries about Mark.

Leaving the house at five minutes before noon, I walked through the doors of the café on time to spot Chrissy beaming. We requested a table outside so we could enjoy the sunshine. We both took our seats and put on sunglasses. Holding our menus, we soaked in the glorious rays. The waitress arrived, suggesting a glass of white wine. Worried about Chrissy's issue, I wasn't going to order any, but she begged me to.

"Seriously, you don't have to avoid alcohol because I do. I know you want that glass of wine. Order it!"

"Why would I do that if you can't drink with me?" I responded. "That's no fun. I don't want to tempt you or make you sad or jealous."

"Sad is the furthest thing from my mind and body, girlfriend. And believe me, there is no jealousy here. Plus you can't make me do anything." She squared her shoulders proudly. "We think we make people feel a certain way, but we really don't. They control how they feel, and that's the beauty." Her response conveyed self-assurance, and I could tell her eyes were twinkling under her large black sunglasses.

"In the old days, I would drink so that I could lose control and let my guard down, have a little fun. But when I relied upon it, that's when it became an addiction, like I had to have it in order to feel good, and I couldn't feel good without it. See the problem?" She hesitated a moment to see if I was following, then continued. "I knew I wanted to feel good all the time, not just when I drank. Madame has taught me a different approach that's much better. When I realized there is something much better than booze, alcohol suddenly lost its appeal." She finished as if she needed to convince herself of her own words.

Cocking my head to the side, I looked at her. I thought, *What in the world is she talking about?* She sounded so much like Mark. "Chrissy, you and I have been going to the same classes now for almost a month. Sorry, but what in the world are you talking about?" I asked, trying to make sense of her words.

"Madame agreed to help me via phone calls away from the studio. She knew my financial situation, and one day, during our call, it just clicked: the power of embracing my sexuality and loving myself … I get it now. Booze is no longer something I need in order to be happy." She must have been able to sense my lack of understanding, and changed course. "Do you like chocolate?"

Confused by her question, I answered hesitantly. "Yes?" I wondered where this was going.

"Well, let's suppose you had never had chocolate before … ever, and you ate a chocolate chip for the first time. It would be wonderful, right? But then one day you are served the finest chocolate in the world. Of course, you're blown away by how good it is. Now, if you were given the choice, would you choose to eat the finest chocolate or a chocolate chip?"

My mind went back to those incredible truffles I ate in the studio. My mouth started to salivate at the thought. "I'll take the finest chocolate money can buy!" I said, laughing.

"My point exactly! My experience is kind of like that. I found something better than alcohol to make me happy. Now I'm free to be who I am all the time, no alcohol needed. That was my biggest desire!" she said ecstatically.

My wine arrived in time for me to "cheers" her water glass in congratulations. Though I understood what it was she accomplished, I couldn't help but think, *Doesn't everyone love themselves? She can't be that happy all the time!* I figured her excitement was merely a temporary response and the buzz would eventually wear off. But I wouldn't dream of telling her that. She was my friend, but I knew better. I finished the toast. "Cheers to making dreams come true."

It was a fabulous lunch. I told Chrissy all about the spirits, about the connection to the L'abeille Palace and the Mystere, the studio, and my budding relationship with Mark. She shared my enthusiasm and was equally thrilled for me, hanging on every word of the juicy story. When I got to the part about Samantha, I must have had a little too much to drink because I began to tell all.

"I just can't believe she would be so blatant about her sexuality. That she would use her body to distract my man. She's a frigging bitch." The words fell loosely from my lips. Yet it felt so good to finally get it out of my head.

I had expected Chrissy to agree with me; to say, "yes you are so right." Having envisioned us acting like schoolgirls again, plotting the ways we would take down our enemy, I was surprised when Chrissy questioned me. I thought to myself, *What does that matter?* With irritation in my voice, I said, "Hey Chrissy, no offense, but she sickens me every time I look at her. I think Lady M hates her too. She's the problem. If she would just go away, everything would be fine. Now, let's figure out a way to vote her off the island," I said, disgusted, with a wave of my hand as if

I were making her vanish. I drained my wine glass to further emphasize the point.

"Dang, girl! She really gets under your skin, doesn't she?" Chrissy said.

"Yeah. If she were gone, my life would be perfect," I answered annoyed.

"Hmm. Have you talked to Madame about any of this? The spirits? Sexuality? Samantha?" she asked.

"Well, I did mention it to her," I replied.

"You desire to trust a man, right? You came to Madame to create that destiny, right?" Her interrogatories seemed almost confrontational.

"Yes?" I answered, wondering where she was headed.

"Well, why not share everything with her? Tell her your deepest secrets, like you have to me, and see what she can do to help you." She leaned forward, reaching out with her hand, and put it on top of mine. "She's safe, I promise. But if you hold anything back from Madame, are you really trusting and loving yourself? We can't love and trust others until we love and trust ourselves first."

What is this girl smoking? I wondered to myself. I wanted to ask her that very question, but her face looked so serious, and she was so happy about creating her own destiny with Madame. I simply chalked her advice up to delusion and didn't want to ruin her moment. "Thank you, that's a good idea." I answered, feigning agreement.

We finished our lunch soon thereafter, hugged, and said good-bye. As I walked back to my apartment, I thought to myself, *Poor girl. Just wait until reality comes crashing down on you. Just wait until you fall in love and some woman pops up and tries to take your man away. Not even alcohol can take away that kind of pain.*

I shook my head in disgust, believing there was no way some "loving yourself" baloney was going to take away this pain. No. Loving and trusting myself meant standing up for my beliefs. I was also very certain Samantha had a desire for Mark, sexual or otherwise, and I was not going to let that happen.

Suddenly, Samantha's words in the studio reverberated through my head: "Men like women who are sexual." The thought of her made my blood boil as my march to the apartment picked up pace until the throbbing in my groin reminded me of my physical limitation.

How can I express my sexual energy with a hernia? I thought, more irritated with each painful step. Stopping at a crosswalk, waiting for the light to turn green, I looked across the street. Next to the corner drugstore was a small lingerie shop with half-dressed mannequins in the window. *Inspiration! That's what I need!*

Making my way to the storefront, I could see four mannequins in various stages of undress. The first one had a peekaboo red-and-black top with black lace panties fastened to knee-high black sheer stockings. The second one had regal purple and black colors with a flogger that would make Madame proud. I closed my eyes for a moment to picture what I might look like as I circled Mark, slowly drawing the leather tassels across his bare chest as he sat tied up in a chair.

A cold breeze brushed across my neck and my eyes immediately popped open. I looked in the reflection of the window. Behind my right shoulder stood Lady M. I watched her lean forward. "I'm here to help you," she whispered in my ear.

"No you're not. You're here to learn from me," I said sternly.

"You are a foolish girl," she replied, half smiling. "You cannot trust this man."

"Why not?" I asked, raising my voice.

"Why do you think he's not returning your calls?" She moved behind me and to my left. "Could it be that he's too busy painting Samantha at this very moment?"

I looked down at the mannequin's feet. The black stilettos were the same ones Samantha wore to class, the same ones she wore when she climbed the pole the day of my accident. My gaze returned to Lady M's dark eyes. "What should I do?" I asked.

"Go to the studio. When you catch him red-handed, you'll understand why you doubted him," she said, as if to reassure me. "I'm here to help you."

My eyes shifted to the left, up the narrow downtown streets, as I mentally calculated the distance to the studio. Seven minutes at most.

"Now go!" she commanded, another cool breeze brushing across my neck in the opposite direction. Mine was now the sole reflection in the window.

Instinctively, I knew had to follow her directions. I changed course back to the studio, hoping she was wrong but knowing deep inside there was no other explanation as to why Lady M would have revealed herself. I looked down at my cell phone. *Still no return text from Mark? Oh my God, what if she's right?*

A few minutes later, I arrived at the studio. The door was unlocked, and I entered. The dampened sound of dance music resonated through the hallway, and I sensed the movement of people in the building. A thought crossed my mind: *I really don't know what Mark does during the day. I know he paints clients, but I have only seen him do that with our group a few times. Where would he be? Would he be upstairs?*

"Hey Lenea, how are you? Are you here for a class today?" My thoughts were interrupted by the sweet voice of Shannon. "I thought you were injured, and ..." She glanced down, scrolling with her mouse as she looked at her computer screen. "I don't think I have you on the schedule."

"Oh, I'm not here to see Madame." I paused, uncertain if Shannon knew about Mark and me. Still, I decided to tell her anyway. "I'm here to see Mark. I ... I came to surprise him."

"Ohhh. Nice. Go ahead and go on back. He should be finishing up with a client. I'm sure he'd be happy to see you." She smiled coyly, probably already knowing we were in a relationship.

"Great. Thanks, Shannon." Walking past the desk, my pace slowed to a tiptoed crawl, not wanting to interrupt his session. It was dark in the studio ahead, but I could see lights coming from one of the rooms to the right. Turning, I approached it and heard a deep, thumping bass followed by voices. I was certain one was Mark's, but I couldn't quite identify the other voice, other than that it was female.

The door was slightly ajar. Peering in, I could see the flicker of candlelight on the walls and pillows on the floor. Then, during a lull in the music, I heard the female voice clearer. "Mark, how is it a single artist like you isn't with someone like me?" she purred, low and sultry. I recognized the voice immediately, and my blood ran cold: Samantha.

Leaning forward, I caught her looking at her own reflection in the mirror. She was dressed in a flowing black skirt with a see-through tunic top covering a black strapless bra. Her hair was long and tousled. She turned and walked away, her silhouette perfectly outlined in the mirror, with each step slow and accentuated, crossing her legs like a model on a catwalk, wearing the stilettos I had seen in the shop.

She reached up and began to unbutton her blouse. A lump grew in my throat. My heart rate accelerated; I could hardly breathe. I wasn't imagining her objective after all. She really did have intentions with my man. *Oh my God!* I stood there paralyzed, watching the scene play out.

"Mark, you can paint my body, but if you really want to know my essence, you must come closer, take a bite." Her blouse dropped from her shoulders and fell to the floor. She stopped and, as though performing a strip tease, took off her bra and began caressing her breasts. "You have to touch me to truly know every curve—intimately. To enter me is the only way to solve the mystery." Her skirt dropped to the floor, leaving her topless with only her black lace thong inversely outlining her muscular buttocks. The mirror may have distorted things slightly, but her body seemed perfect in every way. Had this been a scene in a movie, I might have been aroused. But this bitch was trying to seduce my man! *Who the hell does she think she is!*

She took two more steps then turned abruptly to her right, moving out of my line of sight in the mirror. Leaning in closer, attempting to see where she had gone, what she was doing and what Mark's response was to all of this, I caught a glimpse of myself peering through the doorway. It startled me so much I immediately jumped back, hoping I hadn't been caught. Looking around the hallway, my heart beat faster and I could feel the beads of sweat covering my forehead.

I took a breath, stepped forward again, and strained to hear Mark's response. There was nothing, no sound. With another step forward, I edged closer to the opening, yet I couldn't see any images in the mirror. Moments passed, and still there was no talking. I wanted to burst in and scream, "Get away from my man!" But I waited to hear more.

The music ended, and then silence. The sound of my heartbeat seemed to replace the thump of the bass. Samantha's sulking voice broke the serenity. "I understand. Not enough time during the day; that's too bad." She paused and then continued, this time in a more sultry voice. "What about tonight? You, me, and a bottle of wine? I'll make your wildest dreams come true." Her voice was slightly above a whisper.

"Samantha, thank you for today," Mark answered with a heavy sigh, sounding exhausted. "Your painting is turning out exceptional and is sure to be a masterpiece." I could hear the sounds of him walking around, but I still didn't have clear enough vision to see anything in the mirror. "I do have another client in ten minutes and need to take some time to get cleaned up and stretch. We will need to find another time to finish this; probably one more session. Please get dressed and check with Shannon up front to book another appointment. She knows my schedule better than I do. Have a great day."

Hearing his footsteps coming my way, I panicked. *Oh my God, what do I do?* Looking around for an exit, I tiptoed quickly into the bathroom, only steps from where I was standing, and quietly shut the door. My heart was beating so hard I thought it would jump out of my chest.

My eyes closed as my hand held the cold bronze of the door handle. *Thank you, Mark, for your professionalism*, I thought, almost whispering it aloud. *Thank you for not falling into her trap. Thank you for being such an incredible man.* My eyes opened. Embarrassment crept over me; here I was, hiding in the bathroom.

Faint voices and footsteps entered the hallway. They grew louder until they passed by. I pressed my ear to the locked door, hoping to hear more of their conversation. The dialogue and voices grew faint as they passed by until I could hear them no more. I started to cry—first a sob, then a river of tears—albeit as quietly as I could.

Looking down at my watch, I remembered Mark's words about a next client. He must have been back to back today. My cell phone buzzed with a text. It was Mark: "Hey. So sorry for my delay. Can't wait to see your face. Crazy day! I miss you too. See you around 6pm. Damn. 6pm can't get here fast enough!"

Shit! Now there was no way I could walk out and surprise him. What if Samantha was still there? A fantasy of slapping her face in front of Mark raced through my mind. I shook my head to get rid of such negative thoughts. *Focus on the positive!* my mind yelled again and again.

Yes, it was very exciting to get his text. *There it is. His words clearly indicate he loves me! Yes! More! Be romantic and follow the original plan! Be romantic. Be sexual.*

I texted back: "Excellent. My place. 6pm. Let me take care of you tonight! Purrrrrr. Xoxo"

He texted back immediately: "Meow! I'm all yours."

I felt a rush of sensations from chills up my spine to a longing in my heart. Then I heard his voice and footsteps walking back down the hall, as well as the *click clack* of high heels. He must have met his next client and was walking her back.

Stepping back from the door, I turned to the sink to wash the tears from my face as well as the black lines of running mascara. I was a mess. *Focus on the positive!* I told myself again. "It's all good," I whispered. "You have nothing to fear." The cold splash of water was comforting as it covered my cheeks, eyes, and forehead. I grabbed a paper towel and felt its roughness against my skin. My mind calmed further and I sensed an ease to the tension. "You have nothing to fear," I whispered, looking into my own eyes.

Then it dawned on me: I actually felt sexier knowing Mark had been tempted by a goddess like Samantha and turned down her advances. *He can totally be trusted!* At that moment I recognized how thankful I was that I had followed Lady M's command to come to the studio and see his actions for myself. Once again, she was right. "Thank you," I said into the mirror, expecting to see her face appear. There was no response.

I moved behind the door and put my ear to it to make sure there were no voices in the hallway. *One more minute and then I'll walk out,* I told myself. I tried counting to sixty, but at twenty-two I opened the door a crack. No one there. Stepping outside the bathroom, I saw the door to the room Mark was in was again slightly ajar, and music began playing once again. Turning, I walked quickly toward the waiting area, hoping no one would see me.

Shannon's presence behind the desk startled me. "Did you find him?" she asked nonchalantly.

I could feel my face grow red and became flustered. "He was with another client. I didn't want to bother him and think I missed him when I was in the bathroom. Thanks for your help, though."

I walked toward the door, realizing this might be a good opportunity to ask about Samantha's sessions with Mark. Dozens of questions danced through my head. The most pressing was just how long the two of them had been meeting.

"Hey Shannon, I'm curious, how long have Samantha and Mark met for sessions?" Shocked at my own lack of tact, I realized my question may have sounded a little nosey. Quickly, I tried to cover my tracks. "I was thinking of having a painting done for myself and didn't know how many classes it usually takes."

"Samantha and Mark have only had a couple sessions together," she answered in a matter-of-fact voice. "I believe they have one more session left. But to answer your question, it really depends on what the client is looking for. I've seen it take as little as one meeting for a project to be completed. Other women require multiple sessions as well as multiple paintings and seem to never leave." She laughed at her own words.

"I get it. The man is hot! Who wouldn't want to spend more time with him," I said. It was obvious to everyone Mark was an exceptionally good-looking man and, in his profession, was surrounded by women who wanted his attention and would do anything to be with him. My chest swelled with pride at the thought of me being his chosen one. To know he could deal with the most tempting of situations like this was certainly a relief.

"Well, thanks for the info. I'll see you tomorrow," I said, seemingly satisfied with her answers.

"See you then!" She waved back. I walked out the door.

The sunshine was a welcome change. My stroll home went quickly as I planned the evening in my mind. I would create the most romantic atmosphere for my amazing man. I couldn't believe I had been so worried about him! Samantha sure had a lot of nerve.

Hmm, I thought cattily to myself, *I wonder what she feels like right about now.* Her words from the other day again replayed in my mind: *"Oh yes, men like women who are sexual. They'll do anything for sex."* Sorry, honey, not my man! He's just not that into you. Guess you'll have to take your game on down the road. I beamed delightedly at the thought of the rejection Samantha must have been feeling at that moment.

I was so proud of Mark. It was satisfying to finally be with a man who actually didn't succumb to every temptation. He was a good man. From now on, I would trust him implicitly.

25

The Illusion of Reality

Cleaning the house came easy. The duster in my hand flitted about the furniture, and the throbbing in my groin was barely noticeable. Moving with grace, I danced to the beat of music blaring from the stereo. My thoughts drifted toward fantasy imagining the night together with Mark. I couldn't wait to tell him about the spirits, about everything I had learned the day before, and my plan to overcome them. I was curious to see what he would think. Knowing him, he would probably have some incredible backstory to add. This connection truly endeared me toward him.

Each step of the evening's events was carefully mapped out. I put out scented candles, strategically placed massage oil and sorted through my collection of romantic and sexual music in preparation. Stopping to look around at the ambiance, I breathed a sigh of relief before sitting at the computer to search for a good dinner recipe.

Pictures of delectable meals popped up, each one causing me to salivate. After careful review, I decided to try something new and exotic to demonstrate my domestic culinary skills. Cornish game hens in a white wine and lemon garlic sauce paired with roasted asparagus and wild mushroom risotto was the chosen recipe. The reviews were all five-star, and I even took the advice for a recommended wine pairing, writing all the ingredients down for my trip to the supermarket.

When I returned, I set the bags down on the kitchen counter and hurriedly began the prep work. Turning on the music to a pop station, I soon found myself singing and dancing along and almost forgot about the hernia; it didn't hurt—at least not much.

The apartment was filled with wonderful aromas. Taking a break to catch my breath, I looked around for a last-minute check. *Mark will be blown away!* I thought. *He's going to love this!*

The moment was interrupted by the sound of the cell phone ringing. It was Mark. Looking up at the clock on the wall, I realized it was 5:15 p.m. *Maybe he finished early.* "Well hello, Tiger," I offered in my most sultry voice.

"Hey, Len," he replied, sounding almost dejected and not as excited as I had expected. "Something's come up and … I'm going to have to work late tonight. I'll call you when I'm on my way to your house, okay? I'm sorry for the last-minute change of plans. I can't wait to see you."

What was I supposed to say? "No! You need to come over now!"? I was disappointed but tried to respond without letting my voice betray my feelings. "Oh, okay, no worries. Whatever works for you. We can see each other another night." My voice broke a little at the end. Deep inside, I was saddened by the change of plans.

"I'm still coming over," he said reassuringly. "You can't get rid of me that easy." I could hear the smile in his voice. "I'll call you later. Love you."

"Okay. Love you too," I responded, turning off the phone.

I looked around at the empty apartment, knowing it would continue that way for several hours from that point. I took a deep breath and tried not to be too upset. While I was sad that he wouldn't eat my amazing dinner, I knew it was all for a good reason and lovingly packed away the food for later. *Maybe he can have it for lunch tomorrow,* I thought.

I portioned the other half of the meal on a fine china plate, so it didn't go completely to waste. Sitting down at the table, I cut into the Cornish game hen, savoring the first warm bite while opening my computer to browse the Internet. The pinot noir paired perfectly.

Afterward, I cleaned up the kitchen and decided to prepare the bedroom for his massage. Looking up, I saw that the clock showed a little after eight thirty. The apartment grew dark, still no call. I wondered what he could be doing so late. Before I had time to go down a negative path of thinking, the phone buzzed with a text alert. It was Mark: "Finishing up. On my way. See you soon."

When I greeted him at the door, he looked exhausted. The aroma of the meal still wafted through the small apartment as he walked in.

"How was your day?" he asked in a sullen voice, reaching down to hug me.

I wanted to respond, "Well, it was great until you didn't show up for dinner!" But I bit my tongue. "It was good. Lots of work, lunch with Chrissy. Not much else. How about you? What kept you?"

He looked down, shifting uncomfortably before sitting on the couch. "Just a long day," he muttered. He didn't seem himself, and he hadn't made eye contact.

Joining him on the opposite side of the couch, I folded my legs and tried to engage. Neither one of us said anything for several uncomfortable moments. Something was wrong. He was lying to me; I sensed it in my gut.

"What kept you at the studio so late?" I asked.

"I just had a lot I had to get caught up on," he replied tersely. It was surreal to me, having never seen him display anger before. "I'm really tired. Painting is hard work, you know." He turned on his side to lie on the couch, acting as if he were going to fall asleep. It wasn't right. Something in the back of my mind—or the pit of my stomach, I'm not sure which one—told me something was off.

Trying to ease the tension, I used a more sympathetic offering. "Are you hungry? I made you a delicious dinner." Standing, I walked to the kitchen to retrieve his packaged meal.

"No, not really. I ate on the way. Just tired." His voice sounded drained of energy.

It was surprising he hadn't commented on the aroma of the apartment or even thanked me for the offer. Maybe it simply was a long day. I understood and returned to the couch to give him a massage, hoping that would change his mood.

Looking down, I saw that his eyes were shut and his breathing deep. *Already asleep. Super. Not quite the romantic evening I had planned.* I grabbed a blanket from the hall closet, placed it over him, and went back into the kitchen to finish cleaning.

While wiping the last crumb from the counter, the familiar cool breeze brushed past my right cheek and a movement caught the corner of my eye. Looking up in the mirror, I could see the raven hair of Lady M pass behind me. Time seemed to stand still, and suddenly I experienced tunnel vision.

The wind passed across my left ear. Startled, I pulled back and looked around. The room grew noticeably cooler. "Check his phone," her voice said in my right ear. "He wasn't working late." Lady M's voice moved behind me.

My stomach churned each time I heard her voice, and beads of sweat broke out on my forehead. Looking over at Mark's slumbering body, I knew I had to follow her instructions. She hadn't been wrong so far. I tiptoed over, and noticed he had set his phone and keys on the side table. My heart skipped a beat. I moved forward, reached down, and picked the phone up.

Quickly, I shuffled into the bathroom, albeit feeling like a thief in my own apartment. I pressed the appropriate button, and the phone's screen popped up; my heart felt as if it were going to jump out of my chest. I opened the messaging app and scrolled through the texts. Nothing but the text to me.

Then I checked the recent call log. There it was: outbound to Samantha at 5:18 p.m., not even five minutes after he talked to me. Then I saw another received from Samantha prior to him calling me.

My head began to swirl. I grew dizzy and slightly nauseated. Visions of the two of them together in his apartment raced through my head. It made sense, now, why my gut told me his "working late" excuse was bullshit. It was completely reminiscent of my marriage to Richard. My stomach turned to knots, as if someone had punched me in the gut and walked away. Looking up at my face in the bathroom mirror, I tried to figure out what to do next: wake him now and confront him, or wait until morning?

After opening the bathroom door quietly, I returned to the living room and set his phone down where it had been originally. Standing over his sleeping body, I looked down, disgust filling every cell of my being. Instinctively, I knew something was wrong. There was no way this amazing man could have been with her then come home to me. No way!

Sitting down on the side of the couch next to him, I decided to reach over to wake him up. I was sick of men going behind my back and needed to know the truth.

I touched his shoulder, gently shaking him, when an alternative fantasy of smothering him with the pillow crossed my mind. *How could he do this to me?* He began to stir.

"Oh my gosh," he said groggily. "Did I fall asleep? That's one amazing massage, Len." He sat up, sounding more like a sleepy version of the man I had grown to love, not the lying bastard he had become. Still, my resolve was solid. I seethed inside, barely able to draw a breath.

"Mark, we need to talk." My voice was cold and stern.

"What?" he responded, half dazed, rubbing his eyes before sitting up straight and letting out a big lion yawn.

His lackadaisical response irritated me, and I couldn't keep it in any longer. "So when I asked you what you did in the studio tonight—you know, while you were 'working late' and you gave me some lame excuse about a bunch of stuff you had to do ..."

"Yeah," he responded casually.

"Tell me the truth. Where were you?" My voice was strong and my anger apparent. "You weren't at the studio working late the whole time, were you? Because I know it's not true and I'll give you one chance to tell me what you were really doing tonight." My finger pointed at him accusingly. I couldn't believe how strong my words were.

Mark by now was fully awake and looked like a lost puppy. He closed his eyes, took a deep breath, and then turned to me. "I didn't want to tell you this, but ... I went out with a client from the studio. Her name is Samantha." He saw me react, visibly upset, before trying to backtrack. "Look! It's part of my job! To entertain clients ... so they will continue to buy my paintings as well as continue their sessions with Madame."

He took another deep breath before continuing. "We had a quick bite and a glass of wine at a local restaurant while we discussed how I was going to finish her painting. That's it." He stopped to look at the reaction on my face; I was still overtly pissed. "This is a big project ... and I depend on people like her to grow my business ... our future." His eyes searched mine, maybe for some level of forgiveness and understanding.

It sounded like bullshit—a terrible lie and a made-up excuse. "Oh, I bet you did," I replied snottily. "I'm sure she hated every moment. Seriously. Samantha? The one woman who would sleep with anyone to get what she wants ... and you are so fucking desperate that you believe it is her alone that supports your business. Really? Grow some balls, asshole!"

"Lenea, you're overreacting," Mark responded. "I called her. I knew I needed to finish her painting before her last session next week. I did it for us! Don't you see?"

By now I was past the point of understanding anything. My heart continued to beat out of my chest, and I felt like a freight train steaming at full speed ahead. Nothing was going to stop me from emotionally vomiting all of my anger. "So you didn't tell me because you knew I'd be angry?"

"Exactly," Mark responded repentantly. "I'm sorry. I should have told you." He leaned forward, stretching his arms out in an attempt to give me a hug.

"You're an asshole," I roared, rebuffing his advances. "You know my biggest desire is to trust a man. And yet you chose to lie to me? You know I've been cheated on in the past and now, now, here I am ... in torture, envisioning who knows what the two of you have been up to for the last few hours. But you didn't want to tell me. Why? Because I'd be angry? Oh, I'm not angry over that! I'm angry that you lied to me. And destroyed my trust in you! You know what I've been through! You know how much I hate liars! And yet you lied to me?!" My whole body shook with anger as I sat and seethed, fighting away the tears.

"Don't you see that I didn't want to tell you," he began contritely, "because I didn't want to hurt you. I love you. And I ... I don't want you to be hurt." He put his hand on my knee before continuing. "My biggest desire is to be with you. I'm not perfect. I never will be. But I love you." He tried to grab my hands and put them in his.

Pulling away, I stood up, now even more disgusted at his words and his phony face, pointing my finger directly at him. "Don't throw that guilt trip at me! Bullshit! You did whatever you wanted to do and didn't care until you were caught! Which makes me wonder ... what else have you lied about? What other lies have I not caught you in? Thank you, Mark! All I ask for is honesty. And instead, you've now destroyed the trust I've worked so damn hard to establish in this relationship. Thank you!" I turned and went to the hall closet, grabbing a jacket to demonstrate to him I was ready to leave.

Mark stood, now visibly upset, shaking his head in disgust as he turned, walked to the door, and tried to leave before me. "You know what? I guess my take on you has been off! You know I've had a hard time trusting women as well. They're too manipulative and hold all the keys to the relationship in their hands."

"Fuck you!" I screamed. "You created this problem all by yourself! And until you man up and quit coming up with ways to manipulate my emotions, you're creating your own self-fulfilling prophecy. You have single handedly destroyed my trust in you! You knew about my trust issues with men; about my prior relationships. Why would you do this to me? Did you think you wouldn't get caught? Then ... then you have the audacity to get angry with me for not trusting you? I'm most angry with myself for almost being convinced that I found a man who would never lie to me. Now I'm with another liar? Super! Exactly the relationship I hoped for." By now I had my jacket and shoes on and was ready to leave, grabbing my purse for effect.

Mark moved between me and the door. "So let me get this straight ... You're in love with the *idea* of who I am more than the *reality* of who I am?" He smiled that cocky smile while pointing at his own chest. "This is me, sweetheart. I lie ... I make mistakes ... I'm not perfect. But I am faithful to you. And if you want to blow this out of proportion ... That's your problem." He pointed back. Shaking his head, he laughed a little. "I wonder if you didn't create this just so you have an excuse to leave me. But listen to me ... I'm here," he said, pointing at his chest again. He looked into my eyes deeply. I rolled my eyes in disgust.

His anger intensified. "Look, I didn't plant that seed ... you did! A long time ago! Talk about a self-fulfilling prophecy," he said condescendingly. He turned and put his hand on the doorknob, now obviously ready to walk out.

Suddenly, I felt the familiar chill as Lady M's voice echoed in my ear. "You don't need him! Kick him out! Don't let him walk out on you and gain the upper hand!"

This time it was my turn to stop him from leaving. I put my leg in front of the door to keep it from opening. "So I can trust you now?" My words resonated from a deep anger inside of me, as if I were taking a stand for all women who had ever been lied to. "Don't you see the irony in that? Did you think of me at all when you decided to lie to my face? How the hell can you justify telling me it's all about maintaining a client and that you did it for our future," I said. "That's bullshit! Then you try to make me feel bad for questioning you? Did my feelings, my hatred toward liars, ever cross your mind when you looked into my eyes and lied to me?"

He stood there with no emotion on his face.

"No!" I continued, enraged. "You say you just wanted to protect me by not telling me the truth, when really … you were only protecting yourself! Well guess what, asshole, the truth is … I don't need your protection! Now get out!" I opened the door, pointing outside. Again, he shook his head before walking out.

As soon as he passed the threshold, I slammed the door shut, sliding down the back of it into a ball; tears rolled down my face.

26

Thoughts Can Do Strange Things to One's Mind

Picking myself up off the floor, I stumbled into my bedroom, collapsing in utter fatigue on top of my bed. Exhausted from the angry words as well as the tears, I rolled back and forth on the bed in agony, screaming in pain. It felt as if I were transforming, becoming someone else; some kind of vicious animal was unleashed.

How could I have allowed myself to get so angry, to bite his head off, over a lie? I've lied before! Long-forgotten memories flooded back to me as I thought back to the many lies I told when I was a child, most of which were attempts to please and appease my parents as they dealt with their own insecurities resulting in divorce. I didn't tell lies to hurt them!

What was wrong with me? I thought. *Why did I kick him out of the apartment? That's not like me! This is not my desired world!*

Burying my head under the pillow, I pulled my knees up into the fetal position and rocked back and forth. My stomach burned from physical ache. The area around the hernia was now cramping. My nausea became more pronounced; I wanted to throw up. Grabbing my pillow, I covered my mouth and screamed into it—at Mark, at Richard, at Samantha, at myself, and at the world for causing this pain. It didn't even hurt this bad when I saw Richard kissing another woman. Why would I be in so much turmoil over dinner and drinks?

I was still rocking back and forth, gently weeping, when visions appeared in my head like a horrible movie. I recalled the pain Richard put me through in our marriage and subsequent divorce. Memories of how I discovered secret phone calls and text messages came back, as well as one particular phone call with identical words: "I'll be working late tonight." The thoughts made me dizzy.

Then I remembered back to the very first time Richard was dishonest with me. He had enrolled in a junior college to begin finishing his degree while I worked and supported the household. It was a Tuesday morning when he left for classes, and I realized he had left one of his books behind. Deciding it would be a perfect excuse to surprise him over lunch and bring him his book, I went to the school but couldn't find him anywhere. His car wasn't in the parking lot. I thought that maybe he had left and gone to lunch with friends.

Then something inside of me told me to check with the administration office. I discovered he had dropped out of school two weeks prior. When he arrived home that night, I went berserk, implying dishonesty and even infidelity in our marriage. I remember taking control of everything: his passwords, his account numbers, and where he was at each moment of every day. I didn't trust him and completely emasculated him, believing wholeheartedly he deserved it.

When I questioned him as to why he had dropped out, he didn't tell me. He said it was because "he knew I would be angry." Bullshit. For months I entertained my suspicions by checking his e-mail continuously, looking through his text messages, and following him through GPS. I even interviewed, but didn't hire, a private investigator to ensure his stories of work matched up with what he was actually doing.

It was sad that I desired and expected to have my worst nightmare revealed in order to justify leaving him and moving on. Yet the crazier I went, the more I couldn't find anything to confirm the fear I had inside. After several months, I decided to forget the whole mission. Realizing how useless it was to spend every hour of the day suspicious of what he could or could not be doing, I tried to engage him with romantic dinner offers or sexy negligees, hoping that it was all in my mind.

But the scenarios of suspected infidelity grew deeper, darker, and more complicated as I wondered if he had a separate phone for liaisons or an unknown e-mail account to arrange sex over lunch. Every time I envisioned something bad, my distrust got worse and worse. Would it ever end? Soon I became disassociated from reality.

When I finally stopped and gave up control, it was because I didn't care anymore. Each time I looked at him, it was with disgust. Our relationship became routine and mundane, with more yelling than happy communication. Other people met my needs better than Richard and made me happier too. So we lived individual lives, all under the guise of marriage. I hated him for turning me into such a disassociated human being.

The rocking back and forth stopped and, as I sat up in bed, the waterworks ceased as well. The realization that I was back in the same position I had been in nearly three years before came over me. I had caught another man in a lie and was again turning back into a crazy animal. *Are there any men out there who don't lie?* I wondered. *Or maybe there are other women that are better at dealing with dishonesty than I am.*

How shitty our world has become when relationships are based on the foundation of built-up truth, only to be destroyed by one lie and all the good washed away in one fell swoop. *Who knew what truth and reality were anyway? Maybe it was all lies from the beginning?* My head hurt and my eyes were swollen shut from crying. I rested my head on the pillow and fell asleep.

······•••●••••······

When I woke up, I felt disoriented and confused. It felt like the middle of the night rather than early morning. Gazing around, I could see the mess I had made of the bed. I stood to go to the bathroom when the realization of the previous night's events hit me hard: Mark was gone, maybe forever.

Looking in the mirror, I saw my eyes puffy and almost swollen shut; they were painful to the touch. I turned on the cold water and reached down to splash some on my face, hoping it would make me feel better. With my eyes still closed, water dripping, I reached for a hand towel to blot the moisture from my face.

Feeling a chill in the room and a presence, I opened my eyes. There behind me stood Lady M, as well as several other women. I didn't flinch or move a muscle, not caring at this point. Turning around to confront them, I found nothing but empty space.

"Go away!" I screamed at the top of my lungs to their reflections. "Get out of my house!"

The laughter of these women echoed around me. I turned my head from side to side in an attempt to catch a glimpse of the originator, and the laughter grew louder, coming from all directions. The laughs were directed at me. I began to swat at the air in the direction of each passing laugh, as if to hit them and shoo them away. Nothing but air. The laughter continued.

"Why are you here?" I screamed again. "What's your purpose?" I looked around the room, expecting to see something appear at any moment. Now I knew I had the right target for my anger—Lady M. If it hadn't been for her encouraging me to kick Mark out, he would still be here. I waited for a response as the laughter died down.

A cool breeze moved across my left cheek and the room grew colder still; goose bumps covered my arms. I knew she was there, even though I couldn't see her.

"Madame is a liar too," her voice hissed in my ear. "She and Mark are in on this together. They all are. It's a game for them, and you are the pawn." She spoke from behind me, then over to my right ear. "But you can play the game too and win … if you listen to me. You will know what you need to do."

"No!" I said through gritted teeth. "I don't believe you. You're the liar!" I said it over and over again until I heard her answer.

"No, dear, you have it backward. Why else would I be here? To harm you? My dear, you harm yourself. Get away from them all so that you will understand. You will know what to do." Her voice faded.

Standing in stunned silence, I reflected on her words: "They're all in on it." *In on what? A game? Could Chrissy, Jessica, and Julia be lying? Is Samantha a distraction from it all? Is it some kind of cosmic game God is playing with my life?*

A loud knock on the door startled me. Then I heard it again. I walked toward the door and looked through the peephole. It was Mark. Not wanting him to see me completely disheveled, I ignored the knocking.

"Lenea … please let me in. I know you're home. Can we please talk?" It broke my heart to hear him pleading. "Lenea … please let me in …" He knocked again.

"I'm not sure I have anything to say to you, Mark," I answered through the door, my voice cracking a little.

"Please, Len, give me a chance. Open the door and let's talk," he said. "Please."

Against my better judgment, I secured the safety latch and opened the door slightly, not quite revealing myself.

"Thank you," he said in a softer voice.

"Listen," he said, talking quietly and tenderly through the opening, "What I did last night was inexcusable, and I'm sorry. I never should have lied to you or put you in such an uncomfortable position. I can't tell you why I did it." He paused. "It just slipped out and … it was wrong. It was an easy way out of an otherwise long explanation." He hesitated a few moments, apparently searching for words. "I understand if you need time to think it over and time to trust me again. I love you, and I'm here for you. But your trust is exactly that: yours. I don't control that."

Control. Funny—that was the word both Madame and Mark mentioned previously: "We can't control others; we can only control ourselves." I was sick of hearing the word "control." I became enraged, lost in my thoughts, but said nothing.

"Lenea, are you there?" he asked kindly. "Please talk to me."

"Mark," I began, leaning in closer to the opening, pausing to gather my thoughts. "You lied to me. Aren't lies a form of manipulation, control? You say we can't control others. Yet that's what you did to me. I am not controlled by anyone. Not you, not Madame, the spirits, or Chrissy, and definitely not my parents. Quit trying to control me!" I raged inside thinking of the control he was attempting to have over me at this very moment. I continued.

"Ever heard the term 'once bitten, twice shy'?" I asked, still seething inside. "Well, I think all relationships are bullshit!" I was so angry I didn't recognize myself. Yet the control I felt over him felt good, and I wasn't about to stop there. "What is this life if we can't have relationships? I've obviously failed at two significant ones. Why would I even begin to think that I could forgive you and move on? It's not possible! I will never trust another man in my life. All thanks to *you!*"

"Lenea, can you please open this door so I can see you?" Mark asked.

"No!" I shouted loudly, as some kind of outside anger erupted from within. "Get out of my life! All of you!"

By now I could sense Mark was getting anxious. I was enjoying the control and the attention and decided to scare him as much as possible.

"That's it!" I said, throwing my hands in the air for effect. "I think I'd rather kill myself and end all this pain." A cackling, otherworldly laugh came from my mouth.

Mark shoved the door open; the latch gave way. He looked me straight in the eye. It was gratifying to get this reaction, and I decided to keep playing the role of the crazy woman. "Help me!" I screamed, starting to run in circles, my hands waving over my head. "He's trying to control me! He wants to control my life!"

Mark tried to quiet me down. He turned to shut the front door behind him. When he did so, I took off running for the bathroom and slammed the door behind me. "I'm going to call the cops if you don't leave!" I screamed through the door. "Get out of here!"

"You can't call the cops," he said. "Your phone's out here. Lenea, please calm down. Everything's okay. You're overreacting."

His words made my blood boil, and I thought to myself, *He can't tell me I'm overreacting. I call the shots! I control this game!*

Then I saw the bottle of pain pills sitting on the bathroom counter. I screamed at the top of my lungs, "I'm taking this bottle of pills! I have no reason to live! I hate you, and I never want to see any of you again!" I grabbed the bottle, twisted off the top, and stared at the pills.

The bathroom door rattled behind me as Mark desperately tried to get in. "Lenea," he shouted, pounding on the door, "let me in!"

The pounding continued as I poured a dozen pills into my hand and tossed them to the back of my throat. The pills touched my tongue, and I began to cry hysterically; the reality of the moment hit me. I couldn't do it. I couldn't finish the game. I turned and spit them into the sink, falling onto the floor before curling up into a crying ball of misery.

Mark's pounding stopped. "Lenea, please open this door," he continued calmly. "Please let me in."

It seemed like an eternity until I opened my eyes, finally crawling to open the door. It took every ounce of my remaining energy to reach up and twist the door handle to unlock it. Mark rushed in and held me on the floor in his arms. He allowed me all the time I needed to yell, cry and get everything out I needed to say. The whole time he held me, rocking me back and forth in his arms, repeating, "It's okay. I'm here."

My crying subsided and the sobbing slowed to heavy breathing, while Mark stroked my hair. "Lenea, it's obvious you need help. I'm going to call Chrissy and let you talk to her, okay? When you're done, I think we should go see Madame. I believe she can help you. Does this have anything to do with the spirits?" He didn't even wait for an answer. He stood and went to the kitchen. I could hear him talking to Chrissy in the background.

I sat there stunned, once again realizing what I had created. The thought of swallowing the pills seemed irrational. *How did I let things get this far out of hand?* Yet I still had an urge to fight for control. Mark walked in the bathroom, phone in hand, and I began to laugh hysterically.

"What's so funny?" Mark asked, slightly annoyed.

At that point, I realized that by trying to take control of my own life, I could not control anyone else; I only hurt myself. I remembered Lady M's words—"you are a pawn"—and began to laugh even harder.

Mark set down the phone, looking directly at me. "Why are you laughing?" He seemed irritated.

The biggest unnatural smile crossed my face with the realization that the thing harming me was my belief I could control the situation. Lady M was using me as a pawn. Everyone was, including me. That this was all a game, and I didn't fucking care anymore who won. "Because I'm not in control. And neither are you," I answered, never blinking, never changing my facial expression. A powerful energy filled my mind and body. I felt alive.

Now Mark looked confused, not knowing what to make of the situation. He handed the phone to me. "It's Chrissy," he said.

I took the phone from his hand and I told Chrissy the story of the night's events, laughing and smiling through the whole conversation. "I'm here at your apartment," she said before hanging up. I heard a gentle knock at the front door, followed by her voice. "Hello?" Chrissy must have been driving and talking at the same time.

After coming into the bathroom and hugging me, she and Mark put their arms around me, lifted me up, and walked me down to her car.

Everything seemed funny to me. I felt almost drunk as we stumbled through the lobby. Walking outside with my puffy face covered in tear-streaked makeup, I normally would have cared about my appearance. But today, I laughed.

It only made Chrissy and Mark even more bewildered by my delirium. Yet it felt so good. Lacking control or concern about anything meant freedom. Mark opened the door and settled me into the passenger seat, buckling the belt for me and giving it one last tug as Chrissy sat down and started the car. He bent down, kissing my forehead before shutting the door and getting in the backseat.

We drove to the studio, and my head felt light, as if it was filled with helium; it kept bobbing while I watched the busy bees trudge to their office hives. The sun gleamed off the reflective windows of passing skyscrapers. The local pop radio station played today's hits in the background. The smells from nearby restaurants baking their morning bread filled the car as we drove by. It was as if every sense in my body had been heightened.

My mind replayed the vision of Lady M in the mirror the night before. I laughed. She could have shown up in the backseat and I would have merely turned around and given her a hug. I was in a state of pure bliss, peace.

As we pulled up to the studio, Chrissy told Mark he had done the right thing. Mark jumped out of the backseat and opened my door, lifting me and holding me while directing me up the steps. My laughter turned maniacal as I realized for the first time I had come into the studio not caring who I was.

Looking into Mark's face sobered me slightly for it was truly filled with concern. Leaning on him for support, I was certain I could have walked all on my own. But it felt good to feel his caring, his love. Mark opened the door, and we walked inside to see Madame waiting.

"Bonjour, Lenea," she greeted me, completely devoid of any emotion or compassion for the roiling mess of humanity that had entered her premises.

"Bonjour, Madame," I replied in my worst French accent; then I winked at her and laughed.

"I'll take it from here, Mark. Thank you," Madame said, putting her arm around my shoulder.

"Madame will take care of you," he said softly, reaching up to kiss me on the cheek with concern in his eyes. "I love you. Please know that."

Lifting my hand in recognition of his concern, I walked with Madame down the dimly lit hallway.

"How does it feel to completely lose control?" Madame asked in a manner that suggested a knowing.

"Amazing," I replied, smiling, delirious with the moment and what I had accomplished.

"Welcome home," she offered surreptitiously as we entered the studio. "We've been waiting for you."

27

A Possibility of Success

"Grab a pillow and join me on the floor," Madame instructed. She sat on her own pillow, crossing her legs. I set my pillow across from her and mirrored her position. She took a deep breath with eyes closed, held it a few seconds, then let the air go slowly through her slightly parted lips. Her eyes popped open, "Lenea, do you believe you are going to receive all that you desire and your dreams will come true?"

Still reeling from the delirium of the prior night's events, I laughed out loud at her comment. "I don't care anymore if they do come true. And no! I don't believe you!" It felt so good to be honest with her and not care about any repercussions.

"Good. Thank you for your honesty," she said, the corners of her mouth turning upward, her eyes now closing slightly as she continued. "Now we can get somewhere. Lenea, I don't care if you believe me or not. Your belief does not affect me; it can only affect you. To believe me is a choice. I can offer you a different perspective only because I've been in your shoes. One cannot teach unless she or he has experienced the lessons firsthand. I know you are in the perfect position to make all your dreams come true right now."

Again I retorted with a laugh. "Okay, please explain it to me because I don't understand a word you are saying or how it could even be true."

It felt as though her words were coming straight from a fairy tale book. For a moment I thought she was the one going crazy.

"Ah, now we're getting somewhere." She held a pointed finger up to add emphasis. "Until you ask for my help, I cannot intervene and help you. Now that you have asked me, I will fulfill my promise. After Mark called me and told me what happened last night, I blocked the morning off to spend with you and teach you. I believe that by the time you leave here you will see the world with new eyes. Is this something you desire?"

My mind was dizzy and my focus unclear. Still, I tried to follow her, albeit halfheartedly. "Sure," I responded, shrugging.

"Wonderful." She stood up from her pillow. "I've invited Jessica to join us today and share the rest of her story. I know you have witnessed her personal transformation firsthand. To know the success of another's journey is to know the possibilities within your own. While you listen to her, listen as you did when you watched Elemental Charity and their dance performance. Remember to heighten your senses and awareness. Listen to her music, her words. Follow her emotion. Hear her tone. Place yourself in her shoes and allow her story to move you within your own body. Can you do that?" Madame seemed to tower over me. The seriousness of the moment gave me a chance to sober up, and my mind to clear.

"I still don't follow what you're saying, but I do remember the lesson. I will listen as you say." I bowed my head respectfully before she walked over to the door asking Jessica to come join us.

Jessica still looked as happy as she was when I saw her the week before. Maybe this happiness could last after all. She was dressed for yoga, carrying a black journal held tight to her chest and a pink duffel gym bag over her left shoulder. She surveyed the studio and grabbed a pillow to join us. Madame took matches from a drawer and lit candles around the floor.

Turning the lights down, Madame joined us in the center of the room, perching herself atop her pillow. We now formed a triangle. Jessica looked nervous.

"Thank you for coming." Madame turned to Jessica. "Would you please share with us your story?"

Jessica nodded in compliance, opening her journal before turning her attention to me. "I brought my story today at the request of Madame. If it can help you or anyone else who has been on a similar journey, it's the least I can do in return for all Madame has done for me." Jessica looked at Madame and smiled, then returned her gaze to me. "You already know the beginning of my story, so I'll skip to the part of what happened between then and now. Here it goes."

She opened her journal, flipped a few pages, cleared her throat, and began to read.

"In the days and weeks after the assault, I was angry at the world. I was angry at God. I would think to myself, *How could this happen to me? I'm a good person. What did I do to deserve such abuse?* As I watched others living their dreams, it sickened me, and the anger grew overwhelming. Where was the loving, benevolent God they all talked about when I was being sexually assaulted? I had no choice in the matter. It happened, and I had to live with the painful memories day in and day out—a nightmare that would continue throughout my days. I had no sense of reality and no hope for a brighter future." Jessica looked up at us before turning the page.

"I remember the hatred I had toward all men. I looked at all of them as creeps simply wanting to get into girls' pants. I avoided relationships. The psychiatrist diagnosed me with post-traumatic stress disorder—a stress I received with no choice in the matter.

"One day, shortly after that diagnosis, while on a walk in the mountains, I had a deep thought: *How can I be sexually assaulted physically and end up with a mental disorder? The abuse didn't happen to my mind; it happened to my body!* That one thought gave me the opportunity to share my finding with the counselor and begin a path of healing—but not completely.

"As time passed, and after more therapy, I became attracted to a special man. I opened my heart to him, as well as, eventually, my body. The relationship turned serious, and we moved in together. Then one day he announced he was moving out and leaving me for another woman. I was crushed and felt abused all over again.

"I gave up hope of finding a lasting relationship. I began to have sex with every man on the first date and every date thereafter. It was the only way I could feel loved and desired; alive.

"When one man would leave, it didn't bother me; there was a plethora of other men wanting to have sex with me right around the corner." She looked up and winked. I nodded, knowing exactly what she meant.

"I was never lonely, and everyone seemed to get what they wanted.

Those sexual escapades were short times out of my day and my only vacation away from my thoughts; a form of escape." Jessica paused and turned the page before taking a deep breath and continuing.

"After a while, sex began to lose its appeal, and physically"—she stopped and gestured to her hips—"so did I. I no longer had the body of my early twenties. Men started to reject my overtures, and I channeled all my sexual energy into food consumption. It brought me comfort from the pain—another form of escape. As I gained weight and looked in the mirror, it only provided an excuse to reinforce my belief: that no man would ever love me. How could he? I didn't even love myself. Then the downward spiral; I questioned why I should even be alive. At the depths of my despair, a friend introduced me to Madame." Jessica's eyes moistened with tears as she paused to look up at Madame.

She reached into her gym bag, pulled out a water bottle, opened it, and took a few gulps before closing it. She cleared her throat again before continuing. "When I met Madame, she asked me what my true desires were. I told her that first and foremost, I desired to be married, although I didn't believe it could really happen. We started our work together, and about our sixth session, Madame brought to light a simple thought, very reminiscent of the thought I had on that mountain hike: one bad experience had affected my entire life. She pointed out that I had only been sexually assaulted once—a few bad minutes on one bad day. Yet I had assaulted myself in my mind for over twenty years!"

She stopped to look at me to see if I was following. Without realizing it, my eyes had filled with tears that were running down my face; I connected with each word. Madame pulled a tissue from somewhere and handed it to me. I wiped my eyes and blew my nose. Jessica's eyes grew focused, looking into mine, while she continued to drive home her point. "More important, Madame provided a safe space for me to get back in touch with my sexuality as a woman. I danced and learned to appreciate my body. Looking at myself in the mirror with love and acceptance, I felt powerful and sexy. I learned about the power of being attracted to myself.

"At first I thought it was prideful and arrogant, and I struggled with the concept. But I will never forget Madame's question. She asked me, 'If you think you are sexy and powerful and that you can achieve all your dreams, yet never tell a soul, how is that arrogant or prideful? Don't you want the same for others? Everyone has this ability.' I understood how my mind is my own private imagination station.

"When I learned the power of the sixth sense, or intuition, I discovered a turning point I will never forget. I applied these concepts to all situations in life, and I watched as one dream after another came true, including finding the love of my life." Jessica stopped and looked at all of us with tears of joy in her eyes, displaying the ring on her left hand with pride.

"The biggest 'aha moment' was realizing that it was *my* thoughts that caused the most amount of pain, not the assault from others. The brief moments of sexual abuse that happened to my body were nothing compared to the years of abuse my mind had caused. When I learned to heal my own thinking and warped beliefs ... that's when I learned the power of love: to love myself in order to truly love others."

Jessica finished her story and Madame handed her a tissue to wipe her eyes. Jessica laughed nervously before leaning into Madame as they squeezed each other tightly. "Thank you," Jessica said with her eyes closed. Then they both turned and included me in the hug.

After a few moments, we all stood. "Thank you," Madame said, holding Jessica's hands in hers. "Thank you for helping a sister." Jessica nodded and Madame escorted her to the door. They shared some words before hugging one more time. Jessica left, and Madame walked back over to me.

The message from Jessica's story resonated deep within me, and I was truly happy for her as one of my "sisters." Still, I couldn't help but think back to my own issue: she didn't have spirits haunting her. *How could her story really help me in my situation?*

While I also had a desire to trust a man and get married, I wondered, *How do I heal the pain of dishonesty from Mark and ever trust him again?* Instantly I felt a rush of jealousy for Jessica's healing and where she was in life. *Could Madame help me attain this elusive sixth sense?*

Madame returned and resumed her position across from me so that we could see each other face-to-face. "Lenea, do you know the difference between fear and freedom?" she probed.

"Sure, fear is debilitating and freedom is ... well, free; no limitations," I offered.

"Can you have an experience of feeling fear and experience a feeling of freedom at the same time?" she asked further.

Contemplating, I replied, "No. I don't think so."

"That is correct. There is no freedom in an experience of fear, and there is no fear in an experience of freedom. Fear and freedom cannot coexist. Given the choice, which would you choose?" she asked.

"Freedom," I replied without hesitation.

"Yet here you are, living in a state of fear. What are you afraid of?"

Swallowing hard, I felt the need to tell her everything: my relationship with Mark and his lies, as well as Samantha and my anger at her.

Finally, when it came time to discuss Lady M, I hesitated, remembering her words about not trusting Madame. Still, I felt I had nothing to lose. "There is a dark haired woman who was the madam of the Mystere building that connects to the studio. She and her ladies of the night are haunting me. I've done my research and discovered she was married to a man who cheated on her, and because of that, she didn't trust men. After learning about spirit attachments, I believe she has attached to me because I too don't trust men. I never know when she is going to show up. But every time she does, my life becomes a chaotic mess, from sickness to injuries to just plain fear. I want her gone."

"I see," Madame replied coolly. She squinted and paused, deep in thought. The silence continued for several moments while she stared into my eyes. Growing uncomfortable, I opened up further. "You think I'm crazy don't you? Well, I think I'm crazy too. I've never had this happen before, and I have no idea what to do. I'm tired of living my life in fear!"

"Lenea, *your* reality is simply that: yours. If you try to fight it or refuse to accept it, *that* is what drives a person crazy. To find freedom, you must come to peace with what reality is. Your reality is that you are haunted by a spirit of the past that has caused you to live in fear. Now that we know your perceived problem, we can find a solution. For every perceived problem has a solution."

"No, it's not perceived. It is a problem!" I replied, trying to make her understand.

"It's not a problem for me." She pointed at herself, looking around. "It's only a problem because you see it that way. I'm here to give you new eyes. I have a sculpture and a poem I would like to share with you. I keep them in the basement. I'll be back in a moment." She stood and walked out the door before I could say anything.

Sitting there, I fumed inside, not understanding her words. *What in the world are new eyes?* I wondered. All the thinking made me tired. I needed answers.

When she returned, she was carrying a tall sculpture. It seemed taller than she was.

"Do you need help with that?" I asked.

"No," Madame responded, carefully balancing the piece, "but thank you. It's much lighter than it looks."

Madame set the sculpture down facing us in front of the mirror. It was an odd-looking piece of art. The bottom was shaped from a heavy wood stand, and on top stood a large mask made from reflective material. It was eerie-looking too: the mask had an opening for a mouth but no opening for the other facial features, primarily the eyes and nose. Behind the large mask stood a tall wooden board about three times the size of the mask. The board had an inscription of some sort carved into it. The sculpture also had a cord attached to it. Madame searched the wall for what I assumed was an outlet, and it dawned on me: *It's a lamp.* When she plugged it in, a light from behind the mask shone through the mouth of the mask and illuminated the saying on the wooden board perfectly. It indeed was an inscription. The title was *The Light*.

"This art piece reminds me daily of the lesson I am about to teach you," Madame began. "If you do not understand the message now, know that you soon will." She paused, moved away from the piece, and stood next to me. "Art is timeless. Art carries a deep and profound message that expands and continues long past the time it is created. All art, music, poetry, and dance are forms of expression. The artist, the musician, the poet and the dancer all convey a message to the soul of humanity. As the spectator, many times we feel inspired. Yet we don't always know why. This is because the artist, musician, poet or dancer does not create from the mind. Their creation comes from their untethered soul; that of limitless freedom. Whenever you are in a place of fear in your mind, these art forms will help you remember the freedom we all are inherently born with but somehow forget along the way. May this piece illuminate the freedom that lies within you.

"Don't think about the words," she continued. "Merely relax and accept them, knowing that if you don't get the message now, you soon will." She then read the poem slowly, in a soft tone of voice, caressing each word:

The Light

I have a mask, a mask with no eyes. I wear it often in my mundane lies.
Can someone see me behind the veil? Cowardly hiding in a private hell.
"Remove the mask and you shall see."
Who is this talking to me?
"Darkness lies in a mask with no eyes."
No eyes, you say. Do you not see the pain this world is causing me?
"I see you. I do not see pain. All emotion is
equal. All creation the same."
How can you see me? There is no light.
"Take off the mask. Use your sight."
I removed the mask. Now I see people in masks surrounding me.
The blind lead the blind. Is this true?
"No, they are not blind, and neither are you.
It is the mask that blocks sight; shields the light."
The darkness was better. This sight is no fun.
I prefer my mask than to see no one.
"Wait. Be patient. What is written will be.
Blessed are the eyes because they see."
But how do we see? The mask has no eyes.
"Perceive from the heart the truth in disguise."
A sensation began to envelop my skin. I felt
warmth and vibrations; alive from within.
What is this sensation inside of me?
"Your eyes have been opened. You are beginning to See."
The Light

When Madame finished, she waited, giving me time to reflect on the words. "This poem helps to explain your sixth sense, that of intuition and, for some, vibration. Many times humans pass this off as a feeling of inspiration or an 'aha moment.' Many times they don't even notice it happening or give it a second thought." Her voice faded into disappointment.

"This sixth sense is an internal sense we are all born with," she continued. "It's really not a sense at all, but more of ... an energy transfer. People experience it in different and unique ways. For some it's a simple 'knowing.' It doesn't matter how you experience it, or even why. It is like any other sense in our body: sight, hearing, taste, touch, or smell. And when we learn how to use it, we heighten our perception of all that is around us. Do you remember the lesson with the dancers and the blank canvas?"

Thinking back to the moment in the studio, I remembered Madame teaching about the five senses, explaining that if one went missing, we would perceive experiences differently. *How did this have anything to do with spirits haunting me?*

"Yes," I finally answered. "I remember. And I've experienced this before." After pausing a few moments to digest my own words, I grew annoyed. "I'm sorry, but what does this have to do with the spirits and trusting men? I still don't get it." I glared at her.

"If you pay close attention to these next few lessons ... you will understand." Madame seemed certain before continuing. "And if you choose, you will be able to dissolve the attachment to the spirits. The sixth sense is the first step. If you do not recognize this now, it is because you have not yet experienced it. What you feel and think at this time is normal. However, once you experience the sixth sense, intuition, and understand how it is used, your life will never be the same."

Through all of the night's previous events, the emotions of Jessica's stories, and Madame's insights, I sensed a ray of hope. I gave complete trust and faith to Madame in the belief she could help make the spirits disappear. Closing my eyes, I spoke with genuine respect, asking for Madame's help, "All I want is to get back to a normal life. I will take any tools or guidance you may give me ... if I can get rid of these spirits."

Madame's eyes brightened in response. "Not if ... but when."

28

Mirrors Reflect More Than Meets the Eye

"Lenea, what does the business of prostitution have to do with you?" Madame asked directly.

I was shocked by the bluntness of her question. "What do you mean?" I replied, confused by where her line of questioning was going.

"These spirits that haunt you are a madam and prostitutes. They lived a life of prostitution. Where does prostitution show up in your life? Everything in life has everything to do with everything," she opined, trying to connect the dots.

"I have no idea!" I responded. "I'm not a prostitute!"

She smiled, shaking her head slightly side to side as if I didn't understand where she was going with this. "Prostitution has an obvious meaning. However, it has another meaning as well. The other definition of prostitution is the use of a skill or ability in a way that is inappropriate or not respectable. That is the state of being prostituted." She paused for the words to sink in. "What is your greatest struggle with trusting men?" she asked, trying a different tact.

"I believe all they think about is sex. And they lie and cheat to get what they want. They aren't sorry or think otherwise until they're caught," I said, offering my true beliefs.

"Can you be one hundred percent sure all men cheat and lie?" she asked rhetorically.

"No. But it is how I feel," I responded, annoyed this time by her smugness.

"Okay, then. We've identified your problem. You have a skill and an ability to think anything you want to, yet you choose to believe a lie. Is a lie appropriate or respectable?"

"Absolutely not. I hate lies."

"Yet here you are ... believing a lie," she said, as if providing the answer.

Getting angry now at how her questions were turning into answers, I tried not to get flustered and made every effort to respond calmly. "No. I believe in the reality of what happened to me. I'm living on facts ... and protecting myself in the future. There's a difference." I said firmly.

"Interesting. Yet you have no control of your life. So even your protection is out of your hands," she said. Not satisfied with where this was going, she tried a different approach. "Would you like to live in a reality where all your dreams come true?"

At this point, I had enough of her idealistic approach to my situation. This was complex. *Spirits, attaching to me and haunting me. This is not something that is happening in the real physical world ... but the metaphysical world.*

I grew peeved as she continued, "Reality is living in freedom and knowing that whatever is happening to you at every moment of life is all connected."

Feeling goaded into a confrontation, I was ready to let loose. "You know what? That's easy for you to say. You run your little studio and live in a perfect world and think you have all the answers. But look at you ... you're not even married! How can you be so sure all of my dreams will come true?" Rage filled my body as I waited to see how such mean words would affect her.

Her face remained emotionless. She took a deep breath and released it, giving herself time to formulate a plan before answering. "Your tone tells me you are excited to hear more. So here is your next lesson. I am going to tell you a story about the L'abeille Palace and the Mystere. When I am finished, I am going to ask you a series of questions. I am going to allow you space to gain an understanding of your own thinking. Then, and only then, will I tell you the answer to your question."

My eyes grew wide. Goose bumps broke out on my arms. Fear washed over me. How did she know about the L'abeille Palace? I never told her anything about my research and the connection. I leaned forward, listening intently.

Madame sat upright on her pillow and took a deep breath. "It is early May in the year nineteen oh five. A young family checks into the L'abeille Palace in the afternoon. The husband is a wealthy businessman and the wife is well-kempt, as they said in those days. They are traveling with their seven-year-old son. While standing at the check-in counter, the wife notices all of the beautiful women sitting in the foyer distracting her husband's attention, particularly a striking brunette with big brown eyes. After the family goes upstairs to settle in, the husband excuses himself for an afternoon drink and heads downstairs to make contact with the women. Unbeknownst to his wife, he is invited by the brunette to dinner." Madame looked at me with her piercing eyes and continued.

"The couple is there on a business trip for his company. Upon returning to the wife's room, the husband explains to the wife that he will be meeting with clients for dinner and she should not wait up. He kisses his wife and his son and walks downstairs, where he presents a code word to the front desk. He is then ushered to the back of the hotel, into the coal tunnel, and out the other side into the basement of the Mystere. There, he meets with the brunette, a madam, who coordinates a liaison with a beautiful blonde he has chosen off the menu of her ladies of the night. The brunette introduces him to the blonde, and the two head upstairs, where he is able to satiate his carnal desires. This happens for three nights consecutively." Madame stopped talking and adjusted herself on her pillow before continuing her story.

"On the last day of their stay, the wife begins to sense through her sixth sense, or intuition, that something is off. While checking out, she hears the desk clerk mention 'extra charges' with a separate bill and watches her husband pull out his wallet, taking out an unusually large amount of money to pay the bill. She has a moment of clarity as she recognizes the relationship between the hotel and the beautiful women loitering around, and she is outraged. When she demands to know the truth from her husband about the extra charges, she is interrupted by the hotel clerk who very inappropriately suggests she should be happy to have a man to take care of her. It was the belief of that generation that women in the upper class should accept the infidelities of their partner as a way of life." Madame paused again, clearing her throat.

"The wife went on living in silence and anger, eventually dying of cancer. The husband continued his affairs until her sickness. And the brunette ...?" She paused for effect, "She was the madam of the Mystere. Her name was Margret, or Mattie. Many called her Lady M."

I sat there in stunned silence, the hair on the nape of my neck rose when she uttered her name. How did she know about Lady M and that story? I was awe-struck.

"You most likely want to know how I know this story," she asked, as if reading my mind. "That is not the point. The point is, until you investigate your own thinking, you are not going to understand anything." Madame leaned in, stopping her face inches from mine. "Are you ready for your next lesson?"

It was starting to astound me how much Madame knew, and I wasn't sure I wanted to understand. But if it would help this spirit leave, I was up for anything. I nodded.

Madame leaned back, settling into her pillow. "It is true that in everyday life, thought predicates people's decisions and actions. Yet thoughts alone do not contain any power. A thought only gains power when you believe the thought is true. These beliefs begin to shape your reality and guide your decisions and actions, your will and your deed, and therefore determine your destiny," Madame said, paraphrasing from the Upanishads.

"I am going to walk you through a series of questions to get to the heart of your thoughts. Let's see what happens," she said, smiling. "In the story I shared with you, I want you to stand in the place of the wife; step into her shoes. Remember, we are only looking to find the reality of what is happening in this woman's life. Reality is whatever is happening at the moment. It is truth, not labeled good or bad. It is only good to deal with reality. Avoiding reality or arguing with it only promotes fear. The lesson is to know the difference. Let's begin," she said, looking into my eyes.

"In the story, the wife didn't ask to find out about her husband's actions with the prostitute, correct? She already knew that her husband had cheated on her through her intuition. Why was she so outraged?" Madame inquired.

"Because he had sex with another woman outside of their marriage," I responded quickly.

"Go deeper," Madame said, in a matter of fact tone of voice.

I tried again. "Because he's been with a prostitute and could carry home some kind of disease."

"Go ... deeper. Remember what reality is for the wife in the story. Why are you"—she pointed her finger into my chest—"the wife, upset?"

Recalling the story in my memory, I closed my eyes and tried to imagine being in the wife's shoes. The reality of being this woman was painful. I could feel the woman's anger and what she experienced. Opening my eyes, I knew the answer. "Because they won't tell her about the extra charges, and she wants to know the truth."

"Yes. And what is the truth?" Madame asked, encouraging me.

"That he has spent a lot of money on 'extra charges' and no one will explain to her what they were for. Yet she knows exactly what they were for," I said.

"If he bought you and the child dinner, toys, or flowers and it was explained to you that these were the 'extra charges,' would you be as upset?" Madame queried.

"No," I answered, shaking my head.

"It's not about the money. It was never about the money. What else does she ... *know?*" Madame stretched out the word as if to give me a clue to her question.

"Oh yes!" I answered excitedly. "Her intuition has told her that her husband has been unfaithful."

"Correct. Her intuition is her reality. And any woman who argues against that gut feeling, therefore, lives in fear and uncertainty." She paused. "Now, step out of her shoes and into your own. How did you feel when you *knew* your husband was cheating on you in your first marriage?"

Searching back in my memory, I came up with the answer easily. "It made me angry that he would have sex with another woman, and it scared me that he could have brought some kind of disease home to me. I hated him to the depths of my soul."

"And who allowed him to have sex with you even though, intuitionally, you knew he was unfaithful?" she asked.

Getting her point, I answered sheepishly, "I did. But I didn't have any proof. At the time, I thought I was crazy having those feelings. I didn't want to be the jealous wife. I couldn't tell him that!"

"Yes. And why would you be so angry and disgusted with yourself for having sex with your partner? Why was it okay before your intuition kicked in and not after?" she asked.

Thinking for a moment about what she was asking, it came to me. "Because I didn't know about it; I only suspected it."

"Ah, so you had sex under the reality he was faithful, and then, when your reality changed to the truth, you beat yourself up for not trusting your previous intuition. And you were mad. But were you mad at him … or yourself?"

I hesitated, for I knew the truth but didn't want to say it. "I was mad at myself … and him," I added pointedly.

"So in your world, you had a choice. It is apparent he made his choice to be unfaithful. And you can't be angry, because people change in this world. He is his own person with his own choices. You do not own him. The truth is, you are not a victim of anyone else's choices … unless you choose to be. You are not responsible for anyone else's actions … but your own. You are not attached to anyone else's reputation … but your own. Do you see where you are arguing with reality when you say your husband shouldn't cheat on you? He did cheat. That's reality. Now let's stop arguing with it and get to the heart of why you are so upset. Are you really mad at him?"

The truth of her words really sunk in, upsetting me terribly. "But I am the victim!" I yelled at her. "He chose another woman over me … and it hurts!" I began to cry but continued speaking through my tears. "And I don't ever want to be hurt by another man again!"

Madame paused to let me sob a little, waiting for me to listen. "Ah! Now we have hit the heart of the pain." She gazed deeply into my eyes, as if to console me with looks alone.

"This really hurts to talk about it again," I said, wiping the tears away. "Are you sure this is going to make these spirits disappear?" I asked. She produced a tissue from her side and handed it to me.

"I understand your pain, and yes, this is part of the process," she said reassuringly. "You are safe to share. Nothing bad will happen, I promise. Do you really believe your husband chose another woman over you?" she grilled.

"Yes. It's reality. He did choose another woman over me," I responded angrily.

"Could it be just as true that he was simply horny?" she asked.

"Okay. Fine, he was horny. What the hell does it matter? He had sex with another woman!" I said, completely pissed-off.

"I'm not trying to defend him. His actions hurt you, and that is reality as well. We are simply trying to understand *your* thoughts behind *his* actions. Your emotion of anger is good because it will help teach you. This is not about justifying someone's actions. This is about understanding what is happening in your own mind," she said.

Madame moved closer to me as she spoke. "The truth is, we can never know with one hundred percent certainty what someone else is thinking or why they might choose to do something. Therefore we can only deal with the reality of our own painful thoughts about it and how they affect us. So bear with me a little while longer." She stopped, looking down, reflecting on the moment, and then looked up to continue. "So it's true. He could have chosen another woman over you, and it's also potentially true that he was merely horny and wanted to have sex. It doesn't matter why. What matters is that you understand your own thinking about this.

"So you believe he chose another woman over you? How does this make … *you* … feel?" she asked, hesitating between words for effect.

"It hurts. And I'm angry. And it makes me feel insecure that who I am is not enough for him sexually. That he would choose someone else over me. That somehow I'm not enough of a woman to meet his needs." Each sentence had a painful truth to it as I answered.

"Would you like to get rid of this thought?" she asked.

"Yes. It's a horrible thought, and I would love for it to be gone. But it feels so real." My voice cracked. "How in the world can I get rid of a thought?"

"We have already established in life that you are not a victim of anyone else's choices, that you cannot control anyone else's actions. And we have established that reality is what is, not what we think it should or shouldn't be." She paused for a moment, allowing her words to sink in. "So are you ready to take responsibility for your own thinking and leave the victim mentality behind?"

My insides tingled; numb from the interrogation. I was exhausted from all the events of the last twenty-four hours. I didn't know how to answer her question, and honestly I didn't care anymore.

"Lenea, why would you believe another woman is above you?" she asked me.

"I don't believe another woman is above me," I responded defensively.

"Yes, Lenea, you do. Do you know ... why?" she pushed further.

Sitting there, I tried to find an answer but couldn't. Finally, after a pregnant pause, all I could utter was a simple "no."

"Because everyone around us provides a *mirror* for our own thinking ... even spirits. Do you know what a spirit is, Lenea?" She changed her focus.

My mind swirled. I closed my eyes to concentrate, remembering all the research I had done in the past few weeks, from residual and intelligent hauntings and energy crossing the time space continuum to theories of theology, religion, and philosophy. Suddenly I opened my eyes. My sixth sense confirmed the connection that had been made. I verbalized my realization, "It is the spirit of Lady M that thinks these same things. That's why she's attached herself to me. But I'm not a victim of her thinking!" I said excitedly, pausing as the sound of my own words set in. "Still, part of me believes it is me and my thinking. I don't get it. Is it me or her?" Confusion set in once again.

"Yes. These beliefs are what make up the spirits and how they lived their lives," she began. "Earthbound spirits lived their lives with limiting beliefs, and their strong energy is still present in specific locations. When someone of a similar belief comes into contact with this energy, the spirit attaches to the person like a magnet.

"As you know from science, like thoughts attract like thoughts. Beliefs are a stronger form of these thoughts. The spirits are not here to scare you; they are here to understand. In their lifetime as physical beings on Earth, they were not provided the answers. So they continue to search. This is why spirits can attach to you and even be passed through generations if a person is not aware of the attachment. Addictions, abuse, anxiety, judgment, hatred—any and all negative beliefs are all forms of attachments. They are like invisible chains tying you to the past and holding you back from a brighter future. When you realize your own limiting belief and let go of your pain, they will automatically detach from you. For again, like attracts like." She finished, waiting for my reaction.

What she said made sense. "Oh my gosh, yes! So how do I let go of the belief within myself if she's attached to me?"

"Good question," Madame said. "First we must recognize your own limiting belief. What is the belief you have established that keeps you from accomplishing your dreams?" she asked.

Looking deep into my soul, I thought I found the answer, even though it was pretty simple. "That men can't be trusted and I won't find a faithful partner."

"Okay. And when did this belief start for you?" she continued.

Thinking it may have been Richard, the connection didn't resonate with me. Searching further back in my own history, first high school, then junior high, and finally elementary school, a certain moment felt right. "I think it was the period of time when my parents got divorced."

"And how old were you when this happened?" she asked.

"Five years old."

"So from the time you were five years old you have not trusted men. And therefore you have not believed you could fulfill your own desire to be married. You have lived your life in fear because this belief is your perception, your reality."

Even though what she said was true, it hurt to hear the words. "Yes," I answered.

"Are you ready to get rid of that limiting belief and move confidently in the direction of your dreams?" she asked.

"Yes," I answered quickly.

"Okay. I am here to help you, so you have nothing to be afraid of. Know that in order to heal this belief, we must go to the place of pain where emotionally it all stemmed from. The only way to heal is to feel emotion within the body. Whatever it is you feel you need to do—scream, cry, hit a pillow, run around—it doesn't matter. Do what is necessary to re-create the emotions you felt as a little girl when you first developed the belief that men can't be trusted." She got up and walked toward the stereo system, placing a finger on the top button before stopping to look back.

"In a moment, I am going to turn on music for you to reenact this scene of you as a little girl. Using your body, tell yourself a story of what you, as a little girl, felt like at the age of five, while you watch yourself in the mirror." She adjusted the music in the boom box. My heart pounded in my chest. I had no idea what I would do. *Is this where Lady M shows up?* I

261

wondered. Expecting an upbeat dance song, I began to cry when I heard the music: a lullaby, sung by a mother to her child.

As I gazed into the mirror, all I could do was wrap my arms around myself and rock back and forth, trying to comfort the scared and insecure little girl. I touched my face, while the tears streamed down, I said out loud to my own reflection, "It's going to be okay."

Looking in the mirror, I told the little five-year-old girl in me that I loved her and that it was not her fault that her mom and dad didn't love each other anymore. I fell to my knees on the floor and wept unabashedly; allowing my whole body to feel the pain.

When the song was over, I glanced up, expecting to see Lady M or one of her ladies. It was just me, holding myself, crying and gazing into the mirror at the little girl who never knew any better. The music stopped, and after this realization, I turned to Madame. "Lady M didn't show up."

She nodded and smiled encouragingly. "Now that you have gone back and forgiven yourself for the onset of your own belief, let's go back to when Lady M first entered your life. When did you first see her?"

My mind wasn't clear on the answer. I spoke aloud to help me recall. "I remember flashes of light in the studio. The first time I saw her was when Samantha was dancing for Mark. Yes, she came into the studio and started shaking her head. I thought everyone could see her."

"Where else did you see her?"

"I saw her in the studio … in the sandwich shop … in my apartment … In the window of the lingerie store." Each moment revisited.

"Was there anything consistent about the times she revealed herself?"

After I reflected for a moment, the answer was clear. "Yes, She seemed to reveal herself when I was angry or insecure. The room would become much colder in her presence," I said, recalling the feeling in my body.

"What else? What else was consistent about her revelations?" Madame asked, pushing further.

Thinking long and hard, I envisioned each of the encounters. Then it hit me. "Oh my gosh! I only saw her in mirrors!"

"Yes," Madame said, nodding. "Many times spirits show up in mirrors because they are attached to you. Do you now understand the concept of the mirror other people and even spirits provide for you?" Madame probed. "Every one of us, including spirits, provides a mirror of our own thinking. And sometimes the spirit and person are connected as one. When we deal with our own thinking, only then can we deal with breaking any negative attachments. Do you understand?"

"Yes," I replied. "I believe so."

"Good. You are ready for your final lesson."

29

Reflection, Perception, and an Answer to a Question

Madame pulled two bottles of water from the refrigerator and returned to the pillow to complete our marathon session. Both of us cracked them open, taking long draws until the bottles were completely empty. Madame set the stage, positioning herself across from me. I mirrored her, my legs crisscrossed, my arms resting gently on my thighs.

She closed her eyes to take a deep breath and released, I did the same, letting my ears be my guide. She repeated the process two more times. I matched her each time. Then she paused before speaking.

"Now that you have forgiven yourself for the onset of this belief or attachment, let's move to the next step. I want you to stand up and move over to that mirror." She pointed across the room, past the poles, waiting for me to stand up and move to where she directed. "Now look in it and say these words out loud: 'I don't trust men.'"

Staring into the mirror, I took a deep breath and tried to relax. On the next breath, as I released, I said the words out loud. "I don't trust men."

Suddenly Lady M and her ladies of the night appeared behind me. The room became cold, and even though I knew the spirits could not hurt me, I still felt nervous, not knowing what to expect.

Madame had followed me, only a few steps behind. "Is she there?"

"What, you can't see them?" I turned to her reflection, surprised by the question. "I thought you said you could see spirits?"

"This is not about my reality; this is about yours. Now, I want you to look into the mirror and, instead of stating the belief 'I don't trust men,' talk to the mirror."

"Talk to the spirits?" I queried, not understanding.

"No. Don't blame. Don't play victim. Look in the mirror. Who don't you trust?"

Looking into my own eyes, knowing there was no one to blame, the answer became clear. "I don't trust myself," I said out loud.

Immediately the spirits began laughing at me. The reaction startled me; I wasn't expecting that. Scared, exhausted, and with few options remaining, I forced myself to continue, feeling somewhat safe Madame was there.

"So I'm going to ask you another question," Madame said. "Who chose another woman over you?" She paused to let the words sink in, smiling smugly, "Hot tip ... look in the mirror."

The words hit home like a sledgehammer. Looking in the mirror, I could see the spirits still laughing as I pondered what she meant. "Yes," I roared, realizing the truth, "I put another woman above me. And I don't ever want to hurt myself again!"

It felt wonderfully freeing, the truth of this statement. Her words about "playing the victim" led to another insight. "Oh my gosh ... I get it! I wasn't a victim of his actions ... I was a victim of my own thinking."

"Yes." She smiled knowingly. "All those painful shoulds—he should make me happy, he should love me, he should never leave me—they are all harmless thoughts. But they are damaging ... when we believe them and therefore attach to them." Madame emphasized the last words heavily and slowly, waiting for them to resonate.

Suddenly a flood of comprehension came to me as all her lessons on sexuality and the power of our thoughts made sense now. "Oh my God!" I cried out, tingling from head to toe, "I feel it!"

The laughing stopped abruptly. I looked into the mirror for the spirits. They had disappeared. In their place were orbs of light zooming all around me, circling my head, my body, and my limbs.

I turned around to face Madame, my eyes flashed down and around.

Orbs of light were flying about the entire studio. Just then a memory returned. It was the dance performance in the downtown loft where I had met Madame only three years ago. It seemed as if the same change had occurred. Confused, I looked over at Madame for clarification. "What happened?"

"You changed their energy!" she said enthusiastically. "These spirits have now become orbs of light. You realized your limiting belief, and now you are forever changed as well. Congratulations! You are free."

I turned back to the mirror to confirm the spirits were gone, and the orbs of light began to disappear one by one. Stepping closer, I noticed the lines in my face had become softer and the sparkle in my eyes had returned. I felt an inner peace and deep joy within.

They're gone! The chains had been broken, and I was indeed free! Suddenly the vision of Jessica's words came to my mind as I lifted my right hand and screamed, "I'm free!"

Like a child, I celebrated this discovery, laughing and dancing. Madame turned on some up-beat music and allowed me the time and space to embrace my newfound freedom. When the song finished, I came over to her and hugged her tightly. Thanking her for the lesson, I was in complete and utter amazement at the transformation.

I stood there beaming with pride, while everything that occurred over the last few months fell into place. The clarity of her teachings came to me.

"I get it now!" I said excitedly. "All of us women were trying to let go of our negative attachments around our desires. They may be different desires, but I understand now the whole 'loving yourself' thing and why it applies to our destiny. I get it!"

Madame quizzed me. "What was the common reason all of you women signed up for lessons at the studio?"

I pondered the question before providing a reply. "We all wanted to change something."

"You all desired a form of love," Madame corrected. "What did you want?"

I thought about it for a moment before answering. "Yes. I desired to trust in order to love."

"What about the others?" She asked.

"Well, Chrissy desired to break her addiction in order to love. Julia desired to stop her hatred in order to love."

"Good," Madame encouraged, "keep going."

"Jessica desired to forgive in order to love. And Samantha"—I paused for a moment to consider her desire. "She desires to share her talents in order to love."

"You didn't come to me seeking a Ferrari or a vacation in Maui," Madame stated. "You came to me to discover the most important desire of all: to love yourself so that you may love others. Once you have overcome your deepest fear and attained your deepest desire for love, all other things come easy."

She paused for a moment, walking over to the stereo to turn down the volume, allowing the words to sink in before continuing. "Soon, instead of spending your time wondering what others are thinking or why they are doing what they are doing, you will begin to spend your time thinking about new ideas, desires, and other creative aspirations. Most likely, you have already. By using your sixth sense, you realize that you are being called to do, be, or have something that will increase this joy. The thoughts enter your mind and fill you with pleasure. You begin to see that the most amazing sexual relationship you will ever have happens in your mind. Your *mind* is the single greatest sexual organ. Accepting the penetration of love is the only option. Anything that is not love is adultery of your purpose."

Following her words, I then tried to repeat what I had learned. "I think I understand. The lessons of sexuality, opening up to follow my desires, and trusting myself … that is the sexual relationship I've always longed for!" I almost shouted, beaming from ear to ear.

"Yes, Lenea. It is through the use of your sixth sense you will know love, freedom. It is much like an orgasm that happens in your body, an indicator that you have been penetrated by a thought with purpose and connection.

"In the beginning, it is best to keep a journal every time you are presented with an idea, desire, or any other creative aspiration that activates your sixth sense. This becomes your will or your intention to focus on. Soon your will becomes action or deed, and eventually … your destiny." She had worked herself up into a frenzy, using her hands to describe the feeling, and I hung on, clinging to every word.

"After you set your intention," Madame continued, "you begin to see how you are not separate from anyone else. You see that in order to do, be,

YOU & I, INC.

or have anything, others are involved in the process. All human creation is a conscious creation with the purpose to love one another. Therefore we are all connected."

"You asked me why I never got married," she reminded me pointedly. "It is because I understand and live this concept daily. I am not married, at this time, because it fulfills me deeply to live my purpose with the gifts I have been given; that is to teach and help others—to share my gifts and talents in order to love."

Madame shifted her stance, then continued. "Because I am not married, I can commit to this purpose one hundred percent. But I am not opposed to marriage. In fact, it is the reason I have started the group The Supernal Sacrament. It is my belief that when you desire a partner, and you and your partner look at life using the same lessons I have taught you, life is filled with even greater joy."

I now understood where Mark's words came from. Secretly I wished he were here. I looked around the room in hopes of him walking in.

Madame followed my gaze, attempting to meet my eyes. When our eyes met, she continued. "It is true that two or more people setting a unified intention have a greater return for their deeds and, therefore, a greater joy in reaching their destiny. This concept applies not only to marriage but also to groups of friends, business partners, and all human relationships in general. This new class is designated for couples who really want to understand and apply these concepts in a relationship in order to make a greater impact of love on this planet. That, my dear, is my greatest desire." She closed her eyes, bowing in dramatic fashion.

Standing there, satiated with her knowledge, I yearned to know the answer to another question. "Thank you for your wisdom and insight," I offered gratefully, "but there is something I would like to know. How did you know about the story of the L'abeille Palace and Lady M? I mean ... I never told you about that. How did you know her name?"

A sly smile crossed her full lips. "Once you begin to see with new eyes, life becomes a daily gift to be unwrapped. It is at this stage of life you are given new ears." She pointed to her heart before continuing. "You begin to realize that not only you but also all of creation has a tone and a vibration; that every human, animal, plant, and mineral is connected through these vibrations, and that all of creation, including spirits, has the ability to share wisdom ... if we choose to listen.

"However, this is not something you are going to fully understand today." She put her hands on top of my shoulders and shook her head slowly side to side. "So, for now, trust that your new eyes have been opened. And as you perceive with this sixth sense, you will start to have a deeper understanding and appreciation for the connection we all have. But you must realize that in order to truly love and trust others, we must love and trust ourselves first."

Her answers led to more questions. "Madame, do you see spirits? Did you talk to Lady M?"

"I don't have to," she replied, dropping her hands to her side. "Lady M is me ... and I am her."

I didn't know what to say, furrowing my brow; confused.

She paused for a moment, smiling at my reaction before continuing.

"You are not going to understand this right now. This is part of the new ears I am talking about. Let's simplify things and say that one soul may have many lives."

"Many lives? What do you mean?" I asked, completely shocked by what she had to say.

"I am very aware of my many lives from the past. I have recollection that most people do not possess. I know things about others' past lives as well. People are drawn to me for this very reason. It is a gift. However, I would never rob others of their journey of discovery of their own past lives and tell them what it is I know, for the lessons they will learn on their own are too valuable. It would be stealing another's joy in the revelation."

Now I was confused. *Was Madame the spirit that was attached to me? Did I know her in a past life? Was there some sort of connection we had in a past life that was connecting us now?* Madame could probably see the wheels turning in my head before I asked her the next question.

Peering into her eyes, I cocked my head to the side. "How could her spirit be here and you be here at the same time? I don't get it! And what do you mean by the 'lessons' of a past life?"

"Remember, spirits are the mental energy left in a specific location, like echoes of the past." Her eyes shifted upward, vacantly, before returning to mine.

"Some people are gifted and can see these spirits, and some cannot. Others, like myself, have developed full awareness of our past lives. I believe that we are here to continue searching for the knowledge we desperately need to advance consciously." She waited to see if I was following. "I was a madam then, and I am a form of a madam now. But not all people return with the same purpose. I am here to help women discover and appreciate their own sexuality in order to open themselves up consciously to what you have now discovered within."

The concept was difficult to grasp at first, but it led to another question. "Did we know one another in a past life?"

"Yes, Lenea," she responded happily, seeing my acceptance of her theory. "We did have a connection in a past life. You being here is not a coincidence. It is still part of the journey of accepting who you are and why you are here. However, I will allow you to discover our past connection all on your own. New ears are not something that can be taught. They are discovered on a path that is unique to you. Releasing the attachments and not allowing new ones to form is the first step on this path. Congratulations!" Again she closed her eyes and bowed to me.

"Thank you for teaching me," I replied, beginning to tear up. "Thank you for taking them away!"

"I didn't take them away," she corrected. "You did that on your own. I only showed you how to use the tool you already possess … your mind. My purpose is not to break the attachment for you, but to teach you how to do this for yourself."

"Now"—she stepped forward, taking my hands into hers—"we have only a few hours before our class tonight. Why don't you take some time and journal about your experience. It is a lot to take in, and I don't want you to forget this powerful day." She motioned to my pillow in the middle of the floor, then walked over to the stereo and pushed a button. Calming instrumental music filled the space.

Following her direction, I took my seat and began writing frantically as one revelation after another came to me. An hour passed in a moment. My writing was interrupted by a masculine voice.

"Hey, beautiful," Mark said, knocking on the studio door simultaneously. "Feeling better?" He entered the studio, walking straight toward me without waiting for an answer. I stood and embraced him tightly.

Stepping back, holding his hands in mine, I looked up at him, tears flowing from my eyes. "Yes, I'm feeling much better now."

Sharing with him the events of the morning, I revealed my lessons and what I had learned and how I had turned the spirits into orbs of light. He soaked it all in, nodding acceptingly with each revelation, as if he already knew the lessons well.

"Len, you're an amazing woman," he responded. "I knew that wasn't *you* last night. I'm so glad those spirits are gone."

I hadn't noticed the duffel bag he had set down upon entering until he reached down to open it. "I hope you don't mind, but I went by your place to pick up some of your things for tonight. I knew we wouldn't have much time together before class—assuming you would still care to join me?" He glanced up at me, smiling.

It was so sweet of him to think of me. I put both hands to my heart, grateful. "Yes, Mark, I would love to come with you tonight. And thank you for packing me a bag. I really appreciate it."

"Hey, Len," he said, "I want to apologize for lying to you last night. I really should have taken the time and explained to you—"

Putting my finger to his lips midsentence, I stopped him. "You know what I realized? Those were my own issues. And there's no need to apologize. It really had nothing to do with you, Samantha, or anyone else. It was me all along. I tell you what," I said, stepping back from him, "I'll make a deal with you. We keep this relationship going, and when my intuition veers off again, we'll talk about what it means. Is that a deal?" I stuck my right hand out to seal the agreement.

"Hell yes!" He shook my hand firmly. "A woman's intuition is a gift! You have a deal." He hugged me tightly to confirm it.

As we separated, he looked down into my eyes before continuing, "Hey Len, I also have a belief: I believe our greatest fears are what we push ourselves toward in a relationship. Please, if you ever have any fears about me or us, promise me you will not believe them until we've had an opportunity to discuss them together. Agreed? And I promise to do the same. No thought attachments. Deal?" he said, winking at me.

"Yes, it's a deal!" I responded quickly. "I have learned my lesson about attaching to negative thoughts, to say the least. And I don't ever want to do that again." I reached my arms around his neck, leaned in, and kissed him.

"Okay, crazy girl," he retorted, stepping back, "you'd better get dressed. Madame is bringing in Elemental Charity tonight for a show."

He stopped and rubbed his chin, "Hmm. I wonder what it will be." He smiled with hungry eyes while handing me the bag he had packed for me.

Beaming from ear to ear, I gave him a kiss on the cheek, grabbed my bag, and walked out of the studio to change. As I crossed the threshold, Mark whistled a catcall, to which I stopped, turned, and blushed before continuing down the hallway.

By now, guests were filling the foyer. I entered the ladies' room to change, pulling my makeup out of my bag. Looking at my reflection in the mirror, my eyes were bright and clear. Joy coursed through my veins. In no time, my face was nicely painted and I reached into the bag for my clothes. Everything was neatly folded and in a pile. I even teared up a little as I pulled out the nude-colored dress I had worn on our first date. *He remembered ...*

Putting on the final touches—first hair, then makeup, and a slight adjustment to the dress—I saw the plaque out of the corner of my eye that adorned the adjacent wall. I turned to read it, out loud this time, letting the words resonate:

> It was said of old: The self, which is free from impurities, from old age and death, from grief, from hunger and thirst, which desires nothing but what it ought to desire, and resolves nothing but what it ought to resolve, is to be sought after, is to be inquired about, is to be realized. He who learns about the self and realizes it obtains all the worlds and all desires.
>
> As your desire is, so is your will.
> As your will is, so is your deed.
> As your deed is, so is your destiny.
> —The Upanishads

30

It Comes Full Circle in the End

*A*h, yes, the self must be who I am, I reflected. *Not the spirits, not my thoughts, and not my judgments.* Before leaving, I looked in the mirror, deep into my own eyes; they sparkled as never before. *The self. I like it. This is who I am!*

Upon entering the hallway, I saw people carrying painted canvases. Following the masses, I went down a corridor I had never ventured through before. I knew it led to the basement, but it was unfamiliar territory.

The walls of the corridor were lined with paintings of women from the past. Stopping to look at the details, I noticed their dress suggested the subjects were from around the turn of the century. An older gentleman in a tweed coat was standing a few paces to the right of me. He had also stopped to stare at the paintings. "Pretty cool, huh?" He said out loud, his gaze never shifting. "I can't believe they've kept these after so many years."

"What are they?" I inquired.

"These are the paintings of the women of the Mystere building behind us. Do you know the story of the Mystere?" he asked, turning to me, wanting to reveal.

"Yes," I smiled, nodding my head, "I'm familiar with it. But what do you know about the Mystere?" Silently I thanked Mark for the knowledge he had given me.

"These were the goods for sale," he said, pointing to the dozens of framed paintings of women. "The madam had these women painted so men could look on the wall and choose their favorite; it's a menu, so to speak. I'd say the Madam knew how to advertise well." He chuckled to himself.

I laughed at the thought. The wall of naked and half-naked women was definitely out of the ordinary. I leaned in closer for a better look. Each of the paintings displayed the woman's physical description and a pet name. The gentleman and I had a good laugh. I moved down a few steps until I came upon the largest of the frames, ornately trimmed in gold. From the size, it was easy to discern this was an oil painting of someone more prestigious.

"Excuse me, miss." The gentleman touched me on the shoulder. "I saw this drop from your bag and didn't want you to lose it." In his hand was a money clip with a coin attached.

I took the coin, inspecting it closer. "Oh this isn't mine," I said politely, handing it back to him.

"You should keep it," he said with a smile. "She would want you to have it." He pointed at the large ornate painting. I turned around and saw the subject he was motioning toward: the raven-haired woman—Lady M.

Leaning in, I read the bronze placard below, engraved with the words "Queen of the Red Light District." The hair on the back of my neck rose up, and goose bumps covered my arms. I looked down at the money clip. I flipped it over to the other side, which had a coin with engraved words that read "GOOD FOR ONE SCREW. WHERE THE CUSTOMER COMES FIRST. MATTIE SILKS, PROP."

I smiled.

"She was a brilliant marketer," I said aloud to the gentleman, turning around to give him the clip back. But he was no longer there.

Thinking maybe he went into the large room at the end of the hallway, I moved in that direction. Entering the room, I could see standing easels with paintings placed sporadically throughout the space. Couples were meandering around, and even a few singles—more people than I expected.

The space was identical to the studio above, including the limestone walls adorned with large hanging wall mirrors for dance. The ceilings were slightly shorter, but other than that, it was quite similar. My eyes caught a spot in the wall where a freestanding mirror stood, almost as if it had been strategically placed there. My mind sped back to Mark's story of the voices in the basement and the coal tunnel; a chill ran down my spine. *Focus on the paintings, Lenea; there is nothing to be afraid of. The spirits are gone now*, I told myself repeatedly.

Shifting my attention to the large mirror in front of me, I noticed even Samantha was there, her gaze focused on one of the canvases. *What is she doing here?* I wondered, taking a deep breath. Jealousy and envy had been my downfall yesterday. But today, the new me had eyes wide open. I was not going to let this woman get the best of me. After all, she was merely a mirror of the insecurity I had felt within myself.

Ha! I laughed inside. *Now I feel confident, strong and sexy.*

A hand gently grabbed my shoulder. I turned around to see who it was. It was Mark.

"There you are," he said, a look of delight on his face. "I have something I want you to see."

He ushered me, hand in hand, in the direction of the only painting that was covered in a deep red velvet fabric, placed directly in the middle of the large mirrored wall.

"I will be revealing this tonight. It's quite special. I want you to see it first." We stood holding hands in front of the covered easel.

He reached for the veil, but before he could lift it fully, a voice disrupted the tender moment.

"Mark! I just saw it!" a strikingly beautiful redheaded woman exclaimed. "Oh my God, it is amazing!" She hugged him tight. He dropped the fabric and hugged her back.

"I'm so sorry to bother you, but I have to introduce you to my husband, Dario," the woman said, gesturing to a very handsome man with Italian facial features and dark, wavy hair. The man stepped forward and shook hands with Mark and then with me.

"Hi, I'm Lenea," I said, introducing myself to him. He bent down to kiss my hand with a confident grin.

"It is a pleasure to meet you," Dario said in his thick Italian accent.

"Oh my gosh! You're Lenea!" the redhead proclaimed. She leaned in and gave me a huge hug as if she knew me. "I've heard so much about you! Mark thinks quite highly of you, you know." She smiled at Mark as assurance. He smiled back, hesitantly.

"Oh, where are my manners. I'm Samantha, by the way." She stuck her hand out to shake mine. "It's so nice to meet you! Thank you for letting me borrow your man last night. We didn't complete the project in class yesterday and I just had to finish this painting before the show. And, oh my God, it is more beautiful than I could have ever imagined!" She smiled, looking at both Mark and I with excitement. I turned to Mark. I'm sure the confusion in my mind matched the look on my face. *This is Samantha?* I thought.

Mark shifted uncomfortably in the awkward pause of conversation. I didn't know what to say. Fortunately another voice interrupted the stifled moment; it was Madame.

"Yes, there is a painting of Samantha that is on display tonight as well. It is a gift for her husband," Madame said, gesturing to one of the canvases across the room. She had joined our conversation, unbeknownst to me. I was thankful she had stepped in, as it gave me time to collect my thoughts.

"What do you mean a painting? More like a masterpiece. I can't believe …" The redheaded woman's voice continued, but I had stopped listening. The room was now spinning. I felt nauseous. My mind tried to grasp the reality of the situation. This *is Samantha? This is the woman he was out with last night? This was the woman in the studio yesterday? How could that be? I saw who he was with and it wasn't her. It was …*

I glanced up at Madame, confused. Madame gave me a look of knowing then shifted her eyes as if to direct me toward the answer. I spun around in the direction she was indicating and spotted the blonde woman in the mirror in front of us—the only woman I knew to be "Samantha." She was standing a few paces to the right of me and appeared to be admiring one of Mark's paintings.

The visions of Mark and her began to replay in my mind. Then I traveled back to all of our encounters together. Why is it I never saw her anywhere other than the studio? Suddenly my blood ran cold. Every interaction with her had been around mirrors!

At that moment Madame's words came back to haunt me, "Many times spirits show up in mirrors because they are attached to you. Every one of us, including spirits, provides a mirror of our own thinking. And sometimes the spirit and person are connected as one." I closed my eyes and shook my head. *She can't be,* I thought. When I opened them, the blonde Samantha was now staring at me, body erect, eyes focused in the mirror directly on mine. Her eyes weren't normal. They had a glassy, vacant appearance. Chills moved up and down my spine at the revelation: I knew she was not of this world.

EPILOGUE

The Journal Entry

Looking back over the years, I realize how my thoughts perpetuated all of my beliefs and, by acting out my life based on these undiscovered lies, I lived in a constant state of fear. I desired to love and trust others, but how could I give what I did not have within myself? Today my deepest desire has been met. Never again will I have a need to trust others in order to live a full life, for I know that I am trust. Trust is the sixth sense I embody, and freedom is the rewarded life of following this path.

The key to life is simple. It's loving who I am, what I think, what I feel, what I believe, and what I sense with all six senses. This is different from who I think I should be, from what others want me to be and sometimes even tell me I am. Only I know the truth to these questions, and only the truth can set me free.

To trust the love inside me is the only way to be set free!

The truth is that I am a perfect vibrating light of love under this shell of a body, and so is all of creation. Our purpose is clear—to share this light of love with others. This reminds me of another story:

Once there was a great ball of light. And from that light was created another. And from that light yet another. When the three lights came together again in love, they became one bright light. And it was good.

The beginning of life may not be a story on a linear timeline. Maybe time flows in a circle and what appears as the beginning could be a continuum; the alpha and the omega, the beginning and the end.

ACKNOWLDEGEMENTS

It is You & I, Inc.

What you hold in your hands would not be possible without the influence of the people listed below. Each played a significant part in this story's creation and my life. I acknowledge the following sources from the depths of my soul:

To my husband, William: We have walked together, hand in hand, placing our focus on the cornerstone of our marriage: love, growth and creation. Which was, is, and is to be the legacy of You and I, Incorporated. Thank you for being my partner. I love you.

To the author of "Loving What Is," Byron Katie: Your book gave me the words to create this story and forever changed the course of my life. Though I've never met you, you touched me in unexplainable ways. Thank you.

To Alisa K: They say, "When the student is ready, the teacher appears." This is the essence of our relationship. The words that come to mind are, I wrote this book, "4 You, 4 Love and 4 The World." I know that my greatest offering of gratitude to you is to live my truth. And so the story continues...

To my editors, Luan Ezra, Sue McGinty, Liane Roth, William Beaber and Balboa Press: Thank you for making me a better writer. For encouraging me to step out of my comfort zone, and showing me the ropes of great writing. Our work together breathed new life in me and these pages. Thank you.

To my beta readers, Marsala, Julie, Cheryl, Gina, Shae, Sue, Lauren, Liz, and Mom. Your time, feedback and nurturing support is greatly appreciated. You opened my mind to new ideas. Your influence in my life is honored here in our sharing of this co-creative experience. Thank you.

To my sisters of the Alisa K. Turning Point Retreats, Liz, Alison, Nicole, Elle Ann, Mariela, Charissa, Cheryl, Sara Shine, Amy, Gina, Susan, Connie, Catherine, Jodi, Stacy, Lorie, Shae, Brenda, Melissa, Jenn, Janet, Crystal, Cathy, Ashley, Emily and Twyla: Your love and support is forever infused in these pages and my life through our shared experiences and malas. I will never forget you. Thank you.

And to my family, friends and the countless others who were placed in my life with purpose, thank you for your love and support.

With gratitude,
Andrea